G000089981

Coat with Long Sleeves

Coat with Long Sleeves

Geoff Duck

Matador
9 Priory Business Park,
Wistow Road, Kibworth Beauchamp,
Leicestershire. LE8 0RX
Tel: 0116 279 2299
Email: books@troubador.co.uk
Web: www.troubador.co.uk/matador
Twitter: @matadorbooks

ISBN 978 183859 4060

British Library Cataloguing in Publication Data.
A catalogue record for this book is available from the British Library.

Printed and bound in Great Britain by 4edge Limited
Typeset in 11pt Adobe Garamount by Troubador Publishing Ltd, Leicester, UK

Matador is an imprint of Troubador Publishing Ltd

How dark is dark?

On this June night there are pinprick stars showing in the west; a tenuous moon skulks behind a grumbling, crawling cloud. There are no lights in the landscape. No lamps behind cottage shutters to give even a flicker of flame. No comforting trail to home. No harbinger of dawn in these early hours.

To eyes that have become accustomed to the deep blackness there are milky silhouettes of distant moors on the horizon and outlines of hedgerow thickets in nearby fields, but under woodland trees with their serried canopies of lush leaves there is barely any penetration, only occasional lonely, mottled moonbeams. If you concentrated and you were patient, you could discern your hand in front of you, follow its movement and just about count your fingers. Perhaps you couldn't see around you, but you would be instinctively aware of the branches and the thorns and the brambles and the nettles closing in, their perilous presence pressed on you by a sort of ephemeral and elusive tension you can feel on your skin, and through your skin, that you could not properly describe to a stranger to these parts in words he would understand.

Deep countryside, indeed.

This night is still and warm and a brittle dryness in the air has coated the dead leaves of last year and has given them a satisfyingly delicate crispness that whispers when disturbed by paw or hoof or claw or shoe.

When there is no wind to warp the boughs of the trees there are sounds that reach your ears from far, far away and from under your foot in equal measure. Some miles distant on the other side of the valley a farm dog is barking at a shadow, a little closer a tawny owl is calling plaintively to its mate in a melancholy aria. A toad gurgles and throbs in a muddy ditch and a harried shrew runs for its life.

In this English woodland on this particular summer night there is a faint but distinct shuffling that to the experienced ear suggests the unsteady trudge of two adult human males. They are coming closer to a rocky clearing in the trees where the straining moonlight bathes the scrub with an insipid grey mask. They are trying to be silent, these men, but it's not really working. Every step they take breaks another fragile stick or shifts around the desiccated leaves. The red deer that were grazing on young shoots just a moment before are long gone and there are countless pairs of eyes, all shapes, sizes and colours, fixated on the two shadows from the safety of the darkness. Everything in the wood knows they are coming. They've known since the first warning call. The foxes and the badgers and the rest. They have things under control.

The men are stooped and drawn. It's obvious they don't want to be there. And they have their heads covered on this stifling night. They are not happy bunnies. They aren't speaking. If it were daylight, an observer would notice that the men's expressions tell of apprehension and foreboding and of a sort of primal terror. A visceral dread that is gnawing at the bowels of their souls. But it's not daylight, and the men are keeping their thoughts safely wrapped up in their own minds in the inky murk of the night. Their torments are their own.

Then more silhouettes. They appear from nowhere. There are no words of greeting or acknowledgement. They settle on a fallen tree and wait. They know the time is almost upon them.

Even the owl is cowed.

It is as if the animals and the birds and the insects and all the slithering things, even the trees and the creepers and the fungi, in fact all living things in the wood and some things that were once living, are holding their breath, waiting for ... what? The moon comes and goes and the woodland scents, pungent and fragrant and rank, they waft and mingle with the reek of sweat and the mineral tang of anxiety and fear.

There is lurching and reeling among the sitters, hesitant and uncertain as the inevitable looms near.

Abruptly and without warning, bodies collapse untidily on the mossy floor of the wood and others crouch and bend and double up, foetus-like where they sit. There is no calling out or moaning. No theatricals. These guys are practiced. They knew it was coming. The ones who are left on the bough are swaying gently as if taken by a breeze. It is eerily quiet. Nothing stirs, only a faint burble of water trickling somewhere close.

There is a rustling in the undergrowth behind the tree and something is coming through in a clumsy paroxysm of commotion. Whatever it is, it isn't trying to be quiet. And just as it breaks cover from the brush, another cloud shrouds the moon and the thing becomes indistinct and unfathomable but it's like the forest has come alive and although there is now a vacant stillness in the air, there are branches that are moving when they shouldn't be and the ivy and the honeysuckle and the old man's beard that coils around the limbs of the trees is creeping towards the figures like it does in nightmares and it's twisting and curling around the men's arms and legs and engulfing them. It's all going in their mouths and coming out their noses and they are cloaked in the woodland and have become part of it, and the wood has become part of them. They are the same thing. And now they have become one, there is a quietness again. An immense quietness. It is like the quiet at the beginning of the Earth, before there were things to disturb the tranquillity and the hope. It is another world for a moment. A forgotten world. A natural world. A world at ease, but it feels elusive and vulnerable. It is a fragile thing.

And eventually, there is a stirring from one of the prone figures and a deep guttural sighing and a writhing of unruly limbs and the something that had caused the quietness of the other world and become part of the men is suddenly gone, as if it had never existed at all. It was there, and now it isn't.

The night noises return. The owl and the dog, and a vixen is screaming at her defiler. A startled pheasant bursts from its roost. The cloying air begins to tremble again and branches in the treetops sway unsteadily and as the moon suddenly frees itself from a passing cloud, it glints menacingly on bright metal and the sickly stench of fresh blood fills the piquant air.

Excerpt from the North Devon Weekly Gazette, dated 19th April, 2119.

THATCH FIRE DESTROYS HISTORIC BUILDING.

A fire ripped through the thatched roof of a listed cottage in the village of Crow's Nymet on Tuesday evening, completely gutting the cob and stone property. Fire crews from nearby Chulmleigh and Barnstaple were called to the scene at around midnight but were unable to save the building which was already well ablaze.

No one was hurt in the fire. A police spokesman told the Gazette that the cottage was used as a holiday let and there was nobody staying there at the time. The cause of the fire is not yet known. Forensic experts have been sifting the ruins for clues as to the source of the blaze, and foul play has not been ruled out.

The owner, Mr Nigel Mills, who lives in The Old Church, told our reporter Mike Brown that he feared it was an arson attack. 'Church House has had a volatile history', he said, 'and tends to be given a wide berth by villagers. Nobody has lived there for a long time'.

In an extraordinary twist, on Thursday morning police investigators took away evidence in a sealed bag that may help to solve a hundred year old mystery that has dogged the house and village for as long as anyone can remember.

Mr Mills said, 'After the forensic team had left on Wednesday, I was wandering around the charred site looking for clues myself. I found a tin box that had obviously been hidden but was poking through dislodged flags near the fallen chimney breast, and when I opened it, there was a large bundle of papers inside with handwriting on them. There must have been about four hundred sheets. I took the box back to the church and looked through some of the pages. The bits I read didn't make a lot of sense, but I think it's incendiary. It's going to shed some light on a lot of things that have given Crow's Nymet a bad name.'

Mr Mills handed the box to police on Thursday and there is considerable interest in its contents in the village. Barnstaple Constabulary has not yet issued a statement about this latest find, and enquiries are continuing.

one

It must be about two in the morning. I'll have been sitting here, I realise, since it all unravelled.

It's midsummer. It's the summer solstice, actually, but although there is a full moon hiding out there somewhere, the stewy sky feels dark and uneasy. From my little window I can see that there is nothing yet to suggest even a false dawn to this most portentous of days. It is achingly quiet. I can just make out the faint ticking of my tired long case clock along the hall, on the other side of the door. It's been labouring for three hundred years and hungers for a rest.

This is an ancient house and it is quite capable of groaning and moaning, creaking and murmuring, but tonight it is ominously still. Maybe it's unnerved by the night's events or by anticipation of events yet to come, or perhaps it is just listening silently and waiting and judging. It feels like it might have a natural prescience in its old mud walls.

I'm sitting in my study with just a small brass reading lamp alight on my desk. I'm not sitting at my desk. I'm cocooned in a very commodious armchair next to it and the amber light is shining over my right shoulder, just bright enough for me to write this to you, whoever you are. I've got the wood burner going with the smoke-smudged glass door open and it's toasting my slippered feet. It imparts into the room a comforting ambience that is, quite simply, the very essence of life; a primeval folk memory that is imbedded in the very deepest and impenetrable reaches of our psyche. People who do not have fires in their lives do not have fires in their hearts.

This fire, however, has a tendency to smoke and my eyes are stinging and there is a wispy haziness in the air, dusty eddies of which are picked out by errant rays escaping through loose stitches in the lampshade.

I guess you can have too much primeval psyche.

Portentous days and pretentious ways. Oh dear.

I love this time of day. I love that there are no lights on in any of the houses in this village because every single occupant is tucked up in bed, fast asleep. No one in Crow's Nymet knows what goes on during these hours because they've never been interested enough to find out. They would be very surprised, though, as would you. When was the last time you were out alone in the deep countryside at night?

Ever?

Ever in your whole life?

You would be very surprised at what you found, especially if you happened to choose the fields and woods and tracks around here.

Crow's Nymet is what historians call a hill settlement because it started life when the forested river valleys were boggy and impassable and sensible folk stuck to the higher ground where they chopped down the trees and lumped up banks and planted hedges to shelter their sheep and cattle and divided the rolling land into a patchwork of small irregular fields, most of which are still lying out there today, unchanged by time and progress. Strangely, you mightn't really think of it as being on a hill today, at least I don't, and that's because there are lots of other wooded hills all around and when you're down in the valley you can't look up and see the village on top the hill like you can in, say, Le Marche or Provence. You might just catch a glimpse of a church tower through the trees, but the buildings tend to be squat and spread out higgledy-piggledy, not focused behind some medieval defensive wall or anything like that.

I want you to get the right picture in your mind of what it's like down here. It's different from other places. It's very green and it's very old, and it knows what it likes.

Crow's Nymet is one of the prettier villages in North Devon. It has more than an equitable share of rustic thatched cottages, cob barns and colourful country gardens, and they are all tastefully huddled around its medieval church, the obligatory Georgian rectory and the pub. Yes, we still have a pub. My house, Church House, is possibly the oldest building in the village, and as we shall see, stands (as the name would suggest) right next to the church. It is called Church House because at one time it was a church house, but more about that later too.

We are very lucky. This is an exceptional part of the country, not only because of the unspoiled bucolic landscape and a traditional approach here to all things agricultural and cultural but because there are so many very, very ancient houses to be discovered and digested. Most towns and villages in Britain are fortunate enough to have retained and preserved a core of interesting old buildings. But there's old and old. In the East Midlands, where I spent many years of my life, old means 18th century. Around here old means 15th century or earlier. And these cottages are everywhere and many, including Church House, are substantially intact and original. Some of these places were old when John Cabot stumbled upon Newfoundland in 1497. That's an intriguing little snippet to throw into a conversation when you know one of our colonial cousins is listening.

My study is the service room. I don't want to bore you too much with details just yet, but the classic layout of these old farmhouses has a service room, or rooms, on the far side of a passage that splits the house in two and goes right the way through from the front door to the back. It's called the screens passage because it was formed from crude plank screens either side. The service rooms were the buttery and the pantry, the buttery not being for butter, but for butts. For storage of liquids such as beer or cider or vinegar. The pantry was a pantry, a proper pantry. In Church House the service rooms were separated by a hurdle and mud partition that has long succumbed to the way of all things, but has left tell-tale marks on the main oak beam that holds up the ceiling. This means there is now only one room but two doors, sitting side-by-side in a redundant sort of way and looking a bit silly really. It isn't a large room. It's wide enough to get my big bookcase in next to the desk and stretches the original depth of the house, about sixteen feet, which is a sort of standard dimension in vernacular buildings because it's the longest span you could expect an oak A frame or cruck truss made of local trees to support without bending or breaking. There is a small single casement window, with tiny panes of cheap blown glass set in a leaded frame. One or two panes are cracked.

The service room in Church House is a very original part of an exceptionally original building. The thing with ancient houses like these is that during their lifetime they will have inevitably changed considerably and many times, perhaps once a generation when money became available, fashions changed or technology rendered features obsolete, so it's a delight to find fabric from the very earliest incarnation of the building that remains untouched and intact.

I mean, you can go round a National Trust property, an abbey or a castle or something, and you can gaze in awe at the architecture and the sheer scale of the thing, but more often than not you're just looking at a pile of old stone walls and not much else. In houses like this one you've still got the straw and the hair and the chestnut spars and the oilcloth and the dead moths and the half-eaten hazelnuts. They're over half a millennium old and they're still here. They're all around me now. How amazing is that?

Take the floor of my study.

It's made from thick, wide old oak planks, gnarled and knotty, random widths and hand planed. You can see the dips and irregularities from the carpenter's tools if the light is right. They're all just butted up hard against each other and nailed together with hand-forged blacksmith's iron nails.

I had them put in in 1994.

But don't let that fool you, like it's meant to. Underneath the boards is the original floor, or rather a number of more original floors, that I wanted to preserve, so I left them as they were. The most recent, Victorian I would guess, is a sort of lime-ash slab, but this has crumbled away to nothing except in the corners and has exposed stone cobbles, worn smooth with use. On one side they're formed into a drain which finds its way out through the lower end wall. Obviously the buttery. Or possibly this room was once used to house animals. Where the cobbles are dislodged you could see the original rammed earth floor. I remember, before we covered it up, that on certain types of mild, damp days the earth would sweat with a slimy sheen and I recall thinking that when

5

the whole house had a floor like this it would be running wet, all the time, no respite, even through the summer. If you're not used to damp floors you can ruin stuff very easily. You don't want to put anything on them that isn't glass, ceramic or hardwood or it will rot before you've had time to notice.

What with a waterproof membrane; a little insulation; joists and boards, the new floor has left me with precious little headroom, but the character of my study ceiling is sufficient compensation for that. It really is authentically gnarled and beetle-eaten and rotten. I left it well alone. It's just as I found it and I resisted the temptation to tart it up with a wire brush and beeswax like we did with the rest of the oak in the house. I like it just as it is with its cobwebs and flakes of limewash that scatter me occasionally as I potter about below. Furniture beetles still find the odd bit of virgin sapwood to bore in to or out of and leave little piles of tell-tale yellow dust behind them on smooth surfaces. The heavy square joists are bent and twisted and most have pulled away from both the central beam and the cob bearers where the hunched roof has splayed the walls apart over the centuries. Actually, as I sit here looking up at it, it does rather seem to be defying gravity. There are fantastically crazy elm boards above the joists that are largely eaten away and I think it's only the Victorian pine tongue and grooved floorboards that are clamped at right angles over them that are holding the whole structure in place. Rusted iron nails protrude through the double boards, some bent over, others threatening. They look like some instrument of torture. Along the bottom edge of the joists are three or four jagged lines of nail heads, a sure sign that for most of its life this ceiling has been plastered, and the laths have rotted and pulled away several times and been replaced over the years.

The only beams ever meant to remain exposed were in the very poorest buildings or in the low status parts of better houses. The farmer I bought Church House from had obviously gone to some trouble to rip out all the plaster ceilings that he could reach before he put the house on the market, I would imagine in order to attract a lover of exposed beams. I hope he never thought I was one of them. I expect he'll have got the message when he came around after we'd finally said goodbye to the builders and saw that I'd put all the ceilings back up again. They look lovely in limewash and follow the natural curves of the sagging timberwork.

Except I never had enough headroom in my study, what with the new floor, so it remains the only part of the house with joists and boards revealed in their original form, and I do think it looks well for it, as indeed in this humblest of rooms, it was the way it all started out.

Placed in front of the window is my desk. I can sit and look straight out into the churchyard of Saint Rumon's which comes right up to the wall of the house, and beyond to the meadows and pastures of Beara Farm and further to the brooding, ashen mass of Dartmoor, far in the distance.

This desk and I go back some way. It was the first thing I bought just after we started the company. There was a second-hand furniture dealer up an alley off Loughborough town centre, and I beat the guy down to £12 for a quick sale (maybe? I think he just wanted to get it out of his way). We collected it the next day, dragged it through the alley and lifted it onto the roof of Tim's Volvo Amazon. We strapped it on upside-down with a rope through the windows of the car because we didn't trust the roof rack to hold it. We couldn't tie the knot until we were both sat in the front seats. The windows wouldn't shut, of course. It was winter and it was cold. Tim said he was used to it anyway because the heater hadn't worked for a year. It's a large desk, with two chunky pedestals which were screwed on tightly. It has something of the art deco about it, with its rounded edges and Bakelite handles. Someone had covered the top with sticky vinyl, and under that was a varnish that was brittle and cracked in places, liquid and tarry in other parts, and generally you could perhaps be forgiven for wondering if £12 had been a little on the generous side to give for such an unpromising purchase.

We had yet to open a company bank account. I paid cash from my own pocket and it never found its way onto any balance sheet. It was, finally, the only tangible thing that I walked away with at the end.

So, you see, it's not just any desk. It's had a previous life. It's come a long way with me.

I've usually got both computers running when I'm in here, but this morning they're shut down, silent and lifeless. One is a Dell studio 15 laptop and the other is a Dell tower with a big high-resolution Sony monitor. For a remote, rural spot like this we've got reasonable broadband. It's usually about 3 to 4 Megs download speed and is plenty for anything I need.

I've never had a TV since I've lived here, never felt the need nor desire for one, but now I can watch anything I want online so it doesn't matter. I guess I probably come over as a bit of a technophobe to the people I meet and I'm sure most villagers in Crow's Nymet would be surprised to learn that I can even use a mouse.

The thing is, they don't know what I was like before. They just see a crazy old man in his own little world.

I encourage them in this, of course; it doesn't really take much effort.

I may be crazy, but I'm not old. I'm … 62. Today in fact.

Today is my birthday and it had slipped my mind, what with all the excitement. Well, it doesn't mean much when you live on your own, does it?

I would be first to admit that I look much older. I've always had a craggy face. Lived-in, deep lines were always a prominent feature of my forehead, even when I was at school, but now they're more like ruts. I've been having trouble with my eyes lately, too. They've become rheumy and yellow and red and I've inherited my father's bags which droop and hang where my cheeks should be.

This rather haggard appearance is emphasised greatly by my full beard.

For my 18th birthday my parents bought me an electric razor. Before this I used a sort of clockwork, handheld thing that had cut and tore at my bristles for about five years, (I was always a very hairy person, even from an early age). When I unpacked my things on the first day at college, I realised that I had left behind my electric razor, and from that day on I have never shaved again. I've worn it short or long or very long as the mood has taken me. I let it turn to dreadlocks once during a particularly Bohemian period of my life, but even I have to admit that that was a bit scary. It was black, of course, like the rest of my hair and looked handsome, but now it's white, salt and pepper in parts and perhaps if you were being unkind you might say it was more yellow and white, but not in an elegant blonde way. I have never trimmed the edges and it has always covered my cheek bones and disappeared below my shirt collar. One of the penalties of growing old is that hair starts sprouting from every orifice, so that the hair from my ears and nostrils and eyebrows have now joined up with the beard and moustache to form a curiously featureless whiskerfest all over my face.

I sold my razor back to my father and when later he too grew a full beard he passed it on to my mother, who was by then the only person in our household who shaved. I always felt my father's facial arrangements were provocatively fraudulent. Everyone who subsequently met us together assumed that I had copied his style, but of course it was the other way around.

Once, when some major stuff was just kicking off in the company, Felix took me to one side and told me that there was no future for me as an executive director if I didn't shave it off in line with the clean new image the company was earnestly cultivating. Fucking asshole.

I never even considered trimming it for Felix. Over the years there has been the odd narrow escape involving drunken friends and bread knives and cigarette lighters, but it has always remained a stable and comforting feature of my adult life. No one I know now has ever seen me without a beard. I used to tell my wife that I grew it originally in order to cover an embarrassing birthmark on my chin. Partly true, there was a birthmark, but it didn't look like the phallus that I had described to her. However, it did mean that she didn't hassle me to shave it off. Sometimes I wonder what I would look like clean-shaven and one day, who knows, I may be taken on a whim to clear it all away. I would like to know how it feels to have a wet shave. It is, I guess, one of those nagging little omissions in my life that could so easily, for me, be satisfied. I suppose it may appeal to me one day. Now I've thought about it and written it down, I think maybe the time has come for a change.

Anyway, by now you may have a good mental image of me sitting here alone at night in my little sanctuary. To complete the picture let me tell you that I cut my own hair. Well I'll say no more, but I can assure you that it looks good from the front.

two

My wife once announced to me, while we were still tolerably married and were discussing a forthcoming birthday, that she didn't want to receive anything from me that she would have to dust. I think what she probably had in mind was an item of jewellery or a short break somewhere exotic, but as we had two small children and no money at the time, what she got was a vegetable lasagne and a glass of Chardonnay at our local. A rare treat indeed in those impoverished times. Her disappointment at my lack of romance and enterprise would have been tempered by the glee in notching up yet another failed opportunity on my part to prop up our ailing marriage. One more gratuitous episode noted down on the great clipboard of crimes and petty misdemeanours that by then defined our relationship and I'm sure preoccupied and enlivened her imagination at that time.

Georgia was a fastidious duster, whereas the other woman in my life, notably my mother, never had been. My bedroom, in particular, virtually became a no-go zone as far as my mother was concerned. I went through a phase of collecting televisions and at one stage had a grand total of nineteen sets piled up precipitously around my bed in various states of repair and nakedness. Although this was at a time when practically all households had just one TV in the living room, it wasn't an especially impressive feat because I could still only receive two channels (none of my TVs was capable of getting BBC2 because they were all ancient and none of them cost me more than five shillings).

There are two things to note about taking a TV set of this vintage out of its square wooden cabinet to repair it. Firstly, the metal chassis was always connected directly to one side of the mains. If you lived in a house where there were only two-pin sockets like I did, this meant that there was a fifty percent chance that the chassis was live, and you quickly learned it was inadvisable to touch two at once, in case one was, and the other wasn't. The second thing is that the inside of the TV would be covered in an almost unbelievably thick layer of browny-grey dust that had been enticed inside through the cardboard grill of the back panel by the hot glow of a couple of dozen thermionic valves for a decade or more. This must be where I first developed my laissez-faire acceptance of dust.

I can see little point in dusting with a duster anyway, or a cloth. It just spreads the stuff around; gives it somewhere else to settle. Towards the end of our time together when we had a little more disposable income, we employed a cleaner one day a week. She spent practically all her time dusting. With a feather duster and a dry cloth. What a pointless exercise. I could tell this was what she enjoyed doing and that what she didn't like doing was hoovering the carpets, scouring the cooker or scrubbing the sanitary ware. I could tell when she had been flouncing around with her little wand of ostrich feathers because one of my grandfather clocks had three gold leaf finials that were not fixed properly to the hood. I had mended the case with dowels that were way too small for their holes and they were loose. They were just propped up in the vertical but when Janet dusted them, she left them all leaning at odd angles. She did it every week. Did she not notice? Or care? Was she just doing this to annoy me? Of course, by the time I noticed the finials leaning and put them back properly, Janet was nowhere around, and whenever I did encounter her it was the furthest thing on my mind, so I never did ask her. It will sadly remain a mystery, but judging from the number of breakages and spillages we suffered at her hands I think my conclusion has to be that it was just a combination of careless incompetence, apathy and stupidity on her part, not her interpretation of some weird variant of class warfare or something.

One of the many joys of living on my own is that I do not have to employ a Janet. I like dust, which is just as well because I do have rather a lot of it. I have cobwebs too and I like them as well. I think they go with the territory in a place like this. You can clear the cobwebs away in the evening and then when you wake up they are all back again. It's those very spindly legged spiders, the cellar ones, that are the culprits. They sit there and watch you and then when you come close they start vibrating and laughing at you. Sometimes, if you've not been in a room for a while, the cobwebs brush against your face and cling to your hair and you end up looking like the bloke on the front of the Uriah Heap album cover. It can be very 'eavy, I can tell you.

In a house that's made of mud and straw, that has cracks in the walls that you can put your fingers through and gaps in the floorboards you could lose a teaspoon down, you're going to get wildlife keen to inhabit the same space as you and make their dusky, shadowy presence very evident.

Let me just put it this way. In somewhere like Church House you can't afford to waste your time doing much cleaning; a position that I find myself very at ease with.

The fires don't help, naturally. I've told you about the wood burner, but there's a big inglenook in the living room, too, where sometimes the prevailing draught is down the chimney, not up, picking up soot and ash along the way and filling the room with smoke and debris.

It's lucky that I have no objections to dust really, because my house is filled with the accumulated memories not only of my life, but my parents' lives, and their parents' lives and they're all here quietly gathering the patina of age and the flattening hues of the dust. All this stuff has ended up with me because no one else wanted it. Here in my study I surround myself with little things that at some time meant something significant to me or my ancestors.

On two of my walls there is oak panelling, making the room even darker and cosier, and all along the top is a Delft rack made from strips of old dresser shelves and this is filled with my smaller treasures. The panelling didn't start life out here. It will have come from some nearby church or Big House, though it is of humble quality. Seventeenth century probably, and in poor condition in parts.

I do polish the panelling now and again. I have a cast-iron glue pot that I put on the Aga with a little water in the outer vessel and I melt a block of beeswax with pure turpentine in it. It has to be pure, not substitute. I do it mainly for the smell, which reminds me of a time when I experimented a bit with oil painting as a young man. The smell lasts for weeks. It is powerful and evocative. I apply the liquid mixture with wire wool and use an old toothbrush to get into the corners, and then I polish it off with a shoe brush and it gives it a lift for a while.

As I sit here looking up at the shelf in the quiet darkness, I can make out a pile of Civil War bubble gum cards that I collected when I was about eleven. It was at a time when I first remember having spending money, an exciting development that I can still feel as a tingly frisson in my gut. It was against the rules to skip school dinners, but no one checked and we would buy a Cornish pasty from the corner shop for ten pence-ha'penny, leaving a penny ha'penny from the shilling our mothers had given us for the dinner. Two aniseed balls could be had for a halfpenny, leaving a penny for a pack of two Civil War cards and a slab of the sweetest, sickliest American bubble gum.

I never did complete the set. The manufacturers of the cards probably produced a selected handful in significantly smaller numbers so that it was much harder to get the lot. Certainly, I can remember that some cards held a certain cache and gained a notoriety that elevated them in the hierarchy of swaps to the heady levels of two-for-one or even four-for-one deals. Mostly my cards show the tell-tale signs of having spent some time sharing a schoolboy's pockets with the detritus of childhood and are creased and ragged at the edges and worn smooth in the middle from constant fingering. The rare cards were usually the most gory examples; soldiers with swords, bayonets or wooden stakes sticking out of various parts of their bodies, and with titles such as 'pushed to his doom' or 'crushed by the wheels'. I don't have to take them off the shelf to look at them, even now after all this time. I can see the pictures in my mind because I pored over them endlessly, devouring every little depiction of blood-spattered blue and grey army tunics when I should have been doing my maths or English homework. For a couple of months, it was the most important thing in my life. In the antiques trade they love this phase, when a collector will do almost anything to add to his hoard.

I guess at the time there was a lot of interest in the American Civil War because it was the centenary. I never did history at school. We were very progressive and ahead of the game. We did 'environmental studies' instead of history and geography at a time when no one had heard of the word environment, and I don't remember a single lesson. I learned more from my bubble gum cards than I did from my teachers.

Some years later when I was on company business in Washington, I hired a car and took off on my own to visit some Civil War battlefields in the Virginian countryside and it was a disappointment. These tourist attractions look good to start with, and they naturally have plenty of raw material at their disposal. There are always, always plenty of volunteers dressed in starched period costume and smelling of pot-pourri to engage you in their patter. No, they don't engage you; that's the thing. They're no better than recorded messages. They don't really know or understand what they're saying. They have learned it by heart and know that a smile and an attractive manner is all that is needed to keep the average American happy. It's good sport to interrupt one of these people half-way through their spiel with a trivial question. Once distracted they have no option but to go back to the beginning and start again. You can try this with American waiters; it works just as well.

Once you've got past the period set-piece re-enactments and inspected a conserved huddle of homesteads you proceed to the tour of the battlefield proper. The Americans have a special way of doing this too, and you don't even need to leave the comfort of your automobile. What you do is drive around the site and every so often there is a little lay-by and huge hoardings describing what happened there. You read the details through the windows of your air-conditioned cabin and squint into the distance at the features on the landscape that are colourfully described in the narrative. It's very difficult to buck the system. After the first placard I pulled off the road, though I had to move a couple of whitewashed stones that were strategically placed all the way along to prevent you doing just that. But there wasn't much to see, and soon Abraham Lincoln spotted me from the visitor centre and came and remonstrated with me and insisted I return to my vehicle.

I learned more from my bubble gum cards.

Of the ninety or so cards in the pack, I think I was finally short of only two as the craze fizzled out and we all got excited about something else. I know I never got 'wall of corpses'. I'm sure that somewhere out there in the ether, probably on eBay there is someone who is selling 'wall of corpses' and the other card, whatever it is, and I could finally complete my set. But what the hell. What sort of person would do that?

In the meantime, they're just gathering dust like everything else on my Delft rack.

The cards are in a little pile between two clockwork boats that I used to play with in the bath that I would share with my sister. She had yellow plastic dolphins, I recall, with which she would launch an attack on my fleet. I treasured my boats and unlike most of my toys, I took great care of them. There was another one, an old-fashioned lifeboat, the sort that you had to row, with ropes hung all along the sides, and it was my favourite despite the fact that it had no motor. I took it down to the beach one day while we were on holiday. I wouldn't take

17

my other boats anywhere near the sea, for fear that the salt and the sand would damage the clockwork mechanisms. When we left the beach to go back home to the caravan we were staying in, somehow I forgot about it. I left it lying there in the sand. When I realised what I'd done we were practically at the door and my mum wouldn't go back to help me look for it. The next day it was gone, of course. Someone had taken it. I hoped they enjoyed playing with it as much as I had done and treasured it. Or perhaps I hoped that they became distracted with it, ventured too far out of their depth and drowned.

A rather curious thing happened one day when we were still living in the Midlands. I kept my boats on top of a chest of drawers in the spare room at that time and my father was staying with us and sleeping in the room. He said what a funny thing, but he used to have two boats just like those when he was a boy. He said he also had an old-fashioned lifeboat, which had been his favourite.

I don't want to get so old that I don't remember giving away my toys.

My dad also gave me knives to play with. He was into knives. And swords. Well, I suppose any edged weapon, really. And guns, too, actually.

He gave me my first knife when I was eight. It was a little sheath knife with a bone handle and leather scabbard. I had just joined the cubs and I wore it proudly on my belt to the first meeting. When my dad came to collect me, Akela took him to one side and told him I was too young to be carrying a knife around like that. My dad told her that his dad had given him his first knife when he was six and no one had stopped him wearing it. I don't know what she replied because dad never told me that bit, but anyway, I never wore it again to cubs.

The thing was, my dad liked his knives sharp. He would spend hours honing his blades on a very fine diamond stone that he had illegally acquired from his employer. He gave it to me just before he died, and I keep it in a kitchen drawer and use it to sharpen the breadknife. My little sheath knife was very sharp indeed and was my pride and joy. Had I had any whiskers at the age of eight I could have shaved with it.

I know what you're thinking and you're way off the mark. It was all entirely innocent. I didn't go around pinning spiders to trees or skinning rabbits alive. I whittled. I was a very good whittler and I could make a good feather quill and carve a usable spoon.

When I graduated to the scouts, I upgraded to a four-inch leather handled blade which I would wear on my belt in the small of my back, and then I started wearing it all the time, except to school when even in those days they drew the line at such a visible gesture, though I always carried a penknife. It's difficult to explain to a youngster how different things like this were. People just thought differently. It would never have occurred to anyone that a knife was being carried for reasons of defence. Or attack, come to that.

The one and only time I had hassle was when I was about fifteen and waiting in a queue outside the Vandyke cinema with my mates to see Get Carter. I have to say that by this time I was going through my belligerent period. I was almost certainly experimenting with facial stubble, bought my clothes from jumble sales and was wearing my hair as long as I could get away with. The lady in the ticket office shrieks that that man has got a big knife and everyone looks round at me. To be fair, I think that they had probably had some trouble with teddy boys ripping up the seats in the fifties and had never recovered from the trauma. I had to go through the embarrassment of taking it from my belt and handing it in to the office and because it was at my back I had to take my belt right off, and for a second or two I thought my jeans might fall down. It was an incident that I later dwelled on for some time and in my imagination I had me taking it from the sheath and handing it over with the blade exposed, pointing at the stupid woman. It would have been an unwise thing to do and best kept in my fantasy.

When I collected it at the end of the film the woman gave me a look that said she was eternally grateful that her children hadn't grown up like me.

Ah, what innocent times. The only law we were breaking was being underage to see an X film.

I've got most of my dad's knives here in my study. There are probably about ten of them scattered around. Some are hung on pins on the wall and others lie on the shelf. All razor sharp and ready to whittle. There's a twelve-inch Bowie knife with an engraving of a deer on it; a nasty looking Spanish stiletto; a curious flick knife that looks more like a cut-throat razor and a Hitler Youth sheath knife with a tacky fleur-de-lis stuck over the swastika on the handle. I can see my father using it with a mallet to cut the tongue from a floorboard and saying, as he ruined the butt with the heavy blows that this was a much better use than it had ever been intended for. I still like to carry a knife with me and take great pleasure in selecting one for a night out.

And then there are the Samurai swords. I have those, too. They're all hidden in a narrow oak chest in my bedroom, layered between offcuts of upholstery fabric. Except for one, my favourite, that I have standing next to my desk. Just in case I need to use it in an emergency. It is a wakizashi, a small, one-handed sword that is perfectly balanced in my one hand. I like to take it from its sharkskin scabbard and just look at the blade in various lights. I wonder how many have felt the steel inside them? It is a very old sword. It is signed and dated on the hilt and my father took a rubbing and sent it off to an expert at the British Museum. 1524. In fact 3rd May 1524 was the day the blade was commissioned. Despite the fact it is so old and in good condition, it is by an unknown maker and so is evidently not worth much money at all. In the sixties you could pick these things up in junk shops for next to nothing. Dad never paid more than ten pounds for any of them. I suppose a lot were brought home as souvenirs from the war. Stolen or taken from Nippon officers who had used the family heirloom as a final futile vehicle to relive the halcyon days of their great warrior ancestors.

At least with Japanese swords you don't have to sharpen them. They're sharp enough already. The way the blade is forged creates an extremely hard edge that never dulls. That's why each sword took about a year to make, folding the layers of steel over and over upon themselves. When a blade was completed, the master swordsmith would pop down to his local nick and select a handful of prisoners from Death Row and check and see if the blade was up to scratch. If it could slice a man from shoulder to hip it would pass muster.

Dad tested a favourite blade once, not with a local felon but with the Sunday joint. He took it out in the back garden and put it on a log that he used as a chopping block for splitting kindling. Then he knelt down, took the sword and sliced the rack of beef in half with a single deft stroke. Both pieces fell on the lawn on either side of the block and mum had to wash them again to get the grass off. My sister and I were greatly

21

impressed. It would have been more impressive if he had been wearing some colourful lacquered armour and a bandana as well, but in those days we didn't rock the boat as the garden was overlooked on all sides by the other semis in our road and the one behind us.

I'm looking at the blade of the wakizashi now in front of me, sat here in my study. In five hundred years you must have seen some keen bloodshed, but this house was old before you were even forged.

three

There are many compensations to living alone, as I'm sure you'll know if you've ever found yourself in those circumstances.

One of my favourites is being able to walk into the house with muddy boots on and not get shouted at. Now, if you live in a city or a town this won't be much of an issue for you, but here in the country, mud is something of a way of life, particularly in the winter months. I know, I know, it doesn't take a lot of effort to slip your wellingtons off at the door, and once you've trained yourself to do this, I'm sure it wouldn't be the stubborn problem that it still remains for me.

I opened the back door once to the old farmer we'd bought the house from, the one that I was telling you about. It was soon after the builder had moved in and I was down for the weekend. The place was a tip. Dust and grime everywhere, carpets up, old plaster strewn all over the shop. The first thing he did on the door-step was to take his boots off. He was born in the house; his mother would have instilled this drill in him from the moment he could walk. He could no more pass the threshold booted up than he would go to evensong on a Sunday night without a jacket and tie, even if it meant getting his socks filthy and running the risk of a rusty nail through the sole of his foot. We're made of different stuff, me and him.

I delight in keeping my boots on. No, I delight in being able to keep my boots on, still, after all these years. It's different. Don't get me wrong; I'm not a particularly dirty person. I'm quite happy to go over the carpets with the vacuum cleaner after the mud has dried. It's what I call clean dirt. Wholesome stuff. I don't much care for decaying things in my house, but I don't mind honest country loam.

My dog is of the same bent; she doesn't mind, either. She's not allowed on the furniture, but she has her favourite corners where I can put rugs that can be shaken outside. They can whiff a bit after a while, I suppose, but you do get used to it.

Most dog owners don't realise their pets smell; they've obviously got used to it, too. It surprises me how many people allow their dogs to lie on chairs or stretch out on settees. And share their beds, for God's sake! Rosie isn't allowed upstairs and I would never let her anywhere near my bedroom. All I can think is that other people's dogs must be a lot cleaner than Rosie.

We had friends once who when they visited used to let their yellow lab sit on my armchair as if it were in their own home. I suppose that because the rest of the room looked 'lived in' they assumed that it was okay, and they didn't realise that although the chair didn't really look up to much, we had had it reupholstered in a very expensive fabric for about a thousand pounds. On reflection, they WERE the sort of people who could tell a Sanderson or a Designers Guild from an Ikea, so maybe they didn't care and were wanting to be disrespectful or just taking the piss.

We never said anything. We let it go. We were those sort of people then.

If they came and did it now I would tell them to fuck off out of it.

But, of course, they wouldn't venture anywhere near my home nowadays, even if they could find me.

We never did live full time in Church House as a family. It was always that most vilified of things, a second home. Nobody likes people who own second homes. That's especially true around these parts where empty properties rip the hearts out of communities.

Having been a second home owner, I have rehearsed all the arguments, for and against. I've had opportunity to dwell on the finer points and I've thought it all through. As with most things, I hold a very objective, well-informed and impartial viewpoint. It's starkly obvious that someone who has grown up in and endured a cold, dark, damp hovel is going to want to move to new affordable housing and is delighted to sell it at the first opportunity to an outsider looking for the country cottage idyll, despite what they may have told their friends. And equally obvious that if the outsider didn't buy the cottage with his outsider money, then the thing would ultimately fall down and return to the earth from whence it came. It's obvious, because that's what used to happen before there were outsiders with money.

The fact of the matter is that in the twenty first century, it is virtually impossible to make money in the countryside, whereas it is very easy to make obscene amounts in the city.

So, if the outsider wasn't interested, or wasn't allowed to invest in these rural properties, the money would stay in the cities, and the divide would widen. I know all this. And when we renovated Church House we used only local builders who otherwise would have been scratching around for business. And when we came at weekends we would buy our meat from the butcher in Chulmleigh and our fruit and veg from the market in South Molton, and we would eat at the Druid's Arms in the village. And I know that the summer visitors who book the holiday cottages largely do the same, although nowadays it seems they have probably stocked up at Waitrose in Tiverton, or more likely, arranged for a strategically timed Ocado delivery. They bring into the area much needed cash and they all pay their business rates or full council tax (no discounts anymore).

But.

There's no getting around the fundamental problem that both second homes and holiday cottages are empty for more days than they're full. And when they are empty, so are the pubs and the cafes and the shops. And whether they are full or not, they don't have children who keep the local school going or teenagers who make a dance in the village hall a viable option.

So really, like I say, nobody likes a second home owner.

Whenever we got talking to locals, my stock story would be that we were intending to retire down here, and I was naively happy that this would be some compensation in their eyes. In retrospect, it's plain that the locals see through all this and although they are friendly and approachable they will never treat you as one of them until you are one of them. And that doesn't mean that you've got to have been born here or have three generations in the churchyard. That's become a bit of a cliché. It just means that you have to live here. Full time.

So it's a bit of a paradox that I actually did retire here, though not perhaps in the way that we all had in mind. But although in some ways I most certainly am not one of them, and now will never be allowed to be, I have inevitably morphed into a local and on the rare occasions when I now find myself in the Druid's, I smirk along with the others when a second home owner feigns casual familiarity with the landlord in front of his urban friends. It's a game we all play.

Now that I'm here on my own, there are some parts of the house that I don't use at all. The bedroom that I once shared with Georgia, for example. I haven't been in there since that first day when I crawled in from the Jag when my life went pear-shaped. I couldn't bear to even go in. I probably could now but I don't think I want to. I know it will be in a bit of a state. I've noticed from outside that the window frame has rotted and one or two of the panes have slipped. There's not much of a danger that even driving rain will get in because of the deep overhang of thatch from the eaves but I've noticed that the ivy that clings to this part of the wall has found its way inside. I can see in my mind's eye the greasy creeper wrapping itself around the bed, throttling the fancy porcelain globe on Georgia's side of the headboard and looking around hungrily for its next victim.

More worryingly, I know that jackdaws have been getting in. I can hear them when I pass the door. There's a nest in there this year. God, what a mess it'll be.

I decided when I came back that I would sleep in the green room, as it was always my favourite. It's quite small but I've managed to shoehorn in a five-foot wrought iron bedstead. It's got a good pocket-sprung mattress and a duck down and feather topper that makes the whole thing feel very much like an old-fashioned feather bed. The sort that I used to sleep in when we went to my grandmother's. You can mould a comfy nest in it and it swathes round you and envelopes you in its cosiness. I use Irish linen sheets, which I change every second Monday and the most expensive Hungarian goose down pillows that I could find. They cost over two hundred pounds

27

each and have been the best investment I've ever made. Don't let anyone dazzle you with thread counts of Egyptian cotton or seduce you with silk. It may be a bit of a pig to wash and iron, but you can't beat real Irish linen.

When we were first married I didn't know any of this. For the previous ten years I had, in fact, been sleeping in Redfern Cottage in a bed that I'd bought at a Church fete for fifty pence, with the mattress and delivery thrown in for free. I'd never slept WITH anyone before. The rickety old bed that Georgia brought with her was rubbish, too. When eventually it fell to bits and we had some cash in the bank to buy another it was a revelation. The kids were quite young still. We drove to a converted mill on the Welsh borders that advertised in the back of a period lifestyle magazine. We fancied a Victorian style bed for our newly acquired Victorian style village house. The salesman instructed us all to take our shoes off and get in, which we did, all four of us. The kids were beside themselves with pleasure and awe. We came away with the whole outfit, and never really looked back, sleep-wise. I simply hadn't appreciated how interrupted my sleep patterns had become. On a narrow bed with a crappy, broken-down coil mattress, every movement your partner makes ripples over to your side and disturbs you. With a pocket-sprung Superking that just doesn't happen. The downside is that it's much less intimate, and this perhaps played a far more significant role in our drifting apart than I realised at the time. Sometimes it really was just like sleeping on my own, again.

The kids never did tire of 'four in a bed', however, and we had some lovely family times on a Saturday or Sunday morning, Georgia and me reading the papers and the kids up to whatever took their fancy. Such halcyon days.

The green room is the oldest and most original of all the bedrooms in Church House. It was in fact a sleeping chamber when the rest of the inside was open to the roof and the hearth was in the middle of the floor. It would have been reached by a ladder and was the only private part of the house, when communal living was very much the order of the day. All the unspoken stuff would have happened in here for a century or two. Conceptions, births, illnesses and sometimes deaths. I say sometimes because I guess it wouldn't have been easy to bring a lifeless body down from the chamber with any sort of dignity. Ailing family members were probably encouraged to make their own way down while they still could, and then die somewhere more convenient. You can still see coffin traps in the joists of some of the smaller cottages in Devon and Cornwall, but I don't think they ever bothered with that here.

I know it was a sleeping chamber because the internal walls are smoke-blackened on their outside and in the roof void. I discovered it when I took the paper off the room next door. I'm going to be telling you a lot more about smoke-blackening a little later as it plays an important part in my story. We'll come back to it. It really is the Holy Grail of vernacular domestic architecture and the guys from English Heritage get off on it.

The plaster in the green room is a bit of a mixture of materials from repairs that have been made over the centuries, but the oldest bits have a very fine finishing coat of ... mud. I've never seen this anywhere else. It's just dried mud and hair. No lime at all so it is very fragile. It's just held together by the hair and my builder had to repair it very carefully by squirting a sort of lime slurry underneath to stabilise it and stick it to the next layer down, which is also mud.

So in my bedroom wall in the most unassuming of dwellings is hair that was shaved from children who had become old and grey by the time Henry VIII started his demolition job on the monasteries. Well, a bit melodramatic maybe; the hair was probably from the farm goat or a horse, but you get the picture.

After my builder finished his work I painted the room with a weak limewash, coloured with a minty-green pigment. I was experimenting really and had intended giving it another coat or two, but I was so pleased with the result after only the initial application that I left it as it was. It accentuates the lumpiness of the finish of the plaster and creates a wonderful changing backdrop as the sun or a bright moon traverses across the window. I can just lie and watch the shifting shadows for hours sometimes.

Since I moved in a crack has slowly opened in the outer wall and it's now about a quarter of an inch wide in places and looks troublesome. The walls in these houses are moving all the time. They were built to move. I guess the back wall of the house is spreading out from the weight of the roof at the moment and it will probably carry on like this for another decade or two. Then other factors will take over; a heave in the floor for example, or a drying out of the shale that is the local bedrock, and then the crack will spend the next twenty or thirty years closing up again. I don't worry about it. The house isn't going to fall down.

The window sill is deep and you can sit on it and immerse yourself within the depth of the wall; become part of it. I painted it in Arsenic flat oil, a Farrow & Ball favourite of mine, and I like to keep a jug of fresh flowers in the middle on a crocheted doily of my great aunt's. Yesterday I picked some roses from my Albertine and put them there with some early honeysuckle. What a wonderful, heady scent. So evocative of this time of year.

There's honeysuckle on my curtains too. It's a William Morris print. And on my bed is a fantastic patchwork quilt that I got from eBay. It looks like 1930's offcuts, hundreds of very small hexagons with a purple border and backing. It's seen a lot of use and is very shabby chic. The floor has these massive elm boards, black through age and there's a little qashqai kilim at the side of the bed. It's all very Country Living. I love my little bedroom.

Living on your own means you can indulge your tastes in this way. You can be as contrary and eccentric as you like. I keep my own company and don't need an en-suite bathroom because there's no one to be offended or embarrassed when I walk around naked, as I often do.

If you've ever lived alone, you'll know all these things. I've told you, I'd lived on my own for a decade before Georgia and I bought our first house. She was very brave to take on someone who had indulged his own tastes and peccadillos for such a long time.

I sort of fell into the solitary lifestyle when I was a young man. I was about a year into my PhD and reluctantly had to leave my room in a shared student house at short notice. An acquaintance who I knew vaguely from the pub darts team offered me a room in the house he was renting from his employer. He was an aspiring land agent and the house was tied to a large country estate. It was a gamekeeper's cottage; probably early Edwardian with a pebble-dashed ground floor façade on the front elevation. A typical estate property. It had had nothing spent on it in years. No heating except a ceramic art deco open fireplace in the back room and a little Rayburn with the glass poked out in the kitchen.

It was also extraordinarily cheap. Just five pounds a week, and the rent never went up the whole time I was living there. That was less than half I'd been paying a year previously for a box room in a council house, during an ill-fated, but mercifully short sojourn in Slough, of all places. There were no rates to pay for some reason; I never did find out who looked after that, and fuel came mostly from the surrounding woodland and water from a blue pipe from the neighbouring farm that got iced up in severe frosts.

The land agent unexpectedly got made redundant when his local office was rationalised while he was on holiday, so I ended up living with him for only about four months, and for most of that he was away looking for other jobs. When he left, I inherited his cat Seamus, an ex-pub cat with an illustrious history, and, on what was initially to be a temporary arrangement, his black Labrador Jet. All land agents have a black Labrador. Most of them are called Jet.

I didn't really bother much with Seamus; he could look after himself. I never fed him, though if he was around he would try his luck with Jet's supper if he could get his snout in quick enough. Some dogs wouldn't stand for this, but Jet would let it go without any show of intolerance. She was a nice dog.

I got into the habit of leaving a frying pan on top of the stove when I'd finished cooking with it and it took me some months to realise that Seamus was licking all the fat clean from the surface. So obvious when you know, but not, seemingly, when you don't. Like a lot of things.

I would always throw Seamus out at night. I don't agree with cats staying in overnight. What sort of life is that for them? And cat flaps are just asking for trouble. I don't think you should own a cat if you don't let it hunt at night.

Every country house should have a cat. I share one now. I'm not sure who with, but I know I'm not the sole owner. It's a lovely little black cat that I call Frank and it comes and keeps me and Rosie company sometimes. It leaves me mice on the doorstep and will wait for hours in the kitchen or under the stairs when it senses a kill.

Seamus used to specialise in worrying a particular species for a season. One year it was pigeons (ok); the next, moles (good); then rats (very good). He tried weasels once but gave up after he'd seen off only two, fortunately. I think they were just too hard to catch and too likely to get a bite in first. I like weasels.

Seamus turned out to be an extraordinary cat. He developed a weeping cyst on a hind leg and I was persuaded by a squeamish friend to take him to the vets. I avoid vets if I can. I don't like them and neither did Seamus. The cyst was no problem and he dealt with it simply and quickly but then he said, did I realise that this cat was totally blind. Couldn't even tell light from dark. Here, take a look he added, when he saw my sceptical expression and handed me a torch. Sure enough, when you shone a light in Seamus's eyes you could see that there was absolutely nothing there behind the cornea. Amazing.

When I got him home I tried a little experiment and moved some of the furniture round in the kitchen. Sure enough, he walked into everything that I'd adjusted. Well, he'd been getting by just fine before I realised that he was blind, so there didn't seem to be much point in changing things, so I still threw him out at night without his supper. I did have a heightened respect for him when I saw him creeping along the tin ridge of the woodshed roof, and he continued to have no problem catching

33

pigeons and feeding himself for another couple of years. I don't know what became of him. One day he just wasn't there any longer, and I never did find him.

I was in my element at Redfern Cottage and soon established and developed my full Lawrencian persona. Of course, I had seen and read Lady Chatterley and was very taken by the whole idea, especially as DH had only lived just up the road in Eastwood. I became the gamekeeper. I even took washes outside from a water butt, stripped to the waist. I must have looked a bit of a fool.

It was a truly rural idyll, with no near neighbours and just a dairy herd for company. There was a big timber shed behind the house where the estate carpenters had knocked up all the fencing and woodwork. It had this huge circular saw in it with a single-phase motor and star-delta starter, so when it was cranked up all the lights dimmed, practically went out. It was just like the sort of saw that you see women tied to in silent movies. It had an elaborate guard, but that had obviously been dismantled long ago and lay rusting on the floor beside it in a heap. I bet the blade was over three feet in diameter and it was full of truly vicious teeth. One year, the Post Office decided to renew the telegraph pole outside the garden gate and they left the old one lying in the drive. Before they could take it away, I enlisted a friend to help me saw it up. We couldn't lift it, so we had to drag it to the shed and manoeuvre it into position next to the saw. First, we lopped off a seven-foot section for a new gate post and then started slicing the rest of it up for firewood. It was hairy stuff. After about the third log we somehow managed to skew the pole with a bit of a jerk and it started the blade warping and twisting, just like that Tacoma Narrows suspension bridge in the wind. We couldn't recover it and we couldn't get the pole back out. In the end we felt we had no option but to just drop it and run (not that we entered into a debate about what course of action to pursue. I think it was more just a terrified glance and mutual recognition). As it turned out, there was no time to run anywhere. There was a bang, of unimaginable magnitude, and the blade broke into about a dozen deadly shards that flew across the shed in all directions, ripping several holes in the tin cladding which offered no resistance to the flight at all. It was all over so quickly, we just stood where we were and offered up a silent prayer to whoever or whatever had protected us.

The motor was jammed and started to overheat with that characteristic smell of burning insulation that all electrical engineers know so well. I yanked the handle back and eventually all became silent, marking the passing of this undeniably exciting episode into folklore.

Much later, I found one of the larger fragments from the blade a full two hundred yards away, sticking up in the middle of a corn field; it wouldn't have done a combine much good. The Post Office man came back for his pole some weeks on and when quizzing me as to the whereabouts of his property was oblivious to the fact that he was actually leaning on the part of it that had become the new gatepost. The remaining ten-foot section that we hadn't managed to saw up I fed into the fire in the living room, with the far end balanced on a stool. It lasted most of January, but made the whole house stink of bitumen and tar for the rest of the winter.

The best bit about living at Redfern cottage was the woods. It's where I first experienced the thrill of going out at night into the natural world.

There were about a hundred and twenty acres altogether, in two compartments; Redfern Wood and Pasture Wood, linked by a square about the size of four football pitches that had been clear felled just the year before I got there. All were ancient woodland sites and it was evident that they had been well maintained until maybe the fifties, and then, like so many of our woods in England, had just been neglected. I'm not sure what had prompted the clear felling. Maybe there was a grant or some other funding involved. The quality of timber couldn't have produced any income, especially with the cost of new fencing and replanting. The woods were now just used for hunting. This was Quorn Tuesday country, so the rides were kept clear of brambles and suckers, fallers were sawn and hauled into the side and culverts and drains cleaned out by estate workers with spades every winter.

The woods were wonderful and we had them to ourselves, Jet and me, as long as we kept an eager ear out for the baying of hounds. The trees were mainly oak, mature specimens probably planted after the First World War, which had had a good start in life but were beginning to suffer from lack of management. The understorey was a thicket of briars and brambles, largely impenetrable, with honeysuckle and ivy scrabbling for survival on the dank floor. There were some ash and alder in the wetter parts and at the far end a marvellous glade of beech, where in the spring a carpet of snowdrops and aconites and then bluebells would erupt before the canopy closed over.

Primroses and violets smothered the edges of the rides and the bottoms of hawthorn hedges.

The countryside of the East Midlands is not in the same league as North Devon most of the year but at the beginning of May when the hawthorn is in full flower and the hedges are frothing with cow parsley it comes into its own and there is no equal. England has no equal, I would say, at this time of year. Why would you want to be anywhere else?

I would walk Jet for half an hour before I drove into the lab. The great thing about having a dog is that you have to walk it, no matter what the weather. It gets you outside when you really wouldn't choose to be, if you had a choice. The question doesn't really arise if you have a dog, so you don't even think about the rain or the wind, or the snow. You become aware of the changing seasons in a way that would just pass you by if you weren't out in it every day. My favourite times were in the evening when I came home from work. There are far more noticeable changes then. In the winter it would be dark and cold. Sometimes crisp and sparkling with frost, at other times muddy and bitter. Jet was always frantic with excitement in anticipation of my homecoming and I felt sorry to think of her alone during the cold dark afternoons. I had an informal arrangement with the son of the farmer who looked after the surrounding fields and he would come and let her out most days. He would let me know if he was going to be away and then I would either take her to the lab with me and walk her at lunchtime, or sometimes I would just leave the back door of the house ajar and she could come and go as she pleased.

Ah, more carefree, innocent days.

I had no worries about being burgled despite the fact that the house was unoccupied during the day and was in the middle of nowhere, and in fact the windows on the ground floor wouldn't shut because the frames were rotten and had swollen up and the front door key was on a string behind the letterbox where anyone would look first. I simply had no possessions that anyone would think worth taking. I once, for some reason, became alarmed that I had no contents cover. I think I had assumed that my landlord, the land agent, had got this sorted and he'd told me that just the buildings were insured, and I thought I had better address the problem. I went into a broker in town, filled in a form and handed it in to the guy behind the desk. He looked through it and asked me what level of cover I was looking for. I hadn't really given this any thought. Let's see; carpets and curtains, television, fridge, cooker, twin-tub, furniture, clothes. I thought hard and came up with an answer. £450. The man looked at me with a weary expression and then informed me that the lowest level of protection they offered, on their most meagre of policies, was sixteen thousand pounds. I decided, under the circumstances and now that I'd been able to give it some serious consideration, that I wouldn't bother after all.

When I moved out of Redfern Cottage to live with Georgia, I filled a large skip with the junk and everything else went on a bonfire. All I took were my clothes, my things, my books and my Sony Digicube clock radio that was a birthday present from my parents and still sits next to my bed to this day.

I'd kept a low profile with the estate on the premise that they had completely forgotten about me, and if I gave them nothing to worry about, they would leave me alone. At five pounds a week rent, despite the derisory salary I was drawing as a researcher at the university, I was still able to save, and this enabled me to survive when we came to start up the company on the smallest of shoestrings and I existed with no income at all for the first six months. My only outgoings were on petrol and beer and food, but by then I prided myself on frugal eating and could feed myself easily for a further two or three pounds a week.

It was the long, languid summer evenings that were my best time. Often, I wouldn't get back from the lab till gone eight and then I would be straight out with Jet into those sublime woods.

The thing about summer nights is the smell. Ah, the smell of summer; there's nothing quite like it. It's a cornucopia of scents and stinks from a myriad of disparate sources. You just don't get that in winter. There are maybe a few garden plants like viburnum or daphne that will give you winter perfume but there are none in the countryside. It is a desolate, odour free zone in winter. Contrast this with mown grass, bluebells, hawthorn, cows, foxes, wild garlic, primroses, dog roses, crab apples. I could go on. Honeysuckle, my favourite; wild herbs like angelica and mint and fennel; and fresh badger shit. I used to like to take a rug and spread it out on the edge of the open area that had been felled and just lie there with Jet. Where the sunlight had kindled the flora from dormancy there were swathes of foxgloves, bluebells and primroses that first year I was there.

An arising from a sleep of generations.

All this stuff, the bulbs; ancient seeds and corms; spores of fungi and eggs of all sorts; it's all lying there, just below the surface. We can't see it. We're not aware that it's there. But it is. It's next to us wherever we are. It's just biding its time.

This is going to be a recurring theme in my message to you. It is the very heart of what I'm going to tell you, so just give yourself a minute or two to let it sink in.

four

Among the many things that I inherited from my grandfather, my father's father, was a coat. He had worked on the railways as a porter for most of his life and over a period of time he had accumulated a number of items of clothing from his work. He died suddenly in his sleep soon after he retired, a fate that was alarmingly common in working men of his generation, and one that my father was determined to avoid.

He left behind several coats, boiler-suits, aprons, overalls, sundry steel capped boots and such-like. My dad and I found them hanging in a metal cupboard in the poultry shed at the bottom of his vegetable plot when we were clearing his stuff out. There was also a canvas sun cap on a hook that he always wore on the beach when we took him and my nana to Weston Super Mare for the day. I have a photograph of him sitting in a deckchair, sleeves rolled up and his arms around me and my sister. I'm looking at the hat now. It's on a peg by the window. It's too small for me as I have quite a big head.

My dad gathered up the clothes and the boots and the steel cupboard and put them in his own workshop in our back garden. He took a fancy to a navy reefer jacket that was just his size and fitted him well. It was double-breasted and had black buttons down the front that said 'British Railways' around the edge. He cut the buttons off and replaced them with silver ones that had incised anchors on them. He thought they made him look like an Admiral. He was very aspirational of the sea, was my father and he subscribed to Yachting Monthly which he pored over endlessly, but in reality he had never sailed in anything more exciting than the Isle of White ferry. It didn't make him look like an Admiral. Thank God he never bought himself a bicorn hat as well.

When my father in turn died in his sleep the coat was still hanging there in his wardrobe. I don't think he had worn it much. I suspect that deep down he had realised that he looked a bit of a clown in it. Hanging next to it was a thick black greatcoat made from felted wool, but this one still had the British Railways buttons all the way down the front. I tried it on. It fitted perfectly, but it had rather long sleeves.

Our RE teacher at school, a church chaplain and the nearest thing to a scholar that our school possessed, told us that Joseph's coat had long sleeves. It didn't have many colours. Not even amazing Technicolor ones. It had long sleeves because that meant that you did no physical work, like growing long fingernails or small feet in China, but less extreme I guess, because you could always take the coat off and get stuck in to some manual labour... whereas if you had small feet. It was one of those dodgy bible translations that had crept in while no one was looking, and erroneously assumed a legitimacy of its own. Now I have to say that I have never corroborated this little nugget, nor ever seen any other reference to it, so I don't know if it's true or not, but I have absolute faith in our chaplain's scholarliness. It has stuck in my mind all these years like many other things he taught us about the bible and that just tells me how good a teacher he was.

The arms are long enough for my hands to disappear inside the sleeves, so it wouldn't be much good for wheel-tapping or hauling passengers' luggage. I started wearing the coat when I went walking in the woods with Jet. It was very warm in winter, but its best feature was its ability to absorb rain, which it could do all year round. The trouble with most modern raincoats is that, although they might keep the rain out, they let it drip onto your trousers and you end up with wet legs. Also, most raincoats don't breathe, no matter what you have been told by the salesman or what you have read in the marketing material or how much you have paid for it. It is all blatant lies. Nothing has yet been invented that is waterproof and yet disperses sweat from a briskly walking human. My coat with long sleeves, on the other hand, is so thick that the sweat is absorbed on the inside while the rain is soaking through from the outside. I found that in heavy, persistent rain I could walk briskly for forty minutes without the sweat and the rain meeting in the middle and causing problems and I could remain perfectly comfortable and relaxed and dry. There were only two issues. Firstly, the coat would eventually become extremely heavy and secondly, it would take several days to dry the thing out, hanging dripping over the bath.

At that time of my life I was wearing both my beard and my hair long and unkempt. I grew up during a period when young people were pushing boundaries as never before and the best, literally in your face way you could do this if you were a male was by growing all your hair long. All through secondary school I strived to be the boy with the longest hair and was constantly berated by my teachers who on more than one occasion actually frogmarched me round the corner to the local barbers and stood over me while the regulation length was re-established. No money ever changed hands; the bastards must have had some sort of arrangement. One sanctimonious teacher attempted to take my side and explained that he had no problem with my hair because it was obviously washed and well groomed, whereas other boys were not so fastidious. I could have told him that I hadn't washed it for two years, which was true, but he probably wouldn't have believed me. My hair and I had reached a sort of equilibrium, as I understand will happen to anyone who doesn't flush their natural oils away constantly with detergents and soaps. A downside, I suppose, was that it did get a bit itchy in summer and left an unpleasant greasy residue on my comb, but it did save me a lot of time.

I only ever saw my dad wash his hair once and that was when a sumpful of dirty engine oil made a sudden unexpected appearance while he was tinkering underneath the car one time. He needed most of a bottle of Fairy Liquid to get the stuff out and then a good dollop of Brylcreem to flatten the fuzziness afterwards.

Anyway, by the late seventies I eventually tired of long hair and one morning in a fit of pique and adventure I took the scissors to my black shoulder length locks for the first time. It wasn't really a great success, style-wise but it was certainly, according to all my friends, a shocking development, and it did afford me some notoriety that I was pleased to bask in. It plainly wasn't regarded in my social circle as selling out to conformity, perhaps quite the opposite, I think.

I took to wearing my coat with long sleeves into Loughborough on a Saturday afternoon.

When I first came to Loughborough as an undergraduate it was the most northerly place I'd ever been to. In fact, I assumed it was the North. I was born and grew up in a suburb of Bristol and had enjoyed, by today's standards, an extraordinarily narrow upbringing. Loughborough has a market every Thursday and Saturday, just like South Molton, and I was just blown away by it. It seems nonsense to suggest it now, but I had never actually experienced a traditional market. It is a sad reflection of what was going on in the sixties, but all the markets we had ever been to in Bristol were full of Pakistanis selling anoraks and parkas; West Indians flogging tacky jewellery and children's toys and spivs selling brushed nylon shirts that were two sizes smaller than the label suggested. Basically, all things that you would be foolish to buy more than once, though some obviously did.

Loughborough open-air market had proper stalls and real people. Here were haberdashers, milliners, hardware and kitchenware stalls, a wet fishmonger, two butchers with rabbits and pheasants and occasionally geese hanging on hooks, a stall devoted entirely to cheese (in 1972!) and several fruit and veg emporiums. I also couldn't believe the prices of these things. Although I was a fresh-faced, naïve eighteen-year-old straight from school, I had in fact spent some time during school holidays fending for myself, cooking-wise, and even at that early stage in my life prided myself on being pretty savvy about buying food. I would never have dreamed of getting fruit and veg in a supermarket. I was well ahead of my time and bucking the trend as big supermarkets were becoming ubiquitous and popular, but I was breaking new ground with these Midlands stallholders.

Low as the prices might be, the trick was to see what was left at about four o clock in the afternoon when they started packing up. That's when some astonishing bargains could be winkled out, and all you needed was some strong arms and some enterprising ideas on how to incorporate a dozen cauliflower and a stone weight case of bananas into the forthcoming week's menus.

Over time, I developed what I called my 'Saturday look' as I trawled the streets of Loughborough. To be blunt, the look was basically that of a tramp. My appearance was, I'm sure, greatly informed by the number of beers I'd drunk the night before. I must have looked as rough as I usually felt. I always went out on a Friday night 'whether I wanted to or not' as I pointedly and proudly told anyone I misguidedly thought would be impressed. I did have a close circle of like-minded drinking companions and we had a selection of pubs where we could be confident of finding a lock-in until the early hours. At some places you had to have a damn good excuse to leave before about four in the morning. Drinking and driving wasn't an issue. I know it should have been, but it wasn't. We didn't care. In an idle moment, I once calculated that I had driven drunk a thousand times before I turned thirty. I and my passengers and indeed members of the general public led a very charmed life.

I didn't wash or comb my hair (or beard) before I went out. It was all part of the look. The washing facilities at Redfern Cottage were a bit basic. A walk-in larder, more or less a lean-to outhouse, had been converted into a bathroom, though the outside privy in the back yard next to the coal shed was still functional. There was no shower and no heating. In winter you were lucky to get six inches of hot water in the bath from the combined efforts of the immersion heater and the back boiler of the labouring Rayburn, so there wasn't a great incentive to go for it when you didn't really need to. I wasn't the hardy

Lawrencian gamekeeper all the time. During the really cold months I would often take a shower in the squash changing rooms on campus before I went into the lab if I thought I was starting to smell.

Over time my coat became threadbare on the cuffs and elbows and mud and dirt from the woods clung stubbornly to the felt. When once I became entangled in barbed wire at the bottom of a ditch I ripped the left shoulder open and it really began to look the business. There is something poignant about a torn shoulder, something that is deeply unsettling and loathsome. Ask Leonard Cohen. You can easily test this for yourself with a jacket or coat. Give it a good rip at the shoulder and then go out with it on. It transforms you, instantly. It's better than stains down your trouser front, more noticeable.

I developed a way of scowling. A sort of mean, intense look with the eyes and I could make my jowls and cheekbones dance wildly by forcing the facial muscles. Sometimes I would find a pub and stand at the bar scowling at the other customers. If you go into a strange pub and scowl, you always have to stay for a second pint or people will think they've intimidated you, rather than the other way around.

I found myself looking at the guys in these pubs and the throng in Loughborough market place and holding them in deep contempt and derision. I didn't really like these people very much. I no longer had anything in common with them. Was the Saturday look the cause or effect? And why had I become such a sad, uncompromising misfit?

The funny thing was, the Saturday look was just that. It was only for Saturdays and for walking in the woods. On Sunday I smartened myself up and played darts at my village local at lunchtime, which was as convivial and conventional an occasion as you can imagine. I've always had a bit of a dual personality throughout the whole of my life. I cultivate it and it happens. I like people to think of me as a bit of an enigma.

When I moved out of Redfern Cottage, Georgia put the coat on the bonfire, along with much of my old life. I retrieved it before it burnt and hung it on a peg on the side door of my new garage in my new house in my new life, but I didn't wear it when Georgia was around. I guess for a while I had moved on. Then I decided to bring it down here to Devon and it inevitably became part of my new old life. I think of it as another enduring constant, like my beard.

I find I still have a use for my coat with long sleeves. After my breakdown, during my wilderness years when my 'Saturday look' became my 'everyday look', I found some solace in this link to my previous life.

I wear it to this day. Being black and long, it is ideal to use at night when you don't want to be seen.

five

I want to tell you how I came to buy Church House, so we're going to have to jump ahead some years. We'll go back afterwards, so don't worry. I just want to tell you this now; I hope you can follow it. We're going to fast forward to the spring of 1994 for a spell. We've got kids by then, and the company's flying.

I've always felt I was meant to find Church House. Something guided me here.

I had unexpectedly come into quite a lot of money (I'm going to tell you about that later, as well) and I felt like spending some of it before it burned a hole in my pocket. I thought I deserved to indulge myself after many years of hard graft.

As soon as the cash was safely banked up in my current account, I would buy myself a project. I fancied a nice old cottage that needed some work. I would do some myself and get specialists to do the tricky bits and it would become our family Second Home and we could spend weekends and school holidays relaxing in the countryside and exploring new seaside places with sandy beaches and bracing cliff walks.

I think Georgia had bought into the idea and I'd whipped the kids up to fever pitch. All I had to do was find it.

Georgia would have preferred somewhere on the East coast. Her childhood holidays had been in Whitby, and later on in Robin Hood's Bay and she had fond memories of these times and felt she could recreate them with her own family. We did try it once for a week when the kids were small. I told her she'd forgotten how cold the North Sea could be at Spring half term and I showed her the photographs of Angel and Miriam to refresh her memory, shivering with their buckets and spades and with so many layers of thick clothes on they couldn't bend down to dig the sand. I hear tell it's not much different in August.

I spent all my holidays in the West Country as a kid, where it was always sunny and warm, wasn't it?

We needed to be within about three hours of the East Midlands to make it worthwhile for us to come at weekends. I thought somewhere on Exmoor would be nice. There's some lovely coastline nearby, nice pubs, pretty villages, good walking.

I rang around a number of estate agents and got the details of some promising places. They sent me all sorts to whet my appetite. Cottages, farmhouses, Big Houses, hideaways and hovels. There seemed to be plenty of choice.

A couple of them particularly took my eye. One was an old smithy in a village near Minehead and the other a redundant farmhouse in a wooded valley just outside of Dulverton, which was coming up for auction with an unlikely guide price. I arranged to go and see it, just a day before the auction.

If you know anything about property auctions, you'll appreciate that this was a reckless notion. What was I thinking? The money had already burnt the hole and was playing with my mind. It can do that, you know, if you're not careful. I think

I must have fancied myself as the sort of nouveau-riche bastard we all sneer at who doesn't give a damn about fucking people's lives up, just because he can. I should have been concerned if I thought I was turning into this monster, but of course, I wasn't. Concerned, that is; that's the point. I would be sitting smugly in that auction room with no survey to find the settlement crack that the convenient siting of the dresser is hiding and no search to find the proposed new road through my new garden. And no financial preparations in advance to prove my fiscal propriety. All I would have with me would be my latest bank statement with the fat bottom line and I thought that would be enough. I think I would have been laughed out of the auction room if it had happened. We don't want you time wasters here. Go back to where you came from.

The smithy near Minehead was okay but it didn't set me alight. It didn't tick enough boxes. I was very taken with the farmhouse. I thought it had everything I wanted. I didn't give much credence to the guide price. That was just a joke. They always are at auctions; everyone knows that. I did think that it would end up in my range, though, with enough left over to do a nice conversion job and end up with a sizeable family home. Second Home. The auction was at eleven in the morning in a pub in Dulverton, so instead of trekking back up the M5 and down again, I thought I would go and find myself somewhere to stay the night. A quaint old village pub with rooms would be just the ticket.

And so it was that I ended up in Crow's Nymet. What took me there that afternoon? It's some way away from Dulverton and I'd passed plenty of likely hostelries before I came across the Druid's. What was it that was with me in the car, making seemingly arbitrary decisions on which direction to turn at crossroads, what unmarked lanes to venture down? Who knows? The Druid's didn't even do bed and breakfast, and in any case, it wasn't open when I stopped the car outside and got out to stretch my legs. There was no one about, but there was a cute chocolate-box cottage with a B&B sign swinging in the wind and I was standing next to the front gate. I am a believer in omens and portents and actually the whole day's experience was starting to take on a feeling of not being properly ordinary for a reason I couldn't quite get to the bottom of. Maybe I'm exaggerating or just remembering it wrongly, but I like to think that there were outside forces at work that afternoon.

Whatever, back to Earth. The B&B turned out to be a bit dull. Disappointing, really, because it looked very twee from outside. Even so, I was tired and decided to stay and I brought my overnight bag in from the car and had a shower and a nap and felt good. I could sense something special.

The pub opened at six and the kitchen at seven. I went over for an early pint and booked a table for later. There were some picnic benches out the front against the whitewashed rendering, so I took my beer outside and sat there taking in the last rays of the sun before it disappeared behind the golden thatch of the cottage roofs. It felt good on my face. This place was right. It was where I wanted to be.

It was probably because I was feeling a bit mellow that when I took a walk around the village and saw Church House for the first time, I fell in love with it instantly. Somehow, I wasn't surprised to see it, either. I knew it would be there.

You'll be thinking that it's not actually going to be for sale; that I'll walk up to the front door and make the owner an offer he can't refuse and seal the deal on the spot.

Not quite, but not a million miles away, as it happens.

It was for sale. There was an agent's sign tacked to the picket fence. But I did go and knock on the door, even though the sign said strictly by appointment only. Well, they all do. And the door was answered by the owner, the farmer I've already mentioned, though he wasn't living there at the time so I was lucky to catch him in. Another sign.

He wasn't all that friendly at first. In fact, he came over as a crabby old git. I had to smooth talk him. I don't think he was all that keen on my looks, and it was probably a good thing that I'd left the Jag outside the pub. It might have prejudiced him.

He did let me in and showed me round and I warmed to him. I remember I found it difficult to understand much of what he was saying at first, especially when he got into his stride. I gathered that he'd lived there all his life but had recently moved to a new bungalow he'd had built in his farmyard, which was just down the lane. His daughter wanted to keep a closer eye on him, evidently, now that he was losing it (my words, not his, but it was pretty obvious). He'd already taken most of his furniture out, so it didn't look very homely, and it was in a bit of a mess with ceilings down in the main bedroom and damp dragging wallpaper off here and there. I loved it. I could see past the squalor and decrepitude.

He said he'd been made an offer which he was considering. He told me that right at the beginning when he wasn't all that keen on even showing me around. Then it transpired that he didn't like the bloke and that's why he hadn't yet accepted the offer. This guy was going to do all sorts of things. He was going to jack up the main beam in the living room because he had to stoop to get under it. And that would mean that he'd have to rip out the floors and ceilings of the bedrooms above, and turn the staircase around, and he wanted to put en-suites everywhere and make the barn into an orangery. Yes, an orangery. Church House is listed two-star. He couldn't have done any of that. Except that from the way the farmer described him, he was the sort of guy who would just do it and worry about listed building consent some time down the line when it eventually came home to roost and when it would be too late. Especially if most of his improvements were hidden from prying eyes, though quite how he could disguise his new orangery, I had no idea. He sounded just like the monstrous bastard that I didn't realise I was in danger of becoming. It should have been a wake-up call for me.

Anyway, the farmer didn't like him, and knowing this, it enabled me to pitch my ideas to him in a very favourable light, and I must have laid it on a bit thick with all the right noises. I told him I would take it back so his grandmother would recognise it and I could see he liked the idea of that.

Even before he'd finished showing me around he said I could have it for the same price and I said yes, I would like to buy it please and we both shook hands there and then in the back garden.

Almost as reckless as the fall of a hammer and just as monstrous, I suppose. It wasn't any sort of legal commitment, but it certainly felt like a moral one. I figured that's how things around here had always been settled. You can plead or pledge under oath or solemnly sign a legally binding document, but these things will never be more poignant than nor bear the same longevity as a simple handshake, man to man, eye to eye. There's something primeval about it. It's worth remembering when you're buying a second-hand car.

I was in a bit of a daze. It had only taken about forty minutes.

I told him that if it was alright by him, I'd come back in the morning to take some photographs that I could show my wife. At no time was there ever any possibility in his mind or clue in his face that he doubted that the transaction had already been done, and it was for this reason that I never did bother with any searches or surveys or any other enquiries, much against the advice and protestations of my conveyancing solicitor. You see, I realised that I also felt that the deal had been sealed from that moment. Church House was meant to be mine, and it was going to be mine. End of.

I walked back to the pub with a skip in my step. I didn't say anything to anyone at the bar. I don't think they needed to be told; they would know already. It sort of worked that way, somehow.

I put a new reel of film in my camera and took all thirty-six exposures. It was a dazzling sunny September morning and the rooms were all brightly lit. This was Church House at its best. The gardens were at their autumnal peak, all fuchsias, hydrangeas, hollyhocks and roses.

I stopped at Tiverton on the way back and got them printed on a one-hour turnaround. They looked good; I'm clever with camera angles.

I didn't really expect Georgia to question my judgement, but all the same it would make things safer if she was impressed with my new purchase.

We hadn't discussed it, but I think we had agreed in principle that it was my money and my project, and it would be my time and effort, but it would be our enjoyment and satisfaction. That sounded fair to me.

In my experience solicitors will stretch anything out if they can, but in this case, it appeared that they couldn't. There were no complications. The land was registered. The titles were straightforward and had recently been brought up to date with some probate stuff. No covenants or rights of way. No Chancel repair silliness, because nobody had thought to scam money from it yet. It all went through in about six weeks. Amazing.

So by the end of October I was the proud owner of the oldest and certainly the most interesting house in Crow's Nymet. Time to start indulging myself.

It turned out, and I'm going to be telling you more about this later, it was a bit of a slack time, workwise. For the first time in about eleven years, I felt as if I wasn't rushed off my feet. I had got other people to take over a lot of the things I'd been doing. I felt I could devote some time to myself for a change.

On the day of completion, I was down in Devon bright and early, and the keys were in the front door waiting for me. What anticipation. I knew it would be life changing one way or another, and it certainly turned out that way.

I'd already found a builder and an architect. They apparently worked as a team and came recommended by the landlord of the Druid's. That was a new one on me. Normally these guys are at each other's throats. I hadn't met either of them, but they were both happy to come along on that first day and have a chat. I suppose, really, I should have taken a few weeks thinking and scheming and planning before bringing in any professionals, but I was impatient and wanted to get going.

It was when I met them both on that first morning that I really started enthusing about proper ancient buildings and I quickly realised what an absolute gem I had bought. It wasn't listed two-star for nothing. Our house in the Midlands was an interesting old place with some ancient origins and a prior life, but basically it was just a small Victorian villa made of red bricks and clay pantiles. Church House was in a different league altogether.

The architect knew his stuff. I was in awe of his ability to see through the later additions to the medieval structure beneath. He'd never been in the building before, but he could tell me more about it just by standing there looking around him than the farmer had learned in his long lifetime. He could read it. We pulled some of the gypsum plaster away and revealed the original stone and cob walls, and we exposed parts of the plank and muntin screen that I've told you about, that were concealed by plasterboard. Nothing seemed to phase the builder. There were no sharp intakes of breath or exclamations of horror. We couldn't get into the roof. There was no access. It was obvious that the architect was gagging to see what was up there, but he had to leave for another appointment and there wasn't an opportunity. He told me I had to force an entry and report back to him.

In any case, we had made all our plans even before he left. Basically, we weren't proposing to alter the structure of the building at all, so we figured we wouldn't need planning permission. What we were going to do was to strip out all the modern 'improvements' and take it back to an earlier incarnation by replacing cement-based plaster with lime and by reinstating the ceilings with proper riven chestnut laths while at the same time installing a conventional central heating system and rewiring and replumbing the whole place. We would take up the flags that weren't too fragile and lay some insulation under them and nearly all the windows would need replacing, like for like.

All this would require listed building consent and almost certainly the Conservation Officer would want to take a look around, and the architect was adamant that English Heritage would want to take advantage of the chance to poke about too. He was confident there would be no problem. The combination of conservation architect, local traditional builder and sympathetic owner with deep pockets was the dream ticket that EH always looked for, but sadly seldom encountered.

This was going to take several weeks to set up and organise, but in the meantime he saw no reason why I shouldn't start stripping out myself if I wanted a bit of hands-on experience. That should keep me occupied until the New Year, when the builder would be ready to start putting everything back in again. Meanwhile, he added, I could try and find someone who could make the windows, and a smart new set of ledged and braced cottage doors and frames made of English oak would set the whole interior off nicely.

So that's how it panned out. The farmer offered to dig me a big hole at the bottom of the garden and I managed to fill it up with rubble and concrete, and I kept a bonfire going to burn the rubbish that I thought would spit or stink in the inglenook. I would string a few days together when there wasn't much kicking around at work, maybe leaving early on Monday morning to arrive at Crow's Nymet at sunrise and staying until Wednesday or Thursday night. It was wonderful, and it was indeed an indulgence.

During that first Spring half term, I came down with Angel for two nights and we had the best time. I had a blow-up double mattress and would sleep in front of the big fire when I was on my own, and that's what we did. Angel would be out there with his little wheelbarrow and spade all day, helping me fill that hole. There was no hot water, so I didn't make him wash. He was thrilled. Then we'd go over the Druid's in our work clothes and I would have a couple of pints, Angel orange squash and crisps and then we'd wander back, stoke up the fire and cook something on a trivet in the hearth. It was sausages and beans one night, lamb chops and chips the next, and then we'd lay in our sleeping bags and tell each other stories in front of the glow of the embers. What could ever be nicer than that? It was the best time.

I was keen to explore from the start and had worked myself up into a state of high expectation from the architect's enthusiasm, and that very first afternoon after he and the builder had gone I could wait no longer.

I told you earlier about the smoke blackening and that I would come back to it. Well, this is it.

I've waxed lyrical about the sheer quantity of really ancient vernacular buildings in North Devon, and it's true, they're all over the place. Quite often they don't look old to the inexperienced eye, and this is usually because they've been updated many times during their long lives. Lines have been straightened, walls added, roofs rebuilt. There are some clues that will tell you a lot about the origins of a domestic building, and these are worth knowing as it will make walks through country villages much more interesting for you. That's true of everything in life, of course. The more you know, the more you get out of it. That's why you need to learn things, and remember them.

Look at the chimney stack and it will inform your understanding of the likely age of the house. If it appears to be stuck on the end gable as an afterthought or leaning on a side wall like a buttress, then the chances are that the cottage, or farmhouse or manor house was originally built without a chimney at all. Grander houses and castles might have had fireplaces as we would recognise them, with the flues and stacks designed in from original plans, but these took an awfully long time to percolate down to more humble dwellings. In North Devon, a rule of thumb is that if any updating of a house took place after about fifteen hundred then it would have included the addition of a chimney. These were usually, but not always attached to the outside of a wall. Sometimes it made more sense to use an internal wall and come up through the middle of the roof, in which case you'll be looking out for a huge, squarish stack that clears the ridge of the roof by two or three feet. There'll be a big, big fireplace at the bottom of it. Builders of the day thought that the larger the cross section of the flue, the more likely the fire was to draw. That's now been shown to be a complete myth, and this is why chimneys and flues and fireplaces and hearths progressively got smaller and smaller over the centuries as clever dicks came up with magical formulae for improved smoke extraction, ending up with a fondness for the Venturi effect which imaginatively sucks the smoke through a small slit which would have been wholly counterintuitive to a medieval artisan builder. Happily, the smaller the flue, the less heat disappears straight up the chimney, so the slit is good.

Before chimneys, you kept warm by huddling round a fire in the middle of the floor. Sometimes there would be a kind of reredos constructed to one side which would make it easier to cook things against, but often meals were prepared and cooked in some sort of outshut or shippon in the garden. The smoke just had to find its way through the thatch, which could be up to about six feet thick.

You're probably thinking that the smoke would make life unbearable, but you have to remember that the roofs were high and open to the rafters and if the men of the house had got their act together the previous winter, then the firewood would be tinder-dry. All the same, it must have been a bit atmospheric in those open halls.

You might assume that the poorest of these humble dwellings wouldn't be thatched, but would be covered in some other less expensive material, but you're not using your imagination enough, are you? Thatch was by far the cheapest roofing option, whether it was water reed, wheat straw, heather, bracken or gorse, it was growing in the fields all around, and was all but a waste product. It was free, and labour was cheap. Very cheap. Fast forward a few centuries and your master thatcher won't get out of bed for less than twenty grand, and then he needs scaffolding so he won't fall off your roof and hurt himself. But the problem is that the kind of wheat straw you can buy today only lasts about ten years if you're lucky, and then it's got to be done all over again. And don't let English Heritage catch you using anything else or they'll make you take it off and do it properly.

I'm being a little unfair, perhaps. We've had some very wet seasons recently which rot the straw in the fields in late summer and on your roof in the winter. There's still a strong local market for thatching straw and there are steps being taken to resurrect the traditional long rye straws of the past, that are more robust and resistant to the bruising that causes the rot. They are harvested by old fashioned reaper-binders and stooked up in the field by hand. It is truly lovely to see acres of wheat stooks in neatly swept rows, glowing in the ochre light of an August sunset. You need to see this. It is a tantalising glimpse into an ancient way of life and it's being done today for sound commercial reasons, not to look good for tourists, though of course it does. And it's great to see so many labourers in the fields for a change, even though they're all from Romania. It's straight out of a Bruegel painting. You've got to see it; it'll make your heart sing.

With the chimney in place and the hearth against the wall, our sixteenth century aspiring householders looked around and thought, with no smoke to get rid of, I could easily board over the hall and make some bedrooms on the first floor, create a bit of privacy, and this is what they did. I bet they were pleased the roof was high enough to squeeze in the new rooms. They might not have done the whole house at once, but ultimately the building would have ended up with several upstairs interconnecting bedrooms with proper ceilings and a decent staircase rather than a ladder. The roof voids would be sealed up, often without any sort of access, and this is what happened in Church House. When I bought it, no one had been up there for five hundred years.

When I stood on my rickety stepladder with a crow-bar in one hand and a torch in the other, I really had no idea what I was going to find. I've mentioned that smoke blackened thatch gets the English Heritage people excited. I'd read a bit about it, and I was excited at the prospect of finding it. There are only about a hundred houses in Devon known to have smoke blackened thatch, or SBT as the historians conspiratorially nod to one another.

Shall I spell it out to you why it's so sought after? You probably still haven't got it. If smoke permeates through a thatched roof, it leaves its mark on the timbers and on the thatch. Smoke blackened timbers are two a penny, so although desirable are not particularly rare, but to have SBT means that you know for sure that the lower layers of thatch have never been replaced and that the wheat in your roof was the same wheat that late medieval peasants stooked up in their fields five hundred years ago or more. When there were no tractors or even smartphones. Amazing isn't it?

It also tells you that your house has been in continual occupation for all of that time. Twenty-five or so generations of ordinary families have lived their lives to the background of these walls and roofs. Each time the roof needed rethatching, another layer was added, making it thicker and thicker and preserving like a sedimentary substrate the echoes of these people's lives.

It didn't take much to smash through the laths and plaster of the bulging ceiling in the bedroom of the middle bay of Church House, the one over the living room. I gingerly shone my torch around and despite five centuries of Hammer Horror cobwebs and five minutes of plastery dust obscuring my vision I could clearly see in the yellow light of the beam that there was indeed smoke blackened thatch in the bay above me. I was complete. I felt curiously smug and feverish for more.

I got a longer ladder and a proper inspection lamp and scrambled through the makeshift hole. I was fascinated by the whole concept of all this curious antiquity that I was stooped in. Perhaps a bit like a geologist tapping away at a rock and knowing he's the first human ever to see the remains of some fossilised animal or plant.

Apart from an electrical cable that an enterprising electrician had managed to thread through to a central pendant from below, there was nothing in this place that wasn't just the same half a millennium ago. In my torchlight I even uncovered some smoke blackened insects, moths and what looked like a grasshopper that had maybe died whilst hibernating or perhaps had just expired peacefully whilst enjoying the balmy conditions in the roof as a fire roared below and a group huddled round talking and laughing with a winter blizzard howling outside. Well, it might not have been quite like that, but it's an interesting image to take away.

Sometimes you can find all sorts of things in a place like this. Bricked up skeletons of cats are much loved by fanciful ghost story writers, and witches' marks or other signs to ward off evil spirits. I found none of these things, although I had them in mind when I ventured further into the neighbouring bays. It was not until some time later that I unearthed the object that would become, for me, the ultimate symbol of the remarkable longevity of this building and of the scenes and secrets that it had witnessed during its long, long journey accompanying the inhabitants of Crow's Nymet whose lives it had touched and moulded and changed forever.

I was down for a few days during the refurbishment works. The sparky had alarmed me when he called me at home to tell me he was laying the cables in the roof and he'd had to tidy the void up a bit before he could staple the wire to the joists. He'd bagged up a lot of debris and had had to dismantle a cob wall that was blocking his access. I couldn't figure out which wall he was referring to, but removing any of the original fabric of the roof was precisely what I didn't want him to do. Ask any conservation architect what his worst nightmare is, and very near the top of the list will be sparkys and plumbers. It seems par for the course that a specialist traditional builder will employ sympathetic craftsmen, joiners and carpenters and plasterers and stonemasons who are well versed in artisanal methods, even labourers who have an affinity and an interest in the materials and the styles and the traditions, but when it comes to plumbers and electricians they bring in guys off the street who have spent so much of their working lives punching holes through plasterboard and drilling through pine joists and chipboard floorboards that they can't see the valuable treasure in front of their faces.

In the event, it wasn't as bad as I'd feared it might be. The wall in question was only a thin, non-load-bearing header on a hurdle partition, and he had bagged everything up and dumped it in the barn. I would go through them later to see if there were any treasures (there weren't, unless you count aged thatching spars and empty cobb nuts as treasure). As I was inspecting the new wiring, I was kneeling near where the wall used to be when I noticed something wedged behind a purlin that I'd been unable to see before, when the wall had been in place. It was right there in front of me, a little wooden box about two inches cube. It was black with soot and grime. As I pulled it out from its hiding place, I saw that there was a lighter shadow on both the lath that it had lain against and the corresponding face of the box that the lath had been in contact with. Now this, of course, told me something straight away. I don't know if I have to spell it out to you or not. If you've not realised, then you're not really paying attention to what I've been saying. Okay, well it's this. It's obvious that this little box had remained undisturbed since well before the first-floor ceiling was added. Whoever hid it five or six centuries ago never went back to retrieve it, for whatever reason. That's quite something, isn't it?

Like I say, I realised this as soon as I disturbed the box, so I was treating it with some care, and with some curiosity. It wasn't anything special to look at. It was more like thin matchwood than say, oak or elm, and it had some worm in it. It had a lid that was tied on by rough twine in the way that you'd secure brown paper around a package and it was knotted with a bow that pulled apart as if it had only been tied yesterday. The lid was loose and fell away, revealing what is best described as a ceramic jar, although I always think of it as a phial and shall refer to it as such. It was a little bit like one of those ubiquitous ink containers that you see in antique shops but was slightly larger and with a bigger lip and tiny spout for pouring. It was made of some sort of crude stoneware and had a wooden stopper that looked to be made of cork, but I thought was probably more likely sycamore or holly. This had been dipped in wax or tallow that had provided a seal and fortunately a deterrent to the worm. The wax was brittle and broke away easily when I probed, leaving behind a stopper as clean and purposeful as the day it had been dipped in the sealant.

I shook the phial and could tell there was liquid still in it. I was mesmerised by my thoughts. I was far away in some distant place and time. For a moment or two, it took me over and I was swept along. It was great; it doesn't happen to me very often. I love things that have a story to tell or a mystery to unfold. They hold me intrigued and I savour them. I'm able to keep this up for hours. Like when I get an unexpected parcel in the post or unearth a curious artefact from the garden that merits some research. I'm into delayed gratification. I put the object where I can see it without opening it and for the next few hours I just anticipate what's inside. Now and again, I'll feel it or shake it or smell it, then when the time is right, I'll carefully look at what is hidden within. Even if the story falls far short of the expectation or hope, it doesn't matter because I've already enjoyed the titillation. I do that with chance encounters, too.

The little box practically fell apart as I gripped it too tightly while climbing back down the ladder. I put the bits to one side. I wouldn't throw it away in case it offered up some clues later on as to its origins. I put the phial on the kitchen table and then I went and made a cup of coffee and came and sat back down and looked at it some more. Later that evening, I opened a bottle of shiraz that was lying in the bottom of my holdall and sipped it over a period of about two hours as I sat and wondered what secrets the phial held. A bottle of wine doesn't make me drunk, but it makes me mellow. Several times I picked the phial up and played with it in my hands, moving it backwards and forwards in my palms and now and again shaking it, making it call to me. What could you tell me, I wondered?

When the phial had been hidden, the world was a very different place, and it was intriguing to guess even the appearance of the hider, let alone the circumstances behind his actions. Presumably he had acted alone. Why had he never returned? All sorts of possibilities went through my mind.

Of course the obvious thing to do was to open the bottle and see what was inside, and eventually I could resist this no longer. It only took a sharp twist to release the stopper. Disappointingly, no genies or ectoplasm or miasmic fluid emerged from the jar, and it didn't fizz or bubble or anything. The underside of the stopper was stained a deep brown. It was cork, after all. Portuguese cork, I guessed. What sort of journey had that made from an Iberian forest to deepest Devon in the fifteenth century? Was it a rare or valuable commodity in those times, a specialised sort of material that only influential men had access to? Probably not. I was overegging it, I think.

I smelt the stopper and then I placed my nose close to the opening and took a deep breath. It was vaguely almondy.

I tipped the jar a little until the liquid appeared in the spout. It looked to be quite viscous, with a notable meniscus, but otherwise had the appearance of thick soy sauce.

By now you'll be wondering why I'm telling you all this in such detail, and you'd be right in thinking that the contents of the phial play a significant role later in this story. But for the time being, I'm not telling you anything else. Have a think about it yourself and see if you can come up with something original or interesting. I think it's doubtful you'll get anywhere near the reality.

I pushed the lid on again tightly and left it on the table. When I went home to Hallam I took it with me and placed it on a shelf in my bookcase in my study where I could gaze at it and ponder when in reflective mood. It came back down to its rightful home with Gerald along with the rest of the stuff on my shelves and it sits there now in front of me, just an arm's reach away as I write. There's not much of the liquid left inside now; it's almost empty.

The architect was right. English Heritage was very keen and two of them turned up with the Conservation Officer and spent the best part of three hours prowling around, poking and probing and pondering and making notes in their journals. I could tell they didn't really want to engage with me. They're real snobs, these academics. I didn't speak enough of their language to interest them, and they patronised me in an annoyingly condescending way when I interrupted their thoughts. It was obvious that they were only comfortable dealing with professionals like themselves. All three perked up with interest when I casually mentioned my PhD. They were discussing chronologically dating the cruck beams and I told them I was well versed in cross correlation techniques, but the interest quickly faded when they realised that my jargon was different to their jargon.

Everything we wanted to do was ok by them. One of them was a drinking pal of my architect. Of course he was.

By January the listed building consent was through and the builder was ready to start in earnest. I would try and get down every couple of weeks to see what was going on, and by Easter he had more or less finished. The central heating was drying everything out and it actually felt quite snug.

All four of us came down for the Easter break, from Saturday morning until Monday afternoon. The weather was glorious. We went to the church service on Sunday and then to the Druid's for lunch and we got talking to some villagers who were very welcoming. The kids played in the little park with their new friends. It was all lovely. It was just as I'd hoped it would be.

It was spartan that Easter weekend, but great fun sleeping on the floor and cooking breakfast on a camping stove. There was lots more to do and I was very much looking forward to the next stage, which would be painting and decorating, then carpets and curtains and finally furnishing. I would be looking to get involved in all these things.

I chose the paint for any of the woodwork that we weren't leaving bare. Cupboard doors, window sills, skirting and things like that. I went for loud colours. I learned all about lime wash. We didn't use anything else for the plasterwork. Why would you? It's such wonderful stuff. I experimented a bit, mixing and matching pigments, and was generally delighted with the results. You'd never really know what you'd end up with until the lime wash had properly dried. That's what was so absorbing about it.

I engaged a local upholsterer to do the curtains for me. I went a bit over the top with the linings. Because we couldn't put double glazing in the new windows, I was determined to fit thick curtains that would keep out the cold, but they were very heavy and difficult to hang on the cob walls. You can't just drill a hole and push a Rawlplug into cob, you have to feel your way into the wall with a timber drift and hope you don't find a loose bit.

I put a light-coloured carpet in the sitting room and left the lime wash in there white. There is some original primitive pargetting on the ceiling and this sets it off well. The rest of the floors I left boarded or flagged, with rugs here and there to soften it all up a bit.

I loved looking for furniture. I had some tatty stuff that my parents had given me that I brought down, and the rest came from junk shops, auctions and antique emporiums, all of which are in plentiful supply in these parts. The same with things like cutlery, crockery, kitchenware. It was all unmatched but, I like to think, cleverly coordinated.

That summer I gave myself a whole two weeks off work and we all spent a blissful family time luxuriating in our new world and enjoying our own company. If only it could have lasted.

six

If I turn my desk lamp off and wait for a minute or two while my eyes adjust, I can see that the horizon is beginning to lighten and glow with the faintest of red tints behind the trees. I've been staring at it and thinking. Today is the longest day and the sun will rise at 4:37am this morning according to the infallible and wholly trustworthy oracle that is Google. It sounds about right.

The summer solstice.

From what I could see just now, it has become a clear and still morning. There are stars twinkling so it looks like the clouds have dispersed. If the sun is rising somewhere just North of East, then the full moon must be working its way across the sky towards the West. I should be outside watching this. What a time to be alive.

There really is nothing like seeing the sun break cover over the horizon. You know it's going to happen because you've seen it many times before, but when that first intense shaft of golden lustre hits the back of your eye, it's always a shock. You can only watch it for a few seconds before it becomes so powerful a source of searing energy that you have to look away and then you can see the change that this everyday but extraordinary phenomenon is having on the landscape all around you. How it first caps the western hills with a flaxen glow that spills its treasure onto the lower slopes like honey spreading from an upturned jar and then worms its way into the valleys and transforms trees into orange-green statues before your eyes.

What a special time this must have been for as long as humans have walked the Earth, for hundreds of thousands of years. It would have been an awakening, a rescue from the fears and unknown perils of the dark night, a sudden but promised metamorphosis from the world of wolves and bears; bats and owls; witches and familiars and ghouls and monsters to the comfortable and benign safety of friends and good things.

There aren't many cloudless mornings when I don't see the sun rise, and I try and make a point of being in a special place if I can, so I can get the full benefit. You can understand why the sun has been worshipped and revered for ever, and I think it's very sad that it no longer means much at all to most people. What a shame and a loss that is. It should be a part of us all.

Actually, it is a part of us all. It's another of those primeval things. I can feel it inside me. You should be able to; it's something you can't ignore. It's there.

This is one of the least light-polluted parts of the country and it is easy to see the Milky Way on a clear, moonless night.

Do you even know what the Milky Way looks like? Do you know what it is?

There are a handful of streetlights in the village, but the District Council have decided to economise and have put them all on timers, so they turn off at midnight. It's great when they go off; you can see, then. Some old people complained at the parish council meeting that this would

71

make the roads more dangerous, and that they might get mugged. In Crow's Nymet? When was the last time they were out roaming the streets after twelve o clock? I've never seen them. There are one or two outside lights on cottages which are sometimes left on, which annoys me, and the farmers will keep their barns lit all night at certain times of the year, mainly during lambing. I think I know where all the security lights are. There's only one and it's on a holiday cottage next to the village hall. We don't tend to go in for that sort of thing around here, fortunately.

Have you ever thought about artificial light?

It's one of my things.

Perhaps the most interesting thing about artificial light is that it really hasn't been around for very long at all, and it's my belief that nature has yet to come to terms with it. You only have to go back a hundred years or so and there was nothing but oil lamps and candles in the countryside, and they wouldn't be hanging outside spoiling the night; they would be extending the working day indoors. You wouldn't want to go out at night if you didn't have to. It is really quite difficult to imagine a night-time landscape with no suggestion of a human presence, but it was all like that such a short time ago. It must have been wonderful.

Now that we all use electric lights, it's different. It's not so bad around here, I guess, but when I was in the Midlands, the sky was orange all night long from the sodium streetlamps stretching in all directions to the horizon. There was no escape. It was the most dispiriting thing.

Actually, the most dispiriting thing is now car headlights. They're getting more and more powerful. They're ridiculously bright. What's that all about?

When you're driving your car at night in the countryside, you're in your own little brightly-lit bubble that travels along with you. You don't see the dark fields and woods all around you; they might not exist. You're unaware of all this and yet it's there, next to you.

That recurring theme again, you'll note.

I can tell you this because I'm there in the shadows of your xenon death-ray, and I'm cowering just like the deer and the rabbits; the hedgehogs and the foxes and badgers until you've gone past out of our lives. It's horrible. You have so much power at your fingertips and you don't even know it.

I hate anyone who uses a torch at night. I hate the power it gives them. They don't deserve that power because they don't realise what it does. Just leave us alone.

Sorry about that. Like I say, it's one of my things.

I've calmed down, now.

It really is a wonderful experience to just soak up the vastness of space. It is something that many visitors to the area seem to have never done before. They've lived their lives without stars. They might think they see them, but they don't. Not the real ones. The important ones. They don't see the beauty of the universe from their urban deserts.

When we had friends down in the early days and it was a clear night, I would slip out after dinner while everyone was talking and lay two large kilim rugs out on the garden, one on top the other, and then two camel bags with feather pads in them for pillows and then I'd call everyone out and get them to just lie there under the top rug like so many sardines. It was such a happy time. The kids used to love it too, if they were still up. We'd try to be the first to spot a satellite and we'd count the shooting stars. What a phenomenon that is. They appear from nowhere and are as quickly gone, a transient, ephemeral light show straight from God himself.

Nowadays I can't be doing with the rugs, but I leave a teak reclining chair out on the grass and I sit and watch and let an hour or two slip by watching the heavens. It's heavenly.

Let me try to explain how the house and garden work, in case you've never been here before or haven't made the opportunity to snoop around yet. I've already said that Church House sits next to the graveyard. It's actually part of it. The back wall of my house is the boundary of the graveyard and if you were wandering around looking at the gravestones and crosses and memorials you could come right up to my study window and look in if you were brave enough.

A long time ago this would have been the front elevation of the building. Nearly all old houses were built facing South to maximise the light coming through the tiny windows, but unusually Church House was turned around at some point so that the back door became the front, opening onto the village street, and the front door was blocked up with large pieces of field stone. All the bedroom windows overlook the church and later on a new doorway was formed where my kitchen now is that opens straight out into the churchyard. It is half-glazed and I can stand there and look out if I see anything interesting happening. The cob wall has never been rendered and looks very agricultural, more like a barn than a house. It is a particularly dank and dark part of the churchyard. There's lots of algae and lichen about, even in the middle of June. If you look closely at the cob, you can see that little stones and pebbles sit proud of the mud and this will tell you that over the course of maybe five or six hundred years the structure has eroded by about a centimetre, despite all the dampness and unprotected exposure to the prevailing South Westerly's for all that time. I find that so unlikely that I wouldn't blame you for not believing it, but I can promise you it's absolutely true. Tell that to a Berber tribesman if you happen to meet one and he will laugh in your face. They build their walls in exactly the same way and they're lucky if they last more than twenty years, and they have more sun and less rain than we do. I'm trying to tell you that our houses are very special.

On the road side, the cob and stone walls have been rendered with lime in the traditional manner and a window has been knocked through the kitchen wall, but the only other openings on this side are a small sash on the landing and an opening casement with obscure glass in the bathroom, so it means really that my house looks bleakly unattractive from whatever direction you're looking. Even the front porch, which is embellished with some primitive Georgian-style ornamentation and has a fanlight over the door which is glazed with coloured and patterned glass, can't lift it and comes over as ludicrously ostentatious. I guess the guy who put it there thought it looked good, but it just doesn't work.

Had the house evolved without the churchyard or the street pushing up against it, there would have been a lean-to on the cold side that would have been the dairy, which would have become the kitchen, but there was no room for that. Instead, the kitchen is in the main body of the house at the end where the sitting room should be, and my sitting room, or as I call it, my living room is in the middle where sometime in the sixteenth century somebody stuck on the huge chimney stack bang in the middle of the back wall.

All this doesn't leave much room for any garden around the house, but there is a little courtyard between the study end and the narrow, cobbled pathway that leads the God-botherers through the lychgate into the churchyard. It is quite private because the stone walls are about six feet high at this point, but the only way I can get to it is through a doorway from the front garden. It gets the sun for most of the day and it is nicely sheltered from the winds. I've made it very pretty, very cottagey, and I have a little French bistro table and chair against the end wall of the house. There is a climbing hydrangea that can easily become unruly and has to be cut back every year. It's no problem on stone, but is not really a good idea against a cob wall because it grips and clings too hard, like ivy, and it pulls the earth and aggregate away with it when you try to tame it. There are roses. An ancient and highly appropriate Rambling Rector scrambling through a put-upon white lilac and of course my beloved Albertine hugging the stones. They all look delightful in the late spring. I'm heavily into hardy fuchsias and there are several round the border adding colour well into the Autumn until the first frosts blacken them and turn them to slime. There are self-seeded hollyhocks and foxgloves, forget-me-nots and love-in-a-mist, and the overall effect is of a veritable festival of old-fashioned cottage garden favourites, all mixed up and pushing for light.

I want you to imagine me sitting there on a summer afternoon in a straw panama and linen jacket with a little cafetiere of Columbian coffee, a slice of almond cake from the WI market stall in South Molton and a Penguin modern classic. Idyllic, and a far cry from the Saturday look, I'm sure you'll agree.

I share my courtyard with some amusing little field mice which, thus far, have proven to be too slippery for patient Frank, and a nest of comical common lizards who spend most of their time basking on the South side of the churchyard walls and only return to the sanctuary of the garden when the skies darken.

I can imagine that my little courtyard is a magical place right now. The sparrows will just be stirring from their nests under the eaves and the dawn chorus will have already begun. Bats will be returning to their roosts in the roof void with their appetites assuaged. Scents will be permeating the still air and a rustling in the tangled borders will betray the nocturnal invertebrates and mammals that are heading for home after an active night. It's all happening just a couple of feet away from where I'm sitting, and I'm aware but oblivious of it, except in my imagination and my memory. I want to be there, living it.

The front garden isn't really a garden at all because it borders the street through the village. It is only about four or five feet deep, with the high wooden door that leads to the courtyard and spiky wrought-iron railings on one side of the front porch and a rotten wood picket fence on the other, with peeling white paint and toothy gaps. I don't spend much time here. I don't really like to be seen to be at home when villagers walk past and pretend they're keen to pass the time of day. Sometimes I'll do a bit of light weeding in the late evening or early morning, but it largely looks after itself as it's overgrown with lady's mantle and oregano and choked in late summer with wild geraniums. It does seem to thrive on neglect and despite the fact that at one time it must have had a formal style (I bet there were standard box trees and window boxes full of begonias) it has now graciously settled into a mellow retirement of country calm.

Tacked onto the far end of the house is a semi-derelict cob barn with a corrugated tin roof, straight out of a James Ravilious photo. It has double doors on pin hinges, set back but facing the lane and just large enough to squeeze a hay wagon through. I can get into it from a door in the kitchen and it's useful for storing all sorts of things. Most of it keeps remarkably dry and airy and there is a first floor of sorts, though the boards are mostly unsafe. I used to keep my Land Rover in there, but now it's at the bottom of the garden under a tarpaulin and I rarely use it.

The garden proper leads from the barn right down the side of the churchyard, about eighty or ninety yards of cob and stone wall separating the two. It's draped in ivy on my side and is full of nesting birds and wasps' nests in the summer. There's about an acre of old grass that I'm encouraging as a wild-flower meadow, and further on a little copse of oak standards and coppiced hazel that I manage to keep in good order. There are some ash and beech as well that I cut for firewood. The grassy bit used to be an apple orchard and there are half a dozen or so old bent trees still half standing. They are all old West Country cider apple varieties, and not much use for either eating or cooking with. The farmer told me all their names, quaint and improbable sounding, like 'slack ma girdle'. I understand that Church House once had quite a reputation for its cider, as befitting its medieval origins, but the cider house and the press have long since disappeared. No one round here makes cider anymore, and I have to watch the apples fall and rot on the ground every year. It's a waste, but good for the blackbirds, wasps and slugs, and in the late spring the blossom is simply wondrous and the orchard is a blissful place to sit. I love to watch the flying insects against the backdrop of the setting sun. The bees and hover flies and the moths and gnats, all going about the business of staying alive in their own unique ways and at their own pace.

The land drops away from the village towards the South and there is an impressive view of the moody tors of Dartmoor about twenty miles away in the far distance. Both my copse and the end wall of the churchyard border open countryside and I love that I can go and idly lean against my wall and see the verdant North Devon river valleys stretching out for miles in front of me in their meandering path to the coast.

You might think that the church would be set centrally in its grounds, but it's not; it crowds my house; it pushes its face into my space. This could have happened for any number of reasons. The church would have been rebuilt several times since its original fragile genesis, and it probably crept uphill each time it happened, sneaking towards the village, while the churchyard was no doubt extended into virgin pasture on the Southern side to make more space for the righteous dead. It was common for the North side of a churchyard to be left unconsecrated and I think it likely that this was the case here. It was considered to be a village amenity and was used for all sorts of things, particularly, it seems, ball games. Seems a bit unconvincing to me, but there it is. The denizens of Church House would have had a grandstand view, no matter what was going on, but I imagine it being a touch raucous and unseemly most of the time.

So, although St Rumon's is hunkered down on the edge of the village, the striking verdigris barb of its copper-clad spire means it appears to be more central than it is, and it is notably in the oldest part of the settlement.

I guess it's a bit unusual to find such a large, desirable plot like my orchard that hasn't been spoiled by infill. I'm not going to sell it, obviously; I like it as it is. You couldn't get a five-series BMW through the gap, anyway, without pulling my barn down, and you'd still be left with a blind corner that Highways wouldn't like. It'll never happen; not even when I'm gone.

I'm not overlooked in my orchard because of the way the levels work but I have two neighbours adjoining the Devon bank on its North West boundary and if I choose, I can peer through the thick hedge down into their back gardens and into their kitchens and bathrooms and bedrooms. I can do this expertly and they are not aware of me.

seven

I keep a very bitter lime cordial in the fridge. I'll quite often mix it with a dash of vodka or gin, or perhaps even a little white rum if I have any, but this morning I want to try to clear my head of the red wine I was drinking last night. So, I've just coated the rim of my glass with salt instead, in the manner of a margarita and added a small measure of cold, cloudy lemonade to the cordial and some leaves of fresh mint and crushed ice. It is invigorating. It provides such a fresh punch at this time in the morning and lifts the senses with its sourness.

I've just been outside. It was so still and utterly quiet. I was wrong about the dawn chorus. The birds have seemingly yet to stir, which surprised me, though I heard a cockerel crowing a long way off down the valley. He's early today. How evocative of the countryside is a cockerel's crow, and how comforting is his presence.

I sat and sipped my lime and listened to the deep nothingness for a while. There was a dew on the gravestone which has left a chill in my pants, but I don't mind. Why would you want to be anywhere else on a morning such as this?

The wood smoke from the fire smelled delicious outside and now that I've returned to my armchair, I've thrown another log on and it's crackling and spitting in the wood burner. I think it's apple I'm burning, from one of the old trees that fell over in the storms last winter. That would explain why it smells so good.

The early hours of the morning are very different from any other time of the day. Time can go very slowly. It must be awful if you can't sleep at night because things change then and you can't do anything about it. You can't stop yourself dwelling and fretting about the lightest matter until it evolves into a black shrouded thundercloud that you know is going to break and break badly and it's tearing at your mind and you can't get away from it. It doesn't matter if it breaks or not; the damage is done. You'll never feel the same about it, not even when it comes the next night, as it will. It'll be different then, but just as frightening and hopeless. You've nowhere to go if you can't sleep.

I've been through Hell and back with my sleeping and my thinking, but I'm alright just now. Sometimes I don't like to sleep because it seems such a waste of time, so some nights I just don't bother at all, and guess what? I don't miss it. I don't normally need to catch up during the following day either. 'You can't burn the candle at both ends', my mother used to say, but she was wrong. I can.

However, there is a problem with being on your own and staying up all night and that is that you can think too much.

During my short working life, I did a lot of thinking, but I did it professionally and I was lucky enough to be surrounded by other like-minded, intellectual and academic individuals with whom I could discuss what I was thinking. We created a truly rarefied atmosphere where we debated ideas just for the blue-skies hell of it, and I feel privileged to have experienced it. We were probably some way up our own arses, but at least there were people all around me I could talk to, all the time. There's nobody now.

I guess my eyes were first opened when I started my degree at Loughborough, but although my new friends inhabited a different world to those I had grown up with at school, I have to conclude that our attempts at intelligent discourse must have been naively ill-informed and fanciful, fuelled and ultimately unwound by alcohol and bravado. The proper cerebral stuff came when I returned to the university as a postgraduate, fresh from a dreadful though mercifully brief experiment with industry. My degree was in Electronic Engineering, evidence of my wish to acquire the knowledge to get all those poorly, bloody television sets working properly. In 1975 when I graduated with an upper second (Hons), this was fortunately a topically good subject for finding a job. Well, I suppose in those days, actually, it was no trouble finding a job no matter what degree you had. A job for life, too, if you wanted it. Jobs were plentiful and degrees were rare and appreciated. I came away from an Easter vacation of milk-round interviews holding half a dozen offers of employment with blue-chip industrial household names. Unfortunately, I chose the wrong one. I believe it was just about the only wrong decision that I've made in my life that was entirely of my own making. All the others I was pushed into.

No one was expecting me the morning I turned up for work on the first day of my career. That's awful isn't it? Inexcusable. They didn't know who I was and even after an uncomfortable and embarrassing morning of phone calls and hushed meetings, I'm not confident, now that I can look at the whole thing with a detachment that comes with the benefit of hindsight, that they ever could find any record of my existence. That was a bad start and it shook me up a bit. I didn't really have a lot of confidence in those days; I was still wet behind the ears. Even then they could have recovered from it. Instead, when it was discovered that I hadn't been invited to a shoulder-slapping self-congratulatory orgy of arse-licking that was the annual works dinner (because I didn't exist) they chose not to find an empty seat for me to join them, so I could become one of them. They decided that they would leave me out anyway.

I don't know how much of all of this I told my mother and father, probably nothing because they would have been distraught and indignant on my behalf and would have worried much more than they did about everything anyway. I know what my father would have said. Fuck 'em. Well not quite those words; he didn't swear, at least not in front of me, but that would have been the essence of his response. My dad was never keen on me getting an education. At each stage he saw it as a further departure from the comfortable, formulaic life that he had eked out for his family. He saw me drifting away from him and everything he held dear. He thought I would change, of course, and of course, I did. I was aware of all this, however, and unlike some, I never properly embraced it. I did try very hard to keep it in mind and address the changes as they happened. That's not possible, is it? That's the whole point of change. You don't notice.

Whatever.

I must have changed. A lot.

I did at least manage to keep my Bristolian accent and I still burr my rrrr's. It makes me sound more West Country than I am, I think.

My dad wasn't in the habit of giving me advice, but on that day when they dropped me at my new hall, before I'd missed the razor, he said to me if it all gets too much, you know you can come home. Those were his exact words. I frankly don't know what I thought at the time, though the fact that I've remembered them and can see him in my mind's eye mouthing the words must mean that I took some notice of them. But the thing was, and I came to know this later when things got a bit uptight in the weeks before my finals, I couldn't have done it. I would have killed myself rather than go home a failure.

My mum's advice to me was with a sack of potatoes in the larder, you'll never go hungry, and that was true and ultimately more solicitous than my dad's nugget. Good old mum.

So my first job lasted just long enough for me to know, for sure, that I didn't want to work for a large company in a dreary, featureless office with no windows that you could look out of, with boring non-entities that I had nothing in common with and whose idea of a good Saturday night out was a trip to the local takeaway and the TV, which was always showing dross, especially on a Saturday night, and especially in 1975.

I had always hankered after doing a higher degree, but had never expected to return to Loughborough. In fact, it was the last place I imagined I'd finally end up. For any reason. It's not that I hadn't liked it at Loughborough; I had just expected to move on. I didn't want to go backwards. I applied to several institutions that had funding and opportunities, but they weren't interested in recruiting until the start of the next academic year. I just had to get away from Slough and this awful place where I spent my solitary days testing military radios in an airless Faraday cage. It looked and felt like a prison cell.

I happened to be invited to the annual knees-up at my old hall of residence by some friends who were still there, so on the Friday afternoon I took the opportunity to look round my old department. I stumbled upon the Head of School, quite accidentally because I didn't really know him at all. To my astonishment he offered me a position on the spot with a contract that started in January which would release enough material to start a PhD in October, with funding already in place with the Science Research Council. I think he may have been desperate to fill the post and would have taken the night watchman on if he'd volunteered. I just happened to come along at the right time.

The guy who was supervising the project was unknown to me. I'd never met him, nor had I ever been to one of his lectures. In fact, I was only aware of him because I recalled a friend looking at the staff mug shots in the corridor and describing him as 'the missing link'. He was a wild creature with a full red beard and untamed hair.

The Head of School was bubbling at the way things were unfolding. He pulled me into his office and we made a phone call and I arranged to go and see the man at his home the next day.

Tim lived on the periphery of a small village a couple of miles out of Loughborough on the Nottingham Road in a pretty red-brick cottage. As I pulled up, I could see a woman and four small infants working in a vegetable patch with little forks and spades. It looked like they were planting potatoes or onions or something, or harvesting them. It was a big vegetable patch, laid out very traditionally in straight rows with string lines and cheerful labels, and there were soft fruit bushes at one end and rhubarb and asparagus gone to seed at the other. There were apple trees with hanging fruit which had ladders and ropes and swings draped over them and there were chickens and ducks making a mess in the borders.

I was enchanted. It was all I had ever wanted.

Tim was too good to be true, really. Everything about his life, his work and his family; this was how I wanted to be. This is what I wanted for the next part of my life.

When he invited me inside, I knew what I was going to find. There were jars full of preserved fruit, chutneys, jams; there was freshly baked bread, home-made wines of every colour. And there were the children's paintings and scribblings over every surface, and photographs of smiling people in frames of all sizes and styles, and an upright piano with music open on the stand. I wanted all this.

I didn't need time to think about it. We drank a toast to my future with a glass of Tim's home brew 'Christmas' ale and the die was cast.

To complete a PhD, to be able to call yourself a Doctor of Philosophy, doesn't particularly mean that you have to be intelligent, though of course it helps. It does mean that you have to be capable of a sort of single-minded determination for three or four years, be able to work alone with self-discipline and be able to bounce back when you realise you've been on the wrong track, probably because of your own foolishness and ineptitude and have wasted several weeks or months of your life on worthless effort. That's the nature of research, but it's a wonderful occupation for someone with the right sort of mind. I enjoyed it immensely, and I miss everything about it very much.

eight

Alright, you probably don't know what a church house is, or was, so I'm going to tell you. I'm also going to be using words you've never heard before to describe things like the interiors of medieval churches, so I'll try and explain it all as I'm going along, but if there's anything you don't understand, you need to Google it. It's an important part of my story.

You have to realise that the church, with a big and a small c, has been in a state of flux in this country for ever and it's largely all down to power and control. I used to ask my kids, when I knew them, what is the one thing that someone who has power and control wants more than anything else in the world? I'm going to sneak my answer in somewhere later, but spend a little time to consider it before you look, even if you think you know the answer. Organised religion is by far the easiest way to control people, and as a useful side-line it can also make you very rich, and of course very powerful. You subjugate your congregation by indoctrinating them from an early age and then they can't fight back, especially if you've craftily told them it's wrong to question your ideology.

The Church and what came before it have been moulding shit lives around ordinary folk for all of time.

No one knows what life in medieval times was like for the poor people. Historians can tell you what they ate and drank, how they dressed, what tools they used, how they liked their entertainment. What's more difficult to express is how it felt to wake up in the dark in winter in a cold, damp, dirty hovel knowing that you had a day's toil in front of you, and at the end of that day and the next and the one after, you would still be hungry, cold and exhausted and if you were lucky, you wouldn't have taken a step backwards in your pitiful life by slipping and breaking a leg or falling ill or by looking at your owner in the wrong way. Sure, if you want to get the sense you can choose to live off-grid in the middle of a wood, be self-sufficient, refuse contact with the outside world, but you'd not be a small fraction of the way to knowing what it was like. You couldn't recreate or enact the helpless, desperate treadmill of just staying alive, with no hope, no expectation that anything is ever going to change for the better.

You might have thought that the Church, being founded on a doctrine of loving your neighbour and suchlike, would have taken it upon itself to endeavour to improve the lot of the peasantry. Ease their suffering a bit, like Christ did at the start. I'm afraid not. It was probably the last thing on their minds.

You can most likely tell that I've got a bit of a downer on the Church, but this doesn't extend to the buildings themselves.

Ancient churches have been through many changes of fortune, style, tradition, fashions, and of course they still continue to. We are desperately lucky in this country to have so many well-preserved churches. Although congregations are dwindling and services are often irregular, most of these places are protected and well looked after and are still used for their original purpose. They are amazing. Even if you don't believe in God or Jesus, you should seek out these buildings and spend some time in them just looking around and taking it all in. Why don't you go to a service? I can't guarantee you'll get a good minister but it's worth a try. You could just sit at the back and hope no one comes and blesses you. I love country churches. Don't be hurried or you won't get so much out of it. Give yourself a good hour; read the history booklet that the vicar wrote in 1964. Immerse yourself.

St Rumon's in Crow's Nymet is a delightful example of an unspoilt medieval country church. It has a mellowness that descends upon your soul, shrouds you in awe. It is a quiet and unpretentious sanctuary from the real world. One of the churchwardens comes and unlocks it in the mornings, and then locks it again just before dusk. I have my own key, though nobody knows. A little while back, there was some work being done to the plasterwork and the builder had put scaffolding up against the interior walls. He was there for a few weeks, patching it up. I could watch him come and go from my kitchen window, and I saw where he left the key, under a stone on a grave by the porch. The first place anyone would look, so pretty stupid, really. One night I took it. I think it got him into trouble; it is quite a complicated key and difficult to replace. If you look at a section through it, it's forged in an 's' shape. Not the sort of thing that any old blacksmith could knock up nowadays.

I often let myself into the church at night. I like sitting and thinking in the dark. Sometimes I might spend the whole night there. There is an ancient ladder that leads to a trapdoor into the belfry. It's a marvellous thing and looking at it, I would guess it was made about three hundred years ago from a single long straight oak, and has served this one purpose for its whole life. There are rungs missing and a modern aluminium ladder has been strapped across the front of it, and it clatters and squeaks. The aluminium won't be there in three hundred years, but the oak still will be.

It's a bit awkward getting through the trap door; there's not much to hold onto and you have to watch your step through the bells because there's no floor. You have to jump from one housing to the next through the timber framework. I've been in there by accident when they started ringing below. Scary. Apart from the heavy swinging bells right next to me and the awful noise, the whole tower shook. I thought it was all coming down around me. There's a stiff little ledged and braced door in the belfry that leads out onto the roof. You could easily miss it even if you were looking for it and knew it was there. It's very dark, with only a single 40w eco bulb to light the whole place and the bells and their mechanisms cast shadows in the most unlikely and inconvenient corners. I can turn the lamp on and nobody knows I'm there because both the trap door and the roof hatch are a tight fit and don't let any light escape, and the shutters in the spire are tacked over with Terram and roof felt to stop the jackdaws getting in. I can walk over the lead gulley in the valley between the roofs of the nave and north aisle to the gable of the chancel and I can sit on a stone parapet at the end and have a panoramic view of most of the east end of the village. The roof behind me and the spire above ensure that my profile can't be seen from below, even on a moonlit night. I know this because I took my tripod up once and draped my jacket over it and came back down into the graveyard and confirmed that you can't see it from any angle, and yet nothing obstructs my view when I'm up there. I like to be thorough. I like to know. I usually take my binoculars with me and sometimes my viewing scope with the tripod if there's likely to be anything interesting to look at.

There are some magnificent ancient oak carvings in the nave. The nave is the bit where the congregation sits; the chancel is where the vicar and the choir go. There are some impressive carvings in the chancel, too.

In Devon, you'll usually find carvings on bench ends, roof bosses, rood screens and maybe misericords and sometimes in stone on capitals. These fancy words are coming tumbling out now, aren't they?

Bench ends are the ends of the pews.

Bosses are the joins in the timber of the ceiling that are ornamental as well as functional.

Rood screens are highly decorative timberwork with the purpose of separating the clergy from the great unwashed, as has been fashionable at various periods. We'll come back to them.

You get misericords in grander churches and cathedrals. They are a sort of narrow hinged seat, at buttock height, used to support failing practitioners during long services, so that it still gave the impression they were standing, or at least still awake, or even alive.

Capitals are the stone tops to pillars.

If you look at medieval vernacular church carvings, it will instantly tell you something about the way the church used, and the reverence and sanctity with which it was, or was not, held. Some of the subject matter is a bit surprising. The West Country artisans stopped short of showing fornication, but a Sheela na gig in your face can be a bit unsettling if you're not expecting it.

Up to about the beginning of the sixteenth century there were no pews in the nave and the congregation had to stand or loiter around or jump up and down to keep warm. This large open space was a useful local resource. There wouldn't be anywhere else at all like it in the village, and it was used for a host of purposes, both religious and secular, and for this reason it was often not even consecrated. Just think about it. As well as sombre lengthy Latin based masses and eucharists and dull religious festivals, marriages, baptisms and funerals, there would at other times be singing and dancing, music making, almost certainly debauchery in the dark corners, animal trading and baiting perhaps, storytelling, as well as guild meetings, parish meetings and every now and again some revolutionary militia gathering or civil unrest.

I guess the clergy were ultimately a bit unhappy about all this in the way that the sanctuary and the sacrosanctity was being abused and trivialised and although it must have been deeply unpopular with the proletariat, who were used to such distractions and rather enjoyed them, steps were taken to bring this to an end. The easiest way was to fill the nave with pews, and no dancing in the aisles. This is one reason why bench ends in particular illustrate the vernacular, secular world in the way they do. It was all part of the deal.

Of course, an alternative to the nave had to be found, to keep everyone happy, and this is where the church house comes in. We've got there, at last. Either a purpose-built hall would be constructed on church land, as near to the church as it could be, usually in the churchyard, or an existing suitable building would be converted for the purpose.

First of all, the coarser activities were transferred to the new venue, and then the joyous, merrymaking parts of the religious festivals. Christmas and the like. Confusingly, these are often referred to as 'ales'. Particularly confusing in this case because ales of the other sort became perhaps the biggest attraction of the new regime. It became part ale-house, part brewery and the best bit was that it was all self-funded and augmented the church coffers.

This happy state of affairs continued for a hundred years or more until the puritans went and spoilt it all by outlawing just about anything that gave the people pleasure, and then they had to go and change it all back again. Typical.

Because I know a bit about old houses, I can look around my Church House and work out how it has changed over the centuries. I'm confident that before it became a church house it was a farmhouse, with a very traditional layout. You know, I've already told you a bit about it. Cross passage from back to front; service rooms on one side and open hall living space on the other. Probably just the two bays to start with. Not exactly a yeoman's farmhouse, but rather better than a hovel. More a peasant's smallholding, with a little bit of land, and right next to the church. Excellent raw material for the new village entertainment complex. I'm guessing here, but the churchwardens must have had their eyes on it (if they didn't already own it) and would have been able to put the necessary pressure on the occupants to sling their hooks. It wouldn't have taken much to set the brewery up in the service rooms and the hall, although considerably smaller than the nave, would have made for some intimate get togethers. The hearth in the middle of the floor would be lit for winter meetings and cleared away for summer dances, a step up from the unheated nave, at least.

I learned a lot more about Church House from a man called Godfrey who propped up the bar in the Druid's for a calling. He's long dead now. We're talking over twenty years ago when I first started coming down from the Midlands that winter to get things moving on the house. Although he wasn't born in the area, he'd made it his life's work to unearth anything there was to know about the origins of Crow's Nymet. He ran the local history society and had been the prime mover behind one or two publications; locations of graves, monumental inscriptions, that sort of thing. Crow's Nymet is only a small place. There's only a finite amount of history to somewhere, isn't there? Once you've transcribed and indexed all the census's and parish records, the manorial roles, tithe maps, sundry extant ecclesiastical and legal documents, there's not really anything left. Without the benefit of Ancestry.com or Find my Past, Godfrey had winkled all this stuff laboriously out of the parish chest and the record office in Barnstaple and had written it down on A4 sheets and filed it in his paper filing system and wondered what to do next. If he had lived longer, he could have enjoyed transferring everything to disk, and then a few years later to a website or Facebook page. He would have liked that. He was the font of all knowledge, but in his last days he was reduced to answering queries from lazy or incompetent amateur genealogists from far-flung corners of the globe whose ancestors had passed through Crow's Nymet some time on their life's journey.

Godfrey knew everything and he could talk passionately and attract a good crowd of drinkers around him with his stories, but there was one occasion when he patently had words for my ears only.

I had taken to walking round to the Druid's at around six o'clock in the evening when I was on my own. I would have a couple of pints and then go back for a shower and a change of clothes and cook myself some supper. When you've got lime dust tickling your throat, a nice glass or two of bitter just hits the spot.

Godfrey was in his usual niche at the end of the bar, standing in front of the high stool that he would sometimes jiggle onto if his arthritis was complaining. Everyone knew it was his stool, of course. There were no tired punters in the Druid's who would be brave enough to sit on it, and unsuspecting tourists would never get the opportunity because he was always stood there guarding it, and besides, it was draped in a sheepskin fleece that looked distinctly unappealing. He was holding court with two ancient farmers and I sidled into a space next to them, but was excluded from the discourse by virtue of the fact that they all three had their backs turned to me.

In those days the Druid's public bar was a dark, cosy place with a huge open fire that was always lit; smouldering in summer, roaring in winter. There were stone flags on the floor and old black settles around the wall, reaching deep into the big inglenook itself, and the pub dog would be on its blanket in front of the hearth. Most of that's gone now and it's been lightened up with nicotine-free buttermilk emulsion, and the gastro-diners delight in the wood burner and the novelty jug collection.

After a bit of ooh-ahrring and purposeful grunting, the two old guys shuffled off towards the dart board and Godfrey beckoned me over and whispered in my ear, 'There's something I've been meaning to tell you'.

Well, I don't know about you, but when someone says that to me, I'm always a little nervous. It's usually not good news. We'd spoken about Church House before; it was one of his pet subjects, but he'd obviously got something new for me. He started off with the usual stuff; the sort of things I've just been telling you, then his demeanour suddenly changed, his voice softened and he looked cautiously around as if there might be some interloper in the bar that he hadn't previously noticed and then he signalled with a subtle tip of his head for me to come closer.

A bit melodramatic for the Druid's, where there's usually not much going on.

It was all very comical. I couldn't quite believe it was happening; it was such an affectation. I moved along the bar towards him and stood as close as his garlic-heavy dinner and the tail of smoke from his cigarette smouldering in the brick ashtray in front of him would comfortably allow. He began to tell me a story that he knew I'd never heard before. He told me of a man who had lived in my house. Five hundred years ago, or thereabouts. He didn't sound like the sort of bloke you'd like to run up against in a dark alley. The villagers didn't like him one little bit. They were afraid of him. He had some influence over the churchwardens and was connected in some way with the incumbent rector and the squire and his wife. This is when Church House had just become a church house. It's why I've told you about them, so you'll understand. It was a bit unusual for anyone to actually live in a church house, but this, evidently is what he did. I've since wondered if the sleeping chamber that would become my little green bedroom was where he slept.

Now, I was beginning to wonder how Godfrey knew all these things. I mean, no ordinary person kept a diary in those days and there wasn't much written down at all unless it had something to do with taxes or laws or misdemeanours.

It turns out something very bad had happened. So bad that the ripples of its badness left an indelible stain in the communal

97

folk memory of the village and its inhabitants. It was never written down. It was passed from parent to child over a score of generations; over centuries. That was a bit dramatic too, but you'll get the gist of what he was saying.

This guy had a bit of a reputation for being a shaman. A witch-doctor. And his forte was producing demons. Well, they all do, I guess. What was a bit creepy in this case was that there was some sort of biannual fertility rite, when he would induce a trance-like state in a number of unlucky participants of his choice, so that the harvest and the animals would be at their peak performance for the following six months and babies would be born alive and normal. This would happen out in the woods at the dead of night.

This festival had its origins well back in the mists of time, but the funny thing seems to be that it was a very local affair. It was just a clique of the villagers of Crow's Nymet that had anything to do with it. Everyone else was excluded. It had evidently been a much-loved focus of the farming year until the shaman came along and hijacked it and gave it his own sordid makeover.

Well, it turns out that one time he went too far. Something happened out in the woods that nobody who was there would ever talk about. Two of the villagers never came home again, and neither did the shaman. They all met their end during this rite, whatever it was. No one would bury them in sacred ground, so they're still out there somewhere in the woods.

It's all pretty corny. Do you believe this twaddle? I've seen too many horror B movies to get off on this.

But there was more. Of course.

You might have thought that with the shaman dead and two of their fellows mysteriously taken out that the villagers would have thought that it was maybe a good thing to forget all about this festival and just stick to good husbandry and moral habits, but apparently that's not what happened.

Like I was telling you just now, you have to try to imagine the whole medieval set up. These people's lives would have been influenced and dominated by superstitions and myths from the moment they could first understand a story and perceive a reaction from their peers or family. Every part of their understanding of the world around them would have taken on spiritual or magic or macabre meanings which they would work themselves up into a bit of a lather about at the slightest provocation. This fertility festival had been going on since time immemorial, and to suddenly end it would be just asking for trouble wouldn't it? Why risk it? Before the shaman had come along it had been a bit of harmless, though serious tradition and I guess it made the villagers feel a bit special as it was theirs, and no one else's.

So it continued, but it dropped below the radar. Out of the way.

Not even Godfrey knew anything about how the festival worked for the following three or four hundred years, because the next thing he told me was quite extraordinary. Soon after he'd started getting interested in the history of the village, one of Crow's Nymet's most colourful old characters accosted him in the churchyard one day as he was scraping lichen from a gravestone so he could read the inscription. Godfrey said that this man must have been at least ninety, but his eyes were twinkling with mischief and his mind was keen. They sat down together on a low wall and the man told his story.

The village of his childhood was very different to that of today. The new century had arrived but nothing about the modern age had reached the sleepy hamlets of deepest North Devon. No motor cars had found their way down the narrow muddy lanes with their steep hills and their blind bends. Crow's Nymet plodded along nicely without interference from the outside world, and most villagers would only venture away from their cottages when they had to.

Never mind a century ago, this still happens here today. I've spoken to local people who have never gone further than Barnstaple in their whole lives. And never want to either, nor have the cause. There is one guy who must be in his eighties who will tell you that he still sleeps in the same room that he was born in. I'll bet it's the same bed, too. And the same sheets.

Anyway, if it's like that now, just imagine what it was like a hundred years ago. This man wanted Godfrey to hear his story as he claimed to be the only person left who could or would tell it and he feared, rightly as it happened, that he didn't have much time left on this Earth.

This was when Godfrey learned the story of the shaman and the festival that turned bad. The man had heard it from his father and his uncles as they sat around the hearth on a winter's night. The man impressed on Godfrey that the story should go no further. He reckoned he was the last of the old villagers to know. There was no one left. He told Godfrey that after the ruinous incident, the festival more or less moved underground. It was something everybody in the village knew about, but very few talked of. It had metamorphosed into a grim observance that they had to continue to perform to protect the crops and their unborn babies.

Then the man took from his pocket an age-brown envelope, and in the envelope was a curled sepia photograph. Godfrey looked at the image. The man explained that this picture showed the festival in its death throes. It was the only physical record of the festival that had ever existed. He gave it to Godfrey and told him to destroy it when he had looked at it enough.

At this point, and to my amazement, Godfrey slipped his hand in his waistcoat pocket and brought out the photograph. He passed it over to me. I put my glasses on and took a look. There were a number of figures in a woodland setting. Judging by the appearance of the characters and the motion blurring of some hands and heads with a long exposure, I guessed it had probably been taken in the late eighteen hundreds or thereabouts by a professional photographer, who had no doubt set up his equipment in advance to take the shot. I looked at these characters. There were about six or seven of them, all men. Some were wearing ordinary country clothes and were sat on what looked like a thick bough of a tree. Yes, although the bough was horizontal and about a foot above the ground at the lowest point, the tree was still living because you could see other upright stems with foliage where the bough joined the main trunk. It was a big tree.

The sitting men were all looking at the camera, but nobody was smiling. I guess you didn't smile into the camera in a posed shot in those days. Just look at all those dreadfully morose school children in class photographs of the time. It's only much later that they start to smile. Either they had nothing to smile about, or they were told to look glum. One figure is stood apart and is carrying something that I couldn't make out. Two other guys are dressed up. One looks like he's supposed to be Father Christmas. He has a long cloak with a deep hood that obscures his face except for a straggly beard and he has a sack over his shoulder that appears to be heavy with something bulky. The other guy cuts a really weird image. His legs seem to be wrapped in tree roots, which spread out over the ground where his feet should be. There's no sign of his arms; they're probably beneath his jerkin. Instead, it looks like thick stumpy branches have been strapped to his shoulders. Most disturbingly, out the sides of his mouth and poking from each nostril there are vines of ivy which snake around his body.

I've seen plenty of green men before, but I'd never seen one quite like this. I remember being quite taken aback when I first saw it. This guy looked seriously creepy; as if he had grown from the forest itself.

The man explained to Godfrey that it was his father with the beard and the sack. He said he would have been in his late twenties at the time the photo was taken. It was taken on the morning of the winter solstice.

There was a lot to absorb, and I have to say I was fascinated by it all.

I knew that the barrel roof of St Rumon's was notable for carvings of green men on some of its roof bosses. They all had foliage of one sort or another coming from their mouths; I'd seen them. There would surely be some kind of link with the woodland goings-on.

I also knew a bit about country folklore and traditions, but Godfrey's photo didn't look like any sort of mystery play I'd ever seen. Mummers are very keen on doctors and black men and St George and his dragon to tell their stories, not crazy tree-men. And there was certainly no Morris dancing going on in that photo; it wasn't a scene of gaiety or merrymaking. It was a puzzle and it whet my appetite for what came later.

And you'll no doubt be noticing some connections yourself. The solstices are turning out to be something of a theme, aren't they? And the shaman looks like a prime candidate for some phial hiding.

You'll just have to wait and see.

nine

Isn't it funny how some people plan their lives and others don't? I've often wondered which is the best way; it is a bit fundamental, after all. It's the same with aspirations and ambitions. Some people have them; some don't.

What are you going to do when you grow up?

Everyone gets sick of being asked this when they're a kid. Do you answer with the first thing that comes into your head? Do you tell them what they're looking for and hope they'll be satisfied and go away? Don't say you don't know; that won't keep them happy. My advice is to pick a response and stick religiously to it. I'm going to be an architect. That's a firm enough statement for any godparent, aunt or uncle, and should keep them quiet for a while.

I've never had a plan. If you don't have a plan, then you won't be unhappy when the plan fails, which it will unless you work very hard at it for ever and then you'll probably wake up one day and realise that you've led a very dull life indeed. You'll be smug and your plan may have succeeded, but will you be fulfilled? What else could you have been doing with all your time?

My father's only plan was to keep his head down and he succeeded in making this work all his life. I grew up in a family where my father had no ambition and my mother sought to live her empty life vicariously through my own. My father was happy. My mother was frustrated. I was bright.

Nobody in my family had ever been bright before, it seems. Just a generation or two ago, they all signed their names with a cross and left school at fourteen to become ag-labs or coal miners. My mum knew I was bright and had aspirations on my behalf, but they were cruelly thwarted by Anthony Wedgwood Benn. He was our local MP and he sent his children to private school but advocated everyone else go to comprehensives, which he was just sorting out for us in Bristol. This was my mum's belief, because someone had told her, and then she told me. I've no idea if it was true. Anyway, it meant that instead of surely passing the eleven-plus and going to a proper grammar school, I never took the exam. I ended up at a city centre state school that had been a secondary modern the year before, and had just changed its name and not its teachers or its methodology. My mother was livid and dismayed. My dad didn't say anything, but he must have been secretly pleased. He had a distrust of grammars. They changed people, like universities.

I was always top of my class at school. Top of the year in a cohort of one hundred. A clever bugger in this small pond, but until the fifth form, just before 'O' levels, I had never expected to do more than get a factory or drawing office job and attend the local technical college on day-release. University never crossed my mind, and it must never have crossed my mother's, either. Why should it? No one I knew had ever been to University. Few of our teachers were graduates, and if they were, they never spoke of their experiences to us. None of my friends' parents nor my parents' friends could be described as professionals. We didn't mix with such people.

Once the seed had been sown by a maverick careers master one rainy afternoon, however, staying on to take 'A' levels did seem like an attractive thing to do next, and would put off the fateful day when I would have to work for a living. Our sixth form was small and I enjoyed a wonderful two years, mostly stress-free with little academic pressure and plenty of opportunity for adventure, motor bikes and cars. By then, the idea of University had taken root and promised another three years of hedonistic excitement. It was the easy option again, but there was still no sign of a plan.

I've told you about my ill-conceived move to the working world. Was this a plan? No, not really. It was just another natural progression. It was what you did. When you graduated, you might give yourself a bit of a summer break but then you started your career in earnest with a proper job. No gap years. No casual part-time fill-ins while you sat and thought about it; no finding yourself. Fortunately, there were plenty of genuine career jobs, so it all seemed like the obvious way ahead.

When I had corrected the little blip that was my brief foray into industry, I was immensely happy plunging myself into my PhD and then in the post-doctoral research that followed. I was a little uneasy that this wasn't going to continue for ever, but did I have a plan? No.

So when my ex-PhD supervisor Tim, the missing link, tapped me on the shoulder one day and said shall we start a company together I thought, yes, that sounds like a good idea. Let's do that.

So we did. Did we have a plan? We had a plan to start a company, but was that a proper plan? Not really. We might have expected to get a few free meals out of it for a couple of years, but not much else. We never planned to make any money from it.

Actually, the reason we started it was this, and I used to say this to anyone who would listen. We had both been working on separate, but related, projects for years and years and we could see some true commercial potential in them. We weren't doing airy-fairy blue-skies research on some sort of self-indulgent whim, we had been working on real problems in the real world with real sponsors and we had developed some clever little innovations that were real solutions that people could use. We both felt that if we didn't exploit this research commercially ourselves, not, and here I used to pause dramatically for effect when I was explaining it to another bored listener, not that someone else would exploit it but that nobody would. It would be left on the laboratory shelf and would gather dust until it became obsolete and useless and that wouldn't take long in the electronics industry. And all our hours in the laboratory would have been wasted.

We had a sum total of no business knowledge or experience between us. We read some books on how to start a company, and then we did it.

We sought no funding, because no funding was available that wasn't attached to so many strings that you would inevitably become mired in a bureaucratic swamp that would steal your precious time.

It would suck you down and the money would disappear before your eyes.

The University wasn't geared up to help academics spin out their own companies in the way that they are now. Technology

Transfer wasn't encouraged. We managed to set up a couple of licensing deals with the Registrar so that we could use the University's intellectual property but our first step up the industrial ladder was provided by a very informal arrangement thought up by that same Head of Department who had welcomed me back with open arms all those years before. I guess it wasn't strictly kosher. He was a bit of a wheeler-dealer and had a gift for juggling different accounts with different recipients in a paperless sort of way that kept most people happy most of the time. Put simply, our arrangement was that a research fund that was sitting unnoticed in the departmental closet would supply the electronic components that we would use to build our first product. If, or when, we managed to sell said product, we would pay back the money we had 'borrowed', which would end up in some other fund, and we would pay the department a royalty. Everyone would be a winner. From our point of view, this offered us a risk free, capital free stimulus, just when we needed it.

We started the company with just five hundred pounds each. I simply left the University when my research contract ended. I was footloose and fancy free. I had no commitments or liabilities. I lived alone and I've told you how frugally I could exist at Redfern Cottage. I reckoned I could easily survive for six months or so on my admittedly meagre savings. Tim on the other hand, being ten years older than me, had a permanent, well paid post with full tenure, a big mortgage and four young children. He had a lot to lose, whereas I had only Seamus.

We converted his garage into a little R and D lab and workshop. We told ourselves that this was where all the big technology companies started out. Hewlett Packard, Apple, Atari, Oracle. The Hewlett Packard garage had become a

Silicon Valley shrine. I imagined our humble workshop in rural Leicestershire receiving the same treatment when we had become a Tech heavyweight. It's where it all started, an attendant would tell curious visitors.

It was cold in that garage in the winter of eighty-three. It's hard to solder when your fingers are stiff and numb.

I'm a big believer in, and accomplished observer of, chains set in motion by random acts that percolate through time and change people's lives. How an isolated act of kindness or cruelty in some time and place can result in a seemingly unrelated act at some much later date and in a different place. There must be a special name for it. Yin and Yang but not quite.

Let me tell you what I mean.

I have a long memory. I hold grudges. Once, when we were kicking a football around in the school playground, I managed to slice it over the railings into the neighbouring street, where it lodged under a parked car. There was a lad, a year above me, walking past and I asked him if he could throw it back to me. He didn't break stride, but just looked at me and smiled and then ignored me. I had to go the long way round to retrieve the ball. It wasn't a big deal; it only took me a minute or two, but it did have some repercussions for the boy some years later. I didn't hate him for not getting the ball. It wouldn't have warranted any sort of confrontation at the time, but I did remember the act and I remembered the boy. I tucked it away somewhere in the bowels of my subconscious and when I noticed him one night in a city centre pub one Christmas, I was able to bring it to mind and act on it. Or not act on it, as it happened.

As I watched him with his friends at the bar, I saw the light-fingered girl next to him lift his wallet from his back pocket and hand it to her companion. I believe that if he had thrown that ball back to me I would have intervened, but I chose not to. I heard later that he had a large amount of cash in his wallet and that he had subsequently had to cancel a surprise New Year holiday with his fiancé, and that she had taken umbrage, even though it had been a surprise, and she had left him.

And here's the funny thing. I don't regard what happened as a tit-for-tat. I don't think like that. This boy wronged me, when he need not have, and that's what I remember and that's what matters to me. If another opportunity arose to bring it to mind, I would take it in the same way. Nothing's changed. It's the same with prison sentences. I don't believe that when you've done your time it makes any difference. You still did whatever you did; you just got caught. You can't undo any act. It's not possible. Making amends? What does that mean? You can't change anything that you've done, so why delude yourself into thinking that a punishment will wipe the slate clean?

I know that makes me come over as a right bastard, but you've probably missed the point. Forgiveness is the way to make things right, but that is only within the power of the victim, and in my experience is not given lightly.

Anyway, I'm ranting, and I've realised that it wasn't even a good example; I may have confused or distracted you with my silly story. I was telling you about when we started the company, and I was thinking about an act of kindness, not unkindness, that has stayed with me always and I have passed on to many others who have benefited as a result.

Tim and I were delivering our very first order to a research establishment in the centre of London. It was a box of programmable electronics and we had struggled for some weeks to get the software up to scratch. We were both a bit nervous as we demonstrated the performance of our little baby to our customer. He was European; Swiss or Austrian I think. Very tall with a serious professional bearing. He was the leader in his field and we had been delighted to receive his order. It would convey some credibility and recognition of our design, but his requirements were exacting.

Cash flow was beginning to be of some concern. We were fast running out of our thousand pounds and neither of us wanted to top it up with another tranche. We were naïve, of course, but we believed in ourselves and fancifully trusted in good fortune.

If you don't know how business works, I'll quickly tell you. You can skip this bit if you like, if you think you know.

First, you set up trade accounts with your suppliers. They'll ask you for trade references. If you've only just got going, you'll have no references to give them and no track record. Not good, but it's in the nature of things. Everyone's got to start somewhere. So, the next thing they'll ask for is a personal guarantee, and I guess you have to get used to this idea pretty damned quick because they'll be queueing up. I was a bit affronted by this concept at first. We'd just incorporated a limited liability company with the express objective of enjoying limited liability. Like I say, we were naïve. Incidentally, although you can't avoid them at first, the trick with personal guarantees is to cancel them as soon as you can, or they may come back and bite you in the bum some years later when you've forgotten all about them.

So, let's assume that you've established all the trade accounts that you need for the supply of components, raw materials, services and everything else. In the electronics industry, you'll then get thirty days from the end of the month that you bought them in to pay off the account. When you sell something, your customer will also get credit before they have to pay you. And there's the rub. If everybody paid on time there would be no problem, but they don't.

If I was Prime Minister I would make them pay on time.

There is so much wasted effort, angst, bankruptcies, anger, helplessness, hopelessness just because stupid accountants need to justify their existence by showing how creative they can be; how good they are at making life hard just for the sake of it.

The Professor, the leader in his field, our customer, disappeared into his office with a grave expression on his face, as if he was deliberating with himself some academic question on a higher plane. When he returned, it was with a sheaf of papers and two or three weighty tomes opened at pages of Greek symbols and mathematical formulae. He proceeded to tell us how, in so many ways, our product was deficient and could be improved. We listened intently and took notes.

Then he told us that in his younger days he had made a living selling radios that he had built from scratch from war surplus components, and that he had been grateful to have been paid cash on delivery of his first set and that it had enabled him to buy proper tools that made it easier to build the next one, and that, eventually, the money he earned allowed him to go to college. With that, he handed us a cheque for the full amount of our invoice. He added that he had concluded that our product was the best on the market, he gave us an order for a second unit and advised us to put our prices up.

And it was at that exact moment that I knew that everything was going to be alright.

So you see, a kind act that happened in the fifties in Innsbruck or somewhere meant that we survived an early cash flow crisis and were able to prosper and I was delighted to pass on this gesture many times to small, struggling businesses.

And who knows? The Innsbruck thing might have been precipitated by some other kind act before it, and the people I have helped may subsequently have passed on the goodwill to others. It's a fascinating concept, this causal passage through time, don't you agree?

I've told you; I think too much.

I can't stop myself.

ten

You might think that starting and growing your own successful company is one of the most exciting things that you could do, and it is. But in my case, during this tumultuous time there were other things going on in my life that were even more exciting. Typical, isn't it? You wait twenty-nine years for something to happen and then it all kicks off at once. Ridiculous. I'd spent the last eight years of my life languishing at my own sedate pace, pottering along and getting by. Then we start the company and all hell's let loose and I'm working fourteen-hour days, six days a week and it's still not enough. And then I get my first girlfriend. How stupid is that? Yes, at the age of twenty-nine, I was still a virgin.

You'll be glad to know that I'm not going to bore you with lurid tales of my sex life. I'm an old man. I've lost my appetite for that sort of thing. Suffice to say that from the age of about five, until I met Georgia there was only me involved.

That's right, I really was five when I started wanking. I know because I can remember the fantasies that I conjured that involved looking up girls' dresses as they played on the climbing apparatus in the playground of my infants' school, and I left there when I was six. I had a way of masturbating that didn't involve erections or ejaculation, but was based more on the vibrator principle. I'm not going into details, but it was very clever. This was all fine until I was about ten when I started getting boners, and then I had to change my technique. Then spunk came and made everything messy. For twenty years I wanked at least once a night, every night; five times once before midnight one Christmas Eve when I couldn't get to sleep. I devised ways to hide or avoid the stains and different styles to disguise my actions when I was sharing a bedroom. I guess all boys do that. It's something we don't tend to talk about, so I don't know for sure. Perhaps you do.

I'm sorry. That did turn out to be a bit lurid, after all.

I slipped up once on a family caravan holiday when I hadn't appreciated that the whole thing was shaking like crazy. I don't know if my mum and dad were lying there thinking oh fuck what do we do now, or whether they hadn't perhaps realised what was going on. They lay there mute, but my sister, who was lying next to me, sat up and asked what was I doing. I said I had a mosquito bite that I was scratching but I don't think she believed me. The next night I changed the frequency of my strokes so that it didn't resonate with the natural wavelength of the caravan, and all was ok. You see, even at that age I was a very clever but arrogant little shit, who knew how to put his physics to good use.

You might ask, how can anyone spend three years as a university student and come out the other end still a virgin?

It took a special talent. I think lack of attention to personal grooming and hygiene may have had something to do with it. Whatever, I was happy enough with my own personal arrangements which cost no money, nor required any sort of commitment.

Inevitably, as time went on, it did grind me down; my parents made it clear that they thought I was queer, and the longer it went on, the more likely it seemed to me that this was going to be the way it was for the rest of my life.

And then along came Georgia.

It took me completely by surprise. This was about two years before we started the company when I first met her, just so you know how long it all took. One of my closest friends brought her to the pub one night. They had just started going out with one another. I was transfixed. No one had ever had this effect on me before. I couldn't take my eyes off her.

What is it that attracts one person to another?

God knows, it just happens.

If I'm looking through a magazine and I see a picture of a girl, what is it about that image that might turn me on? Is it the way she smiles? Her eyes? Is she sexier with or without clothes?

I like short skirts that end in a slender waist. Preferably pleated, and long white socks or black boots would be a bonus. I like the skirt to be short enough so that the tops of the thighs have already started to get slenderer. I've spent time analysing photos of girls and this is what I like. I like it in real life, too, except when the girl looks like a whore, and then I don't like it. Breasts? Well, not too big. Small, pert breasts can be very nice, same with bottoms.

Georgia had none of these things, so why was I so smitten with her? She had no waist to speak of, no chest either. She wore dowdy jeans and a baggy, chunky jumper on that first night, hardly an alluring outfit. Her eyes, though. Her eyes were as black and enticing as a rabbit hole, and as mysterious. She had the touch of the Bohemian about her. She was wearing glasses and had her hair in a bun at the back. All men dream of taking a girl's glasses off and shaking out her hair. I know I do. Georgia was a final year undergraduate reading social psychology. Again, not really my thing, but I do like my women to be intelligent. I don't feel threatened by this like some men.

From the moment I first saw her I never really fancied any other girl, and I came to see that this was going to be a problem for me if I had a notion to find a wife who could bear my children and provide me with my oats. I was old-school when it came to morals and scruples. I would no more steal my friend's girl from him that I would shoplift or lie or betray my country. It didn't stop me fantasising about her, of course, and for the next couple of years she became the prime subject matter in all acts of masturbation. I felt my only way out of this unfortunate situation was if they split up, at which point I would manoeuvre for position. All a bit unsatisfactory, particularly as there seemed little chance of that happening. They became very close and when she graduated, they found a flat in town and were the perfect couple. I stayed very much on the side lines, and even when drunk at parties would never declare my hand.

But then something happened that changed it all.

There came a weekend when Georgia had her best friend from school staying with her. She was a year older than Georgia and had a long-time partner who was working on oilrigs somewhere in the North Sea. She was very attractive. Tall, with thighs that narrowed nicely, just below the hem of her very short skirt.

A group of us had been out pubbing on the Friday night and we ended up at Redfern Cottage drinking whisky. It was probably about three in the morning. It had been a good night, but I was tired and past my prime. They all got up to go, but then Georgia's friend, Poppy her name was, announced that she would stay. I'm not sure if this news caused any consternation among the assembled drunken revellers because they all knew I was celibate. It certainly took me by surprise. Up to that point, I hadn't even considered that such a thing could be on the cards. I hadn't picked up any signs that she might be attracted to me but over the next few hours it became obvious that she had had her sights on me for some time. I imagine, now in hindsight, that she had orchestrated the whole thing. She had groomed me, and I was totally unprepared.

Despite an evening's heavy drinking I wasn't that drunk. When I'm drunk I pass out and have to be put to bed or left where I've fallen.

We sat and talked at the kitchen table while I tried to work out what I was going to do. You see the trouble was, although she was very pretty indeed, I just didn't fancy her. I've told you; since I first saw Georgia I had eyes for no other. I was flattered by her advances, sure, but I could have done without all this.

In the end, there really was no choice but to go to bed with her. There was only one bed in the cottage that was usable, and it was in my bedroom. It was a standard width double bed with an ancient mattress and it drooped horribly in the middle where some of the wire loops had rusted through and I had tried, and failed, to repair them with electrical cable. It was, of course, that same bed that I'd paid fifty pence for. The worst thing of all was the sheets. Well, obviously if I'd known I was going to be sharing them with someone then I would have changed them. They were filthy. About as filthy as I've ever let them get, ever. Honestly.

It was all very unfortunate timing.

For some evenings, I'd been working on a problem with the brakes on my car and this necessitated writhing around in the dust and grime of the woodshed floor, which was the only weather-proof outbuilding I had. I've mentioned that the washing arrangements at Redfern Cottage were a bit primitive, and invariably I couldn't face a bath afterwards. Hence the sheets. To be sure, I had intended to change them the very next day, when I had sorted the brake problem.

I wondered if she'd noticed them, and if she had done, would she care? Did she, I wondered, think less of me now she knew a little more of my personal habits? The bare lightbulb in the ceiling pendant was only a tiddler, so she may not have picked them out from the grey gloominess of my bedroom, but she certainly would be able to in the morning.

I don't remember undressing. I imagine it was a silent, introspective affair. I kept my pants on and so did she. She was very kind to me. She wasn't expecting much, I feel, and seemed pleased just to be lying next to me. For my part, I was entranced by the softness of her skin. This was all new ground for me. I had never been this close to a woman before, let alone handled one in the flesh. If you've grown up in a touchy-feely family, then you're used to hugging and kissing. You take it in your stride and consider it the most natural thing. I had only ever been hugged by my mother, and that was a long time ago. As far as I can remember, I never touched my dad. Never even shook hands with him. He would have run a mile if I had ever tried to hug him. This wasn't unusual for his generation and he was a man of his time.

Now, you're thinking any red-blooded male faced with the situation I found myself in would get stuck in and enjoy it, but I'm afraid I just wasn't interested. She must have known this, and she made no attempt to get me aroused, so we both fell asleep with our pants still on. In retrospect, I do feel now that this was a great shame; a truly lost opportunity. My biggest problem, of course, was that I was still a virgin, and I wanted to save myself for Georgia.

Can you see my predicament? My love life was all going nowhere any time soon.

In the morning we lay in bed, Poppy smoking. It was a dull day. I decided to tell her about my feelings for Georgia, as if this would be able to explain everything that had happened the previous night. We talked for hours in that grimy bed. She was my analyst, my sister, my doctor, my confidante, my saviour, my mother even, but not my lover.

She told me that Georgia's relationship with Leo was very much an open one, and that both had taken other lovers in recent months. This was news to me, and I'm not sure I believed her. Not sure if I wanted to believe her. I couldn't really take in all the implications, and had to be helped. The bottom line seemed to be that I had been living in a little fanciful world of my very own where relationships were simple and people told the truth, whereas the reality was that everyone was at it with everyone else, and no one really cared, and I was being left out of it all, a complete chump waiting for the object of my affections to become available, whilst all the time she was sleeping around with anyone who came her way. As was everyone else.

I probably should have said, well, if that's the case let's get on with it, bring it on, but I didn't, and in any case that window had closed. And so the whole sorry tale could have just withered, and I might have been waiting and waiting for the Holy Grail that would never come, and I'd now be a sad old man who had never felt a lover in his arms or experienced the power and ecstasy of giving life to a new generation. There are such men.

But the night of unbridled lust and coupling that never happened, nevertheless changed everything.

Poppy had decided to tell her BFF.

The world can be divided into two parts. Those who have had affairs and those who have not. I wonder which one you are?

The whole point of an affair is that it's secret. If it wasn't secret, then it wouldn't be an affair, would it?

My affair with Georgia was secret because, although I now knew that her relationship with Leo was 'open', I just would never have been able to face him if he ever found out about me and his partner. His wife, effectively. For my part, it wasn't as if I was cheating on a lover with another woman. I was cheating on my friend. I've explained to you, I have morals and scruples. I agonised over what I should do, and in the end my decision was just plain selfish. My continued lack of a steady girlfriend was beginning to affect my mental health, I argued, and I suppose it really was. Also, I wanted children at some point, and I couldn't do this and still be a virgin. I needed a girlfriend, and that girlfriend could only be Georgia.

I realised now that Georgia knew how I felt about her, but nothing had been acknowledged between us. It was a phony time. Then one day I was out drinking with Leo and we were talking about a short business trip that Georgia had just been on, staying in a hotel for two or three nights just outside Birmingham with a group of her colleagues. Out of the blue he announced to me that she'd told him that she'd slept with this guy on the last night. I did wonder straight away of course whether he knew anything about my feelings for Georgia and I analysed his voice and facial expressions for any clues. I was fairly confident he knew nothing, but wondered all the same why he'd told me about it. Was he testing me? He pondered a while and then he added that he didn't have a problem with it, because the guy was such a good bloke. Just like that; a good bloke. Was I a good bloke, too, I asked myself, or was it different being a loyal, trustworthy friend? I was in turmoil with such reasoning, but I guess that's what finally tipped the balance and I resolved to get things moving.

It started one night when there were four of us sat round a table in a pub in Loughborough. It was one of those tables that have been made from an old trestle sewing machine, with a new top and the treadle mechanism removed from the base. I was sat opposite Georgia and we were on to our second pint, the conversation flowing fluently. It was a busy pub and there wasn't much shoulder room. I had my foot on the stretcher of the table leg and I moved it forward so that my heel rested on the ironwork, and then I edged it towards the end where Georgia was sat. I brushed it up against her calf and left my leg there. She didn't move her leg away, but very, very slightly increased the pressure.

You're thinking, big deal. You're right, though not in the sarcastic way you're sneering. It was a very big deal for me, indeed. I can't tell you of the frisson from this simple act that exploded in me at that moment. A sort of electric pulse that discharged through my whole body. The thing that I had been waiting for for so long had started. I would be able to look back, as I am now, and say this was where it began.

Despite all these electrical pulses exploding willy-nilly all over the place, I remained totally composed and gave nothing away in my typical cool manner. Just a momentary, meaningful glance into the limpid eyes of my loved one was sufficient for me to know that this was it.

Have you ever played footsie? Well, obviously I'm not a connoisseur, but I can thoroughly recommend it. It's just like a miniature affair, in that it's secret. That's the whole point. Well, I guess it actually depends on how drunk you are. I've witnessed many attempts at footsie that were obviously meant to be secret, but were patently free for all to observe. The buzz is that your target is complicit and has acknowledged and responded to your advance, and perhaps moved it on a bit. The other useful thing is that it can be a self-contained adventure. It doesn't necessarily have to lead on to bigger and better things. You could save it just to liven up dinner parties, for example. If done sober, however, it does lead to a clandestine understanding between two parties that will never really go away. Try it some time.

You might be thinking that this experience would open the floodgates of lust and desire and it would be an unstoppable deluge of escalation and intensification, but that's not how it happened at all. Incredibly, the footsie period must have gone on for three or four months because we didn't have, or more correctly, didn't make, the opportunity to be alone together. When it finally arose, it was her initiative. She needed a lift back from Nottingham where she was attending a morning workshop and asked me if I could pick her up from the campus as I was collecting some tools nearby. We stopped at a country pub on the way back and had sandwiches and a pint. I realised I'd never been in her company, just the two of us. In fact, I

123

didn't have much experience at all of being with any girl on a one-to-one basis. Just Poppy, really. I was a tad out of my comfort zone, but she was great. We got talking of deep issues very quickly and I was glad we were the only ones in the bar. She wanted me as much as I wanted her, she said. What were we waiting for?

And so it happened. Redfern Cottage was on the way back to Loughborough. We stopped off. There was nobody there, of course; I lived on my own. It was bloody cold. The Rayburn had gone out. It would usually stay in all day if I loaded it up with slack, but it had gone out and looked sad. I hoped it wasn't an omen. I needed a whisky to steady my nerves and we sat for a while in the cold kitchen until we realised that this thing had to be done. We had both contrived it to happen and we had to see it through.

We consummated our tryst in that same squalid bed in the grey bedroom. Clean sheets, this time, though; I had rather anticipated we'd end up here. I wish I could say that it was the best thing that ever happened, but it really wasn't. I was too nervous. I'd waited so long for this and there was a lot hanging on it. I would like to think that it was special for Georgia, too, although she'd had a lifetime of lovers. She said it was, and I chose to believe her.

eleven

Georgia never wanted children. She wanted a career and excitement. When she became pregnant she had some difficult decisions to make, and so did I.

We never really knew how it happened and were certainly shocked, almost disbelieving when we found out. My sperm must have an impressive shelf-life. It seems most unlikely, telling you now, how we had been living our lives since that first flush of lust and consummation. Life had just carried on, on the surface, as if nothing had changed. Georgia was quite happy to continue living in the flat with Leo, and I was content to let her do so. I had enough on my hands with getting the company going to dwell too much on the more enigmatic aspects of my life. We lapsed easily into a sort of routine where we would meet twice a week at lunchtime and go back to Redfern Cottage for rampant sex. We still socialised as a group of friends, played footsie, snatched kisses and embraces when we contrived to be briefly alone. Did anyone know? Did everyone know?

We did give ourselves some rules. Georgia wouldn't allow me to visit her alone at the flat, for example, and I was okay with this. In the summer months we could be a little more flexible, and managed sex in all sorts of places. In the woods, the back garden, the fields and hedgerows and even once in the cruck of a tree in a layby. That was tricky, and I wouldn't recommend it. In darker and colder times, coitus was snatched on the back seat of my Beetle, or in front of a coal fire in the living room at Redfern. Then she started to have some health issues and decided to come off the pill for a while. She was adamant that Leo was no longer interested in fucking her, and suspected he had another lover anyway. I went along with this and was happy to use condoms for the duration. To be honest, although I used to enjoy the coupling, I didn't crave it. I was still of the opinion that a good wank was just as satisfying, a darned sight quicker and much less complicated or risky.

When she first told me that she thought she might be pregnant, my immediate reaction was that it must be someone else's. I didn't know what to say, but my expression must have done that for me. She became a bit emotional and started crying and threatened all sorts of things. She knew it wasn't anyone else's.

The easiest way out would have been to get a termination. No one need have known. I wouldn't have tried to stop her if she'd wanted to do this. I would have accepted it, but I would have been very, very sad for the rest of my life.

Once she had convinced me that it was my baby, (and it was by the way; as it grew up it looked so much like me) a wave of euphoria engulfed me. I can't explain to you how I felt, but it was like nothing I'd ever experienced. It was quite hard to handle manfully. And there was this smug sort of impression that now I knew that all my bits worked. I guess it must be something that's tucked away somewhere in those secret parts of all men. The thing is, does it stay tucked away or does it rise to the surface and interfere with your feelings? I've known lots of men who seem to shrug off the whole idea of their role in the continuity of the species as a macho sort of put-down, but I always wonder how they're really feeling. How is it touching them in the privacy of their own head?

Georgia had never been one for maternal instincts. She would never pick up a child or baby and cuddle it. One or two couples in our social group had already started producing but I hadn't noticed any sort of emotion or even interest from Georgia.

It's a rite of passage; and it ends friendships and ruptures the fault lines of relationships. Put simply, when you've got babies you don't want to talk about anything else, but when you haven't got babies it's the last thing you're interested in. That's it really. Don't let anyone tell you it's more complicated than this. Sure, there will be other factors, such as biological time clocks, barrenness, money, things like that, but they don't count; basically it all comes down to whether you've got a baby or whether you haven't.

But just like me, Georgia changed too, almost overnight, and it was obvious to us both that we badly wanted this child.

But what to do?

It was a bit inconvenient for all concerned. Our relationship was secret. Probably. It had all been a complete accident and was no part of anyone's plan. I had no money. We had no home to raise a family. There was hardly anything that could be described as stability in our circumstances. I had a company to run. I had led a solitary existence for the last ten years in a tumbledown wreck in the middle of the woods, and I had rather got used to my own company. It didn't really seem a promising start.

First of all, we had to decide how and when we were going to announce our news. And to whom, and in what order. In the event it was rather taken out of our hands. Georgia saw her GP several times and underwent some tests for one thing and another. It turns out her sister had suffered a series of miscarriages that no one except Georgia knew about, so there was some concern that there might be some inherent genetic problem that could spoil things. It seemed sensible to keep all this to ourselves until the time of danger was past, which was evidently about fourteen weeks. I don't really know much about these things, as you can tell. What I do know is that when I saw the scan of my baby, it changed my life forever, again, in an instant.

Georgia had arranged an appointment at the Queen's Medical Centre in Nottingham. It's the University teaching hospital and is an enormous edifice, much too big. I took her in on the pretext of dropping her off on campus for a lecture. All the journey there in the car she was telling me stories of the scans her sister had had to endure. How there had been nothing living to see. It got to the point where I realised I was expecting to be disappointed and was bracing myself for the inevitable hysterics.

The pre-natal clinic wasn't in the main building, thank goodness; it was in a shabby portakabin village in the corner of an overspill car park. I still had to park in the hateful multi-storey and was both stressed and slightly dazed when we arrived. I would say I was overwhelmed by events, and not quite myself. Mercifully, we didn't have long to wait, as Georgia was called almost straight away.

They didn't know who I was, that was obvious. This is 1986, remember. It wasn't all that common for ordinary 'nice' women to give birth out of wedlock. I'm not saying it was rare, but it was different to the way it is now. Certainly, it wasn't frowned upon like it was in the sixties and early seventies. We'd got past that rubbish, but it was unusual enough for interested parties to be vigilant. Anyway, they showed me into this room and Georgia was lying next to the machine and there was a nurse standing either side of the bed. They'd just spread some glutinous stuff on Georgia's stomach and were ready to go with the ultrasound sensor. I looked at the screen.

I remember what came next as being properly surreal and other-worldly, but not in the way you're expecting. You see, this was actually my field of expertise. Ultrasonics. Sonar. It was what my PhD and my post-doctoral research was all about, and I had spent years and years gazing at indistinct two-dimensional images of underwater acoustic targets. I was an expert at interpreting the data and even in the poorest conditions, I could distinguish between a mine, a diver and a fish with a transponder stuck on its back, but I'd never seen a foetus before. I wasn't trying to be, but I was fascinated by the interference patterns and the dynamic range of the display, and preoccupied enough by mentally calculating the signal to noise ratio of the scanner that when the actual target hove into view, I wasn't concentrating on it at all. Georgia nudged me and reprimanded me with a cold and frightened expression. The looks of all three women in that room were intense. There was something there, if only it could be brought more into focus. We all squinted our eyes. If it had been a mine, I could have told you its destructive power. Then there it was. The thing that changed me forever. The heartbeat. The new life that I had helped to create. What a wonderful experience it was. A truly seminal moment for me. It was just a little heartbeat amongst the noise and the snow and the fuzziness and the interference, but it was there and I was entranced and would never feel the same about anything, ever again. That heartbeat was all it took.

Even with everything else that has happened, I can look back on that moment and say that it was the only thing that has ever mattered in my whole life.

After the scan, we both felt we had crossed the Rubicon. There was no going back.

You can tell a lot about someone by his or her reaction to an extraordinary and unexpected message. You can tell the selfish ones straightaway, and the hateful ones, and of course you will find out who your real friends are, soon enough.

I really didn't have any notion of how Leo was going to take it. It was the biggest unknown of the lot. I still didn't even know if he was aware of our clandestine relationship, for God's sake. He could have reacted badly and thrown Georgia out into the street. Let's face it, he could have done anything. He might have hurt me, or Georgia, or himself. Some would have. In the event he showed his true colours and told us he was delighted for us. He would move out and Georgia could stay at the flat for as long as she wanted. He hoped we would all remain good friends. Just let him know if there was anything he could do. Now, you can read anything you like into this. Some people would conclude that their relationship had in reality long since peaked, and that this unexpected turn might yet prove convenient for all parties. I just think, what a marvellous human being, what an exceptional friend Leo turned out to be.

My parents were delighted. My mother was overjoyed at the prospect of becoming a grandmother at last and my father was just relieved that I wasn't homosexual after all. Most of our friends stuck by us, and those that didn't were no loss.

Tim took it in his stride, as I knew he would. There wasn't much that could faze Tim. Georgia's parents had divorced and she hadn't seen her father for about five years, so she didn't deem it necessary to tell him. We guessed he would find out if he was interested enough. Her mother's response was reserved and cautious. She made it plain that it was not what she would have chosen for her daughter. We had never met and until the announcement, I'm guessing that she had never heard of me. I have to confess, I probably didn't cut a very good image, and I wouldn't have blamed her for thinking I had very few prospects as a provider and protector of her grandchild.

She did, however, give us some money for a deposit on a house. It seems she had done rather well out of her divorce and this sum was currently surplus to requirements. She said we could pay it back when I had made us rich, but she had patently already mentally written it off.

I had loved living in Redfern Cottage, but even I could see that it was totally unsuited to raising a new-born baby. Dirty, draughty, cold, dusty, insecure, isolated, I could go on. If it hadn't been so ridiculously cheap and I hadn't loved it so much, I would have been climbing the property ladder long before. I'd always hankered after buying a wreck and doing it up at my own pace, but it had never happened. That would have to wait.

I put it to the back of my mind. What we needed now was somewhere that was ready to move into and we wanted it yesterday. I found somewhere almost straight away. I guess that sort of place is quite easy to come by. Most towns have clusters of starter homes, at least they did then. They weren't particularly built as starter homes but that's what they turned into, largely because prices settled at about eighty per cent of the cost of exactly the same houses in slightly better areas or nicer neighbouring towns or suburbs. Young couples would be resigned to buying their first house on one of these estates, with the intention of moving on as soon as finances would allow. It was another rite of passage that you were expected to learn to live with. It was an interregnum for lower middle-class people when I was young and usually went something like this.

Boy and girl both living at home with mum and dad. Boy and girl get engaged, start saving and spend a year planning their life. Boy and girl announce wedding. One or both sets of parents offer a deposit on a house which, together with a mortgage predicated on the boy's future earnings is sufficient to buy a modest house in a cheap area (vis; the starter home estate). They marry and move in. Girl becomes pregnant. Girl leaves work; has baby. Boy gets promoted at work. Girl gets pregnant again. Then, they escape from the starter home estate and buy a decent house somewhere in a pleasant village or suburb and spend the next few years washing their cars on a Sunday morning and putting their children through nice schools.

The starter estate. In Bristol it was Yate. In Loughborough it was Shepshed.

The house I had chosen was a modern two-bedroom semi. It was so cheap that the loan from Georgia's mother was sufficient to buy it outright, which was the only sensible thing to do as I wasn't confident that any bank manager would consider my income a sufficient asset or unsecured property a safe repository of his funds.

I hated that house from the start. I loathed the open plan front garden, the concrete driveway for washing the car on, and the six-foot-high lap-larch fence that enclosed and darkened the postage stamp back yard and stopped the flowers from growing.

I told myself that this was just a stopgap measure and that as soon as I was paying myself a decent salary we would get out and find somewhere better, but of course, that's not the way it worked out. It would be five years and another baby before we moved on.

twelve

But back to the late spring of 1984, (before babies), when things were working out well for our new company. We were bringing in money from our first product which we were now able to build easily and sell at an astonishingly high profit margin. We had received about a dozen orders for these devices, mainly from UK universities, but we were also getting interest from further afield and confidently expected to clinch sales in the USA and even Japan. We had sent out a lot of marketing stuff, attended academic symposiums at which Tim spoke or chaired, and we had pitched our stall at a couple of trade shows. There came an opportunity to expand into new premises which we took with great fervour.

It was perfect timing.

The University was building what they called an Industrial Incubator on a sports field on the edge of campus; a very prominent location and a prestigious project that received much publicity in the local press. The 'Technology Centre' was to be a commercial looking building with modern steel cladding, a double height atrium and lots of glass. It would house about a dozen industrial units of sizes between five hundred and two thousand square feet with a reception area for secretarial services. The idea was to seek out young, technology-based start-ups, enable them to establish themselves within a user-friendly environment and then nourish them and encourage growth and innovation.

Basically, we were made for it, and it for us. We were the perfect tenants and were feted by visiting politicians, academics and industrialists who were wheeled around with weary regularity in the early days of our occupation.

We waited anxiously as the building was constructed. I walked by the site often and took great interest as first the foundations, then the shell and then finally the landscaping and car park were completed. We had taken a lease on one of the mid-range units which would enable us to expand. It was time we took on our first employee.

This is a big move for any enterprise and not one to be entered into lightly, but if you want to grow, you have to do it. As with other business-related things that we knew nothing about, the first thing we did was to read up how to do it. The second was to pay someone else to set it all up for us. That had been our philosophy from the word go. Learn and understand the issue, but if it was something that neither Tim nor I were good at, nor interested in doing, then we'd pay someone else to do it for us. We didn't like filling in forms or jumping through hoops of any kind. We never did our own bookkeeping. I've never written a business plan or a risk assessment and I've never filled in a VAT return or a balance sheet. Our accountant's wife came in every Friday morning to do the books and she turned out to be up to speed on employment law, too.

We did have someone in mind for our first employee. Although Tim was on a year's leave of absence from the

University, he still had research students who were completing their higher degrees and he was supervising several final year undergraduate projects. One of these had been very ably tackled by an outstanding young student who Tim had been courting for some while with a view to poaching him from the grasp of his industrial sponsor. Caspar would certainly get a first-class degree and could have the pick of the best jobs going that summer. If he had chosen academia he would have been welcomed, no dragged, to any research institution of his choice. Fortunately, his girlfriend had another year to go at Loughborough before graduating, so he was keen to stick around for a while.

Tim was a very nice man. Later on, our staff would call him Uncle Tim. He was that sort of guy. You'd feel safe with him. He was able to persuade Caspar to come and work with us for a salary, for the time being, that was about two thirds of what he might have expected in industry. Up to then, I had still been living off my savings, and it now seemed the right time to start paying me. God knows what Tim was living off. I didn't like to ask. I think he had got some sort of lump sum from a pension pot or life assurance policy. Anyway, it meant a huge step jump in our outgoings. Suddenly we were paying out three salaries and rent and business rates and ... this was scary stuff.

Caspar started on the very day that we moved into the Technology Centre and his first job was sanding down benches. One of the lads that I played darts with on a Wednesday night was a retired carpenter and I cajoled him into making us up some benches and tall wooden racking. I ordered in a load of pine tongue and groove floorboarding and two-by-fours and during that first week he built us four twelve-foot-long benches with a half shelf at the back for our instruments and a similar number of high racks of shelves. I guess it all looked a bit artisanal rather than the white heat of technology, but at the time I thought it fitted our garage start-up image perfectly.

I have a photograph of Albert making them in our bare and empty space, with Caspar and Tim standing watching, drinking cups of coffee. How distant it all feels.

Once the woodwork had been sanded and finished off with a coat of polyurethane, and our oscilloscopes and other equipment had been set up, I thought it all looked very professional. We added some bookshelves, a couple of filing cabinets and cupboards and my desk, and we made ourselves at home. We looked good. We now had our name above the glass entrance. It all felt real, at last.

We did indeed prosper. We were now able to work on new designs that would widen our product range at the same time as churning out the proven stuff for good money. I did worry, all the time, if we would have enough cash at the end of the month to meet our commitments. Once or twice, it was a close-run thing.

The next summer we took on another graduate, a software engineer, and made a full time offer to an outstanding technician who had been on work experience with us. We made a good team, the five of us. If only we could have just carried on like that.

Inevitably the time came when we needed more secretarial support. Remember in those days you employed a separate person to do all that stuff. You know, type letters, file things, answer phones, photocopy, make the tea. Again, we looked to the University for our supply, and out popped an admin assistant from our old department. Tim and I knew her well.

She had typed my PhD thesis for me on an IBM golf ball. We didn't exactly poach her. She was going to leave anyway because there was some sort of personality clash going on and we just precipitated it. Angie must have been in her late forties when she joined us, separated from her husband and heavily into bridge and tennis. Just having a woman about the place created a huge impact in our comfortable, well ordered little group, never to be the same again.

The five of us were all engineers; Angie wasn't. Engineers are, by and large, logical, rational people. They don't have emotional needs and they don't have moods or migraines. They don't try and seduce fellow workers when under the influence of an after-work martini. Most engineers are men. They are now, and they assuredly were in the eighties. Most secretaries were women. If they existed today, ditto.

That's all I'm going to say. It was the first of a number of times that a new member of the team moved life on. It's the way of things. It usually seems disruptive at the time, especially if you don't like change, but it needn't be that way.

I've told you we only started the company to get a few free meals out of it. That's not strictly true; I had another reason. I wanted a company car. Most of my peers and contemporaries from school or college had by then got good jobs and invariably they also had company cars too, even the engineers, at least the ones who had sidestepped into management or sales. I was still running my old VW Beetle that I had nursed for ten years. My grandfather bought it for me second-hand after I had agreed to get my hair cut. I was going to get it cut anyway, but it made the old man very happy before he died. It was becoming a bit of a joke. Not my hair; the car. It looked awful where I had touched up rust with grey primer and not finished the job.

Things kept falling off it and it wouldn't go very fast. Tim's Volvo Amazon was even worse. Neither made a particularly good impression on a customer's forecourt. It was time to fulfil my fantasy.

I fancied myself as a bit of a negotiator by then. I felt I was getting the hang of it and prided myself on some impressive discounts on component purchases. Small fry, of course, with what came later.

We didn't set our sights too high. We went for a brace of Bedford Astra vans. I really couldn't believe the deal I came away with. They gave me a special discount for quantity (two) and threw in a two-year servicing scheme (practically unheard of at the time). There was no car tax. We could reclaim the VAT, there were no company car tax issues with vans and you could claim your petrol back through expenses. Why hadn't we done this before?

The day they arrived was, up to that point, one of the proudest of my life. Not proud because I'd got a brand-new car. Van. That's worryingly materialistic, and very possibly a sin. Proud because it was through all my hard work that I was now able to fulfil this goal. And not just work since starting the company. It was the years of research long into the night. The hard graft as an undergraduate. The seven years of secondary school with all the homework and revising for exams and diligent attendance of lessons. That's what it was all about. Only a few lucky people get things handed to them on a plate. Most ordinary folk have to work for them. Just bear that in mind when you question a fat cat's salary, especially if you've been a lazy scumbag all your life. Imagine where you might be if you'd done your homework. Too late now.

The new vans sat there in the car park, gleaming white in the morning sun, with the Beetle and the Amazon lurking shabbily next to them. Tim's van had rear seats fitted for his children. With all four of them in there, it was a bit of a crush. Later on, I drilled some holes in the rear bulkhead of mine and we were able to strap the baby's carrycot in the back.

I can't tell you what a marvellous feeling it was to suddenly have no worries at all about motoring for the first time in my life. It was a big issue for me and was a moment to truly celebrate and savour.

We were doing very nicely, but in the Autumn of 1985 we started work on an entirely new product that was to change our direction and kick start a long period of spectacular growth and recognition. I'll try and describe it simply, so you can get an impression.

One of the large semiconductor manufacturers was about to bring out a specialised microprocessor on a single integrated circuit. It was something quite new and it got the fledgling digital signal processing industry humming.

They needed some sort of vehicle for their customers to develop their own hardware and software around this new device, so that they could embed it into their own products. No such vehicle existed, so we stuck our necks out and said we would make one and sell it as third-party support if the manufacturer would supply us with technical help when we needed it and with early beta release samples of the chip. In this way, we could evaluate it and debug both it and our board and make our development system available at the same time as the launch of the device. It was the perfect synergy. We could see how the arrangement would work well for both parties. All we had to do was make it.

Tim and Caspar could design the circuit. Our software engineer could write a simple operating system. I could work out a layout for the printed circuit board and ultimately, our technician could construct a prototype and then we would all get stuck in debugging it and getting the thing working. What could possibly go wrong?

We decided the actual hardware we would sell would be an IBM-PC plug-in card, and so we needed a PC as a development platform to do this. IBM-PC's were out of our price range. You couldn't get one for less than ten grand. In the end we bought a clone that was the cheapest available on the market at that time. The clock speed was 8 MHz, it cost five thousand pounds and it didn't even have a hard disc (that was an optional extra). We could have got another two Astra vans for that price.

Over the winter Tim and Caspar beavered away on the circuit design and then it was my turn to tape up the board layout. We wanted to introduce this new product at an international trade show the following April. The pressure was on. No one knew if it would even be possible to get the layout on to the PC form factor.

To get it into some chronological perspective for you, this was at a time when Georgia was now six months pregnant with our child and we were in the middle of buying the house in Shepshed.

I was working all hours. Firstly, I had to design the layout on graph paper in pencil, dotted lines for one side of the board, full lines for the other, with x's where the track moved from one side to the other. Then, I had to transfer this schematic layout onto a large, twice real size, translucent sheet using sticky tape of various widths. Blue tape for one side, red tape for the other side. The idea was that during the manufacturing process, red and blue filters would be used to create templates to etch either side of the printed circuit board.

I'm telling you all this, so you can picture me sat at my desk like some Dickensian clerk. Nowadays, of course, the whole process would be automated and done by CAD on multilayer boards. No messing about with pencils or tape or even concentration.

I worked through most of Christmas, into January and just beyond. Although the Technology Centre was a new build, the insulation was woeful, and the storage heaters were useless, especially in the late afternoon and evening just when they were needed, and it was a very cold winter that year. I had a fan heater pointing at me constantly, but it dried out my skin and sometimes took the tape from my shrivelled fingers. I had done much simpler layouts before and had enjoyed the challenge and the creativity, but this one almost had me beat.

When I completed a layout to my satisfaction, I put a serial number on it always ending with the date. I remember the auspiciousness with which I triumphantly but stoically entered the numbers 020286. I've just asked Google what day it was. It was a Sunday. I remember now. I can see me doing it as if it were yesterday, sat in front of that icy cold glass curtain window, looking out at my frost covered Astra van and pondering what the future would bring.

thirteen

Georgia was booked in for an elected caesarean at the Queen's. It was all the rage, but in the event her waters broke two weeks before the planned adventure. I think it was a curry I'd cooked for us. Too many chillies, of unspecified origin. I managed to get her to the hospital without any serious panic and after that the labour was brief but dignified. The nurses were efficient and gave the impression that they knew what they were doing. She disappeared on a trolley and when I was invited into the theatre I was astonished to find about a dozen begowned medical types beavering about. A lot of them were students. I was expecting just an anaesthetist and a midwife and perhaps one or two helpers. I hardly had room to get a look in. A nurse gave me a sticky paper label and told me to attach it to a plastic name tag with a safety pin on the back. It read I AM DAD. I pinned it to my gown. Well, we now know who I am, I thought. Who the fuck is everybody else?

I can't tell you how good it felt wearing that tag. What a moment. I still have that tag. I keep it in the top drawer of my desk. I'm actually looking at it now as I write this. I unhooked the safety pin and carried it around in my wallet for years until the paper started rubbing off. I was on a high that I thought would never end.

I've known many fathers for whom the birth of their first child wasn't a big deal. I've spoken to them about it, and it's fine. I'm just telling you that it wasn't like that for me. Nothing was ever the same again. It was my biggest thing. Ever. Even better than the heartbeat.

They gave me a chair and I sat next to Georgia and held her hand. She was taking it all in her stride. Then there was a brief flurry of activity and I was pushed out the way and then there he was wrapped in a little candlewick blanket and in my arms. I was mesmerised. It was as if my whole life had been leading up to this point and now it had come. That's how it felt.

I wanted to call him Angel. I thought that having an unusual name like that would bestow on him some character that would otherwise be unrealised. Besides, it was very Thomas Hardyesque, and I'd just finished reading Tess of the d'Urbervilles. My parents were horrified and everyone I knew or was related to disagreed with me. They thought it was girlish, but it's not at all. What about Gabriel? They told me he would be made fun of at school. He would be bullied. But I felt that it would sound perfectly natural if you grew up with it, and no one would consider it unusual. I did have to concede, however, that new friends might rate it peculiar or inappropriate and so in the end we settled on it as a middle name. When he was older he could make the choice. So, Zebidee Angel it was, then.

No, just kidding. It was Robert, but I never called him that. It didn't suit him.

I often wondered what that name would have made him.

He was a wonderful child. He could do no wrong. When

his sister came along just sixteen months later, she was a joy, too, but she wasn't Angel.

What a joyous time it was. In little more than a couple of years I had undergone a complete transformation from odd, distant loner with no discernible future path into an upright family man with conventional prospects and a proper haircut.

And against my and my friends' expectations, I embraced it. This was the new me. I loved family life.

I know a lot of people find it hard keeping a sensible work-life balance and I realise that sometimes it's out of your control, anyway. If you ask any successful businessman what they would have done differently, they'll always say they would have spent more time with their kids when they were growing up. I can be smug and say that I got it just right, while it lasted. I've always had the ability to shut out unwanted demands on my time and just detach myself from everything going on around me and focus on the important things. I was a strictly eight to seven man after Angel was born. Arriving at work at eight meant I missed the worst of the traffic and during that first hour I could achieve more than for the whole of the rest of the day. I made a point of taking an hour's break at lunchtime, too. I would go for a walk whatever the weather. If you keep up a brisk pace you can easily cover three miles in an hour in an urban setting. I could walk from the office to the railway station on the other side of town and back at lunchtime. People were amazed, and disbelieving, but only because they'd never tried it themselves.

I would leave at six forty-five in the evening, no matter what was happening. It was my rule. Even if I was on the phone to someone important at the other end of the world, I would bring the call to an end. I was able to make such rules, because I was the boss.

I was back home just before seven. When I was a little boy, my dad stuck two coloured strips of paper over the twelve and the seven of our mantle clock to show us when it was seven o clock and time for bed. I've always since associated the two things, although of course it must only have been for a short time that my parents managed to enforce the rule. Those sticky bits of paper were still on the clock face when I threw it in the skip after dad died. No one had tried, or could be bothered, or perhaps wanted to get them off.

The kids would usually be in the bath when I got home and then I would take over from Georgia and dry them and get them into bed. They slept in the same room and I read them a bedtime story or invented one that I would call the everlasting story because it never ended. Sometimes I would fall asleep before them and then a little hand would reach out from under the bedclothes and snap me out of my slumber, and occasionally Georgia would come and find us all asleep, me bolt upright, book on my lap, but with the sleep of the righteous on my eyes.

That was the only time work impinged on my family life. Apart from the tiredness, I could just switch off, in exactly the same way that I never thought of Georgia or the kids when I was at work or away on business. They were two different worlds and they never really collided, but they were both full on for as long as they endured.

I guess the only fly in the ointment during those early years was that house that Georgia's mother had bought us, and Shepshed, which I didn't much care for. I suppose things were so hectic both at work and at home that we didn't have much time to dwell on such matters, and that's why we ended up living in that damned place for five years. Also, of course, we had no money and we were novice parents with no plan.

I did feel a bit sorry for Georgia sometimes. After all, I had the excitement of the company, and the company of my colleagues. I could escape, too, with the travelling. Georgia was trapped with two babies in an empty space. There wasn't much going on in Shepshed that interested her and for a year or two we only had the van, so she was limited to walking with a double buggy. There wasn't much in walking distance from our house. An unimpressive market once a week on Tuesday mornings outside the co-op, and a few charity shops and that was about it. Shepshed had the dubious claim to fame of being the largest village in the country. I don't know if it was true, but everyone used to say it. Ten thousand souls, evidently. The trouble was that almost all of them lived on the new estates that had promptly encircled and overwhelmed the old village and over-spilled across hundreds of acres of agricultural land, and they all owned cars so would not dream of venturing into the centre when they could go to Loughborough, Leicester, Derby or Nottingham, where they all worked during the day leaving a ghost town in the suburban streets. The only people left stranded in the middle were the old and the poor and they were finding it increasingly difficult to root out any proper shops where they could buy the proper things that they needed. They might have thought they wanted fast food, hair stylists, video rentals and betting shops but what they needed were real things like groceries, bread and toilet paper. There's only so much crap furniture and ornaments that you can stuff in your home; losing horses you can finance; videos you can binge on or ways you can do your hair.

There were some pubs left, but the less said about them, the better.

The highlight of my week – and I'm not joking here or being sarcastic – was walking into town on a Saturday night and getting a takeaway (did you notice how I had become the very sort of person I had previously despised?). It was either a pizza or a Chinese, as the fancy took us. I had a routine, and I guess that's why I looked forward to it so much. Christ, I had only just turned thirty. Old people have routines that keep them pacified. And now I come to think about it, I always ordered the same thing. A twelve inch Mexican or chicken fried rice with curry sauce. Mmmn, delicious.

It would take about twenty minutes (and if it wouldn't, I'd suggest to the lackey behind the counter that it should), which gave me a chance to choose a pub for the scowling and the statutory two pints. We also allowed ourselves a bottle of red wine from the petrol station shop on a Saturday night, which we shared and made last for the rest of the evening. Heady stuff.

The time came when I could take this hedonism no more and we had to get away. Happily, this coincided with my being able to tell a better story to the building society manager, who took on board my accountant's interpretation of my income.

We started looking for a new home for our growing family, but it turned out to be a longer and more tedious task than we'd bargained for, mainly I think because we'd set our goals too high. In the end, the one we chose to go for didn't seem to fit our aspirations very well at all, but we both fell in love with it at first sight. It was in a village on the other side of Loughborough that I didn't know, and didn't particularly like. The countryside was flat, intensively farmed and relatively featureless and uninteresting. It was under the flight path of East Midlands airport skulking only three or four miles away and just for good measure, the main Sheffield to St Pancras railway line was at the bottom of the garden.

Although there's no getting round the fact that it was basically a commuting dormitory, the village of Hallam in the Marle did actually have quite a bit going for it, and our target home, Babel House, was right at the epicentre of the most interesting part.

It was an estate house, and had been neglected. A rural estate, that is; not a housing estate. The word on the street was that there was an urgent need to pay some death duties, so the estate had selected Babel House as an expedient source of funds and were looking for an early cash sale. There was a dearth of cash buyers around at the time, so that looked like the way to go. I've no idea how we managed to do it. I rootled around in the company coffers for a short-term loan, but when we ultimately signed on the line, we found ourselves not only with a new hefty mortgage but also a bridging loan to pay for the urgent updating. How did I sleep at night? Didn't I understand what interest rates of fifteen and a half per cent meant?

Whatever, it all worked out. There was about three months building work to do to get it up to scratch and we found a buyer for Shepshed easily enough and gave Georgia's mum back her money. The sale went through promptly and we moved to Hallam in time for Easter.

Angel was nearly five and Miriam three. It was perfect timing as Angel was able to join the reception class at Hallam School at the start of the summer term. His first school, and one of the most wonderful things about Hallam. The school. It was just great. The teachers were lovely, the children were friendly and well-adjusted and their parents were people like us. It was a lucky escape from the horrors of Shepshed High or

149

the catholic convent that only a few months ago had seemed like the inevitable choices.

Miriam went first to Mother and Toddlers and then quickly to the playgroup and we instantly made friends with other parents from these circles. They welcomed us with great enthusiasm. It was a world that was new to us. It hadn't been that our neighbours in Shepshed had been unfriendly or cliquey, it's just that there hadn't been much of an opportunity to meet up with anyone that we had anything in common with. And most of the time, they weren't there.

It was truly a revelation.

These were idyllic years and they all revolved around the village and its school. It was for me a tantalising glimpse of what it must have been like everywhere at one time.

Hallam isn't really a typical village, actually. It's long and thin, with the new bits tacked on either end, hanging on like strip malls. It follows a parallel path to the River Soar on one side, about a mile away in a wide, flat valley, and the railway line on the other on the edge of a squat, clay escarpment. In the middle are the original parts of the old village. The church, rectory, Manor House, you know, the usual sort of thing. They're all just off the main drag, on the railway side, up the hill a bit and out of the way of the flood plain. Of course, the railway wasn't there when they were built. It must have been quite nice then. The story was that the squire owned all the land on the hill and wanted his very own station for only his use, so everyone could see from the village, and that's why they cut it through where they did. I guess it was a good thing, really; they were going to put it next to the road, otherwise, which would have proven a bit awkward later on.

Babel House was at the top of a quiet lane next to the pretty little church. When the railway had been widened in the late nineteenth century to four tracks they had to excavate a corner of the churchyard, and they took a bit of our garden and built an imposing pink granite wall all the way along the embankment where the cutting is very deep. The disinterred gravestones are leant against the wall, but I don't know what happened to the occupants. There was a footpath that went past our front gate and on to a footbridge across the lines. When we bought Babel House there wasn't actually a gate there, or a fence, and on an old map I found that the original graveyard had actually come right up to our front door. Uncannily, that's a bit like St Rumon's and Church House. Is there a pattern here? I made a point never to plant my roses too deep when I was digging in the front garden, just in case. Georgia was nervous about the open plan graveyard and we put up a picket fence to keep the kids from wandering. They would have found it difficult to get on to the tracks, but that sort of thing is always going to be at the back of your mind, isn't it?

I used to take the kids and sit cross-legged on the footbridge. It was made of an open diamond lattice of wrought iron strips that you could see through. Being a main line, there were trains every few minutes, often in both directions at once. We waved to all the drivers and they all waved back or blew a whistle. Occasionally there would be a steam train come through. You could usually tell when one was due because there'd be blokes with cameras gathering to look. It was a good vantage point for them, evidently. Very photogenic.

The bridge was alarmingly rusty. Some of the strips were no longer connected at either end. One night in the early hours they came and took it away with a big crane, all floodlights and shouting, and they replaced it with one that was sheet steel that you couldn't see through, so there wasn't much point in sitting cross-legged on it anymore and feeling the sun-warmed metal on your bottom. I could put Angel or Miriam on my shoulders, but I had to stand on tip toes because the side was so high that I couldn't see over myself, so I quickly tired of it. Why did they have to make it so high?

The bridge held an attraction for jumpers for some reason. It had this reputation, though no one talked about it. There was one Saturday afternoon when I was idly dreaming in the kitchen when I noticed a man making his way up the footpath. It wasn't unusual; we often got walkers at the weekend. This guy was different. He was deep in thought. Intense. I recognised him, but I didn't know him. He lived in the village. He stopped just past our gate, as if he had walked into an invisible glass screen, and he sort of bounced back as if startled or alarmed. He just stood there, frowning and questioning. He was grey. I watched him for some time. I was going to go out and ask him if he was alright, but he seemed to snap out of it and started walking again.

He didn't jump. That's not the best way, and I could tell that he'd thought it through. You could easily mis-time it and end up being a paraplegic or something for the rest of your life.

The best way is to lie with your neck across one of the rails. I guess it's up to you which way you face. I think if it was me, I'd prefer to see what was coming, but I wouldn't look into the driver's eyes.

They eventually found his head about two hundred yards away, but it took them the rest of the daylight they had left to locate it. You'd think it would be easy to spot, but I guess not.

The incident didn't bother me. I was concerned that Georgia might have a problem with it or that the kids might find out at school, but if it had become an issue I never got to hear about it. The same was true of the graveyard. Some folk might be squeamish about living next to dead bodies, but I think if you can treat anything in a matter of fact sort of way then it reduces its impact and it becomes routine and unremarkable. At least the neighbours are quiet, our friends used to say.

When they were a little older the kids used to love playing in the graveyard. It was overgrown in parts and good for hide and seek. When we first came to Hallam we had a rector who lived in the rectory with his wife. He had lived there for some time. He had raised his four children there, but then they had all flown and the two of them were rattling around together in the cold rambling pile with only a dodgy lodger that no one liked. The rector was a great man and a throwback. He was a throwback; his wife was a throwback and the rectory was a throwback. It was straight out of an Ealing comedy and he was Peter Sellars.

I went over there once for tea. We climbed into his withdrawing room from the overgrown tennis court through a floor length sash window and inside there were lots of old ladies from central casting sat around sipping their teas and testing cakes and talking about nothing.

When he announced that he was retiring and moving into a terraced house in Nottingham, it all disappeared, this magic, unforgettable, irreplaceable world. There was an interregnum with no spiritual leader that lasted almost two years during which the rectory retreated into itself and offered no protection from the world. Doors were jemmied open by teenagers, windows smashed, fires lighted and graffiti scrawled. We all expected it to be torched. We all thought the Church Commissioners expected and wanted it to be torched. It sat in about five acres of grounds and would make a great housing development. In the meantime, it extended the territory in which our kids and their friends played and explored and discovered life. Although they were all under ten, we did encourage them, and I'm so glad we did. It would be more difficult now, I think. I used to dare Angel and his mates to go down into the dark, windowless cellar, and they did, screaming and shouting and goading and living life.

It did eventually get bought up and the inevitable happened. The adjoining field that always had smelly donkeys in it and had forever been the village toboggan run now nursed houses and you can't sledge through larch-lap fences. Once it's gone, it's gone forever. It's true.

I loved living in Babel House in Hallam. I loved the kids. I loved our friends. I loved my life. At that point, I think I still loved Georgia. I'm glad we had that time, all of us.

fourteen

Anyway, I was telling you about our new world-beater, long before we knew Hallam and before the kids came along.

I had made several mistakes in my layout, one of them a fundamental error that was unbelievably obvious to see when you knew about it. It made me feel very foolish. And nervous. Caspar had made errors too, but more subtle ones, and more difficult to find.

We were trailblazing on many fronts. No company in Leicestershire had the equipment to make such a densely packed board, so reluctantly we had to ship everything to an outfit in Cambridge. No one in the country made the little alloy bracket that locked the board in place inside the PC, so we had to handhold a local metal-basher until he made one look good enough.

We had booked our place at the trade show, a prime spot right next to the manufacturer of the chip. We had to be there. It was a close-run thing and meant some midnight oil burning, but we did it, and at the beginning of April the software engineer and I hopped on a plane to Tokyo with the precious board and some floppy discs and a ream of glossy flyers. Even then it could have all gone wrong. We didn't have the time to get a Carnet de Passage and if we had encountered the wrong customs official, we might never have sneaked it into Japan. But it was okay. No one searched the bags.

We stood for the best part of five days in a draughty corridor in the basement of the international hotel where the trade show was being held. It was a bit of a sideshow to the rest of the academic symposium that was the real draw for workers in this specialised field, but during the course of those few days, all the delegates who were attending made opportunity to come and look at the exhibitors and vendors. It was a terrific chance to network and to get our name known. It was another proud moment for me.

Our product was a runaway success and was a breakthrough and game-changer for us. We even took verbal orders while we were there; something that was unheard of, evidently.

The two of us had flown out on seven-day tickets, which was far, far cheaper than a standard economy return. Ridiculous, really. Georgia was now eight months pregnant and was struggling on her own in a strange house, while the software engineer and I flounced around the shady entertainment areas of Tokyo over the weekend on a severely limited budget, twiddling our thumbs, and all to save a couple of grand. I looked forward to more enabling times.

Although we had a success on our hands, I'm still not talking big numbers. There was only a limited, niche market out there for our products. We were only making boards in batches of ten and we would often get held up by component supply problems. Also, these things weren't all that easy to make. There were quality issues with some boards that made both short and open circuits almost impossible to uncover. We had faults that took us days to find. They were real pigs. On top of all that, the chip itself was still riddled with bugs. We and our customers were effectively beta-testing the device for the manufacturer.

But it was fun. An exhilarating time. We sold to countries in all five continents. We had agents and distributors clambering for our patronage. We established representatives in the US, Japan, just about all of Europe, Australia, South Africa, Israel. We sold to corporations with household names, the best universities, government organisations, research establishments of all kinds.

There was always the ogre of US export licenses to add just a little more tension to my life. The US Customs and Border Protection Agency could have closed us down overnight if they had been of the mind, but we kept our noses clean and gave them no cause.

Our success had some knock-on implications. We became very good friends indeed with our US collaborator. They needed us as much as we needed them. We did, however, look further afield and approached other players and made new alliances. A bit risky, perhaps, but by then we maybe thought we could do no wrong. We found ourselves in a unique, privileged position, and we got away with it by not overplaying our hand.

The area where I think we most benefitted was in recruitment. You have to understand what makes a young electronics engineer or computer scientist tick. I'm talking about the good ones now, not those who are content to map out an uneventful career and settle down with the wife and kids until retirement. I'm talking about the high-flyers. One high-flyer is worth ten or more of the also-rans. It's true. What the high-flying engineer wants is to work on the latest and greatest technology that exists. That's one thing that hasn't changed at all in forty years. Just ask Dyson, Tesla or Apple. It will never change. What a rarefied atmosphere such places support. What pure energy. The really successful companies are those that can attract such expertise in the first place and then nurture it and grow it in a closed environment and then keep it. This was us in the late eighties. Jobs in electronics didn't come much sexier than the ones we had on offer.

We all took turns, but it was mainly me who looked after recruitment. We were inundated with enquiries from agencies, of course, but these were pretty much a waste of time. I can't remember anyone we took on from an agency. I did always give the CVs a quick glance just in case anything jumped out at me, but nothing ever did. If you were good, why would you sign up for that?

Most of the individual CVs that ended up on my desk were unsolicited, and that was fine. Unless we wanted someone for a particular job, we rarely advertised positions. Very, very occasionally we would try to poach someone, but in my opinion, there were two major downsides to this approach; you would ultimately have to offer over the odds, and you would very likely piss someone off in the process.

I had one golden rule. If I found any errors of grammar or spelling in a CV, it went straight in the bin, no matter what. I never strayed from this philosophy. Of course, I had the luxury of being able to do this and still have plenty of material to work with. I'm not sure if that would still be the case today.

In the early days I would shortlist anyone that I liked the look of as long as they had a degree or suitable experience. Then I got a bit more picky, and the degree had to be a first or an upper-second, and then it had to be from one of the good universities, and then it had to be a first from a great university, or a higher degree in a relevant field. If you have the choice of the crème de la crème, why settle for anything less?

Interviews were conducted in a very informal manner and often included some little spontaneous executive tests. We used to play with the candidates a bit, which was inexcusable, probably wasn't allowed then, and would be tribunal territory today. Much later, I took an executive board member of Cable and Wireless who we were interviewing for a non-executive directorship to the roughest public bar I knew of in Loughborough and quizzed him on his knowledge of best practice fiscal policies in our target market for an hour over a chilli and rice lunch. His discomfort was intense; I don't think he had ever been in a proper pub in his life or found himself so close to real people. He didn't get the job.

Often, Tim and I would conduct the interview together and we would play the good cop, bad cop routine. Tim would get the candidate relaxed and confident with a series of comfortable enquires about past experience or particular areas of interest and would do some gentle technical probing and then I would descend with some real bastard question that was basically unanswerable or unsolvable. All the candidate had to do was tell me it was a stupid question. One or two did, but most would get well and truly stuck in the mire and had to be pulled out with some benevolent coaxing from Tim. I once, and this went down in the folklore of the company, appointed someone solely on the strength of his ability to play squash, as I was looking for a lunchtime opponent. As it turned out, it was one of my best choices, both workwise and squash-wise.

Once we had appointed someone, we treated them extremely well. We were a very enlightened company. Everyone had a ten percent non-contributory pension for a start, even the seventeen year old with purple hair we took on straight from school to do the typing. It made me feel good inside to think that, although she would have preferred the cash to spend on a Saturday night, when she was old and grey, fifty years hence she would thank me for my insight.

Unfortunately, the pension company was one of those that went bust in the financial crisis. It took my pot with it, and I'm sure it took hers.

I refer to these times as the halcyon days. We were all highly motivated and on the crest of a wave. The company was small enough for everyone to know each other by their first names, but we were growing quickly. From my point of view, this was one of the most challenging aspects of my job. It meant that we were continually adopting new working practices because the way we were doing something last year was no longer appropriate this year. Tim and I were learning on the fly for a decade. Just now and again it meant that some would fall by the wayside because they couldn't adapt or keep up, but this didn't happen very often, and usually it was obvious to everyone if someone had to go.

It was actually not until we had been going for about six years that anyone had left at all; we treated them so well. We had trapped them, really, I suppose. The first to go was a software engineer who got pregnant, and word went round that this was the only way you could ever get away. You could check out any time you wanted, but you had to have a baby to leave. She wasn't all that good anyway and things had moved on, so we didn't invite her back. I don't think you had to then, though I'm not sure.

One of the most difficult things to handle with a rapidly growing company is accommodation. This can easily hold you back, but can also extend your liabilities worryingly if you get it wrong. Most commercial property is held on leases that are either too long or too short, or there are strings attached, or there is no flexibility to expand. When your cash flow is tight, you don't want to stick your neck out and lease too much space that you're not going to need for a couple of years, so you tend to err on the cautious side and put up with the inevitable sardine packing.

This was where the Technology Centre really scored for us because the leases were flexible and so was the accommodation. That was the point of it. The take-up of tenants was rather disappointing for the University, and although at the grand opening we were joined by about half a dozen other fledgling companies, it had proven difficult to attract further tenants with the right credentials. They didn't really want to lower their sights and allow non-tech start-ups and so several units stayed unoccupied. This was good for us, though it's never good to have vacant sites next door to you. It looks bad. It doesn't give the impression of get up and go commerce.

One of the empty slots was indeed adjacent to us and it was dead easy to knock a hole in the concrete block dividing wall and double our usable space. Then we took on another unoccupied unit across the corridor and when our neighbour went bust we took over their two units as well. Before we knew where we were, we had four contiguous units, and the one on the other side of the corridor we used for our production line, such as it was. Although the university was, I'm sure, delighted to fill all the vacancies with an up and growing high-tech company, it went against the ethos of the incubator part of the scheme. You were really supposed to move on to pastures new once you had established yourself. They made it clear to us that they wouldn't encourage further expansion within the Technology Centre, as they were by then getting serious enquiries from other prospective start-ups and needed to be able to offer them space. There had been talk of a full-blown Science Park being built on campus for some while. It was supposed to provide succession to companies such as ours, but it was years away. Lots of talk, but no action. We had to find new premises.

By now we had a fairly healthy balance sheet because Tim and I had never taken anything out and we had been profitable year on year ever since we started. We had about thirty staff on the payroll, almost all of them engineers or technicians. Even our sales and marketing guys were engineers. We needed something prestigious but practical. Somewhere where we could continue to grow, but where we would function efficiently. We looked at all sorts of options. We wanted to stay in the Loughborough area because we wanted to be, and to be seen to be, close to the University, so that rather narrowed the field.

Apart from being a rather dull sort of place, I thought Loughborough had a lot going for it. It was more or less in the middle of the country and had good links by road and air. It was less than an hour and a half to London St Pancras. Despite that, it had sometimes become obvious that we were unable to attract some really good candidates to the area, because it wasn't sexy like Oxford or Cambridge or London or Dublin and it was almost impossible to seduce anyone back from overseas, particularly from the likes of California. However, we felt that this hadn't yet held us back, and in any case, I liked living there and I didn't want to move.

It didn't take long before the quest for more space morphed from an exciting challenge into a bit of a soulless foot-aching exercise. There were plenty of tin-clad industrial units on run-down trading estates, and the wrong sort of business parks. We even got quite interested in a disused chicken shed just a mile out of town on the main road. We spent some time scheming around this and I'm convinced we could have made something of it, but the farmer wouldn't sell us an adjacent shed and we were fearful of opportunists. It was his loss. It's still a disused chicken shed, thirty years on. I've seen it on Google Earth.

Then something came along that seemed just right. I saw it in the residential property section of the Echo one Friday night. I didn't make the connection with our needs at first because we'd only been looking at commercial property, but then I could see it working perfectly. It was a large Georgian rectory in a little hamlet that was just beyond the urban sprawl on one of the quiet back roads by the river. It was a private house, and came with about two acres of garden and parkland. It looked like it had seen better days, but that wouldn't be a problem.

Tim and I went to look at it the next day. The owner was a bit of an unusual character and had clearly been living a hermit's life in a single room of the rambling pile. It certainly had possibilities. We made enquiries at the planning department and they made some encouraging noises about changing use to commercial offices. They couldn't have been more supportive of our plans. We put in a derisory, unconditional cash offer that was accepted without hesitation. It made us think we'd offered too much, naturally.

We were sticking our necks out and it could have all gone horribly wrong for any number of reasons. The sale proceeded without a hitch until a day or so before the proposed exchange of contracts. There was a restrictive covenant evidently, owned by the Church Commissioners, that prevented anything other than residential use.

What I wanted to know was why had it taken our conveyancing solicitor so long to find it? Why hadn't the owner told us about it? The excuse was that the owner had told our solicitor about a restrictive covenant, but his searches had only turned up the one about not calling the old rectory The Old Rectory.

We didn't want to call it The Old Rectory.

The other one was on the next page and no one noticed it.

The Church Commissioners wanted ten thousand pounds for the covenant, almost as much as if it had been the one between God and Moses. We smarted. It was one of those rarest of occasions when I let myself become emotional. I was furious and dismayed and I had to go and sit down for a while.

I was adamant that we weren't paying. We gave the owner an ultimatum. He must pay or we would walk away. Was it a bluff? We didn't think so when we made it, but if he had called it, we would have come to realise that we had invested too much emotional and financial collateral to have backed out. He paid. I've had the Church Commissioners in my sights ever since. Cunts.

Soar Court became my project, and I can see now in retrospect that it really marked the time when I started to drift away from the mainstream of what was going on in the company.

When we started out, I reckon I was a pretty good hardware designer. The first two years of my PhD I had spent designing and building some pretty impressive electronic kit, so that I could use it in my final year to actually do my research. It had microprocessors in it, which was good because Raymond

164

Baxter said they were good every week on Tomorrow's World. It was proper cutting edge, breaking new ground, all that sort of thing. It involved some software writing, too, although this was very much at a fundamentally low level of machine language, not far off just ones and zeroes, but lots of them. I did struggle a bit with the coding and never took to compilers which were then just becoming available.

When we took Caspar on, I realised instantly that he was in a different league to me. Tim had done a good job of bigging my abilities up to encourage Caspar to join us, and I suppose for a while it did look that way. The thing is, I could always get there in the end, but it would take a huge amount of effort to come up with the goods, whereas Caspar could take on board a totally unfamiliar concept, something involving a branch of maths that he had never encountered, for example. He would disappear to the library for an afternoon and when he came back, he would just get stuck in and beaver away on a design that would subsequently prove to work first time.

I've told you how good all our other guys were. They were the crème. It dawned on me that they were all better than me. I felt something of a fraud. How long, I asked myself, was I going to be able to get away with this?

As it happened, quite some time, I think. I was always a good ideas-man. Original thought was my best thing. I would come up with proposals before anyone else, although as you can imagine with so many eggheads about the place, we were never short of new directions. The real trick was to decide which directions to follow, and which to ditch. When to kill your dogs.

As we took on more staff my role became more managerial. Tim had no interest in management, kept a low profile and stuck with the intellectual stuff that he loved and was good at. Whereas initially our business cards had both said Director, mine now read Managing Director and Tim became Chairman. There came a time when I had to hand over all the technical projects I was involved with because I just didn't have the resources to devote to them. I missed the electronics, but I was excited by what would come next.

A side effect of this was that I began to be left behind when it came to everyday competence with a computer. You have to remember that this was a time when individuals were only just getting their own machines on their desks, let alone having them all connected together into any kind of network and communicating with each other. If I wasn't sat at my desk all day doing technical things, I wasn't using my computer for anything, and if I wasn't using my computer I wasn't becoming familiar with all the advances that were coming along thick and fast. And if I ever had a problem with my computer, rather than try and figure out what was wrong and how to put it right, I would simply call over the IT manager who would be only too pleased to fix it for me. So I never learned, and soon I realised that I was becoming a square peg in a round hole in this technological hothouse. I would surely be found out.

Soar Court offered me an escape route and was a massive indulgence for me, and I enjoyed every moment of the project, but I can see now that it was so obviously a procrastination.

After we had completed the sale, I just loved wandering around inside the empty house and around the grounds. Just planning, and thinking, and fantasising about what we could do. I was totally absorbed with the architects and their ideas. When it came to the fitting out I was introduced to a whole new world of interior design which became a passion and a further distraction.

My vision was to juxtapose an ultra-modern high-tech business environment onto a traditional Georgian backdrop. We kept the original features that we were able to save. We repaired the roof lantern on the upstairs landing. It was magnificent. We stripped back pine panelling in what became our reception, and we tore off the woodchip and reinstated dado rails and skirting along their original lines. We restored the shutters so that they worked and remoulded the plaster cornices that were a feature of the ceilings in the principal rooms. We knocked down some shabby utility outbuildings at the back and built a new shower block for when our employees walked or cycled to work or went for a run at lunchtime. We were green before there was green.

I loved choosing carpets and wallpaper and curtains, giving each room its own identity, and was hurt when my style was subsequently likened to a tart's boudoir.

All this took some time to do. I probably went a bit overboard, but it was one of the most satisfying periods of my working life.

Things didn't quite turn out the way we had expected them to, however. The problem was that we had taken on so many new staff while the building work was going on, that when we were ready to move into our prestigious new offices, we had already outgrown the enlarged space. We wouldn't all fit, and it was embarrassing. I had taken my eye off the ball.

There was nothing for it but to split the company into two different locations. We kept on all the units in the Tech Centre and used them for manufacturing, stores, sales, admin, prototyping, and sent off the entire research and development team to Soar Court. Tim had his own office there and I stayed at my desk, where it had always been in the corner of the first unit we had occupied.

It wasn't ideal.

We applied for permission to build a large extension in the grounds of the rectory, but it was turned down flat. I think one or two of the locals didn't approve of us, despite the fact that we went out of our way to keep them all on board with fully catered open days and generous donations to the church spire fund.

Whatever, for the time being we had the luxury of room to spread out in and with plenty of orders in the pipeline, we went into overdrive. By the time we celebrated our tenth anniversary in September 1993 we had sixty staff split between the two sites.

For the big party, we hired a huge marquee and erected it on what had been the croquet lawn. We engaged a famous name in the trad jazz business whom Tim had idolised from a young man. It was a black tie and ballgown do, well over the top and outside the experience of most of us. We invited all our foreign distributors, some local dignitaries and 'friends' who had helped us along the way.

In the crowd that night was a man that I had never met, but who would be instrumental in my eventual downfall.

fifteen

As the company grew, we all changed one way or the other, some for better, one or two for worse. I've told you that my role changed from technical to managerial and that we had to constantly look at new ways of doing things as we expanded. In the early days we used to brag that we didn't need salesmen to shift our products. It was true that the boards sold themselves to engineers and scientists who would buy on technical performance, not on a slick marketing campaign. They could see through hype and didn't like it. But when we had to sell to their bosses, well that was a different matter altogether. We needed a new breed of representative who was good with the smooth talking to do that.

Similarly, it was my proud boast that for the first ten years of our existence, the only time that we employed a lawyer was when we needed a witness for the affidavit to incorporate the company.

Tim and I had walked into the first solicitor's office we came to in town with the documents and had sat for just two minutes while some guy who had been dragged out from the back room by the receptionist glanced at the papers, signed at the dotted line and asked us for £3. He then pocketed the change that Tim and I managed to muster between us and declared that that would buy him lunch today and thank you and goodbye. It was an interesting introduction to the legal profession.

I understand that despite all the rules and regulations that have been forced on everyone since then, it is still how things are done, but probably for more than £3.

Thus far, we had never given any thought to employing anyone you might describe as 'corporate'.

As MD, I felt I had to take the odd initiative, and I entered one or two competitions that the chamber of commerce organised. There were always government backed schemes of one sort or another, mostly involving funding, but practically all of these were a complete waste of time. I could never wrap our company around a box-ticking exercise that was designed for a local high street retailer or small-time back-yard mechanic. On a whim, however, one day I signed up for a series of sessions by a 'company doctor' that was being offered as part of a larger initiative by the County Council. I think I was aiming to be a bit smug when this guy turned up because as far as I was concerned we were not suffering from any ill health that required the attention of a doctor. I hadn't appreciated quite how deeply this man would want to probe into the company's affairs, and I ended up resenting the time that I had to spend collecting data for him.

The scheme consisted of half a dozen weekly sessions, the first and last of which would be exclusively with me as MD, and the others would be with members of our staff who had been selected from my notes as being worthy of further analysis.

Before the first interview I had already decided that this had become a waste of everyone's time, but I couldn't think of a way to extricate myself from it. I could see the looks of derision on the faces of the others, too. Well, I got a bit of a shock. I didn't get an opportunity to be smug, because he laid into me from the word go. It was rather uncomfortable. Despite the fact that we were probably the most successful, most forward looking, most profitable outfit he had seen in his company doctor career, evidently we were doing everything wrong, and he proceeded to show me his whole list, and tell me how he was going to let all my staff know how they should really be doing it.

Probably what I should have done is picked him up by the scruff of his collar and escorted him from the premises in front of everyone. I know some who would have done that. It's not my style, unfortunately, and what I did was this. I thanked him politely for his initial observations and told him I was looking forward to his first session next week which would be with our finance man and our sales manager, and then I bid him farewell and then I wrote a letter to his boss saying I had decided not to go ahead with the remaining study.

It didn't go down very well, of course. Money had already been spent and there would be nothing to show for it, which is, after all the main objective of these exercises. The most important thing is always to tick the box saying that yes, the project was completed successfully in exactly the way that was written down somewhere, and wasn't it all worthwhile. If no one ticks that box, questions will be asked, funding will be denied and someone's spreadsheet will not look very impressive (until the figures are massaged, as they almost certainly will be by the time it reaches a certain level).

They weren't happy, and the upshot was that as a compromise I was persuaded to see a consultant who would try and explain things to me from a different perspective.

This time I was having to pay for it, by the hour.

When he turned up, the first thing he said to me was what a great shindig our tenth anniversary party was, and how he and his wife had so enjoyed it. What I wanted to ask him, of course, was who the hell had invited him and why, and why hadn't I been informed. I thought it was me who had decided on the guest list. I'd certainly put a red line through several names, and we did have a strict fire limit in the marquee that I had to work with. Then it occurred to me that I must have signed it off somehow, and the chances are, I suppose, that I had been introduced to him and his wife during the course of the evening, but I now had no recollection of any of this. It all went through my mind very quickly. I had got quite drunk during the evening, but that was much later after most of the guests had gone home.

There was a photograph that circulated afterwards of me fast asleep on some toilet, still wearing all the regalia and the tuxedo and sporting a ten-gallon cowboy hat that had been brought over by some Texan software writers as a gift.

I decided that I wouldn't ask the question. I didn't want to look stupid and I didn't want to start at a disadvantage with this guy.

He appeared to be about the same age as me. Around two stone overweight with a propensity to sweat at the forehead, it turned out. He'd rocked up in a big black Jaguar saloon and was wearing a pin-striped suit. He didn't look my sort of bloke, really. He was very cock-sure from the outset, and wasn't intimidated by our informal attitude to appearance or working practices. He was at home with the image that he conveyed, but there was no getting round the fact that he looked like a big fat accountant, or a big fat lawyer and so was an anathema to me and the way I did things.

I'd never met anyone quite like Felix before. He had a way of weedling you into his little world. He was very capable of bullying but would try a smarmy, conspiratorial approach first. Later, I saw him do this to other people. I didn't want to like him, but there was no doubt that a sort of nebulous chemistry quickly developed between the two of us.

Felix had never been to University, but he was a really bright cookie. He had an almost magical ability to extract information from a balance sheet in a fluent, intensely coherent manner. Not only could he scan the figures and the totals and the notes, but he could seem to achieve a full understanding of the fiscal health of a company in seconds. He could be subsequently quizzed on any aspect of the numbers without making further reference to the paperwork. Impressive.

He had a bit of a thing about not being a graduate, but this is normal behaviour for such people in my experience. You can pick out the compulsory inferiority complex very quickly. They just can't keep it hidden from their graduate friends, no matter how hard they try. It must be infuriating for them. Some twats make it so much worse by announcing that they've studied at the University of Life or some other embarrassing affectation, but it's obvious that they don't enjoy the breadth of knowledge or deepness of understanding that comes with three or four years of pointless droning into an empty whisky tumbler in the early hours of the morning in some stranger's flat who you thought had something enlightening to say when you met him in the Union bar earlier.

173

Felix wasn't at all interested in how we made our money, only what we did with it. He had no technical ability whatsoever, so it was pointless trying to explain anything about our products or indeed the industry in which we operated. Although the esoteric nature of our chosen niche probably came over as a bit of a novelty when compared with shoes or hosiery, it was fundamentally irrelevant to Felix what we did.

He was incredulous that we had made so much money but had not rewarded ourselves. Well, the reason was that it had never really occurred to Tim and me. We were keen to see the company grow and had been able to achieve this purely from the profits we had made. We'd needed no external investment and had still managed to expand impressively and consistently, year on year. Felix saw the accounts rather differently. He saw a particularly large figure at the bottom of the balance sheet under the heading of retained profits that he felt rightly belonged to Tim and me.

When we started the company, Tim and I had one share each that had cost us a pound. We still had those shares. Sure, we had promised Caspar some equity after we made him Technical Director and we had to do the same for another guy to tempt him to leave his employer and become Sales and Marketing Director, but they were both on 'probation' and the adjustment in ownership would not happen for at least another six months. Why, Felix wanted to know, had we never given ourselves a dividend? All we had done was to apportion a small amount at the end of the previous four financial years to feed our executive pension schemes, and I've already told you what happened to that. It wasn't much anyway, in the scale of things.

And all that time, we'd paid no Corporation Tax because we'd legitimately offset it against R&D. It was a big number on the bottom line.

Felix's philosophy was that Tim and I should pay ourselves all the retained profits – he was adamant this was ours – and any further growth should be funded by borrowing.

I remember asking Tim to join me for a pint after work and I bounced all these thoughts off him. He looked circumspect. Like me, it hadn't entered his head that this was even possible, let alone desirable. You see, even after ten years we were still as naïve as ever.

Tim was a bit of a socialist, even though now he was also a capitalist. His wife was certainly a socialist, going on Marxist. His first response was that it hadn't been just the two of us who had made all this money. Shouldn't we share it out amongst our employees like we did with the Christmas Bonus every year? This annual sweetener was a straight one thousand pounds across the board, to everyone on the payroll. A real bonus to the employee who had joined the workforce in November, but a demotivating source of discontent perhaps to the senior employee who had made a significant contribution from the inception? The number we were talking about now was a lot more than a thousand pounds each. It was a life changing sum for the seventeen year old. She would leave and have a baby.

And this is before you even start thinking about the tax implications of it all, which makes the whole proposition much less attractive. These altruistic intentions start simple, get steadily more complicated and then become ungainly, inefficient and finally unworkable.

Best to keep it simple, then. Two shares, split down the middle, half each.

To say this was a big decision for Tim and me is a bit of a trivialisation. It marked a sea-change in our way of life. Obviously, there were all sorts of ramifications. Should I be talking all this through with Georgia, for example? Well, of course I should, but it would only make the decision making that much harder, so no, maybe I would leave it as a nice surprise. Georgia was seemingly even less interested in money than I was.

Or should I say, than I had been. Because here's the interesting thing. The very thought that had now been implanted into Tim's and my brains changed us in ways that we both would have regarded as impossible only days before.

Have you ever seen those cartoon characters with dollar signs rolling round their eyes like a demented fruit machine? That became us. I could see it in Tim and I'm sure he could see it in me. We felt the lesser for it. It unsettled us.

But we overcame our discomfort and told Felix to do the sums and give us a little presentation that we could mull over. It was the beginning of the end, really.

What he came up with was a proposal for Tim and me to grant ourselves two huge dividends each, one straight away and the other some time after the end of the tax year in April. So huge that it would virtually clear out all the retained profit in one fell swoop.

We needed to talk to the other two directors about it, but they were supportive. I guess they had the long game in mind.

Apart from Tim vaguely saying that he'd always wanted to retire at fifty, we had never discussed any sort of exit strategy at all. For ten years, we had been like pigs in shit. It was a wonderful time. Challenging, exciting and ultimately hugely fulfilling. What turned us on most of all was knowing we could design and make products in our field better than anyone else in the world, and we could conjure these things up from nowhere and be first in the market with them. We were proud of our products. They were the best. We thought they were the best, and it was acknowledged in the industry that they were the best. What a buzz.

Except now suddenly there was another buzz. What would it be like to be rich? Would those dollar signs keep rolling around, or would they eventually get stuck and grind to a sad halt?

You remember my silly riddle about power and control. I never did tell you my answer. What does someone who has power and control want more than anything else in the world? Answer: MORE power and control. Did you get it? It's the same with money for many people. They want more money, even though they've got more than enough. The trick is to be content, and then it doesn't matter how much you have. Few people can pull this off.

Could we, we wondered?

So we went ahead with Felix's plan, but I'm pleased to say that we handled it well. We didn't go out and buy flashy cars. Nothing ostentatious at all. Georgia and I had only recently moved house and were enjoying Hallam immensely and the kids were settled and happy. There was no question of looking for somewhere bigger and better. It was great to be able to pay off the mortgage in a single stroke and there was plenty left in the account even after we had paid the tax burden. It was at this point that I was able to buy Church House. It was my indulgence.

It didn't take us long to realise that Felix had qualities that we could use on a more regular basis, so we offered him a position as non-exec director. Typically, he negotiated himself a very attractive package, but we had convinced ourselves that it was going to be worth it. Felix was going to make us all very rich indeed. He had plans.

Felix's Big Plan was for us to float on the London Stock Exchange. It's what you did. It was the mid-ninety's. Everyone was doing it.

Before we could do this, however, there were quite a few things we had to put in place and this would take some time, maybe years. We had to prepare for the brokers and look good for the investors, and then choose our moment.

We were undergoing so many changes that it was difficult to keep up. Felix circulated in a different world to us. I was finding it harder and harder to reconcile my informal style of management with the more corporate nature of Felix's approach. I increasingly felt that I had become a bit of a spare part.

With the sudden influx of wealth, Tim had been thinking much more seriously about his retirement. I knew he was making plans, then one day he announced that he and his wife were buying a house in Limerick and that from now on he would be working part time and would be taking periods off to attend to his new 'estate' in Ireland. I guess I wasn't all that surprised and had seen that the writing was on the wall, but it was sad. It was indeed, the end of an era.

It also became obvious to me that I was no longer getting quite the satisfaction from the job that I had been, and I thought long and hard about the future. It suddenly occurred to me what the next step should be in the evolution of the company. Felix should take over from me as MD and Tim and I should become the non-execs.

Looking back on it now, I'm incredulous that it was me who thought this was a good idea. That I was wholly responsible for my own destruction. That it was all my fault. That I managed to convince everyone else that this was the way to go. Maybe it was just those dollar signs.

It duly happened and we all adapted to the new regime. The company was still split on the two sites, which was as stupid as it had always been, and we would soon outgrow even this. Then the University announced that the proposed Science Park was finally back on track and would we be interested? Of course we would. We would be the first tenants and could choose a 'landmark' site at the entrance to this prestigious project. It would look good on our prospectus.

It was decided that I would be responsible for the new building. I think this was probably just to find something for me to do. I was beginning to feel I didn't belong in this crazy adventure anymore, but this was just up my street. I jumped at it.

The University was developing the site in conjunction with a large pharmaceutical company who were building a huge behemoth on an adjacent plot and they had all but handed the Science Park over to them to get things moving. They were very London-centric and when I met up with any of them it was obvious that they took us for a load of hayseed-chewing country bumpkins. They were very patronising. They always travelled first class from St Pancras and it all ultimately went on our bill, of course. I got on well with the architect, though he was a bit poncy and spoke a foreign language. He couldn't help himself; it's what he did.

The building that we designed between us was open plan with lots of glass and cast concrete and fancy 'watercooler' areas where ideas would be aired, and a gym and a 'wellbeing' room. As usual, we were ahead of the game. We would have 'comfort cooling' rather than air conditioning because it was better for the environment (it never worked properly so I heard, and the AC had to be retrofitted at great cost and inconvenience).

The reception was all double height and glassy with our name jazzily displayed as part of an arty mural on the wall. Felix had employed a graphics designer to rework my original logo which I was very sad about. I still had my pencil drawing that we had taken all the copies from for the previous twelve years.

I thought the whole build went very smoothly. It came in on time and in budget. I now had to organise the big move, and this is where it all went wrong.

sixteen

In my defence, it wasn't a straightforward move. We were coming from two very different sites and for the first time over a hundred employees would be working in a large, open plan space. It was in complete contrast to the traditional office layout of enclosed rooms and long corridors we had enjoyed at Soar House, and we were uneasy that our designers maybe wouldn't adapt or adjust to this new regime.

There was a false floor for all the cabling and wiring harnesses, and an industrial-chic concrete-vaulted ceiling for lighting and the exposed comfort cooling ducts. On the face of it, it was all completely flexible, and I was starting with a clean slate. We were going to use as much of our existing furniture as we could. We had grown so quickly that it was all new, and of good quality. The challenge would be moulding the ubiquitous screening panels around individual desks to create an efficient working environment in this vast empty shell. We were planning to move over a long weekend, with most of the packing being done on the Friday afternoon, and the objective was for us all to be at our desks, fully up to speed, on Monday morning. I can see now that that was always going to be unrealistic, but the nightmare had actually started unravelling itself some weeks earlier.

I've told you I hadn't really kept up with modern office practice, and was quite illiterate when it came to spreadsheets and CAD programs with new bells and whistles. At a time when most of our internal communications were starting to be done by networked emails, I was still using paper memoranda that I had my PA type out for me. I wrote a 'Founder's Newsletter' every Friday and had it circulated by hand, for God's sake. It makes me cringe just to think about it now. What must everyone have thought? And why didn't I pick it up earlier?

In my office I had cleared my desk and placed on it two A1 sheets of graph paper, then I had Sellotaped them together and hand-drawn the outline of the ground and first floors of the new building. Then I had copied little squares and rectangles in pencil on another piece of graph paper that were the filing cabinets, bookshelves and desks, and then I had cut them all out and arranged them on the plans.

And that was about it.

I was in my own little world. What made me think that this was the best way to relocate a high-tech company on the cusp of the twenty first century. Everyone just let me get on with it. No one queried my methods, or my ability to ultimately do it right.

Perhaps there were some who wanted to see me fail.

As the planned weekend drew nearer, it became obvious to me that I still had an awful lot of work to do. I hadn't even started thinking about where the floor-mounted electric sockets were going to go, or the ventilation grills in the floor panels, all of which needed slots cutting for them. The new phone network was a nightmare, too, and had to be in place and commissioned before the rest of the cabling was down.

What I should have done, in retrospect, was to buy in the expertise and just take on a coordinating, supervisory role, but I was too pig-headed to admit to myself that this job was beyond me. I must have known, surely?

The crisis finally came on the Wednesday before the planned move. I had been working harder than I have ever worked in my life. As the big day approached, I needed to spend more and more time on the project and some nights I wouldn't get home until after midnight. This had never happened before. I couldn't help reflecting that maybe I should have allowed more time for preparation, rather than dwelling so long at Church House over the spring and summer. I had wrapped myself up in the wrong project.

I was still shuffling my little paper desks around when Felix sauntered into my office and sat down at my desk with a very serious expression on his face. He peered at my graph paper. He said he'd been talking to Caspar and some of the others and they had expressed some doubt that the move would work successfully. He wanted to pull the plug and delay the whole thing until he had the confidence that it could be done professionally and efficiently. I have to say that I was affronted. Until that moment, I had never even thought about anyone talking about me behind my back. Now it seemed there was a whole conspiracy of which I had been blissfully ignorant. Suddenly, it all seemed to fall into place.

I suppose most people have been through a similar sort of confidence sapping experience at some time in their lives. The thing I remember most vividly is that my throat and mouth went completely dry and I just couldn't swallow, or even moisten my lips with my tongue. Isn't it funny how you can recall something like that, but not the other things. I don't know what I said to Felix in response to this indignity; it's all become a blur. I know I wanted to sit down, but I couldn't because he was in my chair. I just wanted to escape, to not be there anymore. Then Caspar and the Sales Director and some of the senior engineers walked in and suddenly I was on the defensive and I heard myself telling them that although it might look to them that my techniques were archaic and a bit of a shambles that I had every confidence that things would be fine and we'd all be at our desks on Monday.

I had just blown my only escape route from the impending doom.

No one had really been taking much interest in the move as a whole, other than how it affected themselves individually. They were busy with their own lives. Sure, I had done regular presentations to the board, and a company-wide session where everyone squeezed into an empty unit at the Technology Centre to hear me outline my plans, but generally they had just left me to get on with it and so weren't in a strong position to assess its viability. I managed to convince them that we should go ahead as planned. The consequences of postponing the move would be considerable. Quite apart from cancelling the removal company we had new tenants chomping at the bit to get into our units at the Tech Centre. They wouldn't have taken kindly to being told of delays.

So we went ahead, and I'm sure you can work out what happened. It was, from start to finish, an unmitigated fucking disaster.

First, the boxes didn't turn up on the Friday until about half past four. They were supposed to be delivered early in the morning to both sites, so they could all be labelled and be waiting at the right desks before the workers arrived.

That, at least, wasn't my fault, but I suppose I should have seen it coming. I'd gone for the cheapest quote.

But you can imagine, late Friday afternoon, everyone was prancing around like headless chickens trying to find their boxes, so they could load them up with their stuff in an orderly manner. We eventually called time at about ten o'clock and told everyone to go home. The original idea was that the removal company would come in at seven on the Saturday morning and pick up the boxes which would be neatly ordered and strategically placed, with all PC's and other equipment crated up and ready to go. Only, of course, they weren't. We had to bring our own guys back to finish the packing, and they got in the way of the removal lads who couldn't park where they wanted because there were cars blocking their way. I'm breaking out in a sweat, now, after all these years, just thinking about it. And much worse was to come. Because the labelling hadn't happened properly, things went to the wrong spot or, if unmarked, were just abandoned inside the entrance. None of the desks were reassembled, so no PC's were unpacked. When everyone turned up on Monday morning they were met with a mountain of anonymous boxes and some very angry management.

It took until Wednesday afternoon to get everything in its right place and it was some time late on Thursday when the PC's started talking to each other and the phone system was fully operational. The final straw was that the heating vents had been omitted from the floor of Felix's office. Hence no heating or ventilation. Not good. He called me in, and that was it; I was fired.

Dry mouth again.

A Managing Director can't fire a non-exec just like that. I still owned thirty five percent of the company, and so did

Tim. Between the two of us we could have done anything we liked. Except, that's not the way it works, is it? At least it wasn't for ordinary nice people like me and Tim. Anyway, Tim had buggered off to Ireland so wasn't much moral or practical support for me. I can see now that they wanted rid of me because they looked on me and my values as the dinosaur that was hanging on to their ankles as they struggled to escape from the primordial swamp of old-fashioned ideas. They wanted rid of me because they wanted to move on.

They might have been planning and conniving behind my back, but I knew, or thought I knew, that they wouldn't cheat me. They would do whatever they had to do fairly and legally, but if I kicked up a fuss they would just desert me. I knew I had to go.

It was a humiliation.

I thought of it at the time that it might be like you felt when you lose a baby. The company was my baby. I had given birth to it, nurtured it, watched it grow, protected it from threats and dangers and seen it through to adolescence. I was ultimately to learn, though, that it was nothing at all like losing a baby. Nothing like it.

I never spoke much to Georgia about work, and she wasn't much interested. She had lots going on in her life with the children and her growing circle of village friends. Our marriage was struggling, but I think benefitted from the space this gave us to live our own lives separately, as well as together when we wanted it. Like most wives, especially stay at home ones, she had carved out for herself a comfortable lifestyle of which she was in full control. There was routine stuff like taking the kids to school, regular coffee mornings with other mums, a badminton slot on Wednesday lunchtime, that sort of thing, but also trips into Nottingham for shopping or to catch a theatre matinee performance with friends after a nice lunch. From the early Bohemian identity that had attracted me so much, she had certainly sold out to respectability and had morphed into a stalwart member of the liberal chattering classes when I wasn't looking. I caught her calling herself Georgina once, for God's sake, and George when she was with her cronies.

Me? I hadn't changed, had I?

I was very lucky to have my own study at home. We had built an extension on the back of the house and I had insisted on having somewhere where I could lock the door to keep out inquisitive kids. I now retreated to this vestige of my empire with my £12 desk my sole comfort, only venturing out to make coffee which I got into the habit of drinking voraciously in the manner of someone who chain smokes. I felt I was able to disappear from view so that I would not disrupt Georgia's regime, and not imperil her chosen cosy existence.

Was I moping? Of course I was. In the space of under two short years I had gone from respected Managing Director and co-founder of a hugely successful technology company to a loser whose skills were no longer appropriate nor wanted. I was not yet forty-two years old but was all washed up. What was I going to do with the rest of my life?

It's very difficult to explain what it's like when you lose confidence in yourself. It's one of those things that you have to experience to know. Like dread, or loss, or hate, or love. There's nothing more irritating than when someone tells you you've no idea how they're feeling because you've never experienced it, but the really annoying thing is that it's true. But it's also true, of course, that even if you have experienced it, you still don't know, because your experience of something will not be their experience of the same thing. Can you see how I'm rambling? Can you see how after all this time, I can't quite handle it? Even though after those first timid ructions I've had to endure far, far worse, and managed to come out the other side. Losing your confidence is a very bad thing.

Georgia told me to go down to Devon and sulk there. That sort of crass, throwaway remark didn't help. She might have added to get out from under her feet, but she didn't need to. I didn't feel like going to Devon.

I spent days at my desk waiting for something to happen, but nothing did. When the post came, usually about midday, I would scurry out to the front door and be disappointed at the circulars and bills that would be there on the floor. No, nothing again. What exactly was I expecting?

Every so often, I would get a phone call from Caspar who would fill me in on what was going on at work. Although I was no longer part of the team, I used to think that they were all still my friends. It seemed that Felix was concentrating full time on aligning the company for a flotation. His Initial Public Offering on the London Stock Exchange. It was all the rage. I started getting all sorts of financial guff that I didn't understand fall on the doormat next to the takeaway pizza menus and the gas bill. In the past, I always had someone on hand to explain this sort of gobbledegook to me. I couldn't make much sense of it; I didn't understand the long words.

You would have thought that being a major shareholder would have made me a key player. I should have been, but it was a sure sign of the contempt and disdain that Felix now held me in that he never called me. I spoke with Tim once or twice and he was happy to go along with it all. He was being told a good story and those dollar signs were still spinning round.

If this thing was going to happen at all it was essential that Tim and I were on side. We were being portrayed as the founding academics who were handing their creation on to the Executive Directors to take forward into the white heat of the technological revolution. We'd moved on since Harold Wilson, but that was the gist of it, and fundamentally, it was the truth.

We got invited to a couple of presentations in the City, given by young kids in loud braces and ridiculous spectacles. Tim got his flights paid, First Class. They were courting us. All this was happening so quickly, it was difficult to keep up. I gathered that they were ready to push the button and we were summoned to Felix's office in our bright new building on the Science Park. It was the first time I'd been back since I loaded up my desk and belongings after the fiasco of the move. I have to say I was greatly impressed. It looked the part. I was secretly very satisfied that at least my interior design ideas had come off. Apart from the comfort cooling, of course, which I had been talked into anyway.

Felix had a big table in his big office. Around it sat all the youths I'd met in London, a man wearing a three-piece suit who looked incongruous but important and the other shareholders, who now included Felix who had been exercising his options lately in preparation. We were waiting for a phone call from the rest of the 'team' who were beavering away somewhere in the City. There was a frisson of anticipation and excitement that you could run your finger along as if it were condensation on a mirror, or sweat on a brow. We waited, and then we waited some more.

There were some insulated coffee jugs on a trolley outside the glass wall of the office to keep us all fortified with caffeine and I was refilling my company cup when Caspar joined me.

189

He was looking drawn, rather than excited. He told me he'd been up most of the night talking with erstwhile investors in California. He hoped they were on board. We gazed through the glass like it was a goldfish bowl. We seemed to be looking in on another world in which we didn't quite belong. Caspar counted out the City types around the table. There were eight of them. They were all on at least two hundred pounds an hour, he said, some three hundred. He hoped they were as good as they'd told him they were. We had already spent a million pounds getting to this point, evidently, and there were plenty of bonuses and performance targets written into the deal. If they hadn't already got one, these lads would be looking at stopping off at the Porsche garage on their way home.

We waited but the phone call never came. There was some uneasy shuffling and more coffee. Lots more coffee. Eventually the suited guy got up and asked if he could use a phone in one of the meeting rooms, and he was there for some time before emerging with a dour expression. By then, we all knew it wasn't going to happen that afternoon, and everyone seemed to resign themselves to resuming in the morning. However, the news was that it wasn't going to happen at all. Ever.

'The market wasn't right'.

I would have thought that someone with red braces who was earning two hundred pounds an hour would have spotted that one coming before we had spent a million quid.

No Porsches, then, but they would all have done well out of it all the same. They were the winners, we were losers. We were the ignorant peasants, they were the successful bankers even without the prestigious deal in the bag. Just like their faces told us all along.

How did I feel? That's an interesting one to answer. If you've never had money, you'll probably not understand (yes, it is annoying when someone says that, isn't it?). If the IPO had happened, and all the investors had behaved as we'd hoped, and if the after-market had embraced our story then I would have been a very rich man indeed. I would have started with about twenty million and if the share price went northwards, so would my net worth. There would have been some restrictions on selling, but because Tim and I were no longer 'insiders' we were freer to trade than Felix, for example, who would only have a severely restricted window, even if he decided to sell, which he wouldn't, because it wouldn't look good to the investors and would likely spook the market.

That's a lot of money, isn't it? You could do a lot with that.

It's fairy-story money. Not only could it do things for you, it could do things to you. It could easily fuck up your life if you weren't careful, and other people's, too.

It wasn't for this reason that I wasn't particularly bothered about the failure of the IPO.

It was schadenfreude, like it always is.

The way I was still feeling after my ignominious departure from my company, I was in fact highly gratified that Felix had made a complete pig's ear of what should have been his baby. I caught myself thinking, rather fancifully, that this perhaps might mean that Felix himself would now choose to slink off and that I might be invited back to guide the company through the trauma and into its renaissance.

Fat chance.

In the few months I'd been away, the company had evolved into a completely new beast and was riddled and encumbered with corporate, legal and financial hangers-on that didn't inhabit the same universe as me. I could no more run this new entity than I could now design electronic circuits, or in fact do anything useful.

It turned out, actually, that as a result of the failed IPO, the company found itself in a rather precarious position. The reserves had been sapped. Expectations had been high. Plans had been elaborate and costly.

To put it bluntly, the company was now critically short of cash with no access to capital to invest in this planned growth. How the mighty had fallen

I crept back to my study and got used to no one phoning or writing to me. One day, Caspar called round to see me at the house. It was lunchtime and Georgia was out somewhere. I took him down the road to the pub and we sat there and looked at each other over a pint and a cheese cob. There was some gossip I was mildly interested in. My PA, ex PA, had become engaged to the production manager. Several of the middle management had left, perhaps perceiving a sinking ship. Felix had a New Plan, and its implementation was remarkably far advanced considering I hadn't got wind of it, despite still being a major shareholder. He had approached one of our US competitors and proposed a reverse takeover (as we were bigger than them). They had some cash assets which would be useful to us and were already listed on NASDAQ, the US technology stock exchange. We had a product line which would sit well with theirs and we had a global distributor network that was the envy of our insular US friends. There was a lot of synergy, which was good for the marketeers, because that's a magic word.

It was an interesting proposition. I had had some dealings with NASDAQ in the days when I was still MD. Our North American distributor and licensee, a Canadian company, had listed successfully and I had been on their board at the time. It was a fascinating experience. When we had given them a ten-year exclusive deal to manufacture our products under licence in North America, it was in exchange for twenty per cent of their fledgling company. We chose that point on a graph that they had presented us with during the negotiations, with equity on one axis, and royalty on the other. I remember it. We were in a downtown sports bar and we marked a cross in pencil on a crumpled piece of paper that disappeared into someone's pocket.

The idea was that they would float on the Vancouver Stock Exchange so we would have a market for our investment, and this they finally managed to do after a number of false starts, but they were sailing close to the wind for some years and there was such an overhang on the market that we couldn't sell anything without the price nosediving.

I used to go over for board meetings two or three times a year and it was a bit of an eye opener. I was out of my comfort zone, and it seemed to me that all of my fellow directors were crooks and charlatans. They all flew into Vancouver in their own private jets, often with their attorneys in tow. I think the Vancouver exchange attracted thieves like these, having been based on lumber and gold from its inception. I was relieved when they subsequently listed on NASDAQ. It was an altogether more civilised place to be.

I managed over a period of time to sell all our equity stake in their company without alarming anyone and received more from this highly speculative early strategy of ours than the combined net profit of ten year's spectacularly successful trading. It taught me early on that, sadly, it's much easier to make money from the greed of doctors and dentists and accountants than it is to design and make fantastic products and sell them consistently at a healthy profit, so if you want to make money, that's what I suggest you do.

It was during the lead-up to this new plan of Felix's that I first encountered Ralph Ralph. Now, I don't know about you, but I'm always a bit wary of anyone with a double name like this. It's a bit pretentious, isn't it? Ralph Ralph sounds like a barking dog. He rang me late one afternoon, out of the blue. I used to get a lot of cold calls from lowlife offering to handle my financial affairs. My name had obviously been sold on a number of times, and inevitably ended up on several lists of likely suckers. Normally, I wouldn't even speak. You don't really want to encourage them. Most don't listen anyway, so it would be a waste of time. They have a spiel, like the waiters and the historical re-enactors. They have to get it out, and they can't adapt their dull and unlikely monologue. How do they ever manage to entrap their quarry?

I guess I was feeling a bit mellow. I was half way through a bottle of beer, I recall, and that usually makes me mellow. It was a good time for Ralph Ralph to choose. Right from the start he sounded different from the rest; much more of an individual, not part of a corporate engine. Still, I was obviously very suspicious.

He had a drawling sort of Mid-West accent that I couldn't quite place. He said he had recently retired from a career at an investment bank in Boston and had returned home to New Mexico, so that partially explained it. He knew the CEO of Digital Tsunami, the company that was the target of Felix's bid, and he understood a lot more about the proposed takeover than I did. He somehow knew about me, too, hence his interest. I suppose that I hadn't really given much thought to how I was going to handle my shareholding in this new enlarged company if the deal came off. Georgia and I had quite a cushion, so even if I didn't find paid employment anytime soon, we could coast comfortably for a number of years if we had to and still live in the manner that Georgia had become accustomed to. There was no rush or urgency on my part to liquidate more funds.

He was a likeable guy. He told me his life story, some parts of which I believed. I was still suspicious.

His plan was this. I should open a brokerage account through him as my agent and put all my new shares in it. Whenever I wanted to sell, I just had to call him and he would do it. He would transfer funds across to me into a US dollar account in this country. If I wanted to dabble in trading I could do as much or as little as I wanted. He would be pleased to recommend suitable investments. He was good at picking winners, evidently. Well, he would be. So far, so predictable, and I couldn't really get too excited by this proposal. It all seemed a little unlikely, and more than a little risky. He could sense my apathy. He would have expected it and must have realised that there wasn't much he could do to tweak my interest over the phone.

Come over and see me, he said.

I had been listening without too much enthusiasm, with a detachment that owed more to wondering if there was another bottle of beer in the fridge than if this was a sound investment proposal. A little jaunt to a desert in New Mexico might be just the thing to lift me out of my melancholic mood. Lighten the spirits, perhaps.

Rashly, I told him that if he bought a return ticket and couriered it to me then I would be pleased to visit him for further talks, as long as it was understood that there would be no obligation on my part to sign up to anything at all. I had an empty diary. I wouldn't have normally told anyone this, as it says certain things about you, doesn't it? but it's an indication of how casually I was treating this whole strange series of events that I was happy to let him know that I had nothing better to do with my life.

We decided on a three-night stay, starting that Thursday.

Quick work.

I gave him my passport details and a ticket duly arrived by courier the next day. I was impressed. He must have contacts in the UK, I thought, because it's not easy to buy airline tickets in the country you're flying to for someone who is not you. I noticed it was business class. I wouldn't have expected it to have been coach, but I would have thought he'd been trying too hard if it was first. I think he'd got me weighed up.

I'd okayed it with Georgia. Predictably, she had no problems with me being away for a few days. It was October and there wasn't much doing. The kids were very settled at the village school and didn't take a lot of looking after. I used to look forward to the weekends, which I tried to make distinctly different from weekdays to maintain some sort of structure in my life and I enjoyed spending time with them then, so it was a disappointment to miss this, but just at the moment I had plenty of time to engage with the kids every evening after school. I used to look out for them walking up the lane to the house from school and I'd go and greet them and take their bags.

They were halcyon days for the children, but soon to change.

When I was MD I used to fly maybe five times a year, which was just about right and suited me very well. It was enough for it to remain exciting, as flying was then. I used to feel sorry for the salesmen who spent more time in airport lounges than anywhere else. They all look the same, the lounges and the salesmen; you could be anywhere. That was no one's idea of the glamorous jet setter. I was also lucky in that my trips abroad were usually for reasons of prestige. I was wheeled out to meet other CEO's and dignitaries, wined and dined and generally looked after very well. I flew to Kuala Lumpur for lunch once.

So it was that I caught the flight to El Paso that Thursday morning. It was the first time I'd been in a plane for eighteen months or more. And flying business was good, too; we never did that when I was in charge. We flew economy, me included. It was a part of company culture that I nurtured and was proud of, but it wasn't part of Felix's culture; it was one of the first casualties.

I remembered the anticipation of landing in a strange place and that first blast of an unfamiliar air at the top of the aircraft steps, like a fan heater pointing at your face. Texas was hot, and it felt good. It felt like a new place feels. It felt new. God, it was hot.

Ralph Ralph wasn't waiting for me where he said he would and normally this would have made me anxious, but I think it was a measure of how my confidence had suddenly returned that I preened around the arrivals hall, just like an important person, checking out passers-by and telling myself their stories. I had no idea what Ralph Ralph looked like. I had told him I had a long full black beard, so I hoped he would be able to spot me easily. I had rightly judged that there were no other beards of this type on the concourse. All the same, it would have been confusing if ZZ Top had been flying in.

Then a small man in a large Stetson approached me and shook my hand. He was about sixty and gnarled in a sun-drenched sort of way. He didn't look like a stockbroker, he looked like an oddball. He said he'd booked a table. I guess he was assuming that I wouldn't be jet-lagged and would be up for dinner. It turned out that this table was in an exclusive and very isolated mountaintop restaurant about a hundred miles into the desert, across the border into New Mexico, and his lady friend was waiting there for us.

It was quite an introduction to a rather different sort of life. Very different to my little Victorian village house in the East Midlands.

We didn't talk business at any time that night. We must have covered many topics over the hours, but I can't remember any now. I started to flag at about midnight and we said goodbye to our hostess and left. It was another hundred miles in a different direction to get to Ralph Ralph's ranch, and I fell asleep in the car. When we got there, the moon was out and there wasn't a breath of air. It was eerie. I could hear a coyote or something howling in the distant hills. It was some place he had there. He told me his grandfather had built the ranch house and tamed most of the land I could see in the moonlight. Ralph Ralph had been born and brought up in this homestead and had started his working life as a cowboy. He was quite a guy. Improbable, perhaps, but nevertheless quite real.

He showed me to a room. I showered and went straight to bed. Breakfast was to be when I got up. There was no hurry.

The morning sun woke me when it found the gap in the curtains and cast a burning strike across my face. The blue of the sky was intense, and there were already heat shimmers bouncing from the rocks outside. It was going to be a hot day.

Breakfast was coffee and toast in the sitting room. It had two grand pianos facing each other and the stone walls were filled with books and engravings and paintings, and there were Turkey carpets on the floor. Georgia would have loved it.

Ralph Ralph showed me his office after we had eaten. For a forlorn outpost in the middle of the desert, it was impressive. I guess the array of microwave and satellite dishes on the roof provided the communications as there were no overhead lines. We were off-grid. He had a number of monitors on his desk and two phones of different colours. This is at a time when I still had a dial-up connection at home with laughable bandwidth. The remoteness of the ranch obviously didn't handicap its connectivity with the rest of the world.

Ralph Ralph didn't really need to impress me any further, but when he started scrolling through the portfolios on the screens with a commentary on their performance, he had me a bit dazzled. It could have all been put on for me, of course, and I wouldn't have been able to tell the difference, but by this time I had been seduced. He didn't need to do any more.

That afternoon we drove to Carlsbad and had a beer in a tacky bar and some nachos in a Tex-Mex diner and then we got some more beers from a Walmart outside of town and took them back to the ranch with us and drank them.

The next day, Saturday, Ralph Ralph suggested that I take his car and go and explore the local attractions. I drove to the White Sands and the Carlsbad Caverns in a battered sedan which was alright, but wasn't much fun on my own. I would have liked to have gone to Roswell as well, but it was too far away and they wouldn't have let me anywhere near the good bit.

Sunday was my last day, and I was due to fly out of El Paso at 18:50. I'd told Ralph Ralph that I'd never been to Mexico and would like to tick that one off my bucket list. We'd planned to park up near the Santa Fe Street Bridge and walk over the Rio Grande, pick up a cab and then have a bite to eat and a few beers in Juarez. Ralph Ralph knew a little piazza where there was live music and families on a Sunday. I could tell he was doing me a favour in agreeing to this. Ciudad Juarez was a bad place in 1996, though not as bad as it is in 2016. He was nervous. I saw a glimpse of another side to him. We all have our other sides, it's just that some people hold their masks more firmly in place than others.

I'd put my bag in the trunk of the car and we were sat drinking coffee. It must have been about ten o clock and the phone went.

I could tell straight away from Ralph Ralph's face that something was up. Whoever he was speaking to wasn't giving him much time to get a word in. He was looking at me and he was saying, yes, he's just here, shall I get him for you?

It was one of those occasions when time slows or stops. It was only a second or two before I put the receiver to my ear but in those short moments a whole shedload of things went through my mind. I didn't know anyone in the US who would call me here. No one knew I was here anyway, except Georgia who was in England where it would be Sunday evening. Why would she call me? Maybe she was missing me. The kids had probably gone to bed and she would be feeling lonely. It would have been a first, I think.

It was Georgia. She was hysterical and I couldn't understand what she was saying. I'd never heard anyone in such anguish, such pain, such despair. My Angel was dead. My dear, dear firstborn miracle of a son was dead. I would never see him again.

Helpless. I felt helpless. I was four thousand miles away in the middle of some godforsaken fucking desert and I couldn't help my wife when she needed me more than you could ever need anyone.

What could I do? She wanted me with her, but I couldn't get back any earlier than my scheduled flight. There were no other options that would bring me back sooner.

I had to spend those desolate hours in that ranch house sitting room going over and over in my mind why this had happened to me. What had I done to deserve it?

seventeen

I didn't cope very well with Angel's death. I felt he was my whole reason for existing.

When I finally got back from El Paso things were as dreadful as I had feared. Georgia was inconsolable. She wouldn't stop crying.

She had found Angel lying on the settee in the conservatory mid-morning on Sunday. He and Miriam had been playing outside and they'd been running around shouting and laughing like they always loved to do together. She thought he was just having a nap, but it was a bit unusual for him; he's normally at his liveliest at that time of day. She said she thought he was still alive until the very moment she brushed her hand against his cheek to wake him and then somehow she just knew that he had gone. She panicked and tried to shake him awake, but it was no good. He never breathed again, he only got colder and colder. When the paramedics arrived, they tried desperately to revive him but by then Georgia knew there was no hope. They whisked the two of them off to Nottingham, but it was self-evident to all that there was no expertise there that could raise the dead. By the time Georgia called me she was back home and with a neighbour who was trying to calm her down. I was only glad I left her Ralph Ralph's phone number. I almost didn't.

Angel's body had been taken to the morgue from the Queen's and they wanted to do a post-mortem examination on him. They were impatient, but they had been prepared to wait until I was there, back home with my wife. They wanted us to go and formally identify him before they started cutting him up. What was that all about? What other fresh hell could they think of to put us through?

Plenty, actually.

I'm afraid I couldn't do it. I didn't want to see him dead; I wanted to remember him as he was. I wanted to keep that, at least.

Georgia did it and I waited in the car. I felt wretched. I knew I was no help to her. I guess I'd never been any help. What was the use of me?

You could be thinking that this common anguish might bring us closer together again. It seems to when you watch newly bereaved couples on the TV news. They say it does, and it looks to, at least at the beginning, but it didn't with us. There wasn't enough left, I think.

I began to realise many things after Angel's death. Things that just hadn't occurred to me before.

They sent a Liaison Officer around, a black girl with lacquered hair and a strong Nottingham accent. She was alright. She was doing her best. She tried to explain to us what was going to happen, and I suppose it was some comfort to have her there to lean on.

Miriam was staying with some friends of ours in the village. I'd only seen her once since I got back. I didn't know what to say to her.

And then the police turned up asking their questions and they brought social workers and other people with them who I'm sure were all trained to handle just the sort of sad spectacle that we had become.

It seemed to go on for ever and we only got told anything when we kicked up a fuss and even then it was never the full story. And all the time they were mucking about with Angel's body, rummaging around inside and pulling his organs apart and doing their tests and testing their theories. They didn't have a clue. Not an inkling into the cause of death.

Inevitably, tongues wagged and for a while Georgia was under the spotlight. The police kept coming back and asking more questions. We invented a routine. We would sit on the settee where Angel died and hold each other's hands in an uncomfortable charade. They wanted to know how hard she had shaken him. Could she account for some bruises on his little arms? And did she realise he could be susceptible to epileptic fits? What?

They'd been talking to his teachers and his friends at school, and their parents. Our friends. And, of course, his sister.

There was even talk of taking Miriam away while the investigations continued, and that would probably have tipped the scales into madness and desperation that much earlier.

And then the local press somehow got wind of it and we had to deal with moronic reporters as well as everyone else. What a cruel circus it became.

Then they released the body. It came as a surprise as there was no forewarning this was likely. Did we want to see him? I didn't want to see him, no. I understand they can put back all the pieces so it doesn't show, but I still didn't want to see him. I've already told you why. Georgia didn't want to this time, either.

The funeral was awful. I knew that I wouldn't be able to cope. To be honest, I can't actually remember much about it. I refused to be doped up and had to be helped just to stay upright by my sister's husband. I was no use to Georgia whatsoever, I'm ashamed to say. I've never been good at funerals and start sobbing as soon as I hear Psalm 23. It's unseemly, I think, to be seen to be crying more than the principal mourners, but I can't help it. You can see people thinking, that's interesting, they must have been closer than we thought. There must be some dirty little secret that we don't know about. When it's your child-son's funeral, however, it's alright and you can wail and grind your teeth as much as you want. You're expected to. I was well past caring what anyone thought, anyway. I would never really care, ever again.

It drew a big crowd at the tiny church. They had to set up a PA system outside in the churchyard because only a fraction of the onlookers could get in. He was a popular child with his friends and their parents and his teachers and cub leader, but where had all the other hangers-on suddenly come from? Ghouls. I guess there always are when something's been in the newspapers. If I had had my way I would have restricted it to close family and friends, but it had taken on a life of its own and in the end, it seemed I no longer had any control over my son's death.

The churchyard was a bit unusual for the Midlands in that it still had room for burials. An adjacent slice of land had been donated by the developer who was still erecting his executive estate on what was left of the rectory garden. The fresh graves were being crammed in side by side in two rows, behind a new brick wall which hid them from their future neighbours. Additionally, it had been the practice of the churchwardens to allow the graves of younger members of the congregation who had met untimely deaths to be dug in the spaces between the older, sparser gravestones on our side of the churchyard. There were a surprising number of them, and I was intrigued that no roving reporter had chosen to make some sort of tenuous connection. I couldn't think of one, though in spare moments I had tried.

So it was that when asked for her preference of site, the sardines or the dead children, Georgia had plumped for a pretty little patch of meadowy ground that you could actually see from our living room window. It must have seemed like a good idea at the time, but it was ultimately one of the reasons that I had to get away. I was going to take some time to recover from this but to have a reminder in my face every time I looked out the window wouldn't have allowed me to defeat this thing ever.

So that was where we buried my little boy. What a sad, dejected company we must have all looked on that miserable rainy afternoon.

I was dreading the inquest. I thought we'd be waiting months, but they managed to fast-track it somehow. It was only two or three weeks after the funeral and none of us had yet recovered from that. What would the inquest unearth for the whole world to crawl over?

Inevitably, and you must have realised this from what I've already said, I couldn't get any of it out of my mind, day or night. I wasn't sleeping. I was thinking. It wasn't good for me. I kept going back to the questioning. It seemed to me that it had become relentless and utterly pointless and soul-destroying. At one point, I thought Georgia was going to be arrested. But there was no motive; we all knew that. Georgia loved Angel.

I don't know if you know anything about inquests. Anyone can go and watch. I knew the press would be there; it's their lair. Because I hadn't been around at the time, I wasn't even called as a witness. I wasn't even a Properly Interested Person. That was wrong, surely? I didn't actually, legally, have to attend. I could have just left them all to it, and I have to say, it was tempting. I know what you'll think of me when I say this, but I no longer cared. I was done with it.

It went on for a long two days and at the end, they had nothing. No proper evidence. No idea, really. They wheeled in plenty of experts who talked of Sudden Infant Death Syndrome; cardiovascular abnormalities; respiratory infections; seizures; genetic disorders. They had nothing. Not a clue.

The coroner recorded an open verdict, and that was that. The press didn't like it much, either. There wasn't anything in it for them.

What a debacle.

Georgia knew that I was unhappy about the site of the grave and it was this that caused the final big row between us, the one that ended it all.

It was just before Christmas. I'd been told the headstone was ready for erection. I'd been bellyaching about it; they usually take about six months, for some reason. Everything about it had been a struggle from the start. There are certain things that you can and can't carve into your headstone. All churches have different rules, and churchwardens enforce them according to their taste and power. I wasn't concerned with carvings of teddy bears or cherubs or angels; that didn't bother me, but I did want Angel as the name.

In the end, though, what we came up with wasn't even a compromise. I'd had enough of the whole thing. I just told

Georgia to do whatever she wanted. I washed my hands of it and when the monumental mason rang to discuss some finer point of the design, I wearily told him I was no longer interested. I told him to speak to Georgia about it.

I still don't know what's on the stone because I never actually got to see it.

On the day of the headstone's delivery, despite having distanced myself from the whole thing, for some reason I thought I would prepare for the footings by clearing away the grass at the head of the grave, so I went out early with a spade and started taking the turf off. I've seen too many leaning headstones to have much confidence in the constructional abilities of undertakers. Now in hindsight, I can see that this wasn't the cleverest of actions, but I just didn't think of it at the time. I still wasn't up to thinking clearly about much at all and it didn't occur to me.

The next thing I know is that Georgia is clawing at my shoulder and screaming the most horrible accusations at me. She is beside herself. Uncontrollable. Then she starts kicking me and is trying to take the shovel from my hands. It all happened so suddenly that I wasn't behaving rationally, and I'm afraid that in the melee the spade grazed Georgia's temples and made a bit of a mess of her forehead. There was blood on her dressing gown and mud on her nightie. It must have looked a shocking spectacle.

I realise now that she thought I was digging the coffin up. It is an indication of the depths that our lives had sunk to that such a thing could have entered her head. There was really no going back after that.

I left her standing there by the graveside, spade in hand, blood smeared across her front. She was just staring into space now that the intensity of the confrontation had subsided. She looked like Sissy Spacek in the Carrie prom scene, only bloodier.

She was still there five minutes later when I started the car, reversed out of the drive and pulled away with as melodramatic a manoeuvre as I could contrive, with a shower of gravel and a squeal of tyres making a statement to any neighbours that were curtain twitching. I've never set my eyes on her since that day. I never said goodbye to Miriam. She was still asleep in her bed when I went to get my keys. That was inexcusable, and I am ashamed. She deserved better, because none of this was her fault.

I don't remember anything of the journey to Devon. Normally it would take me about three hours if the roads were clear, but time wasn't really behaving itself on that morning, and I would guess my driving was a bit untidy, too. I do remember arriving at Church House. We used to keep a key under a painted pebble on the doorstep. I let myself in to a cold and empty house. Now I could begin my breakdown properly.

eighteen

I had managed to squeeze my Jaguar S type into the barn and shut the doors behind it. It always looked a bit pretentious in Crow's Nymet, where most of the local folk drive Land Rover Defenders or Japanese pickups, and I wanted to conceal it and me away out of sight. I closed the curtains in the downstairs rooms.

We hadn't made any actual friends in the village. Everyone was always very approachable, and it was easy to strike up a conversation with a total stranger on the street or in the pub, but there was nobody who I would call a friend, and I was grateful for that. I have no doubt that they pooled all the knowledge that they had gleaned about us from any indiscretions I may have let slip during long nights standing at the bar of the Druid's, and from throwaway remarks that the kids might have made in the children's playground, but generally I think our private lives were well hidden from view.

But it was nearly Christmas. People don't like the idea of anyone being on their own at Christmas, and by then they must have known that I was on my own. The busybodies would have seen the light on in the evening, even though I was only using a dim table lamp in the kitchen. They came knocking, but I ignored them. They knew I was inside, but I wouldn't open the door.

I suppose during those first few days in Church House, I didn't eat anything at all. I didn't stir from my dining chair beside the cold Aga. I couldn't muster the energy or enthusiasm to light it and there was no other way of cooking. I must have drunk some water, but I don't recall. I didn't bother with sleeping, although I must have dozed off now and again on the chair.

I think of all the pain I've endured in my life, that was the worst of times, those few days. I was at rock bottom. I don't know how close I came to taking my own life, but if it was ever going to happen, this would have been the time. I probably didn't have the energy to do even that. It does take a little planning if you want to do it right, and I wouldn't have wanted to mess it up.

I've been thinking about how I can describe my breakdown to you. It's really difficult.

There aren't the words.

It was obviously some time ago now, and I'm through it, though forever changed as a result, but it all still remains for me a vivid, hellish experience that I can disarmingly easily bring to mind, and you can't.

In my life, I've known others who have been through similar sorts of episodes, but now I come to think about it, I don't believe I've ever spoken of it with them, either during or after the event. Never been there, at all. Isn't that strange?

I always prided myself on being a good listener, and I've heard many sad and horrific accounts of awful things, but I honestly can't remember speaking to anyone ever about what

211

it's really like; what it feels like; what it is to have your own personal breakdown. Is it taboo? I wouldn't have thought so. I think I have to conclude that it's such an individual experience that you try and keep it to yourself. You're on your own. That's what makes the whole thing so terrifying.

If it hadn't been for a visit from a little guardian angel, I might have succumbed.

I was on my feet, for some reason, holding on to the Aga rail to keep steady when I saw someone at the back door. It was a middle-aged woman I vaguely knew by sight, and she looked me straight in the eye. We stared at each other for what must have been only a second or two, but seemed much, much longer. I had nowhere to hide. I unlatched the door and opened it a few inches and the woman stood there. She had something in her hands. She told me it was Christmas day. There can have been very few people in the whole of England who didn't realise it was Christmas day, but she had guessed rightly as soon as she saw me that I was one of those few. It didn't mean much to me, even when I knew. She put the box she was carrying on the Aga and noted that it was cold. She stood square in front of me, as if trapping me and blocking my way, but I wasn't going anywhere. I must have looked a mess, and almost certainly smelled offensive. She pointed to the package and said she'd brought it because she cared, and I was to eat it now before it got cold and if I wanted anything else I was to knock on her door, and she pointed to one of the terraced cottages on the other side of the lychgate. She said her name was Jean. With that, she turned around and left the way she'd come.

It's funny how those days before Christmas are just a blur, but I can remember this woman's sudden appearance so vividly. I can bring to mind the pale pink cardigan she was wearing, how her hair was tied with clips into a kind of wave, the way my mum used to do mine when I came out the bath, and I can remember how she smelt, of log smoke and cooking. She smelt of life. I just stood there after she'd gone trying to make sense of this unsolicited intrusion and wondering what would make someone be so kind to a stranger.

I could tell you that tears ran down my cheeks in gratitude and that it snapped me out of it, and I was saved, but that didn't happen. I was in too dark a place to be lifted solely by this gesture. It would take a long time for me to drag myself from the clutches of my demons, but I was truly, genuinely grateful to this woman for assuaging the pain.

In the box were several slices of red turkey thigh, some roast potatoes, Brussels and parsnips wrapped up in silver foil; a big slice of puddingy Christmas cake tucked in greaseproof paper and a small can of Mackeson Milk Stout. I sat back in my chair with the box on my lap and took a tentative bite at the turkey. It was delicious. I realised I was ravenous, but I ate purposefully and solemnly with my fingers until it had all gone. The Mackeson went to my head and I felt I was no longer sat in the chair but levitating an inch above it, and the cake weighed heavily but satisfyingly in my stomach. For the first time in days I sat and wondered about the greater world, instead of just about me. I pulled a blanket around my lap and fell asleep and dreamed fitfully.

When I awoke I was stiff and cold. It was dark and I switched my little table lamp on. I found a torch and went outside to check the oil level in the tank, then I turned on the tap, and lit the Aga. I switched on the immersion heater and took a look in the larder. There were quite a few cans of various tempting treats. Baked beans, marrowfat peas, spam, that sort of thing. Some packets of rice and pasta in a square metal biscuit tin to keep the mice out, and some rancid butter in the turned-off fridge. Plenty of tomato sauce in two large unopened bottles. Angel liked tomato sauce.

When the water was warm enough, I ran the bath and filled a hot water bottle which I put into one of the single beds in the 'guest' bedroom, which we kept made up. Sleep came again very easily.

Now I'm not telling you that I made a miraculous overnight recovery as a result of Jean's timely intervention. No, far from it, but I felt and hoped that the worst had perhaps passed.

After her visit, I didn't see a soul for a week or more. I kept the curtains pulled and worked my way through the spam and baked beans. I still didn't feel like doing anything. I couldn't read. In normal times, if I had just a minute or two to spare I would grab a magazine or newspaper to keep myself occupied. I didn't like to be idle. But now it seemed the most natural thing was to simply sit in my chair all day and sometimes all night, just staring into space.

I guessed Jean had reported back on her contact with me and advised that it was best to leave alone until I was ready. I expected the doorbell to ring in the lead up to New Year, but there was nothing. I wouldn't have answered it, but in a curious, perverse sort of way it would have been quite nice. I half expected drunken revellers to try to coax me out on New Year's Eve, but first footing isn't a big thing in these parts. There was some shouting and laughing when they spilled out of the Druid's at twelve o clock to sing Auld Lang Syne, but it was bitter out and they all went back inside after the obligatory first verse to their karaoke and their fancy dress party. There was, indeed, in my mind, plenty of reasons to be wistful for old time's sake.

214

It was several days later and I had run out of the good stuff and was down to just stale tagliatelle with rock-hard parmesan and the tomato ketchup, when I heard a knock at the front door. I still didn't want to see anyone, but I knew I would have to do something soon if I was going to be able to continue to eat. I just couldn't face going out. As I sat there wondering who it might be, I was surprised and alarmed to hear a key turning in the lock. My mind raced. For a fearful moment I thought it might be Georgia come to entice me back home and my whole body spasmed, but then I heard a man's voice call my name. I knew it, but couldn't place it. My brain was in another place. The familiar tongue was there in the bowels of my memory but wouldn't emerge for me. Then a tall, heavily built, rugby-player-in-a-past-life hulk of a man pushed the kitchen door open and I knew instantly this visitor was a dear friend from my old life. I had known Gerald for the five years we had lived in Hallam. His girls were the same age as our two and they had started the village school together and had been inseparable ever since (apart from in death, of course). We did everything together; holidays, parties, days out, school trips. We had both done a four-year stint as school governors. He was my closest friend. When Angel died they had dropped everything and were a great support. They had Miriam to stay at their place when things got particularly nasty, and steadfastly put up with my loathsomeness and obnoxious behaviour. All the same I didn't need to see him just now.

He looked grave. He pulled up one of the wooden dining chairs and placed it in front of mine and sat there with his legs apart and his arms crossed facing me and he told me, bluntly but no doubt accurately, that I looked fucking awful. He wasn't one to mince words.

215

He waited patiently for a response but I'm afraid none was forthcoming. I regret that I started crying. I felt ashamed and immensely uncomfortable and feared I was about to undergo an interrogation, but to his credit he was generous and didn't give me the third degree. He took his time. Told me what had been happening in Hallam over the holiday, which didn't sound like very much to me. Georgia and Miriam had spent Christmas Day with them, and although it was subdued and tearful, they all somehow got through it.

I needn't have feared that Georgia had come to take me back. It was the last thing she would do, evidently. There was no possibility of a reconciliation and she wanted no contact with me and neither did Miriam. That didn't come as much of a surprise, and was what I would have chosen. It was very sad about Miriam, but I just couldn't have coped with sharing her. I wouldn't have survived Georgia's vitriol and anger. I couldn't have done it. It could only be a clean break.

When Gerald had suggested that he might call on me in Devon, Georgia had handed him the key to Church House and told him to empty the contents of my wardrobe into the back of his car along with some other stuff that she had already dumped unceremoniously in the garage. As soon as Gerald said it, I knew that included there would be my vinyl collection and a spelter Art Deco figurine of a running hare that I'd given her one anniversary that was, she proclaimed at the time, a bitter disappointment, as she was expecting an eternity ring.

All these things I could now help Gerald unload from the back of his estate which was parked outside the door, and we piled it up in the service room until I could sort it out later.

He stayed for about two hours. I couldn't talk about any of it to him and once he'd realised this, he didn't push it any further. He was a wonderful friend. He said he missed me. He cared very much for my wellbeing, but just now there wasn't much he could do. He got it out of me that I had no food in the house and wasn't yet ready to circulate in the wider world. There is a little community shop in Crow's Nymet that opens for a couple of hours a day, most days a week, and Gerald almost cleared the place out. He brought back bread, cheese, eggs, butter, bacon, a large brown bag of potatoes and some leeks and carrots and a selection of meat pies and pasties, and a newspaper.

We agreed that he would return the next week with my study in a hired van. I told him to take the files in the bottom drawer of the filing cabinet that contained all the utility bills and bank statements and such-like and leave them behind in a pile on the floor. As far as I was concerned, it was now Georgia's job to sort that lot out.

I had decided that I would sleep in the green room. I've already described it to you. It's a small room and once we'd put a double bed in, there wasn't much space for other furniture, just a little chest of drawers and a tiny wardrobe that looked as if it had been knocked together from cupboard doors and the plank chest with the swords at the bottom of the bed. I selected some favourite shirts and jumpers, my spare jeans and corduroys and enough underwear to last me a couple of weeks between washes and filled the drawers, and hung some jackets and the one pair of decent trousers I owned in the wardrobe-cupboard. The rest I took and draped over a bed in the spare room. Would you believe, after almost twenty years they're mostly still there. Unfortunately, what's left has now become a labyrinthine mouse nest and I should have taken them out and burnt them ages ago. I hope it's just mice.

I put the hare on the dresser by the back door and I look at it every day. I like it. The albums went in the bin. I had nothing to play them on.

When Gerald turned up on the next Tuesday morning, at least I was expecting him and had smartened myself up a bit.

I had resolved to reassemble my study in the service room as I've described, and I had planned out roughly where things would go. When we unloaded the van, everything slotted into place easily. If only my last move had gone so smoothly.

Georgia kept all our photographs and the mementoes that we had salvaged from the kids' childhoods. We had a collection of paintings, birthday cards, homemade mother's and father's day cards, papier mache models and all sorts of school projects that we stored in a wooden box under the stairs. Why would I have expected her to give me any of this? I hadn't and she didn't. All I had was a dog-eared photo of Angel and Miriam sitting naked on the steps outside the back door of Babel House before we built the extension. It must have been just after we moved in and they would have been three and five years old. It was another of those things that I had carried around in my wallet for a number of years. It was a lovely photograph. They were both looking intently at something in Angel's little hands. It looked like a dandelion head which they were about to blow to tell the time. It was a picture of pure innocence and joy, a snapshot of better times. I decided to stop carrying it one day when I showed it to a colleague and she pointed out that it was now child pornography. It wasn't before, but it was now, evidently. That's funny isn't it? The way we've all changed. Who would have thought that such an image of purity could become maligned and offensive and wrong. Who's really wrong, I wonder, and who's the pervert?

I kept it in the top drawer of my desk and now I've put it in a little frame and it's sitting on the dresser in the kitchen. I don't dwell on it, or mope, or mourn, but I do sometimes catch myself glancing wistfully at it. I should take it down and put it away, so I don't see it every day. Despite everything, I'm not one for melancholy reflection.

Gerald didn't hang around after we'd unpacked. He could see there wasn't much point. I still wasn't ready for talking. He had brought me some more provisions, but I could understand that he didn't want to be seen to be encouraging me to sneak away from the world. Nevertheless, I now felt that I was more or less equipped for the years of insularity and myopia that would follow.

And so what commenced was what I unimaginatively refer to as the wilderness years, right up until the banana incident when they evolved into the hostile years. Where did they go, those strange times? It seems, now, that they passed in an instant, although of course that's exactly the opposite of what it felt like at the time. That's the unfairness of life, I think. When you're having a good time, when you're fully engaged with life, it all just disappears, slips through your hands, but when you're going through shit you're seemingly stuck fast forever; fast, but not fast. Slow.

They were strange times, indeed. If you only have yourself for company, day in, day out, and you can't be bothered to do anything constructive, maybe sometimes even get out of bed, but, and here's the point, you still have all your faculties and you're a reasonably intelligent sort of person, then what ultimately happens to you? What I'm getting at is, do you go mad?

It's a question that I found myself asking many times during my wilderness years. It's a broad church, of course. After all, what is madness? Is it, perhaps, the same conundrum as asking 'what is art?'. Well, yes and no, I think. Yes, in that it can be all things to all men. One man's art is another man's shite, and one man's madness is another man's individuality. But no, in the sense that art is subjective and doesn't obey rules, whereas madness is a science that has been studied and reported by some very clever people over many centuries who have categorised it and documented it and given it precocious and complicated names.

On the other hand, if you hear voices in your head telling you to kill the first person you meet with an axe, then I guess most people would conclude that you are, indeed, a madman, in the same way that if you can paint a good picture like Holbein or Constable, then you are indeed considered an artist. I can tell I'm on sticky ground.

Madness is all a bit of a game in which the best players deceive their opponents more than their opponents deceive them.

So, did I go mad? My diagnosis is that during those early wilderness years I was clinically depressed, which is a mental illness, so yes, I was mentally ill (although it was only my diagnosis and I'm not a qualified psychiatrist or indeed qualified in any medical field, so I might have been wrong). I didn't hear voices telling me to do awful things, or have delusions of grandeur or psychotic episodes. But I would say that yes, in comparison with a normal person I did go a little mad for a while. The madness came upon me, and eventually it left. I think.

Those dark days took their toll on Church House, too. For years I did no cleaning or maintenance, and an old house like this needs constant attention. The gardens grew wild and were a disgrace and if I had cared I would have been embarrassed; Crow's Nymet is such a pretty, tidy village.

I was lucky that during those first few painful weeks, I was just about able to hold things together in order to keep living. I did eventually pluck up courage to go to the community shop by myself. I tried to pick a time when there were few villagers about. I reckoned just before school ended was a good choice, when all the mums were already at the playground gates waiting for their brats and the pub was closed. All the same, inevitably there were times when I couldn't avoid the villagers I met in the street or in the shop, and I came to dread them. I was very aware that my appearance had deteriorated alarmingly, although by that time I guess I had resumed showering and washing my clothes. I must still have looked grey and lifeless and remote.

I'm trying to tell you that I sort of fell into the wilderness years. They just happened. If ever there was no plan in my life, this was it.

You might think that it would not be possible to just retreat from society like that. To disappear from life, but still be there. To go off-grid, abruptly and without warning. I wouldn't have thought it likely, either, but like I said; I just fell into it. I kept myself to myself, and it worked.

I soon came to realise that I couldn't survive solely on the inventory of the community shop. They didn't sell toilet paper, for a start, and there's only so much newspaper you can put into a cesspit without it blocking up. I speak from experience. I couldn't persuade the shop owner to buy stock in for me, so I had no option but to catch the bus to South Molton market on a Thursday morning. I had already decided I wasn't going to drive again; it was that confidence thing. I couldn't overcome it.

It was uncomfortable for me to sit on that bus with all the bubbly, laughing, local characters. It was always busy. It was the only day out in the week for a lot of them, so they made the most of it. It was for me, but I wasn't looking to be cheerful about it. I could have walked, I suppose, but I didn't want to traipse back with heavy shopping. It was a nuisance having to wait all day for the return bus. There was only the one.

But I began to realise that I might just be able to live the life of a modern-day hermit. I suppose I always expected that things were going to catch up with me in the end, one way or another, but guess what? They never did, and they still haven't. I've been hidden under the radar for nearly twenty years and still no one bothers me.

I think it's got to be a good thing, actually, that something like that can still happen in this scary, regulated, connected world. Is it just me, or are there others out there?

I've no idea what headaches it might have fostered, though I used to ponder it occasionally when I needed to amuse myself. Georgia never forwarded mail on to me. It would have all gone straight in the bin, and maybe eventually folk just stopped trying. Perhaps Georgia told them I was dead. She wouldn't have found that hard to do, and it was true in a sense.

There was a lot of money in our joint accounts, but fortunately I'd had the foresight some time before to open a spare one with another bank in my sole name that I didn't get round to mentioning to Georgia. It was useful as a syphon for sundry homeless funds. I had inherited more when my parents died than she knew about and I put a big chunk of this in my account, too, and I transferred some tax refunds that I also kept quiet about. There was a sizeable sum that could keep me going for a while, and then I could always cash in my premium bonds. I didn't think money would be a problem, although without bank cards I always needed to think ahead.

I let the landline account lapse, which was a mistake that I came to regret because when I wanted it back some years later it was a hell of a job to get it reinstated. I think I had been blacklisted, and they probably had a little note in the call centre by my name saying be as vindictive and obstructive as you like.

There wasn't much else that mattered. There was council tax to pay, water rates and the quarterly electric bill and the oil tank to occasionally fill and that was about it. I didn't spend much on food, and there were plenty of charity shops for clothes; my tastes were simple.

Nothing else from my past life has ever caught up with me. I ignore any post that looks official that I don't recognise and pop it in my little wood-burner out the way. That seems to do the trick.

Life in the wilderness years was, indeed, very cheap and very simple. I miss it, sometimes.

But although I've obliquely suggested to you that after Gerald had brought my stuff down and I'd plucked up courage to go and buy my own food, that the worst of it all was over, that's really not the case. I didn't get away that lightly. I was an empty carcass of a man. There was a void in my life that stretched out in front of me whether I was awake or asleep. I couldn't get away from this emptiness, nor could I hide.

I lost all sense of time and was unaware even of the changing colours of the countryside with the passing of Winter into Spring and then Summer. I was a shell. I wandered around stuck on autopilot, but never landing, never regaining control.

Most days I would stay in bed until late morning, just day-dreaming really, that's all it was. I would casually drop in and out of reality. I wasn't sleeping much during the nights and, as we've discussed, that inevitably is the worst time. Things are different then. They engulf you in their desolation. I was in a sort of stupor from which I couldn't break free, I guess because I had no wish or need to do so. I was, as I've said, a bit of a mess.

I suppose this must have gone on for several months, because one night it had already become summer and it was just too hot for me to sit inside the house and I went and lay on a fallen gravestone in the churchyard to get some air. I'll bet it was July or August and we were in the middle of a heatwave that had hitherto passed me by. Church House warms up very, very slowly with its thick earth walls and heavy thatch. It takes a couple of weeks or more of relentlessly sunny days to make any sort of impact, but then when it has absorbed the heat it holds on to it and gives it up again only reluctantly. It can be stifling. As I stretched out, I could feel the energy radiating from the West facing cob wall that had been soaking up the sun's rays all day and late into the evening, and from the depths of the gravestone itself. It was a heat that bestowed, not sapped.

It was wonderful lying on that slab looking up at the stars in the intensely black country night, with perfume from the recently mown grass and a myriad of wild flowers left uncut among the dancing graves with their heavy pungency and chaotic mix. For the first time since that December night when I stumbled weary and numbed from the Jag, I actually felt a notion that I had become alive again. It seemed I was just now bobbing my head above a seething ocean of hopelessness and despair and was witnessing again the emergence of a life that had been taken from me and locked away somewhere out of reach.

Yes, that was the moment that I started to mend. I still feel warm and safe inside when I think about it now, even with the gaping chasm of time. It marked the beginning of my laboured re-entry into the real world and a tentative rediscovery of the wondrous things that fill ordinary people's lives.

I lay on the hard, warm slate being alive until the sun came up and I heard the voices of early risers in the village. It's all very well becoming alive again but the rest of the good inhabitants of Crow's Nymet probably wouldn't relate well to such a concept. They had had their lives all along, after all.

It was a little bit like coming round from the effects of a flu bug or a very bad hangover. When you're in bed with a fever and aches and pains you just don't feel like doing anything at all, do you? But to someone looking on at your bedside, that doesn't really come over and sometimes this gets people upset, especially women. They can't seem to understand, despite having been through the same experience themselves. They just forget. But when you wake up recovered, suddenly you want to do stuff again. That was how I felt after those many months of deadness.

I guess it would have helped if I'd had someone to tell all this to, but I had no one. This never bothers me in normal times, but just then I remember I got a little pang of loneliness that made its presence known on and off all that morning, but then thankfully it was gone.

It's come back to me tonight, actually, now that I think about it. It's a horrible thing to be lonely.

nineteen

The wilderness years consumed sixteen years of my life. That's too long a time to just take up a couple of pages of my story. It's almost a lifetime in itself. Where did it go? I went into it a broken man, dragged myself through the early trauma and was reanimated on that hot slab of stone with the awe of the natural world and the cavalcade of ever-changing life in the countryside around me. I rose from the depths of despair to embrace a sense of intimacy with my surroundings and eventually a nagging desire to assimilate myself back into village society that was then, in turn, cruelly crushed by a conspiracy of misfortune.

Sixteen years. That is indeed a long time to be alone with only your own company to keep a solitary, enquiring mind active and occupied. And that was the trouble, of course. It precipitated my downfall, and then my hesitant renaissance, and sadly, finally my end.

But we'll come back to all of that.

On the afternoon of the hot grave awakening, I took a paper bag from the oddments drawer in the kitchen dresser and spent a good hour just wandering around the churchyard, filling it with all sorts of plants. There was a sultry airlessness in the lush grass between the graves and the ether was filled with busy, noisy insects of all shapes, colours and sizes. It was still hot as hell.

It was alive.

I was alive again. It was my resurrection. I had my resurrection in the graveyard, so that was neat, wasn't it?

Graveyards are wonderful, wonderful places. They are serene, tranquil oases in a hostile world. They're very special.

In this country we have buried our dead for centuries in consecrated ground that is accessible and still part of our living world. We don't hide them away or put them in some poor isolated corner, neither do we banish them to some godforsaken square of ground a mile out of town like the French do. We don't pile the coffins up in a multi-storey necropolis and we don't plaster gaudy mausoleums with enamelled photographs of the deceased. We like our graveyards simple and pleasant.

In North Devon we have the best churchyards in the world. I mean it. They are very special. The loveliest of them are just left wild and unkempt and have been allowed to evolve as they please. I know that not everyone agrees with this. Some people like to see neatly mown lines, and weeds strimmed to within an inch of their precious lives, but I think this is a great shame. It might look appropriate in a city cemetery, but is a squandering of opportunity in a country churchyard. You see, the thing is with graveyards, they have never had animals grazing on them and they have never had farmers emptying gallons of herbicides and pesticides all over them, either. And they'll have been protected from the harsh realities of farming and the worst extremes of the weather by an ancient stone wall or thick stock-proof hedge. You can find things in an English churchyard that have long disappeared from open country. And anyone can

227

go and walk around them at any time. You don't have to be a Christian, or even believe in God. No red-faced character with a shotgun will tell you to get orff their land. You should get out there and soak up this unique survivor. They are at their prettiest in the springtime but are wonderful at any time of year. Take a stroll through an English churchyard in the dead of night and you'll be transported to a different world. There's no need to feel uncomfortable or be afraid. Try it and see.

I emptied the contents of my paper bag on the kitchen table and spread out the stems and flowers, and I was able to identify all of them with my ancient dog-eared Collins Wild Flowers book. It was my mother's. It has her name in the front and was a present from her cousin. The next day I collected a dozen more, different ones, and I identified all those too. Who knew collecting wild flowers could be so absorbing?

I found myself spending more and more time outside in the countryside, at all times of the day and night, in all weathers and in all seasons. I grew to love being at one with everything that was going on around me, and I started to take notice of things of which I'd been oblivious. There was so much to look at, smell, hear, taste, experience, and it was all on my doorstep. I was keen to learn. I had a voracious appetite for knowledge. How I would have loved a teacher. I had to do it all myself and longed for someone to just walk with me and point things out that I had missed or ignored or simply undervalued.

I immersed myself in the natural world. I became a part of it in a way that I'll explain to you later. I possessed an abundance of that most valuable and elusive of things.

Time.

With no one to talk to, and no internet, I had to rely on the books that we had collected in the cottage and some that came down with my study, and fortunately these were very good and full of revelations. There were all sorts to choose from in my bookcase, but I also picked up some more fascinating oddities from the second-hand bookseller in the market in his fifty pence box. Books about flora and fauna don't really date like other subjects and a two hundred year old manuscript is just as relevant as a recently published coffee-table picture-book. And the drawings and plates are inspirational. It seems the Victorians were heavily into naturalism and writers were keen to explore some unexpected angles. Although it might come over as dull or eccentric to you, it was heady stuff for me. It took over all my waking thoughts for a few months and I look back on that time with great fondness and serenity.

I should add that I actually started with a good background knowledge that I had gained at my mother's knee. When my sister and I were small we went on endless walks in the countryside, so I could tell the difference between a primrose and a celandine, a purple loosestrife and a rosebay willow herb and a frog and a toad, and that gave me something of a head start, but everything that came afterwards, that was self-taught.

I started walking by myself along the Devon lanes and on footpaths and bridleways and through woodlands, and would spend hours exploring new ground. I got to prefer wandering at night.

Most of England's wild fauna are nocturnal, or at least crepuscular and this suited me very well as there were fewer people to bother me at night. In summer I would be up just before sunrise, or perhaps while it was still completely dark and for several hours I would enjoy the stillness and solitude of that special time of day. On summer evenings I would be roaming the fields as it got dark and taking in the sounds and scents as one half of the natural world went to bed and the other awoke. In the winter, when it gets light at eight and dark at three it's not so enticing to be out in the twilight. It's a busy time in the civilised world with folk scuttling about going to and from school or work, but there's not much happening in the natural world. It can be bleak in the winter in the deep countryside, no matter what the weather. There isn't much moving. Everything slows down. Nothing wants to waste the energy it's conserving. It looks like it's empty of life out there, although of course it's not. In winter I much preferred going out at about midnight, maybe earlier if I wanted to cover some ground, and often I wouldn't get home until gone seven. It was a very seminal, enchanting time, and informed a lot of my subsequent thinking.

I was eager to explore as far and as deep into the local countryside as I could, and this was very easy for me to do. As well as the best churchyards, North Devon has the best hedgerows too. They are a hidden gateway to a bucolic past that has sadly disappeared from most of our land. They remain a fascinating vestige of medieval life that you can discover all around you in this lovely place.

Let me explain what a Devon hedge is like.

It's a bank, rather than a hedge, which is why they're often referred to as Devon banks. The bank is usually about three to five feet high, sometimes much more imposing on sloping ground. The interesting thing is that no one really knows why they were made like this. After all, it would have been a significant effort to pile up all this earth, and you can see when a bank has been disturbed that it's made of good earth, not stones or clay or rubbish. Why waste that good soil on a boundary when you could be growing your crops in it? And unlike hedges in the rest of the country, nearly all of Devon's hedges really are medieval or earlier; they aren't enclosure markers or verges for new roads. The earth was piled up hundreds, sometimes thousands of years ago, and it's been there ever since, hosting the flora and mammals and birds and insects and fungi that make them so special and continue to provide a natural conduit for these creatures and plants between adjacent habitats. It's why it's such a tragedy when they're grubbed up and destroyed. A thousand years of the natural history of our island annihilated in an instant, never to be recovered. Thankfully, it doesn't happen so much nowadays, and we have plenty left, though sadly, they're often flailed mercilessly and cropped so tightly that they no longer provide the shelter for sheep and cattle that they once did, nor such sanctuary for nesting birds. In times past, they were managed for the harvest they yielded and the garnering was an integral part of the farming year. Notably, in the depths of winter when other work was sporadic or impossible, the banks were carefully denuded of the season's growth of whips and young stalks with slashers and bill hooks, and repairs to the stock-proofing would be made by bending over the bulkier, partially severed stems to plug gaps or encourage perpendicular growth from the laid branches. Nothing was wasted. The most important crop was the next year's fuel, which was faggots of twigs, bound by hazel spars and stored in the farmyard in a covered stack to dry. These would fire the clay ovens in the farmhouse inglenooks and bake bread for the family the following year, so it was a vital resource to get right.

When I'm walking the lanes, I try and imagine what it must have been like in those days. The countryside would have been swarming with workers at all times of the year, bustling away, trying to survive. Now it's empty, and no one is interested. A tractor with a flail attachment can trim a whole farm's hedges in a day and a night, leaving only splinters and ragged wounds. Quite often, the only hedgerow trees on the landscape are the ones that have hung on next to telegraph poles where the driver couldn't get close enough to rip them off. In older days, the most promising oaks and elms and ashes would have been left to mature for the carpenter, especially if their shadow fell on a neighbour's field, not your own. It would have been a lot woodier, more vertical.

The most likely reason the banks were built was to provide shelter from the biting winds blowing across from Exmoor or Dartmoor and funnelling through the valleys, and at least they still perform this duty, and although from what I've just told you, you know that they're just a shadow of their former selves, I need to emphasise that they are still wonderful things and should be applauded and worshipped as a treasured remnant. I love them. I can't get enough of them. Even in winter I can stand and stare at one for a half hour or more and soak up its power to endure and its benevolence. And in the Spring, well I'm afraid I just don't have the words. You need to see them then, to know.

When Angel and Miriam were small, Georgia and I used to take them on country rambles as often as we could, just as we had both enjoyed in our own childhoods. Sometimes it was a bit of a struggle to keep them engaged and then there would be some whinging and sulking, but I remember that we had made one or two favourite walks from Church House that first summer and it was these familiar routes that I first started to explore. They took me over fields, down farm tracks and along quiet country lanes. I used to think about Angel a lot and on occasion struggled with a deep sadness, but mostly these early memories of our walks together did lift my spirits as I remembered happier times.

I found my walking to be very therapeutic and was keen to explore further afield.

I had a number of Ordnance Survey maps of the area in the house and I spent many hours poring over the two and a half inch ones which showed me not only the bridleways and footpaths but also the field boundaries and the positions of isolated farmhouses and worker's cottages. It was fascinating to compare the ones that had been surveyed a hundred years ago to the modern ones. It then became quickly clear how many field boundaries have disappeared during the century and woods diminished in size and moorland drained and improved. It was also evident how many workers cottages have either vanished back into the ground from whence they were hewn, or have evolved into much larger edifices or have become farmhouses in their own right.

I have always been mesmerised by maps. I can visualise the ground they portray in my mind as if they were laid out in front of me like an architect's model and I can fly through the valleys and bob the trees like an unlikely alliance of Raymond Briggs' snowman and the Google Earth satellite. Not everyone can do this, I know. It can keep me absorbed for ever and it used to irritate Georgia very much. A good thing about old maps is that they show all the farm tracks, not just the public footpaths and bridleways. It's very useful to know where the old paths used to go, because most of them are still there and you can easily find them and use them.

I looked at nearby hamlets and villages that would be in easy walking distance and worked out the best routes to these settlements that would keep me away from the roads as much as possible. I was keen to try these out. If I stayed out all night I could easily reach places that were seven or eight miles away.

I became very familiar with all the lanes and paths around Crow's Nymet. They belonged to me at night when there was no one around. And there was no one around. Between the hours of about eleven thirty when the last pub customers would career homewards and, say, four o clock, it was rare to see a vehicle of any sort. I had it all to myself. It was the way I liked it. I got to know the nature of the ways. I harboured a mental image of the contours of the land and the meandering routes of the watercourses. I took note of and remembered vantage points where I could scan the road ahead for any approaching traffic. At night when it's still and black you can see headlamps for miles around and hear engines and tyres above the ambience. You've usually got plenty of time to hide yourself, if that's what you need to do. I knew where all the farm gates were and if they were locked, ajar, broken, climbable or jumpable. Similarly with gaps in the banks, deer jumps mainly, and whether they were barred with barbed wire, a pallet or a sheet of tin and if they would safely provide access or an escape route. Lanes that had none of these made me nervous and I tried to avoid them except at the quietest of times. Some of the deep Devon lanes have grass growing in the middle of them and banks so confining that you can almost grasp the shrubs on both sides with arms outstretched. Here there is nowhere to hide. If the lane was a little wider with a grassy verge, it would be easy in the summer to disappear from view into a ditch or a rut if headlights threatened, like a hare finding a shallow scrape in a field. In winter it wasn't quite so easy, or dry.

The seasons and the weather did have a marked effect on how easy it was to follow paths. Wet winters were the most problematic and I would stick to metalled surfaces if I could to avoid the boggy pastures and overflowing field drains. In summer, or in dry winters or heavy frosts, you can go just about anywhere without much trouble if you know what you're doing and where you're going. Some of these woodland tracks I know so well that I could do it in my sleep.

I always slipped a small torch in the pocket of my coat, but I've never used it. Ever. I've told you what I think about artificial light. It was just for emergencies or if I was taking a look inside a church or an empty building or something. You don't need a torch in open country, not even on the darkest of moonless nights. If you can't see the moon anywhere in the sky, chances are that it will be hiding somewhere helping to lighten the heavens, even if it's below the horizon, and even if your nearest town is ten miles away, its rude yellow lights will be reflecting off the clouds or the hills. Regrettably, it's never completely dark in this country, no matter where you are.

If you're not in a hurry and you have your night eyes, then seeing your way in the dark is not a problem. The trick is to open your eyes as wide as possible so you look like a startled lemur and make sure you don't stare directly at any point source like a distant streetlight.

I also carried a pair of secateurs with me and a serrated knife to trim back any suckers or undergrowth that could catch my ankles or my eyes. I have always been nervous of branches springing back into my face and if I was exploring somewhere new and overgrown in the dark, I would often wear safety glasses which would give me the confidence to cover the ground faster. You only need one vicious dog rose to rip your cornea out and you'd be in a bit of a state for the rest of your life.

Now and again I would also take my forked hazel stick with me. It's amazing what you can do with one of those by your side. It can be some comfort.

When I went out at night, sometimes I had a goal, a definite route that I wanted to cover or a destination to reach, and on other occasions I would just see what took my fancy and I could end up anywhere. It was those more relaxed outings that I preferred. Then, you could put some effort into moving silently and stealthily. Humans don't usually do this. They're like most dogs; they'll just walk without placing their feet, so they make sticks snap or leaves rustle or mud squelch. I learned to walk like a deer or a cat and could be silent when I wanted to be and had the time. I also had no problem standing still for long periods, maybe for an hour or more, and so I was able to observe wildlife in a way that would not be possible for you. Sometimes, badgers and fox cubs would come right up to me and sniff my wellingtons and didn't seem to be in the least alarmed at my presence. I also noticed that as I became more skilled at this, and as, I suppose, I became a more familiar sight and sound in the woodlands, the birds wouldn't be issuing their warning calls quite so vehemently or so early. It felt as if they were accepting me into their world.

Over the years I got to know all the outlying houses and farms quite well. I certainly took note of which ones had dogs loose or chained outside and I gave these a wide berth. Occasionally I would set myself a challenge with the leashed dogs or ones that were kept in a compound and I found I could actually get reasonably close if I was clever enough. There's not much of a better burglar deterrent than a bored, territorial dog with aggressive ambitions, so apart from these odd fanciful interludes and experiments, I tended to leave well alone.

That still left me plenty of choice. I had my favourite hiding places and was very resourceful. I could spend hours nestled in a conveniently sited tree, or even a garden seat if it afforded a quick getaway. I was very anxious of being discovered and dreaded being confronted by an angry householder. I don't like embarrassment in any form.

Well, it never happened. Close, once or twice when I slipped up or hadn't prepared properly, but I'm glad to say, I believe I got away with it. Voyeur extraordinaire, that's me.

In fact, paradoxically perhaps, it's a bit of a rarity to see anyone out and about in this deep Devon countryside, apart from the dog walkers and joggers who tend to keep to the lanes and the daylight because it's easier. The countryside can be a very lonely place. There are few farmworkers in the landscape at any time of the year. Most farms are worked by only one person nowadays and all modern machinery is designed with this in mind. You don't see anyone with a hand tool anymore unless it's some sort of heritage event like hedge-laying. Some days you don't see a soul for miles around and hours on end. What a shame. And it's only going to get worse. Soon, tractors will be driverless, cows milkerless and combines harvesterless. It's a sobering thought, even for me who likes to keep himself to himself.

I don't know what you think about blood sports, but at least it gets people out. It's all very sociable; it oils the cogs of the community and that's got to be a good thing. Around here we've got pheasant shooting, rough shooting, foxhounds, stag hounds, mink hounds and beagles. I've got opinions about all of them and the people who do them. My unhappy inference is that if I'm going to see anyone out and about in the woods or in the fields it's going to be someone preparing to catch or kill animals or birds for fun. So on the very rare occasion when this rule is broken, it's something of an event and an oddity. And this brings me to the first incident of two that I need to tell you about.

twenty

It happened about five years ago, out of the blue. Nothing particularly eventful had occurred in my life for some time, years maybe, nor was I expecting it to. It was late one afternoon, I guess it was probably in September or October as I remember the leaves were just starting to turn. I was about three miles from Crow's Nymet. I had followed the course of the stream that flows in the river valley just down from the village. You can track it under cover for its whole length until it reaches the main road and joins the Taw at a humped back bridge, and during the summer when there's not much water you can walk along the cobbly river bed in walking boots and it's easy going.

I was about half a mile from the bridge and I had a good view from the stream along the tree lined valley. It was sunny and the woodland was speckled with dappled light from gaps in the canopy. When I'm walking in the river bed, I tend to look down most of the time to be sure of my footing on the slippery pebbles, then stop now and again and look around. I was stood there doing this and I saw a figure about two hundred yards away coming towards me along the deer path a little way up the incline from the stream. I could see it was a girl. Woman, really. She was carrying a bag over her shoulder. I didn't know what to do. I kept still in the water and she kept coming. I didn't want to encounter her or speak to her. This was my wood; I didn't share it.

I was next to a bank where there was a bit of a bend in the stream and the outer shore had been eroded and undercut. I took a tentative, slow-motion step back towards it and then another and when I could feel the cool moss of the bank on my palm I carefully lowered myself on to it and sat motionless just as if I was a big cat stalking its prey, never taking my eyes off the girl. There were the remains of a long-fallen tree in front of me which gave me cover. I slid behind the mildewy stump and peered through its rotted stems.

I watched the girl come closer. I didn't know her. She was in her late twenties, I would say. She was wearing jeans and a red jumper and a beige duffle coat and she had a scarf partly covering her brown wavy hair. She looked a bit retro. Sixties. She was nice. When she was about forty yards away from me she stopped.

She looked straight at me, but I could tell she hadn't seen me; I was well camouflaged. In the daytime I always wear greens and browns, the colour of moss and tree stumps. She stood like that for a while; she had an intense expression. She looked pensive, and then sad, and then angry and then pensive again. She had things on her mind.

She looked around her and stepped back up the hill, walking a few paces until she came to an old oak tree that had leant over at a bit of a crazy angle with one of its larger boughs bent right over into the earth of the hillside so it looked like a huge crab. I'd often gazed at it with interest as it was an unusual natural curiosity.

The tree didn't seem to interest her; I don't think she even noticed it. There were a number of logs lying around. It must have been a young ash faller that someone had taken upon themselves to crosscut into manageable pieces, but for some reason had never come back to collect. It was obvious they had been there for some time because they were covered in moss and young ferns sprouted from the bark. She eased one into an upright position and sat down on it. It made a good seat.

She sat there for maybe twenty minutes or more, her bag by her side, and I was beginning to wonder how long this might go on for. She took her phone out and looked at it quizzically, frowned and put it away and then got it out again and jabbed at it erratically.

I was very relaxed. I could stay there for as long as she could. My diary was empty.

At one point I could see that she was crying. I saw tears dripping down her cheeks, but it was as if she was in denial and wouldn't acknowledge them. Eventually they dried without her having to wipe them away. She would be a very pretty girl if she smiled, I mused. For a fleeting moment I imagined her naked. Just for a moment, though; I've told you, I'm over any of that stuff now.

I thought I saw her expression change from one of sadness to an unsettling mix of bitterness and bleak resolve. From her bag she produced a coil of rope. It was that awful blue polypropylene stuff that everyone seems to use nowadays. It was tied with some binder twine and sprung apart when she released the bow. Nasty stuff. There looked to be about twenty feet or more of it and it was lying on the ground like a limp spring.

For the first time, she looked around her self-consciously. It was the first sign of cognition that I'd seen in her face; a

241

purposefulness that enriched her countenance and gave me a glimpse of another self that she had not shown me before. By then, I knew what she was thinking. I'd seen that expression before.

As luck would have it, she was sitting right under the most convenient bough in the whole wood to hang herself from. I wonder, did she feel that was an omen when she realised? Perhaps if it hadn't been there, things might have turned out differently.

She stood and looked up at the branch. It was only about three feet above her head. If she had jumped, she might have been able to touch it.

Did I see a flicker of doubt in her eyes? If I did, it was gone in an instant. She had to make several attempts to get the rope over the branch. She threw like a girl. Once over, she had to stretch on tip-toes to reach the coiled end. I could see that she had a handsome body beneath the duffle coat.

The end of the rope had started to fray into strands and was unravelling. You need to melt it to stop it coming undone. She tied a single knot in it instead, then she put it around her neck and tied a granny, and the frayed end looked like one of those bootlace ties on her collar. The blue didn't go with her top.

She arranged the stump so that it was directly below the bough and then she stepped up on to it and checked her balance. It was wobbling on a stone and she looked unsteady. There was an untidy broken limb on the bough that she could reach and she wound the loose end of the rope around this several times and then tied it in a loop which she then hitched on the ragged spur.

The way she'd tied it, she had to stand up straight, as if she was standing to attention and she had her hands and arms at her sides. She was still looking in my direction, but I could see that there were no tears now. There was nothing, actually, nothing at all. Her being had already left her hollowed, abandoned body.

When she kicked the stump away, I thought for a moment that she was looking me straight in the eye, though I think maybe not. I could see she had no regrets and she didn't struggle to release the loop. She kicked for a while and jerked about and her face went bright red and then her tongue popped out and her eyes bulged (I thought they were coming out, too) and she dribbled down her duffle coat. And then she was still.

I was fascinated. I'd never seen anyone take their life before.

When she stopped twitching, I got up and took a closer look. I walked around the hanging body and scrutinised it from all angles. She didn't look so pretty, now.

I didn't touch her, though I would have been interested to see how long it took for her skin to cool. I realised, of course, that this was quite a big thing. I may have made light of it in the way that I've told you, but I knew that at some stage there was going to be a lot of wringing of hands, grinding of teeth, questions being asked and authorities of various kinds wanting answers. I also realised that if there was even a hint of foul play then someone would be coming knocking on my door at some point.

I looked around me at the soft Devon earth and the disturbance it had lately encountered. I pride myself on my self-taught tracking ability. I've become like one of those Indian scouts you see in westerns getting down off their horse and peering at dried sweat stains on baking rocks and pointing to a dust cloud in the distance. I can tell a lot from all manner of clues that you wouldn't even notice. I could see my footprints in the earth leading from the stream where I had been sitting. No doubt there would be some crushed moss and disturbed pebbles, too, that I could find, but the average plod would ignore.

I retraced my steps taking care to mask and obscure any signs I could find and then I walked back to Church House through the stream and paths by which I'd come. They do that in cowboy films, too.

The girl-woman haunted my mind that night. Should I have prevented it? At the time it seemed to me such a natural thing for her to do, for some reason. Her anguish, perhaps? The desolation in her eyes? Now, I wasn't so sure anymore. She had a lot of life to live. There would be others whose lives would never recover from this act. I had a very disturbed struggle with sleep until the early hours when I drifted away.

The next afternoon, I found myself retracing my steps and when I got to the scene I stayed in the stream and looked at the hanging body. There were dark stains on her jeans, front and back. Her face had turned much redder, a black red and her tongue was purple and flies were grubbing round her open mouth. I think her belly had swollen up, too. I think it had. She was just swinging round slowly in the gentle breeze, first one way, then the next, in her own time.

I had made peace with my demons and felt no guilt for my inaction, but I knew that there must be friends and family for whom the nightmare was very real and only just beginning. Although you probably won't believe me, I did agonise over this. I knew I really should tell someone.

But I didn't. I didn't want to risk any involvement and I couldn't think of a way to do it without the possibility of being identified and dragged into it.

The agonising did pass, and I continued to be fascinated by the whole experience. I went back again the next day, and the one after, and the one after that and I stood in the stream and gawped as the body deteriorated and decomposed and blackened and bloated and oozed and started smelling. On the fifth day I saw the white hasmat suits and the police do not cross tape from a good two hundred yards away, so I didn't venture further.

It was over.

The other thing that I need to tell you about was nowhere near as dramatic as the hanging, but it is more important to my story. It wasn't so much an incident as a revelation.

It was the finding of The Clump

I found it about two years after the hanging, so that would be round about the summer of 2013. You might ask why it had taken me so long to find it when I had been traipsing the wilderness of my wilderness years for the whole sixteen of them, and The Clump was only a few hundred yards from Church House, practically next door.

In mitigation, perhaps I should say that for the most part my expeditions tended to be further afield and it was my habit to ignore the woods on my doorstep, choosing only to use them as thoroughfares. On this particular afternoon, I hadn't gone far when I came over all weak at the knees. I get these funny turns every now and again. I think it's something to do with blood sugar levels because it soon goes if I eat a chocolate bar or something.

On this occasion I didn't have a chocolate bar with me, so I needed to sit down until it passed.

I was in the woodland that starts just beyond the churchyard, so I wasn't very far away at all. There's a path that the hunt used to use that was probably a firebreak once. Hardly anyone goes in there; not even dog walkers.

I ventured off the path through the understorey, which was mainly brambles and holly and not dense enough to be problematic finding a way through. It didn't take long for me to come across a fallen trunk to sit on, and as I rightly surmised, the blood sugar eventually corrected itself of its own accord and the malaise left me as quickly as it had appeared.

When I looked around me, it was one of those occasions when something just clicks into place and I realised instantly where I was. I was sat in exactly the same spot as the local yokels in Godfrey's old sepia photograph. The bough was growing from the base of a huge yew and was just as I remembered it from the image. What an amazing thing. This was where it all went on. This was the sacred grove where the festivals were held, for centuries probably. It sent a shiver through my spine. I'm not one for histrionics, but there was something not quite normal about that place and for a short moment I was spooked and considered running away from there as fast as I could. I don't normally suffer such things. I laugh in the face of fear.

But it wasn't fear, exactly; it was more an uncertainty, an abnormality. I couldn't quite put my finger on it. It's very difficult to explain how I felt. Anyway, I bore it and it went. This place just exuded history and mystery. I wondered if anyone now knew of its existence, tucked away in this inconsequential place. Did anyone recognise the significance of the site anymore?

You'll guess that someone did, or I wouldn't be telling you about it. You'd be right. That's how I came to know that the sacred grove was known by those who knew as The Clump, and the yew was known as Yew Magna. Not the Yew Magna, just Yew Magna. The big yew, I guess.

I was quite chuffed at my discovery. I would have liked to have told someone, except that I wanted to keep it for myself. It exercised my imagination, and of course, there was the direct connection with Church House and the Shaman. That was so intriguing. It rekindled in me an interest in all things folklorish which ushered me with a natural urgency to the next part of my story and my life.

twenty one

Once I'd realised what I'd found, it focussed my attention and I kept coming back and sitting there on the yew, on Yew Magna, feeling its strength and age and mystery coursing through me and in the following weeks I made two further discoveries.

I was trying to think myself back to the time when this tree was young, but that in itself was a real problem. How on Earth could I know how long it had been growing there? Let me describe the tree to you in case you haven't got the right idea yet. Yew Magna is not a tree with a trunk from which branches grow and form a mushroom or ball-shaped canopy of thick green needles. It may have been like that once many hundreds of years ago, but it's not what it's like now. The main stem rotted away long since, and in its place grew other stems that have, in turn, also rotted and been replaced by new growth. If Yew Magna were one trunk, that trunk would be more than thirty feet in girth and you could measure it with a tape and do some calculations and arrive at an estimate of its age from the number of growth rings that you thought would be inside. But that's not the way it works with very old trees, especially yews which can go into a stasis where they don't grow at all for centuries. Yew Magna may indeed have a girth of thirty feet, but that girth is made up from dozens of stems of all ages, sprouting at different angles, some showing vigorous growth, others none and still others a morbid decline. This tree could be a thousand years old. It could be two thousand. It could be five thousand. It will have seen a few changes in its long life.

Curiously, yews don't usually grow in woodlands in the South West; they're more solitary animals. And if they're going to freely multiply in the wild, they ideally need limestone or chalk to tickle their roots. But then you have to ask yourself, did it grow naturally, or was it planted, and if it was planted, who planted it and for what purpose? And following on from that, is this a sacred grove because it has a yew growing on it, or was the yew planted here because it is a sacred grove? And while we're at it, what is this grove business? A grove is a number of trees, surely? Was it like that or was it just always the one in a clearing all on its own? And why is it called The Clump? A clump is a group of trees, too, isn't it? So many questions, and no answers apart from the easy one. It is a very, very, very old tree.

For a start, I knew the bough upon which I sat hadn't changed in over a hundred years and compared to the rest, it looked like a youngster. It was about a foot diameter and pushed and poked its way through the undergrowth, layering and seemingly sprouting new growth wherever it touched the earth.

I tried to imagine what this place was like, how it had changed during the lifetime of the yew. Perhaps it had changed many times?

I'll try and describe the surroundings as they are now. Yew Magna is growing on a slope in the middle of a deciduous woodland of native broadleaf trees, mostly oak and ash and beech. It is ancient woodland; this is obvious to anyone who knows about trees and woods and I can easily tell that these companion trees were never planted. They grew there of their own accord and are themselves much older than a hundred years, and what's more, their parents did too. That suggests neglect and abandonment. The question in my mind was: were they here when the festival was being enacted, or did they spring up after the fracas with the dead shaman when the whole thing upended?

It is growing in the middle of a rocky outcrop, a sort of crude amphitheatre in the hillside. In these steep Devonian river valleys, the shaly bedrock is never far below the surface. It's why the meadows and pastures are so wet and boggy and acidic. We call it the culm measures.

You see old overgrown quarries wherever there is an ancient house, where seams of decent building stone have been mined from the sedimentary layers of shale. It's the same with tracks and paths and roads; it beat hauling the stuff for miles with a pack animal. Nowadays, the ones on the side of the road are usually full of old fridges and plastic feed sacks and the hidden ones with half a millennium of midden. The rock formation surrounding Yew Magna has nothing to do with quarrying. I pondered whether it was a natural concave bowl in the rock face, or if it had been hollowed out by primitive tools, but then one day when I was just mooching around, I made my first discovery and I think I know now, why the tree is there and why it was a secret grove. Suddenly, it all began to make sense. I found a spring.

It wasn't any old spring, either, because there are plenty of those about, too. This spring looked very special to me. I don't know why I hadn't spotted it before, or heard it, apart from that it was a very small spring. In fact, I think I must have even stepped over it numerous times and not seen it. It was just down the slope from the yew and it flowed from a vertical face of rock, down a smooth channel carved or worn into the surface and then it gently dribbled off the underside of a protrusion like a tap open a quarter turn. I'm sorry to be crude, but where it came out of the rock face, it looked just like a cunt. It was just the right height for sticking your head down into the gully and taking a drink from the lip of the overhang. I stared at it. It was a lovely thing.

One of the reasons I knew it was special, apart from the cunt thing, was because the water then disappeared from sight. There was no sign of it reappearing anywhere; it went straight back into the bowels of the earth as if a moment's exposure to the outside world was all it was giving. That may sound a bit silly to you, but I'm trying to explain how it was different from other springs. I mean, there are springs and wells everywhere around here. We get a lot of rain. Every farmhouse and worker's cottage in the countryside will have a spring or well. Of course they will; that's the reason they were built there.

A well is a hole in the ground that is dug below the water table and you extract water from it by hauling it up in a bucket or pumping it. The water stays in the well if you're lucky no matter what the weather has been like lately because the water in the well fell as rain a long time ago and has had plenty of time to percolate through the rocks to smooth out any periods of drought or excess. A natural spring is rainwater that follows the course of a porous sedimentary layer that borders an impervious one and either releases it from the side of a slope or pushes it up under pressure like a fountain. In either case, you would then expect it to form a water course which will eventually find its way down a valley and beyond. Most natural springs keep going even in prolonged dry spells. If they don't, they're more likely to be field run-offs or drains, and don't count.

I could see why my little spring might be looked upon as a magical thing. It was just so lovely. A mystic, sacred, spiritual, magical thing.

I think the spring was here first, and then the yew. The yew was here because of the spring. Someone had planted it here because of the spring. A long, long time ago. The spring was more important than the yew. It must have a name as well. I wonder what they called it?

I was getting quite into this. First, I had found the sacred grove; now I had found a holy shrine in the same spot, and I'd only just got going.

My next discovery was derived from human, not natural origins. It was this. It was the remains of a Celtic cross. It was just lying there, poking out from the mounds of leaf mould that were blanketing the rocks. I was sat there, on the bough, as I had by then done dozens of times, and I noticed it. It was obvious to me what it was, straight away, mainly because it was a different stone (it turned out to be granite). It had certainly been brought there from somewhere else. Why hadn't I picked it out before? It was just the top of the shaft that I could see, but I had no doubt that the rest of it would be round about somewhere. If you've never come across a Celtic cross I'll just tell you that it's an ordinary cross with an added bulky, circular hub in the middle. It made them easier to carve from stone because the arms were less likely to drop off. In fact, sometimes they didn't bother with the arms at all, but then it doesn't really look much like a cross, to my mind.

A lot of them were lopped off during the reformation and turned into sundials.

You do quite often see Celtic crosses in the West Country, but they're usually in churchyards or built into the fabric of churches themselves, so it was very curious why this one wasn't. It either never had been, or it had been brought from the churchyard to here. Curious in either case, but reinforcing in my mind the importance of this site as a very special ancient place.

My guess was this.

The holy well, the spring, had always been there and roughly in its current form, though the markings on the face would have matured with climate and erosion. What I'm saying is that it hasn't changed, maybe for tens of thousands of years, in fact it's been there since last there was any geological or volcanic activity in these rocks. I'm not a geologist, but that would be my guess. Now obviously, a lot of other things have been happening during that time like any number of ice ages (though the glaciers never got this far), land bridges to Europe, successive migrations of humans of one sort or another, that sort of thing. But I'm thinking that maybe this little magical spring has been there all the time and hunter-gatherers chancing upon it at any time in history would have realised it was special and they would have revered it and preserved it and worshipped it or what they perceived it represented. It wouldn't have mattered that it was tiny and there was plenty more water around. I believe it would have acquired some special status by whoever knew of its existence.

I have no problem if you think this is fanciful. There's no way of proving it one way or the other, but what an absorbing idea, isn't it? The things that might have taken place at this spot that were core to people's lives, for tens of thousands of years.

Anyway, I accept that it's speculative. Let's move on to, say, five thousand years ago. That's the Neolithic. There aren't many folk about; they're all hunter-gatherers using flint tools, but they've discovered fire and domesticated dogs and pigs and are mainly nomadic for most of the year. The land is densely wooded and full of game and the tracks and paths are on the high ground. Because there's plenty of food and land to go around, these guys are likely to be fairly peaceful and mix freely with one another in small family groups or tribes. They've probably got some spiritual thing going that is based on the natural world around them. The sun and the moon and the changing of the seasons; the providence of food and water. I'll bet they all do their own individual stuff and there's not much in the way of power and control yet. They'll have some sort of special way of dealing with their dead that has become a tradition or rite and they will probably have established festivals and other customs, and maybe built henges or earthworks where these took place, and where tribes or families would want to be on these occasions and be prepared to travel to.

Ok, I haven't been able to find henges or standing stones or barrows or astronomical calendars here, but it's quite possible there was something once. Anyway, I'm going to stick my neck out and say that I believe the spring became one of these places. I'm trying to tell you that I could feel something special as I sat there on the bough that seemed to be trying to reach out to me over the millennia and draw me back to nature in its rawest form.

If I'm right, at some point any nearby trees were probably felled and tidied away and the site would become a clearing in the dense oak woodland.

Then, at some later date, Yew Magna is planted as a young sapling to be nurtured to maturity by generations of supplicant custodians. This goes on for centuries and things change. Metal tools come along and there's a pressure on land as new waves of migrants roam the countryside and want to try their hand at farming rather than hunting and gathering so are seeking just the right place to settle down and raise a family, and there are going to be conflicts and trauma while all this is going on, but I think the little spring and Yew Magna could have transcended it all as a spiritual sanctuary for all-comers.

There are going to be more upheavals, the coming of the Romans, for example. New ideas, but most significantly, more people with their eye on the main chance. Power and control, of course. That's when the whole thing gets spoilt.

In more recent times, the arrival of Christianity to these shores must have been tumultuous. So many new ways of doing things. So many clever, but ruthless bastards keen to ruin people's lives.

I'm surmising that's where the Celtic cross came in, though what the full story was, I'm afraid, is lost in the mists of time. Just think of it like this. If you want to subjugate a people by introducing them to a religion that you already control, then the best way to do it without upsetting them too much is to craftily assimilate the way they do things with the way you do and hope they don't notice or mind. So it was that the new churches were built on existing holy sites, and the festivals and traditions that the local population knew and loved were incorporated into the new Christian calendar so even if they noticed, they wouldn't bother about it too much. Apart from the druids, I suppose (the priests, not the pub), who got a bit of a raw deal because they remained troublesome and wouldn't adapt, but ultimately because they didn't want to lose what power and control they had already managed to wrest from the peasants. They had to go.

It must have been a bit tricky in what became Crow's Nymet, because they've got a long-established sacred grove with its well and its yew, both of which couldn't be moved, but it's not a very suitable place to build a church. It's much better two or three hundred yards away at the top of the hill.

It must have been a bit of a conundrum for the decision makers.

St Rumon's is about eight hundred years old, but in all likelihood there were other wooden churches there before it, and maybe just the preaching cross before them. Here's what I think happened.

Round about the time that Christianity made an appearance in these parts, there was a small community who lived in a ramshackle hamlet where Crow's Nymet now lies, and they had on their doorstep a sacred grove that had been there for as long as anyone could remember and was used in religious rites throughout the year, mainly concerned with harvests and fertility and prosperity which was overseen by a hermit or shaman or druid who lived near the grove and eked out an existence from tithes or gifts or penances or other contributions.

I think by this time, the sacred grove had become the property of the erstwhile Crow's Nymet. They no longer shared it with others or endorsed pilgrims. It wasn't big enough to share and it had always done them well and that's the way they wanted it to stay. But it was a throwback to pagan ways.

I think, ultimately, that's why they built the church where they did. They wanted to keep the two things separate. They wanted to keep them both. They were hedging their bets.

I could think up many reasons why the Celtic cross had ended up there where it was, but whatever the cause, I bet it involved some unpleasantness.

I have to say that my mind had been occupied by this absorbing introspection ever since I found the Clump. It was very satisfying how things seemed to be falling into place, how things started making sense.

This sacred grove had had an intimate influence on the village of Crow's Nymet for ever. Everything that now existed in Crow's Nymet could trace its origins in some way back to the existence of The Clump. You only had to look at the grotesque carvings of green men in the bosses of the church roof and the obscure symbolism of the primitive images on the bench ends. The guys who carved these either had overactive imaginations or they were benefitting from a lifetime of superstition and myth, or both, or something else as well.

And why was the Druid's Arms called that? And what about Godfrey's shaman?

So many questions. And indeed, it was these questions that then next influenced the direction of my story.

I've told you that the last time my life had dramatically changed, the realisation whilst lying on that sun-warmed gravestone that I wanted to be part of the world again, when I went on to discover the miracle that is the natural world, that I was able to feed my knowledge from the vast depository of books left to me by my mother and supplemented by the odd snippet from the second hand bookseller in South Molton market. They had served me well and I had fed on their facts and inwardly digested a whole literary canon from their texts and learned well from it.

I realised that I couldn't do this, this time around. No such books existed on my shelves. I would need to invest in other sources.

I am an intelligent man. I knew what I had become. I understood what people must think of me, and the sort of words they would use to describe me to others. I didn't care about this. I've told you, if anything, I promoted and relished it.

I did feel now that it was maybe time for a change. To tell you the truth, I was getting a bit bored with my own company.

I think I've given you a good picture of what I looked like at that point. Long, uncombed beard, self-cut hair and the coat with the long sleeves and the torn shoulder for dark nights and cold days.

Of course people talked about me.

So I combed my beard and gave it a bit of a trim and smartened up my hair as best I could and I found a presentable, mouse-free jacket from the pile on the bed and I took the Thursday market bus into South Molton with the aim of seeking knowledge.

South Molton has a most satisfactory library in the council building on the main drag. It is a bit limited, as you would expect of a small market town, but it does have an excellent local studies section with all sorts of treasures in it.

The woman behind the counter wanted me to join the library. I should have expected it, but it hadn't entered my mind that she'd ask me to fill in a form before I could see anything. I know it's not a big deal, but it's just that I hadn't been involved in anything 'official' for so many years that I was scared of it and I hesitated. I'm telling you this because you need to know the sort of man that I now was. You would probably change, too, if you'd just spent sixteen years with only yourself for company.

Anyway, I managed to overcome my fear and filled in the form and signed it. I remember being intrigued that my signature had weathered the unused years with impunity.

She let me into a back room that had bookshelves on three sides and filing cabinets on the fourth, a table in the middle and a small desk with a microfiche reader in the corner. There was an old guy sat squinting at some indecipherable scrawl on the screen. I asked her for stuff on Crow's Nymet. It turned out there was quite a bit. I gathered from what she said that after Godfrey had died, the history society didn't have the heart to carry on without him, so they donated all their paperwork to the library. I got the impression that it was a mixed blessing and the bulk of the duller, unindexed stuff was taking up room along with all the rest of the library's detritus in a shipping container in the car park.

She pointed me to two whole shelves containing books, folders, pamphlets and lever arch files and I started leafing through. I didn't know what I was looking for, exactly, but at this stage, anything would help.

The first thing I took out was a folder with a printout of census returns and I had just got myself comfortable at the table when the bloke at the microfiche reader got up and came and stuck his face in mine.

He was too close for my liking; the closest I'd been to anyone for a long time.

He told me he couldn't help but overhear that I was interested in Crow's Nymet and wasn't that a coincidence because he had lived in Crow's Nymet for the first sixty of his eighty years. What was I looking for especially, he wondered?

I wasn't sure I was ready for this, but it did seem to represent an unexpected opportunity. These omens, again. I told him about the photograph that Godfrey had shown me. He had known Godfrey vaguely and he knew about the photograph, so that was a very auspicious start. He also had a good idea who the man was who gave Godfrey the photo.

He told me that when he was a boy, he and his mates would tell each other stories about the festival and what went on during it, to frighten girls and themselves. They invented and embellished most of the stories for added effect and it all became a bit of a game for them. They would dare each other with taunts but ultimately, the guy said, none of them would have dreamed of being there in the wood after dark.

It soon became obvious that I knew more about the sacred grove than he did, who was born and raised in the village and spent the whole of his working life farming the fields that bordered the woodland. He knew where the yew was and he had been there often in company, but never alone. I didn't tell him about the spring or the cross or about any of my theories, and I'm pretty sure he knew nothing more about the site than he was letting on.

He did tell me its name, The Clump, and he only referred to the yew as Yew Magna. That's how he'd always known it. The festival itself was called the Rousing and it took place twice yearly on the eve of the summer and winter solstice, so you were right, weren't you? It's all going to tie in.

He told me he'd never actually seen the photograph, but he'd had it described to him by those who had. It had evidently acquired something of a cult status in the imaginations of the village lads. Rather stupidly it made me feel privileged to have already been party to it, like some sort of honorary member of a secret club.

The way he described it to me was exactly like I remembered from my brief exposure. He told me that the guy with the sack was supposed to be the old man of the woods, and he was indeed a kind of primitive Father Christmas figure. His job was to conjure up the green man from the living energy of the forest and then the green man would bless the fertility of the crops in the fields and the fecundity of the young folk of the village. I think it was the green man that all the local lads were afraid of. They'd probably spent many an idle hour during morning prayer on a Sunday looking at the macabre images in the ceiling of the barrel roof that were staring back at them through foliate masks.

I have to say that I found the whole thing entrancing. I was caught up in it already. I wanted to find out more.

Unfortunately, it seemed that I had exhausted this man's repository of knowledge of the festival, or Rousing as I shall now call it from time to time. I probed gently, but if he did know of the shaman and the regrettable turn of events in medieval times, then he wasn't giving me any of it. I don't think he knew, and I found that rather curious. I would have thought it would have ratcheted up the level of suspense and communal fear in these local boys if there was a witchdoctor up to no good and locals dropping like flies and never heard of again. Why had no one been tempted to tell them about this bit? Perhaps he had forgotten, but I don't think so. Maybe this part of the story had been purposefully held back from him and his peers for some reason?

Perhaps it was the fear. Real fear, I mean; the sort that loosens the bowels. Not the fear you cultivate with your friends; the fear that's deep inside you that no one else can see. Simple lives are ruled by fear and superstition.

I've dwelled on this and after giving it some serious thought, I have concluded that superstition is a very personal thing. The only time I can remember talking to anyone about their superstitious beliefs was with my mum, oh and her cousin when the two of them got together. She had quite a few and she was keen to let me in on them, and this is what I mean. You get these beliefs from a very early age from your mother's knee or your father's side and they are, of course, very, very difficult to shake off. That's the point of them, I suppose.

I have never thought about this before, but I've just managed in my head to come up with over twenty of my mother's superstitions, most of which are still influencing my life in some way. That's extraordinary. Fortunately, they're all trivial. They don't stretch to raising spectres on the night of the full moon, for example. On the other hand, I don't believe I ever spoke of my real gritty beliefs, the deep and unerasable stuff, with my schoolfriends, college friends, mates, colleagues, strangers, even intimates, anybody at all. What about you? Do you have fears that loosen your bowels?

The guy was spent. He looked at his watch, turned the microfiche reader off and filed the envelope in a card tray, and then he politely bid me farewell and left. He said his name was Harris, and he only came in on Thursdays if I ever wanted to see him again. I doubted I would. I felt I had sucked him dry.

I went back into the main library, selected a couple of books on medieval folklore and ordered two more on green men at the counter for delivery the next week. I was just on my way out, feeling quite buoyant that I'd managed to accomplish such a lot on only my first attempt, when I noticed a computer on a desk in the corner. It was turned on and displayed a home screen with scrolling local ads. I asked the woman if this was for public use and she said it was and I was welcome to log on and did I need any help? I said no I didn't and went and sat down at the desk. The screen and keyboard were facing away from her, so she couldn't see what I was doing. I rested my wrists on the table edge and extended my fingers as if I was typing. The truth is, I didn't have a clue what to do.

I stared at it and finally managed to access a browser by trial and error and much overuse of the return key. I was like a fish out of water. My, how things had moved on.

I think I was mesmerised by the whole experience. It was very strange. For the whole of my wilderness years I hadn't once missed this wormhole to the world. I'd never even given it a thought in all those long nights and days, and yet now that I was sat here with my fingers poised and mind alert it was just as if no time had passed at all and I felt completely at home in this surreal habitat that was so mystifyingly familiar. It was as if I had been magically transported back to my desk in the Technology Centre or to my study at home in Babel House. What a strange feeling it was. It was like the long years of solitude and introspection had never existed at all and I had suddenly been able to cast them aside as if that were another life that had never been.

I probably looked a bit of a picture, like a kid with a new toy that he can't quite get to grips with. What was all this stuff on the home screen? So many ads. So pushy. It never used to be like that.

I looked for Yahoo but the computer gave me Google. I thought I would try searching on green men and was astonished at the breadth of the response. I was blown away by Wikipedia; what a brilliant idea! So much stuff. Such variety of sources. So many oddballs and saddo's out there.

Wow, it was a Eureka moment, to be sure. I needed all of this.

twenty two

It seemed to me that I was ready to start my rehabilitation with the twenty first century. That's how I remember it feeling at the time. I had been to hell and back, but had come out relatively intact and unscathed by my experiences. I had not sought help, nor had I been given it, though as you know it had been offered. I'd managed to pull myself out of the mire without assistance. Now I felt I was ready to take back control of my life.

Yes, that was the thing that was most important to me. I had the confidence that I could once again control what was going on around me.

When you lose control it's a terrifying thing. I'm realising now for the first time as I write this that that's what it was all about, that strange moment in my life. It was about the regaining of control. That's what had been missing in my wilderness years; I had been unable to choose the path my life was taking.

It's extraordinary how cathartic just putting pen to paper can be. I've spent all this time thinking about stuff but not necessarily understanding anything at all. I find that a bit worrying. What else haven't I understood, I wonder?

Anyway, that's for you and me to discover on our journey together, I suppose.

What I'm saying is that I had some decisions to make, now that my confidence had returned and I was in control. Did I still want to be that sad, reclusive, old man that people avoided in the street? Sure, it was a life without goals, or pressure, or threats, or risks and it had suited me well, but was it time to say goodbye to all that?

I think at that stage the jury was still out, but my epiphany in the library had shown me I wanted to be a part of the wider world again and I needed to be connected to it all in the comfort of my own home by my phone line.

I've already told you I had trouble getting the line back. It was a fucking nightmare, and I very nearly gave up and crept back under my stone. It was not a good introduction to the way things had become. I'm not going into it; it still makes me mad. Suffice to say, and I'll leave this to your imagination, with no phone, no internet, no transport, no credit rating, no help it was difficult just making contact with the right people. I was at the end of my tether, and then I happened upon an Openreach man up a pole outside the parish hall. I think I must have left an impression on him that he'll take a while to forget. I don't think you're supposed to speak to them. Anyway, he sorted it for me and a few days later the line duly made its presence known with an automated call welcoming me to the brave new world.

My computer had spent the last few years in a heap of wires, cables, mouses, keyboards and modems, just where Gerald had dumped it by the side of my desk. I didn't hold out much hope that I would be able to extract any sense out of it after all this time. It took me a while to remember how to connect it all up together. I couldn't help but feel as if I was on the outside looking in. I was out of my depth and drowning.

I couldn't get any sense out of it. I didn't even know what I was supposed to do with my new router. I needed help.

I realised, of course, that this new sunlit upland I was seeking was a different animal to the one I had withdrawn from all those years ago. Everything had moved on without me, and at a pace that was itself increasing. I had no idea what was out there. I'd picked up the odd snippet from newspapers and I knew what a smartphone looked like because I'd seen people using them in South Molton, but I didn't know what they could do. What was Twitter and why would you want it?

I looked at the sad tangle of parts on my desk and the blank CRT screen. I needed to kick-start this somehow.

Now it might be easy for you to buy yourself a new computer, but for me it wasn't. I didn't have a debit or credit card, no internet of course; I wasn't confident enough to go to PC World in Barnstaple and there was nowhere in South Molton that sold anything more technologically advanced than a light bulb. I tried phoning one or two stores in Exeter on my new phone line and told them I would send a cheque through the post, but they just weren't interested.

My, it was a tough, unfamiliar place out there. I wondered if I really wanted any part of it.

It was a frustrating time, but in the end, I solved the problem very elegantly. I had been rash and unfair in mocking the good retailers of South Molton. On my next visit I discovered a compact corner shop that I'd never noticed before, up a side road I rarely bothered with. It sold all things computer. It was run by a little man about my age who, he told me, had been in the TV and radio repair business all his life but had recently diversified into computers on the recommendation and instruction of his son, who was staring intently at a screen in the workshop behind the counter and stabbing at keys. Between the two of them, they guided me through what I would need, and the best thing was that as soon as it was all delivered to the shop, the lad would come out and install it for me and get it working, and then give me a tutorial on using it for as long as I needed. And they took cheques.

I had no regrets in being extravagant with my purchase and I bought the laptop and the tower together. I had quite forgotten what it feels like to treat yourself to a nice new toy. It felt great. It lifted me in a way that I hadn't expected. Look at all those brand-new colourful, glossy cardboard boxes and cable and connectors in shiny sealed plastic bags. What anticipation.

The first thing the lad did was to dump all my old gear in the back of his van and clear my desk. He seemed amused by its antiquity. I wondered fleetingly whether there was anything on the hard drive that would be of interest to anyone, but I thought it unlikely. I don't really remember what exactly I ever used my computer for.

The kid was good. He knew what he was doing, and he gave me a running commentary all the way through. I was impressed. Who knew such things had reached South Molton?

He asked me for passwords and PIN numbers, but he might just as well have asked me to decipher an Enigma code. Well, it didn't matter, and we set it up with new ones. The only thing I remembered was my email address, but I thought it very unlikely that it would still be active.

It was.

We played around for a while and downloaded and installed some clever things and he took me through browsers and search engines and showed me how to use Google Earth and YouTube. I was blown away. I was truly amazed. I must have looked a picture. I bet my jaw had dropped and I was drooling. That's how I felt.

We found my service provider, who remarkably was still providing a service, and with a bit of jiggery-pokery and some smoke and mirrors, we managed to log on. I looked in my inbox, which I could tell you held sixteen years of accumulated intellectual correspondence, but it didn't. There was some phishing and Nigerian money-making opportunities but the rest must have dropped off the server into the ether long ago.

The lad was just creating some files for me when we stumbled upon a spam folder that looked innocuous, so we opened it.

Among all the rubbish, I was drawn to a message that turned out to be from Ralph Ralph, of all people. It simply said, 'are you still alive?' and was dated about four months previous.

Ralph Ralph. I'd forgotten all about him. It seemed such a long time ago, and was a painful episode. I had no one personal to send an email to, so the lad encouraged me to fire off a response so we could test the new set-up. I told him it wasn't much of a test because the likelihood of getting an instant reply would not be great. Ralph Ralph would be in bed, for a start.

I wrote back 'I'm still here, battered and torn but surviving'. Of course, there was no reply, and in the end, we sent a test email to the boy's father in town and he responded straight away, so at least we knew it was working. I was so impressed with the kid's work that I slipped him a twenty-pound note as he left and told him to buy his girlfriend dinner. It was a bit of a creepy thing to do and not like me at all. I'm sure he would be dining out on the whole experience for a while anyway. I saw the expression on his face when I led him through to the study. The house was in a bit of a state.

It was later that afternoon that I had an email back from Ralph Ralph. I was absorbed in my new toy and was studiously examining a cut-away drawing of a rare umbellifer on some obscure website on folk medicine when my computer pinged and a little window indicated new mail. In a curious sort of way, it made me feel as if I had been accepted into the new technological age. It was as if the computer itself had generated the greeting.

I think Ralph Ralph was as surprised to hear from me as I had been from him. It was a short email and to the point. It said something like great to hear from you, let me know your phone number and I'll give you a ring directly.

I have to say, I was a bit hesitant. It was all very well hiding behind the anonymity of a worded message, but I was concerned that just the sound of Ralph Ralph's voice could trigger some sort of relapse. It was such an awful time, that afternoon long ago in New Mexico, and I've relived it so many times that it's turned into a bit of an ogre in my imagination. I still can't seem to shift it.

Did I even want to speak to Ralph Ralph? And what did he want after all this time?

I decided, reluctantly, that I would have to go for it, that perhaps this was one demon that would be relatively easy to exorcise. He called me back straight away. His voice did indeed take me back as soon as I heard it. It hadn't changed at all. I felt sick and I told him to hold the line for a minute or two. I took deep breaths and composed myself and returned to the phone with what I hoped came over as an upbeat, jaunty sort of air.

What Ralph Ralph had to tell me was fuck-off crazy. I don't know why I'm passing it on to you, except that now it doesn't really matter anymore who knows.

I'll keep it simple for you. It went something like this. Just before I left the ranch to return to Georgia's nightmare, Ralph Ralph had said he was very sorry that my beloved son had just unexpectedly died, but could I just sign here and here and here before I left. Evidently, I had opened an account with Ralph Ralph's agency, transferred my shareholdings into the new account and then, just for good measure, had given Ralph Ralph the power of attorney over my affairs in the US. I don't think it's the sort of thing that I would have done if I'd been thinking straight. I don't think it's the sort of thing that a respected broker like Ralph Ralph should have been doing no matter how straight he was thinking. What sort of moral code do you operate by if you take advantage of someone's misfortune for your own gain like that? When he told me all this, I had this great sinking feeling inside.

It must seem unlikely to you now, but during those wilderness years I hadn't actually given much thought to my shares. Sure, I knew that if the takeover had ever happened they would presumably have been worth something, if anyone had wanted to buy them. I think that perhaps because I never heard anything, I assumed it hadn't worked. I don't know. It didn't seem part of my life anymore. I'd had no need for more money. If I had, then I guess I would have needed to make some enquiries to see if there was anything left of value. Much rather that than to try and claim welfare of some sort from the state. Not that I've anything against that as a concept, it's just that I couldn't have faced the horrors of the benefits office and the awful creeps that work there. And it would mean that they'd found me.

In a nutshell, this is what Ralph Ralph told me over the phone, and you have to believe me when I say that I knew nothing of any of this. I was busying myself with nocturnal nature rambles while the markets buzzed and popped.

Nothing much did happen for a couple of years after they managed to do the deal. The performance of the new, enlarged company was unimpressive, and management were struggling to make the new organisation work. Then, in 1999, for no apparent reason apart from the fact that a cartel of greedy people wanted to make a lot of money before the telecoms bubble burst, everything went mental. Someone, somewhere with enough clout and spunk had decided that the Digital Tsunami Corporation was the vehicle they would use to bolster their pension pot and had started buying all the stock they could get their hands on. It was a shrewd move that wouldn't work in normal times, but these times were anything but normal. When you have those dollar signs rolling round your eyes, you don't do normal things and you can sometimes get away with the extraordinary.

The share price went through the roof in a matter of hours. Up from three dollars with no volume, to over eight dollars with trades in the thousands. Everyone knew that there was nothing in the fundamentals of the company that could justify anything like this price tag, but of course, that didn't matter.

Ralph Ralph told me he kept his cool. He waited until it reached twenty dollars before he started selling, and then he trickled it out over the next six months as it continued to rise until, when the bubble finally did burst with the new millennium, my account was sitting on mainly cash. When the dust settled, Ralph Ralph started reinvesting the funds and this time spread it out to widen the risks. Ralph Ralph's forte is with NASDAQ stock that you've never heard of, with emerging markets so obscure and risky that nine out of ten fail. It's the one that succeeds that pays for the rest.

He told me the balance in my account was now into eight figures. About twenty-two million dollars.

This news, as you can probably appreciate, came over as a little surreal. It's like a big lottery win, I suppose, and just as sudden as far as I was concerned. Surreal and distant. I didn't need or want this kind of money. What use would it be to me? I would need to give it some thought. I asked Ralph Ralph to call back in a few days after I'd had time to mull it over.

And mull it over I did, and this is what I decided.

The thing was, as far as I could tell, nobody knew I had this money. Not anyone in the village; they didn't know how I managed to live, not Georgia and not the Inland Revenue, although all three would probably take an interest if they found out. I'll admit that I was tempted to ask Ralph Ralph if he had heard from Georgia. She would surely have got wind of the share price from someone. What did he tell her? I bet he'd thought of something clever; he would be good at things like that.

When Ralph Ralph rang back I told him that I wanted to keep things just as they were. I trusted him to manage the portfolio in any way he saw fit, and I also told him that I wanted him to send me some cash every so often from the account. He was to send it in handwritten brown envelopes, several notes at a time, and if by any chance he could get hold of some pounds sterling, that is what I'd prefer, as they don't accept five hundred dollar bills in the community shop.

And that's what he's been doing ever since. When they're not in my special hiding place, I keep them in the grey tin box that sits upright behind books on the bottom shelf of the bookcase in the sitting room. I haven't spoken to him since that day. He gave me the log-in details and passwords in case I ever wanted to take a look at the portfolio online, but I haven't bothered. Like I say, I've not much use for it.

twenty three

I remember how I felt rather pleased with myself at that time. I felt I had finally left my wilderness behind and I could actually, tentatively look towards the future. I had no idea what it would hold for me, but I knew it would be different from what had gone before.

I had smartened myself up. I'd got myself a credit card, for God's sake, and made my first online purchases. That would have been unthinkable just a few short months before. I'd bought some new shirts and jeans and a Barbour coat which I wore to the market. It felt good in a way that I wouldn't have predicted. It was as if it gave me this veneer of legitimacy, somehow. I was treated differently in the street. I could see that people didn't go out of their way to give me space on the pavement. They no longer avoided eye contact or ushered their children from my path. It was only the little kids that would ever look at me, and they couldn't keep their wide eyes off. I'd revelled in all this when it was going on, but now I wanted something different. I wanted to join their club, but the question was, would they let me in?

I tested this dilemma one Thursday afternoon when the market bus dropped me outside the Druid's and I plucked up courage to go inside and have a drink. It was just gone two and the lunchtime eaters had come and gone and there were only a couple of lads standing talking to the landlord at the bar. He came over and with a smile he asked me by my first name what I would like to drink. I think I may have told you that he's good at that sort of thing, haven't I? I pointed at his session bitter and he tapped it off the barrel behind the bar.

What a nice place this was, and what a nice man.

I sat on one of the stools at the counter and pulled the local paper from a pile and scanned the headlines. I noticed with interest that Godfrey's stool had become a shrine. There was a photograph of him on the wall behind it and his walking stick was still propped up in the corner. The lads left and the landlord pulled himself a pint and came and stood opposite me. You know, we chatted together drinking our drinks as if it were that first day when I'd gone and introduced myself as the new owner of Church House. I wouldn't have thought it possible. Was this what he was able to do with all his customers, I wondered, or had he made an exception for me for some reason? There was no recognition that there had been an interruption of nineteen years; maybe that was trifling to him.

I enjoyed my little treat so much that I vowed I would do it again the next week, and this is what I did, and it was just as convivial.

I decided that I'd tidy the garden up a touch at the front, so I got a wheelbarrow out and a weeder and a small fork and set to work on the patch of oregano and lady's mantle by the picket fence that was getting a bit scruffy. A quick trim now might mean new growth would colour things up for the autumn.

I was sat on the doorstep sipping a cup of stewed tea when who should walk past but Jean, the one of the Christmas dinner. I'm ashamed to say that we hadn't spoken since she made that kind gesture; not in the whole time that I had lived in the village and she was only three doors down. She stopped and looked at me. Something was puzzling her. I could see it in her expression; she was thinking something through.

'I wonder if I might have a word with you', she said.

I offered her a cup of tea but she waved her fingers dismissively as if she was still thinking hard and couldn't multitask.

'I've got a bit of a problem that you may be able to help me with', she added at last. And she explained her problem to me.

One of the oldest inhabitants of the village had just died, apparently; an elderly lady who everyone loved and was sorry to see go. I remembered a big funeral a few weeks back. It seemed like the whole village and more had turned up for it.

The old lady's closest companion was her dog. It was a collie/labrador cross and it was pining for her. Jean had offered to take it while she tried to find it a new home. It was a bitch, only about seven years old, but aged before its time as it'd only had the elderly lady for company and had rather gotten used to spending its days sat with her by the fire when it should have been out chasing rabbits and sheep.

Jean wondered if I would like it.

She assured me that it was no trouble. It didn't bark or whine and would walk to heel and come when I called. The old lady's grandson had trained it for her when it was a puppy. It was a good, well behaved dog. It might be just what I needed, she observed.

I hadn't had a dog since Jet at Redfern Cottage. We were going to get one when we moved to Hallam but somehow never got round to it. It would have made our little nuclear family complete. That's what dogs do. When we had a break-in and some low-life nicked the TV from our kitchen I was adamant we needed a dog and we went round the rescue kennel the next day, but I couldn't convince Georgia to take one, even though she picked them all up and they muzzled her and loved her and the kids were crying when we left empty handed. I think we'd needed one; not to catch the burglar, but to keep us all together.

I remembered how I'd loved taking Jet into the woods and across the fields. I don't know why I hadn't thought of getting one before. It would have been something animate to talk to, at least.

Jean told me that Rosie came with everything I would need to start me off. Leads and choker; a whistle that she responded to; her bed and blankets; food and water bowls and a big sack of the dry all-in dog food that she ate twice a day. What could possibly go wrong?

I would have felt mean not to have given it a try. It sounded like it could be just what I needed to break some ice. Dogs are good mixers.

I said yes, I would take her. It was on the understanding that if it didn't work out one way or the other, then Jean would take her back, so I felt I had nothing to lose, except perhaps hope.

She brought Rosie and her accoutrements around later that afternoon. She was a lovely dog. She had bright eyes and a cold, wet nose and she was pleased to be with me. She settled instantly. As soon as I put her bed on the rug in the kitchen in front of the Aga, she was in it and curled up and eyeing me with great interest. Her expression said, okay, what are we going to do next? I'm quite happy to stay here in the warm, but if you want to go out, I'm game for that, too.

I eased into life with a dog again. I didn't go mad. In fact, once I'd had time to think it through, I wondered if I had done the right thing. I had got rather used to doing exactly as I pleased without taking the needs or wishes of others into account. When Jean was entreating me with her suggestion I must admit that I was imagining taking Rosie on my long walks at night, but now I thought about it, it didn't seem right at all. I couldn't have her on the lead; that wouldn't work. She would chase or frighten the wildlife away. She wouldn't be likely to want to stay sitting for hours contemplating or watching nature and she'd probably set guard dogs off too. She was black so I wouldn't be able to see her easily at night, and that would make things more awkward still.

On the other hand, it would be my guess that Rosie would much rather be tucked up in her bed at night in the house than roaming the countryside with her mad owner. She wasn't used to long walks, after all. The main benefit for us both would be that we could venture out during the day and not arouse any cause for concern, suspicion or alarm. The dog legitimises the man (that's why it's called dogging). A man alone in the countryside without a dog is a man to be avoided, even if he has a map and a pair of binoculars in his hands. If he has a dog, then he's okay (unless he's dogging, natch).

And so it was. Rosie pretended not to notice when I crept out at night and feigned sleep when I returned and during the day, we went out together and had a great time.

I put her on the choker when we were walking through the village, as she did pull a bit, but when I let her off she was so happy coursing over the fields and exploring the doggy delights of the woodland that I felt she was probably making up for the lost time the old lady hadn't been able to give her. We developed a close bond that came naturally to us both.

One early evening in late summer we were returning from a lovely walk along one of the quieter lanes. I remember I had been picking off blackberries from the laden brambles in the hedgerow and throwing them for Rosie to catch. She had grown a taste for the berries but rarely took the trouble to find them for herself.

As we passed the Druid's I just fancied a pint. It was that sort of night. It would finish it off rather nicely, I thought. There was a throng of punters inside. Mostly when I went in at lunchtime, there were few people around, so I was a bit taken aback. Had I realised how crowded it was going to be, I probably wouldn't have bothered. There was a lot of noise. The acoustics aren't too good in the Druid's and it only needs a big raucous group for the volume to ramp up.

There was a big raucous group. I saw them as soon as I got through the door. Big, red-faced men with boots and dirty working clothes, some with shirts open at the chest and bellies hanging over straining belts. Men of the land. Salt of the earth, perhaps. Perhaps not. They were farmers, all of them, or farm labourers. The pleasant evening and a few phone calls had probably got them there on their way home to supper. There was a crowd of about nine men, all standing and drinking and laughing and shouting. And then they saw me.

You've probably seen the scene in Withnail and I or American Werewolf in London, (and Straw Dogs too, I think), where the guys go into the pub and everyone looks round and there is a hushed silence and murmuring. It's become a stale cliché; much used. Well I'm telling you it was just like that.

They all turned and looked in my direction and to a man they all stopped their talking and their laughing and their shouting. It was instantaneous and it was spontaneous. It had happened as if it were the most natural thing. Not one of those men had stopped shouting because their mates had; they were all acting as individuals. I could see all this on their faces.

When they went quiet, the rest of the pub went quiet, too. They wanted to see what was going on.

I don't like to be the centre of attention. What I should have done is turned round and walked straight back through the way I'd come. What I did do was make my way to the bar with Rosie at my feet, pushing past inert, unmoving bodies, saying excuse me, and could I just squeeze past you please. I could smell their sweat and their salt of the earth dirt. They watched me pass and like in the clichés they started up their chatter again, but now with a conspiratorial and cliquey menace.

The landlord wasn't there. It was a spotty youth behind the bar who I didn't know. He looked sullen but had perked up with the excitement of my entrance. Our exchange was mechanical. He didn't call me by my first name. He was obviously trying hard not to position himself in my camp, and he kept looking at the farmers to see if they'd noticed. I sat down at the corner of a table where there was a free seat and Rosie lay down by my feet. I have to say, I felt uncomfortable. I didn't think there would be any chance that I'd be staying for a second pint.

Looking around the bar, I could see that it was all village locals who were filling the place tonight. All sorts. Middle-aged women with dyed hair and risqué lipstick slouching with their fat husbands, and earnest youngsters drinking lager with snotty kids around their legs sucking lollies. The nice evening had brought them out, too. Did I want to be one of them? They were certainly having a good time. Easy in each other's company and at ease in their natural habitat.

It was obvious they were hefted to the place. They were at home.

I became aware that one of the farmers was standing close behind me. I could feel it. His presence was piercing through my back. I half turned, more out of nervousness than efficacy. He was young and very broad with a bull's neck and huge hands with dirty nails. Rosie noticed him, too and stood up. Then the young farmer made a gun shape with his thumb and forefinger and pointed it at Rosie and made a clicking noise with his tongue and palette and Rosie keeled over, just like that, poleaxed, on her back, her legs in the air, mouth open, eyes closed, still as the dead. It all happened so quickly. It had taken me completely by surprise.

The group of farmers erupted. It was literally a roar. A roar of whooping, shouting, whistling, jeering and clapping. They were crazed, lunatic.

Poor Rosie was just lying there on her back. She had started to dribble. The roar subsided and now it was most certainly me who had become the centre of attention. Everyone in the pub was looking in my direction. What was I going to do?

What was I going to do? I tugged at the choker, but her head was floppy and it flipped the drool from her mouth on to the flagstone. I bent down and petted her and ran my hand down her chest and tummy. She remained motionless. I couldn't understand what had happened and I didn't know what to do. I felt helpless, humiliated, angry and fearful, all at the same time. The pub was completely silent; you could hear a pin drop.

Then the young farmer, who had meanwhile moved to the bar and turned round with his elbows leaning back on the wooden counter, clicked his fingers and Rosie instantly stood up and wagged her tail and the whole pub erupted a second time and the farmer turned round and ordered a beer.

Well, you've probably worked it out, haven't you? But it had all happened so seamlessly and I felt so intimidated by it that I hadn't cottoned on.

With all the excitement, I needed the toilet. I looped Rosie's lead under the table leg and went to the gents. And as I was stood there at the urinal, of course it came to me. The farmer was the old lady's grandson, the one who had trained Rosie for her, and he had obviously taught her the trick. Simples. I'm sure he couldn't believe his luck when we walked in.

When I came back into the bar, she was gone.

It's not over yet, I thought.

I stood there wondering again what I was going to do now.

The group of farmers had reformed and they were all looking at me. Waiting. Sipping their drinks and boring their stares into me. And then they sort of shuffled apart in a sidestep and behind them I could see Rosie on the end of her choker hanging from a hook in a beam. She was struggling and kicking and spinning around wildly.

This time I didn't bother with the thinking, or speculating or musing or agonising; I lunged towards the hook, arms outstretched to support my dog. I was grabbed roughly from both sides and restrained and held there with Rosie swinging about in front of me, convulsing maniacally.

This can't be happening I kept telling myself.

How long can a dog swing on a rope before it dies? What gives out first?

It felt like it was never going to stop as they held me there, and then this one guy with the reddest face of the lot came and stood in front of me so that his nose was touching mine and his spit was going down my throat. He was no longer of this world. His brain was in some other place along with his senses and any cognitive abilities he may previously have had. I've never seen anything like it. He was a frightening sight.

I couldn't understand what he was saying. He was so close to me and his words were coming out all mixed up and wrong. This man was insane. He was not of this world.

And then I was suddenly released and someone pushed the man from my face and he stumbled backwards into the crowd.

It was the landlord.

'Not in my pub', he kept yelling. 'Not in my pub'.

He grabbed the lead from the hook and threw the lifeless Rosie into my arms and turned to face the man.

'Not in my pub you don't', he added for good measure, but the man was still incensed and it took four of them to hold him. He was still spitting and screaming and his eyes didn't look right.

The landlord took me by the shoulders and frogmarched me out of his pub. 'Get out', he said simply. When we were outside in the street, he didn't let me go. We stood there panting; he still had me by the shoulders from behind, and I still held poor Rosie in my arms. He drew closer and he spoke softly in my ear.

'He thinks you watched his daughter die', was all he said. It was all he had to, really.

twenty four

I don't like violence. I'm not a violent man. Quite the opposite. Throughout my life, I've managed to avoid being on the receiving end of violent acts. Admittedly, it's been a close thing now and again, but I've always been able to talk my way out of any unpleasantness without resorting to a physical solution. So you can imagine how this incident had unsettled and upset me.

I thought Rosie was dead. I carried her all the way back to Church House and lay her limp body on the kitchen table. She wasn't breathing and I did, for a moment, wonder about mouth to mouth. How would you get a decent seal? I thought that I had lost her, and we'd only known each other for a few weeks. In that short time, she had become my only friend and now that was all gone. Oh dear, I was becoming maudlin again. Those were my first thoughts when I got back, and had she not recovered I think I would have been in a very bad way.

But then it was just as if she had had this new life breathed into her. If I had been the sort of person to believe in miracles, that's what I would have thought had happened. It truly looked to me as if she'd been raised from the dead. I've had time to ponder it a lot since, and I've considered many explanations, some bordering on the ridiculous, most of them unlikely. It was this Church House thing making its presence known again. What was it about this place that made me think this way?

I was looking straight at her on the table. She was only about an arm's length away from me. She wasn't breathing, and then she was, simple as that. She was reborn.

And as soon as she started breathing, she opened her eyes, and as soon as she saw me, she started wagging her tail, and then she raised herself unsteadily on her hind legs and I held her very tightly and I cried and cried. I wanted her so much and I hadn't known.

I found that I was shivering, even though I was standing next to the Aga and it was a mild night. I would say I was convulsing. I couldn't stop it. I couldn't steady my hands and I had to turn round and grasp the Aga rail and I lowered my head onto one of the hotplate covers and rested my forehead there. I realised I was sweating. It was a cold sweat and it was dripping down my neck and off my nose and I could feel it running down my leg.

It was a bit of a low point, I suppose. I'd gone through a few, like I've told you, but this was something new. I guess the thing that was different this time was that I had been full of hope and optimism, and now that had been dashed. I'd had hope that I had a new life ahead of me, waiting for me to reconnect with it, but now I knew that this just wasn't the case at all. I'd been fooling myself all along. These people weren't going to let me into their lives. I was never going to become like them. I would always be on my own. Nothing was going to change.

I felt like I had been really hit back hard. The memories of my breakdown had never truly gone away and I can tell you that as I lay prostrate over the Aga, I was very afraid that it was going to start all over again. I didn't think that I would be able to cope with it a second time.

The shivering went on all night and I didn't get to sleep till well past five in the morning, but then when I woke at about midday I was strangely relaxed and other-worldly. I lay on the settee, quite still, eyes open but not seeing, but not shivering any more.

And as usual, it all seemed different to how it had been the previous night.

I think if you're going to avoid relapsing into morbidity, depression, anxiety, hopelessness, whatever you want to call it, you really need some sort of goal to drag you out of it. My goal had been rehabilitating myself with the outside world but that had been cruelly taken from me by the lynching of my dog. I needed a new goal to replace it.

I thought maybe it would be to teach those cunts a lesson. That might do the trick to get me sorted.

It certainly made me feel better, just thinking about it. I spent the rest of the day brooding on it, and it lifted my spirits and aroused me.

It would be a long, unstructured campaign, I decided. Nothing too dramatic to start with, and it would need a bit of thinking through. I would savour it. I wondered if it might prove to be an opportunity to put some of Ralph Ralph's cash to good use, but for some reason it didn't feel appropriate and nothing sprang to mind anyway. It would be much more pleasing coming from only my ingenuity, and indeed that's how it worked out, but I did have a shrewd idea that the money was going to come in handy eventually.

And so it started.

Subtly. It started subtly. It is quite easy to frighten someone. You don't have to dress up as some creepy monster and jump out at them in the dark. That's silly and for kids or Halloween, and it only lasts for an instant. I felt I could do a much better job. I knew I could upset lives over a much longer period. I felt I was easily placed to start the ball rolling. After all, I knew a lot about these villagers' lives already from years of careful observation. I knew when they were going to be out, or away from home. I knew how to get close without being seen. I was good at stealth. I'd had a lot of practice.

What unnerves people the most is if they can't understand something. In my experience, something, some event or phenomenon that doesn't have any rational or sensible explanation is a source of anxiety for most folk. It doesn't have to be anything big or far reaching. It could easily be as simple as something not being where it should be.

One of my first exercises was just that. There's a pretty cottage near the school that has two big ceramic pots on either side of the front door, under the porch. They are both the same colour and both have hydrangeas growing in them. They look the same to you and me, but their owner would be able to tell them apart. One night, I swapped them round. It probably wouldn't be immediately obvious even to the owner that they were any different, but at some point, she would notice and she'd not understand how this could be. It wouldn't be newsworthy enough to tell her friends and perhaps she'd even think she might be getting a tad unhinged, but I reckon it would be gnawing at the back of her mind for a long time. Every time she looked at them. I like to think so, anyway.

It gave me a great thrill to do this and I now know why cat burglars and shoplifters do what they do. It's more for the buzz than the gain. It brings you alive.

I'm sure it doesn't seem it to you, but I think it might have been a bit daring for my first time. Trivial, perhaps, but daring nevertheless. After all, anyone in the street or looking out of a window could have seen me do it. On the other hand, it was a very dark night, and it was near four in the morning. All the same, I didn't make myself conspicuous and I wore a hooded sweatshirt under my coat that covered my face in shadow. I didn't want someone taking a picture or video of me. Not likely in Crow's Nymet, I know, but there's no point taking chances. I wouldn't have been able to handle the shame of discovery; then and now.

The thrill of the act, the frisson, was something that I hadn't thought about before I started my campaign, although I had always found it stimulating to simply stake a place out and sit and watch what was going on in other people's houses. I could tell you some stories.

Most folk round here don't lock their doors when they go out. This is particularly true of those more isolated places where you'd think it might be most prudent. The thing is, there is virtually no crime at all, so it all gets pushed to the back of your mind. Also, you'd be amazed at how regular people are in their habits. They do the same thing every day and every week. Take and collect the kids to and from school at the same time, always shop the same day, down the pub same nights, skittles, badminton, bowls, pilates, yoga, bellringing, darts, all at the same time and predictable.

These were the easy ones to target, so I started here first. If I was confident that I had identified someone's routine, then I only needed to briefly prepare beforehand to make sure there was nobody left at home.

I was used to the titillation of looking through windows from the outside, but it was so much more of a thrill to go into other people's houses uninvited. I expect you can imagine. I was very careful and made sure I left no trace. No muddy boots. I was meticulous. Usually, I didn't know what I was going to do in advance; something would normally present itself as an opportunity. Piffling things at first like moving stuff around, eating things from the fridge, altering settings on TV's and radios, rearranging books in a bookcase or ornaments on a mantelpiece. There were occasions, I have to admit, when I thought perhaps some of these things were too trifling and would go unnoticed and I was just wasting my time, and the most disappointing thing of all, of course, was that I was never there to witness the deed being uncovered, and I found that most unsatisfactory.

Inevitably, I did become more brazen and I began to venture more deeply into houses, into bathrooms and bedrooms and these were much more interesting. Much more. And so much more scope. You wouldn't believe what some people get up to.

I guess it became like a drug to me, and I needed a bigger hit each time. Eventually, I fancied I needed to go into properties when the owners were still in them. And not just at night when they were asleep, but during the day, too. This certainly fed my habit. I had to be confident my homework was up to scratch and I needed to keep alert and aware and I always worked out my escape route in advance and left doors ajar and gates open. I don't think I've ever done anything as exciting in my life. Nothing really comes close to that exhilaration. Knowing that someone was upstairs in bed while you were trampling unseen through their private world was just so compelling, so arousing.

Now I might be giving you the impression that I went out every night doing these things, but it wasn't like that. It couldn't be. I knew that if I wasn't careful, I could overdo it and there might be some sort of organised retaliation if they realised it was me. I would seek out new tricks only about once a week, and I was still keeping it very low key. I wasn't shitting in their beds.

I never did disturb anyone. Never did need to use my planned quick escape routes.

But still there was this nagging annoyance that I never actually got to see the results of my endeavours.

I suspect it would have gone on much like this until one night I would have slipped up and got caught or discovered or exposed and that would force an end to it and it would come to a disappointing conclusion, but something occurred quite unexpectedly that put a bit of a skew on the whole thing. Made me think about it all differently.

It's funny. Some things in life can seem to come along without you noticing them at all. They arrive one day on the very edge of your little world without an invitation and settle comfortably down on the periphery of your consciousness, and grow slowly, slowly until you are aware that they have become a part of you. Like a fondness for almonds, for example, or an infatuation with the way a particular bird behaves with changes in the weather.

On the other hand, some changes come about like an express train exploding from a tunnel into your life.

I can pinpoint the exact moment when my comfortable, familiar way of doing things was turned on its head, and in a completely unexpected way. One moment I was just a mad, sad old man, and the next moment I had become a mad, sad, but especially bad old man.

I had taken to walking Rosie across the playing fields on the edge of the village hall car park, to get to the lane that took me down to the stream. They weren't much used. There are two or three rides for the kiddies, a slide, swings, that sort of thing, and a small football field with a single goal marked with white posts. I had just reached the penalty spot when the dog decided that it needed a shit. Now I can tell you that I have always been a responsible dog owner. When I'm in the village with Rosie I always carry poo bags and I have no problem using them, unlike several people I've known, mainly men, and mainly men of the 'old school' variety. You probably know some of these types as well. In fact, in my experience you can pick them out in advance from their attitude to life in general and categorise them. This man won't pick up shit under any circumstances and is proud of the fact. This one will find some excuse that he can smugly justify to himself and won't be in the least concerned or possibly aware that the excuse is risible. Others pick up only if they know someone is watching and still others just pretend not to notice. The same men always park in disabled slots, too. I see them behaving like this in South Molton all the time. It's rarer in the village because they seem to be better trained; the owners, not the dogs.

I was fumbling around in the pocket of my coat with long sleeves for a poo bag that I knew was there somewhere. The pockets are deep and I do keep a lot of debris in them, so I had difficulty extracting the bag from the rest of the flotsam. I guess in my distraction I might have wandered a little away from the steaming pile, and by then Rosie had moved on to other attractions. The next thing I knew, there was this woman stood right in front of me, sort of blocking my path. They all do it, it seems. I must attract them. It does appear to be a recurring theme. My life is full of recurring themes. I recognised her, but I had never spoken to her. She lives in one of the council houses and her husband drives a pick-up with a trailer permanently attached. She started ranting on about her little Gavin who plays with his mates on the field and that my dog would blind him with some hideous disease, and that she would come and put the stuff through my letterbox (I don't have a letterbox, actually), and that I was a miserable cunt. And one or two other things that I forget now.

You might think that I would get mad at this unfair diatribe from the stupid woman. Unfair and unwarranted. In other circumstances I might have done. If the whole thing had happened the day before when I was feeling more argumentative, I probably would have laid into her about her brat Gavin and how I'd seen him pulling a little girl's trousers down behind the recycling bins or how her husband always parked his van with the trailer sticking out on the corner so you were on the wrong side of the road round a blind bend. On another day, I might simply have gone back and scooped the offending pile into the poo bag and chucked it in the bin like I had been intending to do. Had I done this, then things would have turned out very differently, for me and for the good burghers of Crow's Nymet.

What I did do was this, and I suppose that in order to get a full picture of what happened, you need to appreciate that at this point I would have presented a bit of a spectacle visually, what with the torn shoulder and all (I had reverted to type). I had a banana in my other pocket. I just stood there, still and quiet after she'd stopped for breath. I took the banana slowly out and held it like a gun and pointed it at her. I don't know why I did this, but I guess I was still smarting from the guy in the pub and might have got the idea from that. She looked at it, and then she looked at me. I said 'Bang'. There was a pause while we stared at each other of what must have been about seven or eight seconds, but seemed, and still does seem in my memory, much, much longer, and then I added 'You're dead'.

That was all, and in my most normal sounding, unhurried, unflustered voice.

Now, like I say, this just happened. It wasn't planned. It's just how it was. I didn't know what was coming next. If the woman had just burst out laughing and repeated that I truly was not only a miserable cunt, but a crazy one, then things probably would have passed so unremarkably that I wouldn't have needed to tell you the story. What she did do took me a bit by surprise. Her whole face changed completely. I've heard people talk of the colour draining from someone's face, and indeed this is what occurred in front of my eyes. From being a ruddy, farmer's-wife's complexion, her cheeks and jowls and throat turned an awful insipid, cloying grey as if someone had held open a tap and the blood had just drained away. Her expression went from indignation and anger to one of pure fear. I had, up to this point, never seen such sheer terror in a person. And do you know what? Although I'm sure I didn't show it, this response had an immediate effect on me as well. I got off on it. I had power in a way that I had never experienced before in my life. I knew that I possessed the means to do anything to these awful people who had been so cruel to me. It was all so simple. If I could achieve this effect with a banana, just think what I could do if I really put my mind to it.

The woman turned and walked away from me. I wouldn't have been surprised if she'd wet herself, the way she was. She was probably going to find Gavin and give him a hug and a cuddle to keep him safe.

I refer to this little incident in my mind as the banana incident, for obvious reasons, and I may bring it up again, later.

It changed everything. Again.

Word gets around quickly in Crow's Nymet, and over the next few days it was obvious that the story had been widely circulated. I wondered if it had become embellished in the telling. After all, it's not much of a big deal. This weirdo gets a banana out of his pocket, points it at me and says bang, you're dead isn't really going to cut it in these days of hardcore internet violence. Maybe it morphed into that psycho came up to me, told me he knew where I lived and that he'd come and slit all our throats as we lay sleeping in our beds.

It's a thought. I do know where they live.

The change that I'm trying to tell you about was this. Up until the moment when I saw that woman's face change, all my extracurricular activities had been pretty inconsequential. Moving things, adjusting things, changing things, all a bit tame and only intended to unsettle. And I couldn't go too far. I didn't want word getting round. I didn't want someone in the pub to say, well this funny thing happened to me, and then someone else say, me too, and another, and another. I was hoping they'd keep it to themselves and just be frightened on their own. And like I say, I could only speculate on the effect it was having on them. I didn't know for sure. I never saw it.

Whereas, I'd just seen with my own eyes the effect I might have on people if I chose. It gave me power over their lives. I felt great again. I felt strong. I could do anything I wanted to these creeps.

I felt things were going to escalate.

I really began to hate the banana woman. The things she had called me. I had bad thoughts. Thoughts that would keep me awake at night. I've said before; too much thinking is not good for me.

I put them away in the back of my mind, at least the more extreme ones. I don't want to go to prison. I couldn't survive in prison.

But I did make a plan, and it turned out to be a very successful one.

The banana woman's husband, the one with the pick-up, was a bellringer. I'll call him Ted because that's his name. Bells are part of the country idyll here in Devon. We ring them differently to everywhere else in the country. Nearly all churches have six or eight working bells. It's nowhere near as popular as it was, but many villages can muster a quorum of ringers on a Sunday morning or for a special celebration. If you go into any church tower around here, the wall is filled with dusty and faded framed certificates of notable peals rung and competitions won in times past. Team photos of long dead ringers look down on the ropes, hung out of reach of casual visitors and inquisitive youngsters.

I need to explain to you briefly how bellringing works, so you'll understand what happened to Ted. Six or eight people stand around in a circle and coil the loose rope into one hand, and then grasp the sally – that's the thick furry bit with the candy stripe pattern – with both hands. On a signal from the caller, everyone starts pulling. Now, the rope disappears through a little hole in the ceiling, you know, the hole that people are dragged through when they don't let go the rope in time, and in the belfry the rope is wound round the edge of a big wooden wheel that is attached to the axle of the bell. The idea is that when the rope is pulled, the wheel goes round. The harder you pull it, the higher the bell is lifted on its rotation, back and forth. When the bell gets to the top of the cycle, a 'stay' prevents it going any further, and it can be rested at this top position.

The objective is for all the bells to be rung in sequence. If the ringers are good, this can happen from the word go until the bells are going full swing. It's at this point that the caller starts calling changes, and this is the clever bit. He or she will call two bells by number and they will simply change order by one slowing down and the other speeding up a fraction. It makes for a very pleasing tune, unless you're a second home owner trying to get to sleep on a Sunday morning.

Ted is a big bloke, and his bell was the tenor, the heaviest bell. It takes a bit of effort and muscle to get this one up. I knew the ringers were having a practice session on the morning before a wedding in St Rumon's. It was a big wedding. The daughter of the churchy people at the Old Rectory was marrying a lad from up country and the bells would be a big part of their staged exit from the church doors for the usual prolonged photo session. Ted was a good friend of the father, so I expect he was looking forward to a good drinking session later, and I'm sure he was proud to be part of the peal of bells to mark the occasion.

The belfry is my domain. I own it. I know all the nooks and crannies and can climb around the mechanisms in quite an agile manner for a sixty-two year old. I was up there one day in the dim light looking at the bell wheels when it struck me that there was an opportunity for some mischief here. I tucked the idea away in the lower reaches of my brain until the emotional turmoil of the banana incident released it in a most demanding way.

And so it was, the night before the wedding I let myself into the church as usual and climbed the ladder to the belfry

296

in darkness. I had brought a wooden mallet with me. That's all it took. The stays in St Rumon's are made of thick staves of ash of about four by three-inch section. Ash is a strong but springy wood, and is used so that if the ringer is a little overenthusiastic the stay will not break, but will bounce back unharmed. An inexperienced ringer could manage to break the whole thing – that's the point – the stay will break and can be easily replaced without doing any further damage to the bell or headstock, but an accomplished ringer like Ted would never find himself in this position. He would be able to feel his way through the pull of the rope so that he could gently nudge the slider with the stay that would just take the bell over top-dead-centre to rest.

My job that night was to adjust the height of the stay so that rather than nudging the slider it would just miss it altogether. Most stays are clamped into a socket somehow, normally with a couple of bolts, but amazingly, the tenor stay in St Rumon's was just tapered for a tight fit. It took a bit of fiddling around with a tape measure, but only about ten seconds to tap the stay a further inch into its metal socket. I rubbed a bit of dirt over the top afterwards. I knew that if things worked out the way I hoped, there would be an inquiry of some sort and the bell captain and his team would be puzzling for an explanation and would be looking for signs of tampering. Best of luck to them. I was confident they wouldn't be able to trace it back to me, even if they managed to work it out. It would really bug them.

I wish I could have been there the next morning when the ringers assembled for the practice. I watched them all troop down the cobbled path through the churchyard. Cocky buggers. Carefree and laughing and joking. I heard them start to ring the bells up. I was trembling, virtually beside myself with anticipation, like a naughty schoolboy.

I've had to rely on accounts that I've picked up from snatched conversations that I've overheard to put together the way it all happened next.

I could hear the ringers were well into the first peal. Evidently, someone missed a change and the caller called to set the bells in. In other words, everyone was to set their bell in the upright position so that they could start again. Now, Ted would be just looking to rest the tenor gently on the stay as he always did. He wouldn't have been expecting what happened next. If he had been, he most certainly wouldn't have had the loop at the end of the rope wrapped around his wrist. Stupid wanker. It's a fundamental error but one that confident ringers are happy to make. It served him right, really. He deserved what he got.

The thing is, as he wasn't expecting anything, he wouldn't have been bracing himself. He probably didn't realise something was amiss until the bell was half way round and the rope was suddenly snatched from his grasp. The way I heard it, his shoulder came clean out of its socket. He was lifted off the ground, and in an immaculately choreographed manoeuvre managed to unhook a certificate from a twenties peal competition from the wall with one foot, and kick the two front teeth out of the caller's open mouth with the other. The certificate flew across the room and shattered into a thousand pieces, one of which lodged itself into the ankle of another ringer. There was much blood and crying and tearing of hair, especially as the caller was the bride's sister. I bet they put her behind someone tall in the wedding photos.

How I laughed. I wish I could have been there.

I had so much fun with the bellringers that I was getting a bit of a taste for it, and that was how I met up with Pinky. Pinky, however, was in a league of his own when it came to terror.

twenty five

I say met. I've never actually met Pinky in the conventional sense, as far as I know.

It was only a week or two after Ted's adventure with his tenor. I was still on something of a high and was wondering what I might try next, when another bizarre incident came along, totally out of the blue which would have a profound effect on everything. Again. My life seems to work like that; have you noticed? Why is it?

I was at the market in South Molton on Thursday morning as usual. It was always an early start as the bus travelled through half a dozen villages before eventually arriving at the solitary lay-by in the centre of town that sufficed as a rather unlikely bus station. I'd got into the habit of finding something for elevenses to see me through until lunchtime. The cheese stall sells the most delicious scotch eggs and I had invested in one of these for the purpose. The yolk is sometimes a little runny, which you don't often find in scotch eggs and I didn't like at first. Runny yolk can be a little problematic for me because if I dribble some on to my beard, sometimes I don't realise it's there and it must make me look a bit wild. A bit Mr Twittish.

Anyway, I was sitting on the island outside the market hall on one of those metal benches that are made back-to-back, so you're looking outwards on both sides. It's a busy spot. There are always lots of lazy drivers who can't be bothered to walk from the car park who are looking for a slot on the side of the road and there are shoppers walking between the bank and the High Street to the market. I was there carefully eating my scotch egg out of its brown bag, concentrating on containing the aforementioned runny yolk, when I became aware that the person who was in the seat behind me was leaning backwards and had the back of his head uncomfortably close to mine. I couldn't see him but could sense him there and I was aware of his body heat next to me and I could smell some sort of eau-de-cologne on his collar.

He whispered in my ear in a gravelly voice that I shouldn't look round.

Now, I have always prided myself on my ability to be unfazed by sudden unexpected changes of circumstances. I've hinted at this, I think. Once, a long time ago when I was a young man, this guy pulled a gun on me while I was pissing in an underground public lavatory in Nottingham city centre. I could see in the mirror that he was wearing a battered bomber jacket but had no shirt on underneath. His torso was bronzed, dirty rather than sunburnt and he looked as if he'd been sleeping on the streets for a few days.

What would you do? Well, for a start, things are probably a bit different now to the way they were forty years ago. Nottingham had not yet received the dubious accolade of gun crime epicentre of the UK, so the concept of carrying small arms was unfamiliar to most ordinary folk. Nowadays, you might react a little impetuously, a bit panicky, perhaps. What did I do? I turned to him expressionless and emotionless and looked him in the eye. I continued pissing until I was done, trying not to piss on his feet in case it upset him, then I zipped up my flies, turned around and left. Just that, and the guy stood there looking vacant.

It was probably a toy gun, anyhow.

In the same manner, I rather nonchalantly carried on eating my scotch egg as if this sort of thing happened every time I came into South Molton. Some few seconds passed then he added that he knew who I was.

I could sense that this was now getting more serious, so when he further revealed that he also knew where I lived, I knew it wasn't going to go away. That's the phrase that always ups the ante. I know where you live. Still, so far, he had said nothing that any fruitcake off the street couldn't have said.

There was what's best described as a pregnant pause. Thus far, I hadn't responded in any way.

'I know you've got money'.

Another pause, but I suspected now that he could have been doing some due diligence on me, and I was becoming alarmed. No one knew about the money.

'... and you have no friends'.

He was on the button with that revelation, too.

I'm still eating the scotch egg, but there's not much left. Despite my apprehension, I decided that I still needed to play this coolly, so rather like in the underground lavatory in Nottingham all those years ago, I just said nothing. I didn't turn and look him in the eye, though. I did think that might prove to be unwise.

'I think I may be able to be of some help to you'.

'I can do almost anything that you want me to'.

I must confess, all sorts of things go instantly through my mind, all of which I don't want to share with you. What sort of things did he have in mind?

'I could even do things for you that you don't yet know you would like me to'.

This all comes over as a bit surreal, doesn't it? It's not the sort of thing that happens in South Molton town centre. A collision between two mobility scooters is about the most exciting thing I've witnessed here in twenty years. Perhaps this sort of thing goes on all the time and I've been blissfully unaware of it.

Doubtful.

So, I'm sat there wondering how to respond. This guy could still be a nutter, and a dangerous nutter at that. Should I just walk away? That would have been the sensible thing to do, but my mind is beginning to spin this over. There are perhaps one or two jobs that have been on my list for a while, somewhere near the bottom where they're likely to languish. He knows I'm interested.

'Think about it, and I'll see you here next week, same time, same place. It would be much better for us both if you never see my face'.

I know, I know. You're thinking all this is too ridiculous to be true. There's no place for cloak and dagger stuff of this sort in this story, but I swear to you that this was how it all started with Pinky. It was none of my doing. He approached me first.

I had absolutely no idea who he was. I don't know why I call him Pinky. That just sort of came to me. It seemed right. Who was this guy?

He disappeared from behind me before I knew he'd moved. I didn't look over my shoulder. There were lots of people milling about anyway, and I didn't even know what he was wearing. His voice suggested he was in his late forties, I would say. I didn't pick up an accent. Did I really want to know who he was?

I had a week to think all this over. I was still coasting from the bellringing incident. I had the power. I could frighten people very easily. I could make them pay. Did I need any help?

My biggest worry was that I didn't want to get caught. That would have been unthinkable. I wouldn't be able to bear the shame. I've got used to people pointing their fingers at me, but they know nothing. I don't mind them pointing fingers, and I know they talk about me all the time, but I wouldn't like to be made to answer publicly for my actions.

So, of course, over the next week, I thought a lot about Pinky's proposal. My mind went into overdrive, and I had to try and calm things down. I spent the next three or four nights out, watching and thinking.

It was with an air of self-suppressed anticipation that I travelled to South Molton the next Thursday. For a couple of hours I wandered round the market, but I couldn't concentrate on my shopping. Usually I buy some fruit and veg from the grocer and pick up the bag just before the bus is due to leave, but I couldn't stop analysing every man I saw and wondering if it was him, and whether I was doing the right thing.

Of course, I went and sat on the bench at the allotted time. I didn't bother with the scotch egg this week. I wasn't hungry for a start and I felt, curiously, that eating while we were conducting our tryst would put me at a disadvantage. Before I knew it, there was a presence behind me. For a moment, I thought it was him, but it turned out to be two fat women vaping. I panicked a bit. Would this frighten him off? Would he even come?

How do you get two gossiping, self-obsessed women to get up off a seat? Well, imaginatively, I farted rather loudly. I have to admit, it smelt very bad. They could have been in no doubt about its existence or its origin. Then I started singing. They moved. One of them muttered something.

So I'm sat there, arms crossed, waiting, waiting. I'm beginning to think I've been stood up. A good quarter hour passes and I'm starting to feel a bit of a chump. How was I taken in by this charade? Why have I wasted a week of my time, preoccupied with this game, this scam? Who is this bastard who's been stringing me along, playing me for a fool?

I was very dejected. I don't like being let down. I don't like changes of plan and I don't like not being in control. I don't cope very well with lies, either.

I stood up and looked around. I wondered what to do. I felt stupid. I was stupid. I have always been stupid. There was a big ass's head where mine should have been. I ran my hand through my beard, as I do when I'm feeling stupid, and there it was. It was just a small, rolled up piece of paper. I knew it was from him. How did he do that? How could he have done that without me noticing? I sat down. I thought back over the last twenty minutes. Nothing. No, nothing.

This morning had been a bit of a roller-coaster emotion-wise. Up and down. Up.

I unrolled the paper, and this is more or less what it said.

I can do anything you ask of me. I work alone, but I have resources. I will be your friend. I would like you to pay me a monthly retainer for my services. If I do something that delights you, you may reflect this in an additional consideration if you wish. Yes, it was those exact words. Retainer and additional consideration; I read the note many times. He didn't tell me how much he wanted. It went on to tell me where I should put the money. There was an old tobacco tin in a crevice of the churchyard wall on my side, about eighty yards down the garden from my back door. I would recognise the spot because there was a lilac rooted in the wall there, the only one. When I had put the money in the tin and hidden it in its hole, I was to put a broken clay tile that I would find there in the grass, on top of the wall so it could be seen. Pinky would replace the tile when the money was taken. Should I have any 'errands' for him, I was to include these with the money. There weren't any instructions on how Pinky was to get messages back to me, but I guessed that if he could plant a note in my beard without me noticing, then he could probably find some way of letting me know. If the tile reappeared on the wall, I figured there would be something there for me.

You're thinking that all this stuff is a bit unlikely, aren't you? You're just a little uneasy that I might be stringing you along with a fantasy. Or that I'm just plain lying to you. Well, all I can say is, it's up to you what you think. And I can tell you that if you think the Pinky bit is unlikely, then you'd better brace yourself for what's to come. There's some really weird stuff on the way.

On the other hand, the bit about the gun was lies. I just thought it looked good when I wrote it down and it added dramatic effect. So now you've really no idea what to believe, have you?

I mulled over this new opportunity for some time. It did seem to represent something of a natural progression in the way my life was suddenly panning out. There'd been lots of ups and downs, but suddenly, I did feel my life was back in the ascendancy. I felt as if I was in control of things again. I felt like I could do anything I wanted to do.

But there were some jobs on my wish list where a little bit of assistance would come in handy.

Money would be no problem, though I would perhaps need to test Pinky's penchant for US dollars, as I had rather a lot of these. I hoped he wouldn't think it was cheeky. Should I give him a task to prove himself, or should I just wait and see what he came up with on his own? I thought, the latter. There would be more suspense

I left it a couple of days; I didn't want to appear too keen. I found the tin easily enough. It was all there as Pinky had said it would be. I put two $500 bills in the tin and tucked it in the hole in the wall, then put the broken tile on top, as instructed. It felt a bit like putting dubious tokens in a charity box, but I imagined that a thousand dollars would probably satisfy him, at least in the beginning. As long as he had a way of laundering them, I supposed. Would that test his 'resources'?

Then I waited. I thought a lot about Pinky. Presumably, I thought, Pinky knows that I like to wander around at night. He'll have been watching me while I was watching others. He'll have been there in the background, on the darkest of nights. Now I knew this, I knew things would never quite be the same. Every time I heard a twig snap that I couldn't identify, I was going to think it was him. Every shadow that looked in the wrong place. As long as he was still on my side, that was no problem. I just had this very uneasy feeling that if I ever crossed him that things would turn nasty very quickly, and after what he did to Mrs Gogwell's cat, I must confess I did occasionally have some misgivings about the whole idea of Pinky.

I really hated Mrs Gogwell. How did Pinky know that? Mrs Gogwell resented me and my family right from the start and went out of her way to let us know. It upset Georgia so much it put her off the idea of coming down here at all as a family. In fact, now I come to think of it, Mrs Gogwell's reaction to us as neighbours was instrumental in driving us apart. It was all Mrs Gogwell's fault. Well, I could be exaggerating. She was probably a very nice old lady.

She had an elderly black cat by the name of George, of which she was extremely fond. It was overweight and its shaggy coat made it look very scruffy, almost feral. I didn't particularly mind it, though I'm not much of a cat person. I like animals. It came in the house sometimes and would make itself at home for a couple of hours in front of the fire. Rosie didn't mind it, and neither did Frank. I liked to see them all there; they looked like they all belonged. I wouldn't have dreamed of hurting it. I think all animals deserve respect for their welfare. Unfortunately for George, it became obvious that Pinky didn't share the same philosophy.

I don't know how he managed it, but somehow he had wound a wire tightly around the cat's neck, not enough to kill it, but sufficient to stop it screaming, and then he had tied the wire to the rear bumper of Mrs Gogwell's VW Polo. She had a regular session at the Christian Aid charity shop in Chulmleigh on a Wednesday morning. She worked to save heathens from 11 o clock until 1pm and then came home and polished her halo. The car was parked in her drive, half in and half out of a tumbledown timber and tin carport. She didn't notice the cat, which Pinky had kicked underneath the back end of the vehicle. The first to notice it was Mrs Oliver and Mrs Keen who were chatting at the post box by the Druid's as Mrs Gogwell drove past and up to the junction with the main road. She is a very safe driver, rarely venturing above thirty miles an hour no matter what the circumstances, and she's very cautious around corners. She never reverses for anyone (though if she had, she might have discovered her unfortunate George a little earlier and ended its suffering sooner by running over it).

By the time the two women at the post box had taken in the scene and realised what was happening, Mrs Gogwell had turned the corner and was out of sight. There wasn't much they could do. When they later relayed the story to appalled friends (I'm speculating), they described how the cat's eyes had been popping from its head, a look of abject terror and incomprehension on its face. Well, maybe. Mrs Gogwell had reached the beacon on the hill just outside Chulmleigh before the first car caught up with her and was following her slow progress. The driver must have wondered what on Earth this was being dragged along the lane. When he eventually realised, he started flashing his lights and waving and gesticulating. Unfortunately, Mrs Gogwell never looked in her mirror, and even if she had done, she'd have taken little notice, the flashing of lights being a staple of her country drives. It wasn't until she slowed down for a speed ramp outside the school where the road widened out, that the other driver was able to overtake her and prevent her from going any further. She was most indignant. She was used to people offering their thoughts on how her driving might be improved, but she had never been the victim of a road rage incident before. At least, not any incident of which she had been aware.

I understand that initially there was a bit of a fracas, and then lots of wailing and gnashing of teeth. The whole debacle was inflamed because just at that moment, a crocodile of year three children was passing by on their way to the gym. It's probably a scene that will stay with them forever. The cat was somehow still alive. Most of its fur had come away and was hanging loose, and the flesh was red raw and gritty, and some organs were exposed. Legs were broken. And still those accusing, uncomprehending eyes (I made that bit up; I wasn't there, but I'd like to think that that's what was waiting for Mrs Gogwell when she stepped out of her car to see what all the fuss was about). The cat was soon dead. I don't think she ever drove the car again, which was certainly a result for all the other road users around here. Despite being the unpleasant woman that she was, she had many friends and neighbours who rallied round and supported her. They helped her arrange a little funeral in her back garden the next day and someone made a simple wooden cross with the words RIP George written on it and planted it on the mound of earth as a headstone with a little posy of flowers in a jam jar. How very English.

She was never the same. You might be thinking that Pinky had made an impression with his first mission, and indeed I was in great admiration. However, he was not done. He had saved his piece de resistance for further gratification.

It was about a week later, and I think it was probably me who would have noticed it first as I spend a lot of time in the churchyard, and it wasn't particularly easy to see. There are, of course, many gravestones of all sorts in the churchyard. It's a big plot. Mostly, they are slate stones standing at precarious angles, and newer marble ones with fancy inscriptions and naff engraving reflecting the predisposition of the occupant, or the occupant's benefactor.

Around the back on the North side are the poorer, older graves but there are one or two family mausoleum-type edifices too. I may have told you that normally the richer families would have pride of place outside the porch or at least somewhere on the South side so that the peasants could admire and revere and remember them on their way to services. There must have been something not quite right with the ones that got shoved around the back.

Not many people bother to venture here. It's dark and dank with the overhanging branches of the ash trees in my garden and there are no new graves. You might possibly walk through it if you were throwing spent flowers on the compost heap, but there are other routes you'd prefer to take. It has a neglected air about it.

I was wandering around, communing with nature as I do. There were still primroses out and bluebells and red campion were making headway in the long grass. One of these ugly mausoleums has a sort of stone spire about twelve feet high ending in an iron cross at the top. There are railings all around it, and there's been some subsidence that has caused the flagstones to split and list at uneasy angles and there are cracks in the side of the sarcophagus. It doesn't look right in this pretty churchyard. This would never have been a particularly uplifting place to lay your mortal bones for eternity, but now it was positively squalid. It looked out of place.

But there it was, of course. You've probably guessed already. Pinky had only gone and dug up the bloody cat and stuck it on the pointy end of the cross. It didn't look much like a cat by then, but I knew what it was straight away. I wasn't repelled by it, but as soon as I saw it, I was a little nervous. After the cat's impromptu excursion to Chulmleigh, there were, of course, mutterings and shouting. Something like that isn't easily forgotten, especially by the ones who were there. No culprit could be found, but obviously someone was responsible. Unfortunately, there aren't many ne'er-do-wells or teenage belligerents at large in Crow's Nymet to blame for things like this. It's a nice place. I'm sure the finger was pointed mostly in my direction. I was the ideal scapegoat, after all. No one said anything to my face, but they were all thinking it, and this put a bit of a downer on the whole thing for me. What was the point in getting someone to do your dirty work for you if you ultimately got the blame for it anyway? And now this. I couldn't see how this could go any other way than straight back to me. What injustice there is in the world.

But here's the funny thing. I don't think anyone ever put two and two together and made cat. Pinky had made a good job of reconstructing George's grave, because I checked (I wonder what's actually under there in George's place?), so no one was expecting to find a missing feline corpse hanging around. I've told you; it no longer looked like a cat. It's still there to this day, two years on, and I'm sure that nobody realises that it's Mrs Gogwell's former pride and joy. I take a good look at it every time I pass, and smile to myself. I'd expected that as it decomposed it would start smelling like badger road-kill, and if you've ever smelt that you would know that the game would be up straight away. You'd be able to smell it as you were kneeling for communion at the altar. But the thing is, it didn't rot; it dried and shrivelled and became even less like a cat.

Mrs Gogwell doesn't get out much nowadays, but if she ever upsets me again, I think I might just point her in the direction of the North side of the graveyard.

twenty six

I thought I'd better let you know about Mrs Gogwell's cat, because that was Pinky's first job, and in terms of shock and awe, probably one of his best.

I'm conscious, too, that I'm starting to come over as a really callous bastard. Up to now, I've tried to make out that I've actually been a rather nice person for most of my life. Worked hard as a kid. Bit of a loner, maybe, some odd ideas here and there, but basically a sound, dependable sort of guy who became a loving family man and created some good jobs and prosperity for many along the way, before falling victim to circumstances. But even then, in my wilderness years, I was kind and considerate to animals and gave no one trouble. Now, there's suddenly a departure from all that; I've become a monster before your eyes.

Well, it happens. It happened to me, it seems. I must have been a callous bastard for a while, because that's how I remember it. It was just the way it worked out. I blame the banana woman.

Anyway, I've mentioned that I was a bit nervous about the cat episode and how it might find its way back to me. Also, I didn't feel that we would be able to keep up this sort of pace without the whole thing blowing up in my face.

So I'm going to move on six months or so, if that's alright with you, because nothing further emerged after I hinted in a little note to Pinky that he might cool it for a while. I still kept putting the thousand dollars in the tin, and I suppose there were one or two things that surfaced in the village that were probably attributable to Pinky.

One of the farmers who was at the Druid's lynching had the wheel nuts on his pick-up loosened one night while parked up outside the pub and didn't discover it until he was sliding sideways down a very steep hill on only three of his wheels, before rolling it over the bank into a field. It was okay. He walked away; walked home in fact, and didn't go back for it until he'd sobered up.

Another of the farmers had an unexpected call from the police enquiring about a rifle they had reason to believe was unregistered, but that could have come from anybody.

All pretty tedious stuff, really. I'm sorry to disappoint you if you thought we were just building up a head of steam.

Anyway, although there wasn't much overt activity during this time, I continued my nocturnal mischief and I did feel that Pinky was out there looking after my interests in his own discrete manner. I did think that on more than one occasion when I was out and about at night that he was somewhere nearby, in the shadows looking on. I never saw him, but I could feel him there.

In all that time there was no communication between us and then one day when I was putting his dollar bills in the tin, I discovered that he'd left me a present.

In the tin was the photograph.

I recognised it as the same print that Godfrey had shown me because it had a ring mark on the back and the word Uglow written in pencil in the middle of the stain.

I wondered where on Earth Pinky had found it, and why he had offered it up to me like this. Godfrey had told me he was going to burn it.

It sort of rekindled my interest. What with all the excitement of Pinky coming on board, and then the vacuum of the lull in activity, I realised that things had become a bit humdrum again. I was bored. I needed stimulating.

In fact, sitting here writing this now in the comfort of my study, it's intriguing to marvel at everything that subsequently happened in the following six months between that photo arriving and last night.

When I ponder on the nature of my life after Mrs Gogwell's cat, I realise now that it was going nowhere. It didn't seem so at the time; I was quite content and I did actually feel I was living life to the full, or as full as I wanted it to be in the sense that I had the freedom of a man in control.

Okay, so I was a strange old man, a loner, an outsider who was despised, feared, pitied, avoided, all these things, but that had never bothered me unduly, and now I accepted it would always be the case and was quite happy with it. I enjoyed the power it gave me over the peasants, and the simplicity of not having friends. I was on my own, and that was good; self-sufficient and reliant on no one. I had Pinky should I need to do something more far reaching, and I had Ralph Ralph and a seemingly bottomless supply of ready money, but I didn't need either of them. I could have managed without, just like I'd done before. I had my broadband connection, so I had easy access to the outside world when I wanted it. I had no desire to travel any further than South Molton or Chulmleigh. My needs were simple and all here. Yes, it's funny looking back at those benighted times. I really had no life at all.

Well I was telling you how Godfrey's photo gave me new direction, and I got the sense that, somehow, lots of things were coming together in my mind and aligning themselves from the chaos. Ever since I got my library card and then my Google account, I'd been dabbling in and exploring local folk tradition, and its connection with the occult and the paranormal. Ghosts and the unexplained had always whetted my curiosity and I'd taken the opportunity to indulge myself in a feast of learning and discovery during the long days and nights of my erstwhile rebirth. I thought I knew a lot.

And I certainly felt I was in the right spot for it. I've tried to illustrate for you the otherworldliness of the sort of deep countryside you get around here and how this enclave of nature in the raw hasn't changed for centuries. The ancient customs and traditions and superstitions that until just a few generations ago were what guided and ruled the lives of ordinary people who lived in this place, some of it is still just beneath the surface. It's latent. It's there and will make its thereness known if poked with a big enough stick.

I'd been greatly intrigued by Godfrey's original account of the festival, and then by Harris's take on the Rousing and was captivated with how these ancient rites had continued underground for hundreds of years and why ultimately the practice had finally died out. Now I dwelled for nights on end on Godfrey's crumpled sepia photograph that depicted the final days, possibly the very last festival. The expressions on the participants' faces. What were they trying to tell me? What did they know of these sacred and archaic rituals and their origins and their meanings? Maybe they knew nothing. Perhaps they were just happy to go along with it. If they were farmers, they would be hedging their bets, anxious to seek out any strategy to help protect their crops and harvest. Why wasn't there a shaman in the photo? The original one had been a loose and dangerous cannon. Had they done away with him altogether by the time the photo was taken? And that green man disguise? Was it fancy dress, or was some of it for real? And who was the guy who was standing looking at the camera? Was he the shaman?

I pondered, too, on why the Rousing had remained so seemingly localised, how they'd managed to contain it within the boundary of the parish That must be a bit unusual. I know many places have their own customs; Padstow with its Obby Oss and Ottery St Mary with its burning tar barrels for example, but I don't think it's quite the same beast. Traditions like these have always welcomed spectators or observers or even new participants. Crow's Nymet had different ideas. It was secret, secret, secret; even, I gathered from what Godfrey had been told, from some villagers themselves who were not party. It had always been a bit cliquey.

Could it be that they'd stumbled on something so special that they wanted to keep it only for themselves? It was hard to believe this. I didn't believe it anymore. If the special something was related to successful harvests, this wasn't reflected in the wealth or prosperity of the village which showed no variation from its neighbours. It didn't have a bigger church or grander houses. Its villagers still died of poxes in their droves. What was it that made it different?

I had discovered their sacred grove, of course. The Clump. That hadn't been difficult. I've already said, the yew tree hadn't changed much in the last hundred years, and was easily recognisable in the picture. A hundred years was just a twinkling in the eye of its long lifespan. It would still be there in another thousand years, just the same. The spring, too, that only I seemed to know about.

Godfrey had told me that the festival always started at midnight on the eve of the solstice. I was curious to see if I could get a sense of the mystery of the occasion a hundred years or more after the last gathering. Was there still a power out there in the woods waiting to be unearthed and perhaps harnessed in the age of the smart phone?

I resolved to be in that sacred grove at midnight on the eve of the winter solstice. It wasn't far away, now. Partly for my own amusement and enjoyment, but also just in case it might make a difference, I thought I would get in character as best I could. I would go as Father Christmas. Father Christmas, the old man of the woods, not Coca Cola Santa.

Although in my mind I recall this proposed re-enactment of the Rousing as a spontaneous impulse, I'm afraid I have to conclude that it was not, and that actually I'd had this purpose in mind for some while. I guess it was always going to happen, it's just that now I can't remember any build up to it. I must have always been intending to do it and I'll tell you how I know.

Some weeks before, I'd bought a Moroccan djellaba from a charity shop in South Molton. It was hanging there on the clothes rack in the men's section at the back of the store. A bit exotic for South Molton where nylon twin-sets are more the order of the day. Maybe it had been an unwanted impulse buy by a pressurised tourist on a Casablanca cruise liner stop-off. Whatever, it fitted me like a glove. It came down to my ankles and the baggy sleeves concealed my hands. The hood was magnificent and drooped over the front of my face like a monk's habit, so it was in shadow and just my beard showed below it. If it had been a proper cloak it would have opened at the front, but you can't have everything. It was dark brown with narrow cream and blue stripes down the whole length, and some spiral piping on the cuffs, which I cut off. I bought some green dye from the pharmacy and soaked it overnight in a dense solution and it came out a very dark verdigris and you could no longer see the stripes. I was quite taken with it. I hung it in the yard outside the barn to dry where no one could see it. I don't want people to see things like that. I remember thinking that this new outer garment might even prove more appropriate for my nocturnal excursions than the grand old original black Saturday coat with long sleeves, but it was obvious that it wasn't robust enough to cope with brambles and barbed wire and to keep out rain. You probably don't get that sort of thing in Morocco, especially if you're a holiday-maker on a cruise liner.

Whatever. It was always going to be my old man of the woods outfit.

When the eve of the solstice arrived, I was spiked with tension; I was alive with the thrill of the unknown. I put on some wellington boots, mandatory on a December night's route march through the woods whether you're Father Christmas or not. The figure in the photo had been carrying a sack with some mysterious contents. Not likely to be toys, I fancy. That would have been an unknown concept around here, where an orange and a sugar plum would have been considered extravagant. I did have an old hessian chicken food sack in the barn and I filled it with some rags that were lying there, then I tied the top with binder twine. I was ready.

319

The night of the twentieth was cold and starry, but not yet frosty. There was something of a northerly breeze that freshened the cheeks, but apart from that it was still and quiet in Crow's Nymet and it was very dark. It was just how I like it.

The route to Yew Magna took me through the graveyard, so I slipped out of the back door and hugged the wall down the overgrown East and North boundaries, past a platoon of lichened slate gravestones that had been hauled from their original sites as they fell and leaned roughly against the stone wall like drunken soldiers. Although the nettles and docks had died back for winter, the yellow limp grasses and bristly thistles still clung to the stone and the lumpy hillocks they created obscured the path and made the going heavy. This wasn't a problem for me. I was familiar with every part of the graveyard. I knew it better by starlight than by day. The exit at the lower end was by a stile that was built into the wall in the manner of over-long keystones laid through the body of the construction. It marked one of those footpaths that appear on some maps, but not on others, and are a bane in the lives of confused ramblers. This one isn't a public footpath so isn't accompanied by a finger post or way marker of any sort and so remains enigmatic and is no doubt a curiosity to casual visitors. They don't know where it goes. I know that no one else apart from Mrs Keen and her Labrador and occasionally Ken Bower and his two border terriers ever use it. I can see the stile from my window, and in any case, I go this way quite frequently and can spot any new activity easily. I've mentioned, I think, that I'm an excellent interpreter of tracks, both human and animal. In the winter it's easy-peasy, what with all the mud and dead plant life. Even on this dark night, I can tell that the last walker of this path was me, about four nights ago.

I almost lost my balance as I negotiated the far steps of the improvised stile. There's quite a large gap between the top and middle slabs and I'd forgotten that the djellaba didn't allow much freedom of movement of the lower legs. I had to lift the hem to my thighs. It no doubt appeared a little ignominious even though there was nobody to see it. It's not what you expect Father Christmas to do, after all, especially as apart from two thick jumpers, I wasn't wearing anything underneath.

The path crossed a rambling, wet, moor-like field. Unimproved grassland is the agricultural term. Culm measures to you, now I've told you about it. It was more rushes than grass, with squishy bits where the water courses came to the surface and mole holes scattered along the drier parts. There were no sheep grazing here tonight. It was resting. I kept to the banked hedge to avoid the worst of the waterlogged quagmire and came to the wooden five-bar gate that marked the entrance to the wood. It was quite a small one; not big enough to get a modern tractor through, but sufficient to let a horse and rider pass. It used to be a favourite track for the hunt to take, but it was years since it had been last used. Maybe the wood had changed ownership or perhaps more likely the landowner had fallen out with the hunt. It used to happen quite often because the hunters and their followers were an arrogant, self-important bunch. Like most things to do with people, whatever had caused the dispute only ever needed to happen the once and that was it for the rest of time. Nowadays, I think the huntsmen have a more enlightened attitude towards the serfdom, but it's only because they have to.

The gate was loose at the bottom hinge and so hung at an unusable angle; one of the staves had rotted and broken in two and the whole sorry structure was tied with binder twine to a mossy post. I could show you a thousand like it in the Devon countryside. It wasn't worth bothering to try to open it. I always got into the wood a little further on where there was a deer leap and the barbed wire was loose and easily scalable, but it meant that I needed to lift my skirts again. I know you must be thinking it all sounds a bit pervy and you've probably got a mental image of me with my djellaba up around my waist and my bits hanging loose, and with the rubber boots and the hood it does paint a bit of a picture, but I can tell you that although I had never, ever contemplated going commando like this before (except, I suppose in my dressing gown on the odd occasion, but that's different), I have to say that I found it a rather sensual, exotic experience. Not sexual, sensual, and not erotic, exotic. I didn't get an erection or anything.

As soon as I was inside the wood under the canopy, I felt much more at ease. I feel it's my natural habitat, somehow. No matter how bright the stars or how prominent the moon, it's always a lot darker under the trees, even in winter when they're bare. I knew the ride well and so was able to keep to the drier parts almost by a sense of feel rather than sight. The Clump is just about in the middle of the wood. It's probably only about twenty acres in area, gently sloping where I'd entered but with a steeper incline towards the South where it joins the twisting valley. I imagined Yew Magna in all its majesty, standing where it had been for millennia anticipating the coming of the solstice.

I felt electrified with anticipation. What would I unearth? I approached purposefully, but cautiously, and then I stopped suddenly in my tracks as a bolt of adrenalin coursed through my body like a shock of lightning. I could scarcely believe what I'd sensed.

I could hear voices and they were coming from The Clump.

This was something that I assuredly hadn't foreseen, and all sorts of explanations raced through my pounding brain.

Variously: that I had imagined them – no, not likely; my mind may have been on high alert, but there was no cause for hallucinations; that the voices came from living human beings – if that were the case, who the hell were they? I couldn't come up with any reasonably likely answer to that; and finally, that I was witnessing for myself the explanation for why the yew existed, that this was a paranormal phenomenon of some sort. A spectral memory? A portal to another world and if so, what world? – the world of the dead, another parallel existence of the type that I've mused and pondered over for years? A natural occurrence that couldn't be explained because we had yet to discover the laws of science that described it? Was this a sacred, otherworldly survivor from another time?

All these possibilities seared through my brain, causing much excitement to synapses and neurons and bringing on in me the sort of mental apogee I expect you get from an acid trip, a probing awareness that clears the path for an awakening of the inner reaches of the mind. I'm sorry, I'm just trying to find the words to tell you that I stood there transfixed with terror and wonder at the edge of the Clump on that black, starry night.

I literally couldn't move. My legs wouldn't work. It sounded to me like there were three separate voices. In all my years of nocturnal wandering through the woods, I'd never encountered another soul, ever. The nearest I'd come had been with farmers out lamping, and they'd been easily avoided. I think my greatest fear has always been of discovery and exposure, but no matter what the explanation behind the voices, there was no way I was

323

just going to slink away back into the night without getting to the root of this.

I fixated on the sounds. I couldn't make out anything from where I stood, but occasionally there was grunting and raised exclamations both in volume and pitch. Then I saw that there was a flickering light and I could make out dim reflections of faces. It wasn't a fire or a candle. It was the wrong colour, and anyway, I would have smelt the smoke long before I heard the voices. The three figures were sat hunched on the horizontal bough, just like the characters in that sepia photograph. My heart pulsed and pounded in my chest as if it were trying to break loose. My mind was in one of those places where you can't stay with the one big thing; it was wanting to skit all over the shop.

I just stood there, not moving an inch, not even twitching in case they detected me. This must have gone on for several minutes, while I took stock and tried to figure out what I was going to do. I was only about thirty feet away from the bough of the yew on which the figures sat, and was hidden by the holly bushes which had self-seeded on the forest floor and formed the understorey. It wasn't much cover, but on this dark night would easily suffice to hide me. I could take another five or six paces and still be concealed by the holly, but I was worried about giving myself away by making too much noise. It would only take one brittle stick snapping under my wellingtons and the game would be up. There was a carpet of dried holly leaves under my feet which in the quiet of the copse would sound like the rattle of a tambourine. I'd never encountered this situation before, where the person I was stalking was right there in front of me, out in the open and close enough almost to touch. There had been plenty of times when I'd been much closer to my 'prey', but they'd been behind a stone wall, or on the other side of a curtained window. It was unnerving, but I was pleased with myself for the brazenness of a tactic I now employed to approach to within a whisker of the nearest figure. I waited until there was sudden laughing or shouting and in that instant I took a long stride in the direction of the group. Curiously, there seemed to be much jollity and hilarity in their discourse and there was easy opportunity to make progress in this way. I had inferred that this assembly, whether mortal or supernatural, would be an occasion for seriousness, maybe even melodrama or solemnity, but not laughter, so it just tweaked a little bell of uncertainty in my mind, which made inroads into the trepidation that I had first experienced. At the final outburst of laughing, I crouched down behind the holly on one knee. I could have reached out and touched the nearest figure; I was that close. I still had the damned sack over my back; there wasn't a lot that I could do with it. What on Earth was I thinking of to bring it with me? The winter mud of the forest floor soaked into the djellaba and felt cold and earthy. A holly leaf dug painfully into my kneecap and the top of the wellingtons chafed against my shin. It wasn't very comfortable, but I felt I could quite easily stay like this for a very long time if necessary.

For a moment I thought I was going to panic as one of the figures looked up and straight at me, but it quickly became obvious that he couldn't see me in the dark. I had excellent camouflage. With the hood down over my face, I couldn't have wished for a better outfit for just disappearing into the background of that inky black copse.

I was able to see all three faces through a gap in the crown of the holly. Mostly they were all in the dark, and then every now and again the ashen-faced masks would be washed in an eerie glow. I could see that all three were young men, and that they, too, were wearing hoods. They were talking more quietly now and I had yet to make out anything of their conversation. Then there was some banter and they all threw their heads back as one and the glade was ringing with throaty laughter. I was alarmed by the suddenness of it, and it was at that moment that I realised just what I was looking at. It wasn't some paranormal phenomenon at all. It wasn't even some earnest souls performing an ancient fertility ritual in front of me. It was that fucking little shit Gavin and a couple of his cronies getting pissed and stoned on God knows what and snapchatting and instagramming and sexting on their fucking imbecilic phones. I was furious, and dismayed, and saddened, and incredulous and many more emotions that I didn't know I possessed. I was beside myself. I was truly astonished at my stupidity and naivety. I wore that big hairy ass's head on my shoulders once again, which I couldn't prise off. What a moron I had been. I'd had far too much of my own company recently and it wasn't doing me any good at all.

I'm trying to tell you that I didn't like myself much, just then, for a few moments. However, things did move on quite quickly, as I'll show you.

What to do? You can see that I was in a bit of a vulnerable predicament, crouched there just behind them spying on them like that, and dressed as I was, too; that wouldn't go down well in a court of law, or in a fist fight. I felt that I had absolutely no option but to remain hidden for as long as it took, inches away from this little gang of rogues.

I can tell you that in that brief interlude I learned more about the modern teenage attitude to life than you could pick up from a year's supply of earnest Sunday paper liberal bleeding-heart articles on parenting. Basically, they haven't got a clue, have they? The parents, the writers, the psychologists, the psychiatrists, the agony aunts and uncles. Not a clue. They have no idea what goes on. If they think they do, they are either stupid or naïve or most likely both. It's another world, and they're not invited.

It was illuminating, and in other circumstances I guess I might possibly have got off on some of this. I've always enjoyed eavesdropping as you know by now, and this was riveting stuff, some of it. I would have been quite interested to take a look at the image that the biggest lad traded for a selfie of his erect prick. It certainly elicited some laughs and raucous approval from the others.

I was tiring of this, but still nervous of discovery, and I started now to view this revelry from a more detached perspective. I got to thinking; it was a bit of a coincidence that they were here the same time as me, wasn't it? A big coincidence, really, exact same time and place. I certainly hadn't given anyone any clues that this is where I would be on this night. Why would I? I thought some more. I was here to see if this was a special place at midnight on the eve of the solstice. So – it now seemed very likely to me all of a sudden that this was why they were here too. Now, I'm sorry if I'm patronising you. You probably worked that out for yourself some pages back. I was otherwise occupied with sordid teenage adventures to get it as quickly as I should have, but once the thought took root, it got me all excited again. Just where could they have got the notion to venture out to the sacred yew grove at this specific time? It must surely have been that they'd been told about the Rousing by someone. But by whom? Well, the most likely source of

327

such knowledge that I could think of was their parents, and this is what I found suddenly electric. It would mean that even if the festival was not celebrated any longer, the essence of it had survived within the village community of Crow's Nymet purely by word of mouth from one generation to the next. That was the genuinely exciting implication of the little get-together I was now witnessing. And just as soon as I'd worked all this out for myself, I noticed that things in front of me were beginning to take on a new character.

There was less laughing.

I could just make out on my watch that it was now about five minutes to twelve. One of them was saying that as they'd taken the trouble and made the effort and the preparations to be there on this bloody freezing night that they'd better get on with it. The phones were slipped in pockets and the eldest lad took something from inside his coat. It was a plastic cola bottle, not quite empty. From what I could gather, the other boy, the one who had held back from the most lurid of the sexts and was more soft-spoken than the other two had had something to do with providing this. The liquid in the bottom of the bottle wasn't cola but was some mysterious mix of infused herbs and other suspect ingredients. Eye of bat, bile of newt, that sort of thing. It was the pressing of magic mushrooms and the lad's story of how he had picked them back in the summer and preserved the juice in a marmite jar that most interested the others. And me, too. They were asking things like was this the original recipe and was it going to work, but the lad wasn't saying much. I could visualise him looking quietly confident as they joshed him about his ingredients, but I couldn't actually see much at all because it was dark without the phones and I'd not got my night eyes back.

It was obvious from their prattle that they'd all eaten the mushrooms before and knew where they grew. Psilocybes are easy to identify because the stems go blue if you pinch them. I've taken them, too. Only once, as it happens, but I'll briefly explain to you what they do, in case you haven't had the pleasure.

I was at a beach party when I took them, in the sand dunes at a place not all that far from here actually, called Braunton Burrows. There are about three square miles of dunes and scrub and you can easily get lost. I guess I must have been in my early twenties. We were in Devon for a few days on holiday. We built a fire and humped the booze and sounds across the dunes as a little hunting party went out in search of the fungi. It was some time later that I noticed the mushrooms were doing the rounds. They were in three plastic carrier bags which were being passed to anyone interested. Now, it probably didn't help that by then I'd already doped myself up with weed and got through several pints of cider, but for some reason I'd got it into my head that these weren't the right sort of mushrooms at all. After all, I'd never been able to find one anywhere, and I had looked quite hard. Because I thought they wouldn't have any effect, and because there were quite a lot left when the last bag got to me, I determined that I would eat as many as I could get down, so whereas most of those present satisfied their requirements with about ten stems, it would seem, judging by the analysis and subsequent mythology that evolved in my social circle around the incident, that I managed to get about ninety of the slimy little buggers down my throat. Of course, if I had been sober and thinking clearly, it would have struck me that if indeed they had not been psilosybes, but some other poisonous fungi, that I might have ended up with liquified kidneys rather than a temporarily addled brain.

Anyway, I'm rambling. What the mushrooms did was this. It made it impossible for me to tell what was real and what was not real. That's a very unnerving experience.

If your senses are telling you one thing, and your brain is telling you another, then I can tell you, it's unsettling. The mushrooms cause you to hallucinate in all your senses at once, and you don't know where you are, or even if you are. My only anchor on reality was if I made a noise like a clearing of the throat, I thought that I could be reasonably confident it was actually happening in real life. It was the only control I had for a while over a very tenuous grip on reality.

That's what they do to you.

When I awoke, it was daylight and I was on my own, lying face down in the sand and barely lucky, perhaps, to be alive.

The eldest boy took the half empty bottle of supermarket gin that they'd been drinking and poured a measure into the cola bottle, then he shook it around a bit. It fizzed for a moment while they scrutinised it. There seemed to be some hesitation and nervousness. I could pick it up in the air. Then the biggest guy put the plastic bottle to his lips and took a big glug. He grimaced, but as the acknowledged leader of the group he quickly corrected his expression to one of determined sense of purpose and passed the bottle to the youth next to him. He said something inane like he preferred his gin with ice and a slice of lemon. The bottle went round the gang a couple of times in the manner of a spliff and soon it was empty and tossed away into the undergrowth. How long was it going to take, Gavin wanted to know, and was told it would be spot on midnight. I thrilled with delight. We waited. The three lads sat fidgeting awkwardly and I crouched and knelt stiffly on the wet ground. One tried to make out that he'd seen something moving in the bushes, but fortunately, he was pointing in the other direction to my hiding place, otherwise, I may have overreacted.

Then, it must have been just before midnight, there really was something in the bushes. I heard it too. It was just behind me, whatever it was. I didn't move, even to turn my head round to look. The kids were shitting themselves, and that was before they even saw me. Gavin had stood up and was looking my way, his face a mixture of terror and curiosity, but mainly terror. The night rang with expletives in a way that's only possible when coming from the mouths of three unhinged adolescent boys on drugs. You can probably imagine it. They were each trying to solicit courage and command, or at least support, from the other two, but it wasn't quite working and they were indeed a sorry shambles, the lot of them.

Then I felt something pulling on the sack on my back and it was my turn for loosened bowels. I stood bolt upright as best I could with my creaky knees and numb thighs, and I may have let out a sort of groan. At that moment, the big lad who was still sat on the branch must have got the torch on his phone working, and he shone it straight at me. In all my life, I have never seen anyone move so fast than those three kids. They set off in three different directions into the undergrowth as fast as their legs would allow. It all happened so quickly. By the time I turned around they were gone, and so was whatever had been behind me. I was left alone in that mystical yew grove and felt sure that something very important had just slipped through my fingers. It had been so close, but alas we'd screwed up and lost the moment.

There was nothing for it but to go home as quickly as I could without anyone seeing me. All of a sudden I was feeling very vulnerable again. I had no idea which way the boys had gone, or if they'd met up or made their separate ways. They did have the advantage of technology on their side, but I would think with the way they were probably feeling just then, something a little more primeval than 3G reception was top of their priorities.

I easily found the gate from the wood and jumped the wall in the same place as I'd entered, and I hugged the bank again and tried to keep as low a profile as I could against the hedges. I climbed the stile back into the churchyard, and as I manoeuvred myself swiftly through the gravestones I heard voices again and my blood chilled. They were coming down on the opposite side of the wall through a long overgrown private garden which also had an entrance into the graveyard. If they carried on down here and through the gate, they would be standing directly in front of me. Like they all seem to do.

Not good.

There was a makeshift compost heap next to the wall near where I stood. It was just chicken wire held up with wooden stakes, but it had a little earth bank piled up on two sides to disguise it. I slipped over the wire and crouched among the dead florist's chrysanthemums and soggy, holed oasis.

The talk was animated and sounded threatening and aggressive. Three figures hesitated at the gate and an argument ensued. I recognised Gavin's contralto whine. I was so close behind the bank that I could hear everything they said. They were shouting and cursing. Their fevered voices were loud and penetrated the still night air like death metal through a brick wall and I feared the commotion would be heard in the village and the bumpkins would come running, looking for a witch to hunt.

As they stood there at the gate, it soon became obvious that Gavin wasn't a willing participant in this jaunt, but was being dragged roughly by Tenor Ted, his father, with a tight grip on his wrists. My guess is that the magic mushrooms and whatever else he had ingested had just kicked in. I could see through the dead thistles on top the bank that he had a feral, vacant stare and he was gibbering, rather than contributing. He didn't want to be there.

I'm not much good with dialogue, and I don't remember the exact phraseology or words that were used, but the gist of it was this, and I can tell you that I found it a fascinating insight into the way these people thought and lived their lives.

Basically, it seems that the other guy, who I guessed must be the father of the quiet child, was being accused of putting all sorts of ideas into the head of his son, who had then managed to talk the others into this unhappy adventure. This other guy was, however, unrepentant and stood his ground aggressively. He defended his behaviour and indignantly goaded Ted for the ridicule and censure which I'd heard him spit out. He invoked their grandfather several times. Evidently, they shared the same grandfather. First cousins, then, or brothers. I think there was some sort of deep-rooted resentment and hostility between the two and this was a good excuse to give it an airing. They were both unhappy men, each with a lifetime's turmoil and sad waste on their shoulders.

I thought it was going to end in a good old-fashioned brawl but it seems that they weren't quite ready for that. Probably needed to poke a bit deeper and rawer, and besides, they had something of a common cause tonight. They both wanted Gavin to show them everything that had happened earlier. Had he been capable of coherent thought, it was probably the very last thing that Gavin would have wished to do.

The two men pushed through the gate with Gavin in tow, tugging his arm like a toddler with a tantrum.

Call me reckless, but this is what I did. I realised, of course, that as soon as they were level with the compost heap I would be discovered. I was crouching there with just the chicken wire to hide me. For the second time that night, I managed a spectacular entrance. I stood up and took three big strides up the earthy bank and took up a commanding position in front of the three figures, legs slightly apart, sack over my back, hood drooped. What power! I love it. Gavin was off like a flash, again, as the rush of adrenalin enabled him to break free of his father's grip. The other guy stood askance, mouth wide open with a look of wonder that quickly changed to uncertainty and unsettlement and then to fear. He was off, too. He wasn't hanging around to lynch the witch. Ted was the only one that wasn't having any of it. I could see it in his face, the fury and the hatred and the disgust that must have been the last message from mankind given to many a poor, wretched misfit.

First, he called me a fucking paedo, and it was at that point, while I was assessing my chances of a painless escape, that I realised my djellaba had split right down the right-hand seam from ankle to waist, probably from the barbed wire, and I was displaying rather more flesh than I would have wished. I could understand that he might have felt that my intentions, or indeed my actions, had not been honourable.

He lunged at me and managed to grab my calf with a vice-like grip, and he went to climb the bank to achieve a closer and more advantageous fighting stance.

I do believe I have lived a charmed life. Someone is looking after me.

On his first step his foot vanished into some soft earth, conveniently excavated by a considerate rat or mole or suchlike. His other foot then slid backwards on the mud on the path and he released me and fell legs spread-eagled in a heap clutching his ankle. I had heard something click like a ligament tearing or a bone breaking. Whatever had happened, it was a game changer. He was in agony in the mud. He was in a real state. Pathetic bastard. At least it had taken his mind off me.

Now, I figured that he must know that it was me in the cloak. If you didn't believe in the supernatural, then there was no other candidate but me, really, was there? I wondered if he'd be inclined to go to the police? I was under no misapprehension that if he did, I could be in very serious trouble. Paedophiles aren't particularly fashionable at the moment and the police tend to devote substantial resources to catching the creeps and then locking them away for a very long time in an unfriendly place. I thought it was unlikely, actually. I guessed that there were many aspects of his life that he'd rather not lay bare for the constables. He'd try and sort it out his own way, in the cherished tradition of little England.

Just to discourage him a little further from broadcasting his actions far and wide to anyone who would listen, this is what I did, and this was indeed reckless, I suppose. I lifted the loose flap of the djellaba out of the way and I pissed on him. He couldn't do anything. One foot was still stuck down the hole and the other one, I could now see, was pointing at a funny angle in the mud as he clutched at it. His legs were splayed apart and I pissed all over his groin, so that it looked just like he had done the pissing himself. Try explaining that to the good folk at the Druid's. It was exhilarating.

I can only think of one suitable word to describe his demeanour. Apoplectic. Yes, that's about it. He was very upset.

I just smiled at him and stepped back. He couldn't see my eyes because of the hood, but he knew they were smiling, too. I walked back through the graveyard to my kitchen door, a little brash I know, because now there could be absolutely no doubt in his mind that it was me.

So. What an evening. It hadn't turned out quite as I had expected and it had left more questions and uncertainties than it had solved mysteries. I opened a bottle of beer and went to my study and proceeded to unravel the night. This is what my post-mortem pointed to.

Firstly, the knowledge of the festival was still very much alive in the village among a select few, just like it had always been. This was exciting.

Secondly, there had definitely been something out there at midnight that was unexplained. I had come as close to it as possible without seeing it. I knew it had been there. Even so, I had to still keep an open mind about this. It doesn't have to be supernatural or paranormal. It could have been a deer, say, or an owl or something. Much more likely, it was perhaps one of the kid's mates who had got wind of the little party and was looking to give them the frights. It might even have been Pinky. All these were possible, but in my opinion unlikely. I favoured the supernatural, myself. I think between us we had raised the spectre that was the root of everything that was the reason the festival existed.

Thirdly, and best of all was this, and I'm sure you're one step ahead of me on this, too. You'll have figured it out. Now that I knew about the quiet lad's magic potion, I could easily speculate what was inside my little stoneware phial, that five-hundred year old relic of festivals past.

I was a bit nervous that a mob might still come knocking on my door in the early hours wanting blood and revenge, or that the police might rock up with their blue lights flashing, but it never happened. I guess if I'd really expected it, I would have showered and changed into something a little less controversial for the purposes of answering questions, or answering for my behaviour, but I didn't, I was too occupied by my conjectures.

It was fairly obvious that it was going to be more or less open warfare in the village from now on. Maybe I would have to have another word with Pinky.

twenty seven

Gavin's dad had broken his ankle. I saw him on crutches, smoking outside the Druid's. He wouldn't be working for a while. You can't drive a pick-up with a plaster cast on your right foot.

It was interesting to speculate how much of the story of what happened that night had percolated down to the friends of Ted and the other guy. What would they have been comfortable spreading around and were they both singing from the same hymn sheet? Were they so protective of their Rousing that it would be kept concealed in the family skeleton cupboard away from their uninvited, nescient neighbours?

It was difficult to say, because the open hostility I encountered had now become a fact of everyday life.

But as for me, well you might be thinking that I was cowed and frightened and anxious, but I wasn't. Quite the opposite, actually. I was feeling greatly empowered and oddly 'protected', somehow.

Invincible? It felt like that, yes.

I resolved that I would put it to the test sometime soon by venturing back into the Druid's and seeing what sort of reception I got there. Fuck 'em, I thought. I would need to be in the right mood to do it, all the same, and I wasn't going to take Rosie this time. I wasn't that stupid.

After the revelations of the winter solstice, I was itching to find out more about the contents of the phial. I took it down from the shelf and placed it on my desk and sat and looked at it and wondered at its origins for some silent hours. I twisted the cork stopper off and smelt it again and the almondy scent was still prominent, with maybe a hint of ammonia.

This was an action that I was going to savour. I left the phial on my desk, right in the middle on its own where I could see it from my wing backed chair. I felt I would know when the time was right to go one step further and taste the liquor.

In the meantime, following on from what I now thought of as the enchantment of that night in the woods, and it being that time of year, there arose in me an urge to widen the appeal of my Father Christmas persona. I was quite taken with my outfit and I sewed the seam back up. I learned to sew from my grandmother and I can darn a sock, should I ever see the need.

I have strong views about Christmas. Whereas I appreciate that in a liberal country such as ours everyone should be free to enjoy it in the way they wish, I do regret that so many folk have simply lost their way. Nowadays, it's all about money, of course. I know people have got to make a living and in retail if you don't make Christmas work, you're dead in the water. I know all this. The sadness is that the magic has been lost. In my opinion, that's the true meaning of Christmas, the magic. It's gone for most of us. Whether your thing is the birth of Christ, the goodwill of friends and family, the giving and receiving of presents, the eating and drinking and making merry at the very coldest, barest, darkest time of year, any of those, I would suggest to you that the magic is no longer part of it. If I was able, I would make it my life's work to restore the magic to Christmas.

And I would start with Father Christmas. There's no better way to illustrate how the festivities have been misappropriated and corrupted than to take apart the modern Santa. Big black boots with furry tops; red trousers and red jacket all with furry bits; big black belt; red bobble hat of various designs, also with furry bits; rosy cheeks; big white beard. That's about it, isn't it? About as far removed from any of the origins of the figure as you could get. Then there's the sleigh bells, the sleigh, the reindeers, Rudolph and all the others, the North Pole, elves, I could go on. What's that all about? Okay, well you say it gives a lot of people a lot of pleasure, and that's true, but what I'm simply saying is that it's lost its magic. That's all.

I felt I was in a unique position to bring a little magic to the children of Crow's Nymet. I would do my bit. I thought very hard about how I could do this. You don't need to be blatantly in someone's face to influence thoughts or beliefs or memories. A surreptitious or even subliminal message can work and can remain forever in the mind.

When I was in my infants' school, there was an occasion when we were all excitedly awaiting Father Christmas's arrival in our classroom. While all the other children's eyes were on the door where he would soon burst in, I glanced out of the window. We were sitting cross-legged on the floor and the window ledge was quite high, but for that instant I saw what I knew were the tips of a reindeer's antlers flash past in the playground. I've no idea in retrospect, now that I'm an adult and know better, just what it was. Probably just a janitor's broom handle or a blowing branch. What it really was is of no significance. What I thought it was, was Rudolph pulling Santa's sleigh through the sky and I held this as the proof of my beliefs until I was about twelve. I remember arguing the case for Father Christmas with some schoolfriends who were incredulous and rather unkind, and this is the very argument I used. I knew he existed because I had personally, with my own eyes, seen the evidence in his reindeer's antlers. The janitor had a lot to answer for. I'm just glad the tooth fairy never left such an impression.

I tried to come up with ways that I could implant some similar memories in the village children. See, I'm not all bad. I considered going abroad through the village on Christmas Eve, and trying to present myself at bedroom windows or such like, but logistically, that was much too difficult and risky. I thought of offering my services at the school Christmas party as a sort of alternative traditional Father Christmas figure, but I knew that was out of the question, and in any case, they'd already had their party back in November.

I was fresh out of ideas, but then I saw one of the churchwardens tack a laminated notice to the telegraph pole outside the lychgate that declared there would be carol singing at the church porch at five o clock on Christmas Eve, followed afterwards by mince pies and mulled wine in the nave. It was especially for the children, probably with the intention of promoting the true meaning of Christmas, as understood by the vicar, before the kids were whipped into a frenzy by network TV. I sensed an opportunity, though quite how it might pan out I wasn't sure. I would be there waiting for a chance to spread my magic.

If you're as old as I am and you venture out on Christmas Eve, you'll know that it's not like it was. When I was a boy,

Christmas Eve lunchtime was the start of the festivities for most people. Men would leave work early and make their way to the pubs, which would be heaving. After a few pints, suitably lubricated fathers and husbands would call in to toyshops or jewellers or women's apparel shops and buy the most inappropriate presents for their loved ones, and would go home and put the tree up and decorate it with the kids and trim up the living room and then become very mellow and ready to enjoy a short but well-earned break. None of that happens now. The shops and pubs and markets are empty on Christmas Eve because we're all at home looking at our screens, and in any case, the shops aren't selling Christmas anymore. They're getting ready for the post-Christmas surge. We put the tacky decorations up weeks ago and the pine needles are already in the vacuum cleaner. It's all about the anticipation and not the real thing. That's where the money's to be made.

I wanted to be the real thing. I had hunted out an old pair of green corduroy trousers and was wearing them over some sober black leather shoes and I emptied my sack a little so it wasn't so bulky to carry. This time I would be able to make a quicker, more dignified escape if needed.

I can't say I had high expectations, but I felt I had to make an effort.

Some time before the singing was scheduled to start, I crept into the church. On the left when you go in, there's an area reserved for the children to play during services, to keep them occupied while their parents do the serious stuff. It used to be used for Sunday school as well, but that was abandoned years ago through lack of interest. There were about a dozen little wooden chairs set round in a half circle and there were some toys and wooden jigsaws scattered around on the floor.

342

In a bookcase were a number of children's religious books, heavy on the lambs and angels and Christ looking serene and trustworthy. There was a large straggly Christmas tree, donated annually by a local farmer who hoped he would get his reward in Heaven, which was nicely decorated with home-made tinsel and dangly paper ornaments. It was propped up in half an oil drum at an angle that was about three degrees off the vertical. It's one of my pet hates. Nothing looks less natural than a cut tree that is planted crooked. It would never grow like that. Doesn't it annoy anyone else?

I couldn't be bothered to do anything about it. The truth is that I had already done it once, soon after they'd brought it in, but by the time a class full of enthusiastic infants had scrambled all over it with their baubles it was sadly leaning again. The roots were lodged tightly in the stones at the bottom of the drum. I wasn't going to mess around with it again. It was destined to spend all the Christmas services looking not quite right.

Just past the tree, before you get to the tower, is another small oak door in the wall. It's covered by a long mauve velvet curtain that drags on the ceramic tiles, and opens outwards onto the gravel path outside in the churchyard. It's locked internally by two huge iron bolts, top and bottom. No one uses it, of course; there's no point. I don't even know why it's there or what its original purpose was. It's only a few feet away from the front porch, after all. It is certainly ancient, so perhaps it predates the porch. The first time I managed to heave it open, it felt like decades since the iron strap hinges had moved, and generations of dead creepy crawlies fell from the space between door and jamb and sprinkled me with their earthly remains.

There was room between the door and the curtain in the thickness of the wall to completely conceal an adult, and this is where I hid to see how things unfolded. Naturally, I had sprung the bolts.

I have to say, the carol singing was very uplifting. I love carols. Silent Night is my favourite and can bring tears to my eyes, especially when sung in the German. There was quite a crowd that entered the church afterwards, and the churchwardens and churchy helpers brought with them a big urn of hot wine, carried adeptly between the leading pair and there were baskets with tea towels over them that doubtless contained the mince pies. The church cups and plates were already laid out ready on the souvenir bench by the door and this is where the carol singers congregated. There were quite a few children, of all ages. The older ones stood with their parents or sat in pews with their social media while the infants ate their mince pies and sat and played with the familiar toys in their little chairs. It made me think of Angel. It was all very convivial and I had no idea how I was going to be able to make any sort of appearance, not even to individuals that I might be able to isolate from the rest.

Then, as the adults began replenishing their cups with a second mulled wine, I noticed that a number were vanishing into the vestry with most of the older children. To those left chatting tiresomely in the nave, the vicar then made an announcement that there was to be a modern interpretation of the nativity to be given by the schoolchildren of years seven to eleven during which there would be some audience participation. Meanwhile, the infants would be receiving a special pre-Christmas visitor of their own around the Christmas tree. I couldn't believe it. Everyone filed into the vestry excitedly, leaving about eight little children sat in a half moon around the tree. They were all alone. The youngest looked to be about two and was holding hands with his sister and none of the others were older than four or five. It was just them; all the adults had gone.

Extraordinary.

Of course, I had to act quickly, and I swished back the curtain with a flourish and stepped into the centre of the little group from behind the tree. To my delight, not one of the children started crying or screaming or even looked startled. I can remember back to when Angel and Miriam were this age and Santa Claus made his entrance at the playgroup party and there was pandemonium with kids blubbing and holding on tightly to their mothers in panic. Maybe without their parents there, these kids had no reason to react.

They did look very vulnerable sat there on their own.

I hadn't rehearsed what I was going to say. I thought that if I got the chance, I would know what was right when the time came. I just stood there calmly and serenely and the kids were entranced. I told them I was the real Father Christmas of the woods and that they were special and that I would look after them and I would always be there for them and that Christmas was a very special time of year because in the darkest, coldest, scariest bit of winter magic things happened and made people's lives better, but you had to believe in the magic for it to work.

Before I'd come out, I'd picked a little posy of Christmas roses from my front garden, and I gave a single white flower to each child. As I turned around to go I said to them to remember me; I was real, and with that I stepped back out of view and disappeared behind the heavy curtain. As I pushed the old wooden door open, I just glimpsed the other Santa entering the church through the porch. I wondered what he would tell the children. Would he have a carefully chosen, tastefully wrapped present for each one in his sack and would they like their gift from Santa better than my Christmas rose? I hoped he wouldn't fill their heads with silliness and would just tell them to go to bed early and make sure they were sound asleep when he called later.

So, do you think I made a lasting impression on these village children? Do you think that in years to come, maybe in decades or at the end of their lives when they're sat under their rugs in a nursing home, dribbling, that they'll think back wistfully to that night when they briefly experienced the true magic of Christmas? I would like to think so, but then I am a bit of a romantic.

I hope the adults didn't spoil it for them. I guess they probably figured out that something had gone on while they were neglecting their offspring, what with the Christmas roses and all. That would have been difficult to explain. There were two Father Christmases, mummy; one was red and the other green.

I hung around in the graveyard for a while afterwards before going home, until they started drifting away to their cosy Christmassy cottages and no one opened the little door. No one was curious enough to follow the real Father Christmas back into the woods.

Later on, in the early hours of Christmas Day, I let myself in with the key and closed the two bolts and just sat there for a while wondering at it all.

twenty eight

It was in the first week in January when I felt the time was right. I'd been savouring and wondering for long enough and I was now in the right mood for a little experimentation. I congratulated myself on my will power.

I sat at my desk and uncorked the phial, and gently tipped it so that the thick, brown liquid just filled the little lip that had been moulded into the stoneware jar.

What was I expecting? Well, in the light of what actually did happen, and the consequences of that over the last six months, I'm afraid I can't actually remember what was going through my mind as I sat there, fixated as I was on shamans and magic spells. I guess a part of me probably suspected that it would all be a disappointment, a damp squib. Even if the recipe had been concocted five hundred years ago to achieve some specific result, the potion would most likely have lost its effectiveness after all this time. On the other hand, of course, exactly the opposite might have been true. Like an uneaten takeaway curry left in the fridge overnight, it might have matured with age and its potency boosted. And I was only just speculating on its original purpose, which I surmised to be a vehicle for raising spectres on the night of the solstice in the sacred grove. It was neither the solstice nor the sacred grove that I had chosen for this curtain raiser, so what were the chances?

I touched my little finger on the lip of the jar and a tiny globule of the sticky fluid attached itself. I looked at it. It was all so innocent, like an errant splash of soy sauce on a plastic tablecloth. If I had known that from this moment there would only ever be a before and an after to my life, would I have hesitated? If I had just washed it down the sink, what direction would my fate have then taken? I think it would have been an empty void. Rather like I now feel about the first sixty one and a half years.

It might have smelt like almonds and ammonia, but it tasted only salty on the tongue. Almost immediately, I felt something changing. I pushed the cork stopper back in the phial and scrambled to put the jar back onto the bookshelf. It was as though my heart, my whole metabolism, was slowing, and I felt weak and my muscles weren't responding properly. I just had time to kneel down on the rug in front of the stove before the rest of my body collapsed and crumpled and I fell forward in a heap. This was the first time. I realise that in your mind you're seeing some sort of Mr Hyde character grasping at his throat, tongue lolling, so I'm sorry, I don't know how to describe it any other way. It must have looked a bit like that, but not quite so hammy. I remember it like a car crash, in slow motion. I managed to protect my forehead from slamming into the slate hearth by heaving my limp arm wildly across my chest and face and then I just shut my eyes and that was it.

It's difficult to keep track of time when you're unconscious, but as all this was new to me then, and as I was feeling my way, I did subsequently note when I looked at my clock in the hall that it was only about ten minutes that I lay there. It could easily have been much longer. It could have been a lifetime, actually.

Now, I have the job of telling you what it was like, that first time. It's difficult for me, because for a start I don't know what you've ever experienced in your own life that you could relate this to. What words can I use?

If I say it was a Near Death Experience, if you know anything at all about Near Death Experiences it might make you want to put this account down now and not finish it, and that would be a real shame because we're just getting to the bits that you need to know.

When I came round and was lying there on my back on the floor looking at the rotted boards in the ceiling, this is what I thought I had just had. I was actually feeling as high as a kite. It was like I had died and then I had come back to life again, and here I was to tell the tale.

Let me give you my take on Near Death Experiences. I know quite a lot about them because as soon as I thought I'd had one, I asked good old Google to tell me all he knew.

As you might expect if you'd had time to think about it, there is quite a lot of raw material online to get your teeth into. About nine hundred million hits. It's the sort of subject matter for which search engines were designed. Although Near Death Experiences have been analysed and raked over ad nauseum by all manner of amateur enquirers; scientists, of course; medics of all sorts, especially psychiatrists; alien abduction conspiracy theorists and religious nuts of all persuasions, they remain essentially very similar in nature in lots of ways, and I can't make out whether this ought to mean you should be more likely to believe in them, or less.

This is how it goes, in almost all cases: Firstly, of course, you almost die, and probably your heart stops beating for a while. Then you have an out of body experience and you're likely able to look down upon your prone, inert physical body, rather like if you were astral projecting. You have a feeling of unconditional love and security and maybe the sense of the presence of dead relatives, sometimes a 'guardian angel' with the role of guide to the afterlife. There's usually a perception of enhanced colour or visual effects and often the concept of a light at the end of some sort of tunnel that you're approaching, where you will reach your goal which is probably acceptance by some divine figure who is waiting there for you. If you think about it, if I had asked you to use your imagination to describe to me what you thought a Near Death Experience might be like, then let's face it, you'd have probably come up with something quite similar, without any help from the internet or from me. I think most of these fruitcakes so desperately want to experience something like this that they are able to delude themselves into thinking that it has actually happened.

Because the most dispiriting thing about these online accounts is the number of contributors who claim that they have evidence or proof of their experiences, but when you delve deeper into their diatribes, no matter how thorough they appear to be, there is never any proof at all. Not a jot or a tittle. Nothing. Just like winning roulette systems. What drives them, I wonder?

So, what WAS it like for me, that very first time? I'm still not sure how I'm going to tell you. You can see, I'm procrastinating. You have to understand that over the last six months I've done this many times, and each time I return with a more profound understanding of the way it seems to work. Profound, but also cryptic and enigmatic, like I can't quite pin it down. I don't know where it's coming from, but I'm certain that when I wake up, I have a clearer awareness and appreciation of many things. It's just sort of implanted there in my brain, somehow, where before there was nothing. During that first ten minutes there was just a nothingness, but not an unpleasant nothingness, there was a sense of union and togetherness and yes, security. An impression that my whole being was at ease with the natural world. I felt I was in good hands. I felt that everything around me was on my side and was protecting me from harm. I was in a very safe place.

That's how I remember it feeling.

There were no spectres or divine figures, or indeed form of any kind. No sounds or structure. Just nothing, really, as I say, apart from a feeling that there are no words I know to describe that some meaning, some explanation was being unravelled in my brain.

That was rubbish, wasn't it? It sounds cheesy and pretentious, now I've read it back. I've been wondering for a little while how I might tell you all that I've learned from these raw experiences. I thought I would perhaps drip feed them to you between further anecdotes of my increasingly isolated and hostile village life, but I can't imagine that's going to work. It's too important. What I have to tell you will change your life, but I don't think it will sit well with the rest of the narrative. So I'm going to give you some tools, so that when I decide to tell you all I know, you'll be more prepared. I'm coming in, all guns blazing, with some Big Ideas. It may put you off, and I may lose you, and that would be a pity. You've come this far. It'll be your loss if you give up now.

Look, I've marked the top of this sheet with red pen, and I'll do the same at the end when I'm done. It's so you can easily come back any time you like and reread it, or you could skip it altogether for now if you don't feel like exercising your brain and want to get back to the story. It's up to you. There's a lot to take in.

Let's get the biggie out of the way first. There is no God.

This means there is no creator. There's going to be no one waiting for you. It also means that every religion that there is or ever was in the world is based on a fallacy. God does not exist, in any form.

This is a bold statement and you may not like it. I don't care if or why you believe in a god. If you do, then I hope you will keep reading anyway, for your sake.

The proof is, quite simply and boringly, evolution by natural selection of the fittest. I shall refer to this as Darwinian evolution, for obvious reasons (there are other kinds). Sorry if you were expecting something more sagacious. I'm not going to attempt to explain anything about Darwinian evolution to you; there are mountains of literature on the subject that you can easily find, and of course there are also lots of writers out there who dispute the facts, and some put up good and learned arguments. I am obviously aware of all this and I'm not going to waste my or your time by discussing them. What I am saying, and I know it's arrogant and provocative, is this:

Darwinian evolution explains EVERYTHING about our natural world and how every cellular thing that has ever existed got here. It DOES. It also explains, of course, why there is no God.

I understand that there are some highly educated and intelligent people in this world who appear not to agree with this simple statement, and it remains for me one of life's mysteries why this is so. Okay, I can see why some support the views that they profess to hold and there are good reasons for them to do this that have nothing to do with a quest for knowledge or understanding and everything to do with power and control and money and face-saving and sometimes, I suppose, just naïve hope. A large number of these guys will be in denial. I'm afraid that I have to conclude that if you believe in a creator that does not obey the laws of Darwinian evolution in the privacy of your own brain, then you are nowhere near as intelligent or educated as you probably think you are. Simple as that. I'm glad we got that one out of the way, as it's rather fundamental. Sorry to be so blunt, but I really don't have the time to argue about something so obvious. There are plenty more esoteric things that are much more difficult.

But by the way, if you're an atheist I've got some good news for you: although there is no god, there is an afterlife.

So if you've read this far and have an open, enquiring mind and want to go on, then there's some other pretty big stuff to follow that you'll need to concentrate on, too.

Let's take eternity next, and combine it with Heaven and Hell. This is a little trickier because there is no large body of evidence that we could produce as proof of the existence or non-existence of some eternal immortality, so I'm going to ask you to just think a bit about the concept of eternity. It's a long time.

I wonder how many people who believe in an eternal afterlife have actually ever sat down and really thought about it hard, or even discussed it with their friends? It's a subject that you sort of take for granted, isn't it? For a start, you sort of assume that it would be a Good Thing, but that's only because you've never thought seriously about it. Or possibly, you've never thought seriously about it because you want it to exist and to be a Good Thing.

I'm going to go back to my old favourite, Father Christmas, to give you a bit of an analogy. Children believe in him partly because they've been indoctrinated by their parents, their peers or the media and partly because they want to, because it's a Good Thing. Children who believe in Father Christmas have never thought deeply about it, either because they don't yet have the mental faculty, or because they don't want to, because it's a Good Thing. If they did think hard about the concept of Father Christmas, then it would quickly become obvious to them that he couldn't get round all the world's children on a single night, that he would get stuck down chimneys, that reindeer don't fly and a score of other good reasons that would tell them straight away that it just wasn't true (unless, of course, you believe in magic).

So when you start thinking hard about eternity, it turns out that it might not be a Good Thing after all. Even if you were pretty-well set up in the hereafter, what would you do with yourself every day for the rest of time? And how old would you actually be? Are you going to spend the rest of perpetuity as an old man? Or a child perhaps? Your first wife will be there, too, but then so will her second husband, so who's going to be with whom? And will she still be a cow? And if you're looking forward to having a bit of fun with seventy-two virgins and a permanent erection, what happens when they're not virgins anymore? Will they be replaced with new ones? And all the shagging's going to become a bit tiresome eventually, anyway. Will there be other things to do? For the rest of time?

And what if you'd wasted your life on Earth being devoutly and piously religious instead of having a good time, in anticipation that Heaven was going to be much better, but it actually isn't? That would be a bit of a downer. But not so much, I suppose, as if you'd been a Bad Hombre and you ended up in the other place.

You could spend a whole week coming up with other shortcomings of eternity, but no one does because they're afraid of what they might realise.

What I'm trying to say is this. What happens when you die is such a Big Thing, that it's just incomprehensible to me that the vast majority of people HAVE JUST NOT THOUGHT IT THROUGH.

You might say, well, the thing is we don't really know what happens and that's the best thing about it, but my point is that most of the people who haven't thought about it ARE the people that think they know.

By the way, I do know what happens when you die, and I'm going to tell you at some point. And after what happened last night, I have the proof to show you, as well.

Let's move on from Eternity to infinity. It's not the same thing. Most people think they know what infinity is, but they don't. It is, actually, a scientific and mathematical construct that can be approached in a very structured and thorough manner, but I'm not talking about that. I'm referring to the popular understanding of the concept of infinity.

Most people could envisage the boundary between the universe and the nothingness that lies beyond. Stars are extremely few and far between in deep space, anyway, with lots of nothingness in between, but this border occurs when the stars finally run out and there are no more. That's got nothing to do with infinity.

Let me try and give you an example of just how big infinity is. I'm afraid it's become a bit of a cliché, but you'll have to bear with me. I've changed it slightly. If you're sat reading this wearing a pair of socks on your feet, imagine this. If the universe is infinite, then there is another place somewhere that is exactly the same in every respect as the world you inhabit, apart from in this place you are wearing not two, but only one sock. Everything else is the same. Not very likely, is it? Not as likely, I would say, as ten to the power of all the atoms in the known universe to one against, which is very unlikely, though not particularly mathematical. What's more, there would also be a world where the Nazis won the war (natch), and another where the sea is orange and yet another where gravity pulls the other way. In fact, and to spoil the image slightly I think, if the universe is infinite, then there must be an infinite number of worlds where you are sat there with just one sock on but everything else remains the same, and an infinite number with two socks, and triumphant Nazis etc.

What I'm trying to say is, if you believe in infinity, then our existence on this tiny planet is a bit inconsequential and your life doesn't matter much at all in the scale of things.

Right, we're done with three Big Things, and there are three more coming up. I want you to think about them all, because when I start telling you what I know, you'll need to refer to them if you want to understand.

The next three are: Other dimensions; sixth (and more) senses; and parallel universes. They are all linked together in some way, and I'm afraid that they all sound a bit science fiction, but that's because I can't think of different names for them.

First up, other dimensions. We don't have to get too technical or mathematical, here, although we could if we wanted to. We live in a physical world of three dimensions that we all understand because we have always lived in this world and are familiar with it, and we have evolved in it. Nothing is more natural to us than thinking in and experiencing these three dimensions. You might think that time is the fourth dimension, but it isn't really; it's a red herring, and it just complicates things, so we'll forget about it (Sorry, Einstein). Anyway, it's just relative.

There may be other dimensions out there, but if there were, or are, we wouldn't necessarily know anything about them.

As an example, let's take a snail sliming along a piece of flexible vinyl. This snail happens to be a bit flat for a gastropod, and for all intents and purposes, lives its life in only two dimensions. The vinyl has no hills or valleys and the snail cannot fly or jump or in any other way enter or interact with the third dimension. He is unaware of its existence, in fact. Let's say he is there with his girlfriend, minding his own business, but he has a task, and that task is to find some lettuce and to bring it back so that they can both have lunch. He slimes in a straight line and finds the lettuce, but then a godlike figure bends the vinyl over in such a way that the snail is almost touching his girlfriend. They are virtually shell to shell, but are totally unaware of each other because the small distance between them is in the third dimension of which they have no knowledge. There's nothing for it, he slimes all the way back to where he started, oblivious to how close he had been to his loved one. He could have popped the leaves into her mouth. He was so close, and yet he was not close at all. And in the meantime, his lettuce has wilted.

I'm simply suggesting there could be other dimensions of which we know nothing, but it or they would exist all the same in some embodiment, and would likely be a tad tricky to get our heads round.

That was a bit clumsy, and it is a difficult concept to grasp, mainly because by definition we have no idea what those other dimensions could be like. All I'm asking you to do at this stage is to be open to the possibility of there being other spaces around which our lives revolve but about which we have no knowledge or experience.

That brings me on to sixth and more senses. Imagine the Earth about four billion years ago, maybe about half a billion after it formed and settled down as a proper planet, but before there was any living thing on it. What's the point of it? Apart from in an astronomical sense, it might not be there at all. An alien a thousand light years away might possibly be looking at it through his telescope, but apart from that, no one or nothing would know. It only had meaning when the very first single cell creatures arrived and started interacting with it, and once that miracle happened, Darwinian evolution simply did the rest, and here we are. We human beings have ended up with five senses that work reasonably well, and are, of course, by default absolutely ideally suited to our survival. It's why there are seven billion of us. We can't see as well as an owl; smell as well as a dog; hear as well as a bat; taste as well as a catfish or feel as well as a spider, but we can do all these things sufficiently adeptly to survive and thrive as a race. Some species have additional senses that have evolved to exploit their environment, such as sonar in bats and porpoises or magnetic homing instincts in birds and bees. Senses are very interesting and very clever. Quite often they work together to enhance their effectiveness. If you give a malt whisky connoisseur a blind tasting with a clothes-peg over his nose, he can't tell you whether it's whisky or brandy he's drinking, let alone if it's an Islay or a Speyside. Try it; it's fun. He needs his nose to tell the difference.

Usually, if you can't or have never been able to use a sense, you have absolutely no idea of its existence. If you were born with no ears and associated bits and pieces, then you would have no conception of sound, in all its subtle, or not so subtle variants (you might be curious to feel a shockwave from a bomb on your skin or your internal organs, for example, but you wouldn't associate it with noise). You would have no idea that acoustic waves travelling in air could enable you to interact in any way with your surroundings. Let's face it, even when you know and understand it, it seems unlikely, doesn't it? Same with eyes and reflected light waves. And smell, come to that. All our senses are gobsmackingly ingenious and so, so unlikely.

When someone talks of a 'sixth sense', what they're often thinking about is telepathy or some way of communicating with the mind over long distances. Well, I'm pretty sure that no living thing has developed a scientifically, consistently provable system for doing this – but it could easily have happened. If Darwinian evolution is capable of coming up with something as complex as an eye or a liver, then it would have had no problem with radio frequency transmitters and receivers. It just never happened, but it could have done. That's a bit of a pity, really; it would have saved having to invent the phone.

It's an interesting little subject to ponder over when you've got the odd hour to spare. It tickles the curiosity, and has plenty of latitude for an active imagination.

Finally, on to parallel universes. These are much loved by science fiction writers because they have so much potential. If you can cast your mind back to our analysis of infinity, then if other worlds like this exist, and they have some sort of convenient wormhole connecting them, then you could just flit between them causing havoc and interesting though overworked story lines. That's not what I'm meaning by parallel universes. I shouldn't have used the word universe at all. Parallel lives is better.

There are examples of parallel lives everywhere. I've illustrated some already; you might have picked them up. It's when people occupy the same space and apparently do the same things and evidently experience the same stimuli but in actual fact are living totally unconnected existences.

The little girl who comes to school with bruises on her arms and legs may be sitting in the same classroom, being taught by the same teacher as the child who is met at the gate by a loving, caring parent, but she inhabits a totally different world. She has different experiences. She lives a different life, yet seemingly is as much part of the same human condition as everyone else.

The car you overtake on the motorway that is all misted up and has a rear passenger who is drooling, propped up against the window like a zombie may be travelling along the same road as you, in this case in parallel lanes (a good analogy, then), but will ultimately arrive at a destination that is in no way the same as yours, because the occupants of the car, though occupying the same road as you, live a different life altogether.

These are trite, and I'm sure you can think of many examples; they're all over. I think about this concept very often.

For our purposes, I'm particularly interested in three different kinds of parallel life, which I shall call the natural world, the supernatural world and the soul dimension. I'm going to come to the latter one in more detail when I start telling you what I know and by then I'm rather hoping I'll have come up with a better name for it.

A parallel life in the natural world is when humans live in very close proximity to the natural world, but are totally oblivious to its existence. Ditto, the supernatural. More on that later, too.

I might have annoyed you, but I hope I've got your intellectual juices flowing. We've touched on some big concepts that you'll need to be able to handle to understand what I'm going to tell you.

This is just a taster to whet your appetite.

Every cell that ever existed in the history of the world had or has something attached or linked to it that does not exist in the three physical dimensions, but in another dimension that is not governed by laws of science that are known to us. I shall call this something a soul because I'm feeling a bit provocative. Most people think of the soul as that part of you that remains when your physical body dies, but they normally associate it with some religious belief, and I've already told you, there is no god. It IS the bit of you that survives the death of your body, but it's got nothing to do with god.

From the very beginning, souls were an integral part of the evolutionary process and their continued existence and development were a vital part of the survival and selection of the fittest, though there was no direct or linear interaction between the soul's dimension (or dimensions) and the physical world. In order to survive and evolve, a living thing needed both healthy cells AND a healthy soul. One or the other wouldn't do; it had to be both.

Anyway, fast forward a few thousand millennia and nature has picked up on the idea of sex. It's a brilliant idea, at all sorts of levels, and it's why it continues in this very modern world to bring diverse human families together to widen the gene pool. You may not thank your prospective brother in law for getting drunk at your sister's wedding and pulling the prettiest bridesmaid, but believe me, it's one of nature's best ways to join up parallel lives.

Generally speaking, in nature there is a moment of conception when an egg and a sperm (or their more primitive counterparts) join together, and from that time on a new generation is started and a new soul is created. Cells start multiplying and so does the attached soul. As time went by, living things became much more complex. Cells started to specialise, and the cellular structure started to become highly sophisticated. The same thing happened to the souls. They were linked or attached to the physical cells from the word go, but the soul itself only exists in this other dimension, the soul dimension.

So, how far have we got? We've established that every living thing has or has had its own soul that is attached to it and is existing in another dimension, and that the soul is necessary for the survival of the living thing and is in fact evolving with it. The big question now is, as the soul and the physical living thing go through life together, do they interact? Are they aware of each other's presence? Has the evolution of the one been influenced by the other? – and here, I have a bit of a problem. I don't know; I'm still working it out.

It is, I believe, a uniquely human conundrum.

Some tens of thousands of years ago, human beings started developing consciousness. I think I'm right in saying that it's unique to humans, though I'm sure there are other theories. Consciousness is part of the mind, which originates in the brain, the physical brain. It follows that consciousness disappears as soon as your brain dies. I think that if there ever was any interaction between the soul and the physical body, then that link was weakened and then finally extinguished when consciousness took over as the predominant survival tool in humans. The human soul probably stopped evolving round about that time, too.

There are quite a few implications to this theory, and the most interesting one is that other living things have a closer relationship with their souls than we now do. This includes your pet dog, your aspidistra in the hall and the mushroom in your salad.

I'll just let that settle in a moment.

I want to emphasise that all living things have souls. All this is speculation, because we lost touch with our souls long ago, but it seems likely that if, after we developed consciousness, we no longer had use of or for the soul, then it would have stopped evolving, whereas creatures with no such intelligence or cognisance would continue with both the link to and the evolution of their souls.

That's enough for now. There's plenty there for you to think about. Thanks for listening to me.

Now, back to the story.

twenty nine

Although my degrees were in Engineering, I do like to think of myself as a scientist. I have an enquiring mind. I'm intelligent and I have a grasp of enough scientific principles to make a stab at analysing anything I encounter that is unfamiliar. If I don't understand something, I look the subject up in books or online and read about it until I do understand it. I've always been like that. If you want to pick out future scientists or technologists or engineers from a class of primary school age children, then this is the trait you should be looking out for. I get very unsettled when I can't understand something.

You can imagine then, that when I came round on the floor of my study that first time, there were a lot of things I didn't understand. I felt very unsettled.

I also felt animated. I had been building up to this moment for some time, after all, and had been fearful that it would turn out to be a disappointing failure. I saw it as some sort of pinnacle. It could so easily have backfired on me. I got back up off the floor and slumped in my chair. The elation was tempered with fatigue. I felt groggy physically, but my mind was active and engaged.

I thought hard about it.

In a nutshell and to summarise, I was fairly confident that the phial contained a liquid that had been contrived and prepared by some sort of shaman in the late medieval period for the purposes of enhancing participation at a festival held twice yearly on the occasion of the summer and winter solstices as a traditional and customary fertility rite. But I couldn't surmise much more than this. Everything else was just speculation and conjecture. It seemed that the last 'official' medieval festival had ended badly with the death of the shaman, and then it had disappeared underground, probably in some lesser form, maybe a pastiche of its former self. So it seemed reasonable to suggest that the shaman had hidden the phial himself and had been unable to retrieve it because he was dead. It could quite easily have been someone else, though, for whatever reason.

The next question I asked myself, and I've already bounced this off you, was had the contents changed in the five hundred years it had had time to mature? The answer was: no idea. Maybe. Maybe not.

That left the two biggies: what was it made from and what was it for? And was there anything about it that was in any way not of this world? That's three.

I pondered that there was maybe some way in which Pinky might be able to help me with the first one. He was evidently a man with self-professed resources; he would have contacts and I had the money. I couldn't really see it happening, though. Academic institutions are always on the lookout for funding, of course, but it doesn't usually come in the form of used fifty-pound notes. I suppose he might have been able to find a bent researcher who would ask no questions and do it quietly in his grubby, back-street lab or he might care to approach some illegal drugs operation who had a facility with spare capacity and a penchant for developing a new market. And that was the trouble with that whole concept. I thought I had something a bit special here; I really didn't want it to slip through my hands and neither did I want to share it. Also, I didn't know how much of a sample might be needed and I didn't want to let any go at this stage. That's a lot of negatives. I felt I'd drawn a blank on the whole idea; the recipe would remain a mystery.

As for its true use, well now I could make a few intelligent guesses, just like you could, but we would both be clutching at straws. I think most of my guesses would revolve around the exploitation of simple country folk for gain or just for the hell of it, but I could be well off the mark.

The final question is fanciful and not necessarily for the scientist. Nevertheless, it's a fundamental one. Is the liquid simply a poison or some type of nerve agent or suppressant that just shuts the body down until it is virtually, but not quite, dead, or is there more to it than that? Something that would need new laws of science to explain, perhaps?

My mind was running wild. The biggest single problem with being a miserable loner is that you have nobody to discuss ideas with. How I longed for some proper intellectual company during those turgid days, someone more original and informed than the anonymous online creeps that I had to put up with. If you have no one to bounce concepts off, you soon find yourself going down blind alleys or round in circles. It's why secretive research is so desperately stupid. I understand why scientists do it, but it is just so stupid, and a tragic, wretched waste of time.

My very first thought, of course, was hmm, that was interesting, let's do it again, and it would have been very easy to get too zealous without considering the consequences.

366

I exercised some more self-discipline and resisted the urge to dip my finger in again. I would think further and I would savour this and I would keep my composure.

Sorry to be so boring. I've told you; I'm a scientist.

I did realise it could be dangerous, obviously. There was no doubt that I could be risking death or serious health issues, especially with extended or prolonged use. I knew I was in uncharted territory. A thought suddenly occurred to me that if I didn't come round from one of these adventures, my body might lie on the floor for weeks before anyone discovered it. Poor Rosie would probably eat me. That didn't worry me, though it would be a loss if I died because there was so much to do, but I was intrigued to imagine the scenario that would follow such an unexplainable death. How long would the village take to recover its mojo from something like that?

I resolved to repeat the procedure in exactly the same manner the next day. I would do it as scientifically as I could. I would attempt to reproduce the same conditions, from eating and drinking the same things to exercising and resting in the same way. The only difference was that this time I'd have prepared by lying on the floor with a cushion under my head, and I'd have already sealed the jar and put it back safely.

As I licked my little finger, I lay gently back on the cushion. It didn't disappoint. The experience was very similar to the first time, the nothingness and the feeling of wellbeing and safety and a hint that I was in the company of a friendly, benign, natural environment. I got the impression, like the previous time, that there was this transfer of knowledge that I've spoken to you about as being ultimately the most significant thing that was going on in my head. On this second occasion, I could sort of feel it was happening but I couldn't quite put my finger on what the knowledge was or what it represented or how it was all functioning. But it was exciting, and when I came round I was eager more than satiated. I wanted to do it again.

Over the next couple of weeks, I conducted quite a few 'experiments'. I restricted myself to one only per day. I was rigid in my observance of this. Play safe and stay in control was my policy. On one day, I tried diluting the liquid, to see if it reduced the potency. I dripped a single globule of the liquid into a test tube that I just happened to have in my desk drawer, left over from a table decoration holding single stem flowers, and I diluted it with ten parts water and shook it around. It was interesting because the mixture turned a light shade of blue. I wasn't expecting that. I lay down as usual and dripped a single bead of the weakened fluid into my mouth from a pipette and swallowed it and waited. Nothing. Nothing at all. That was interesting, too. I lay there thinking about this.

What actually went through my mind more than analysing the unexpected results of my experiment was did this constitute today's ration of exposure to my magic potion? Did it count, because nothing had happened? Of course, I knew it should have counted, and I knew that I had intended for it to count, but now that it had had no effect, I felt bereft and unfulfilled and anxious. Rather like I imagine a junkie feels who has just discovered his longed-for hit has been a dud. I'm ashamed to say that my self-discipline evaporated and I snatched the test tube from its stand and drained the contents down my gullet. I must have really looked like Dr Jekyll doing this, and indeed this had been an image that I had been wrestling with for some time. There was worse to come, because that had no effect on me either. I just slumped there on the floorboards feeling like a dummy. At that point I could have panicked and reached for the phial, but instead I just started crying inconsolably where I lay and I rolled into a foetus. I must have looked pathetic. I couldn't stop. Where was it all coming from? Up to that very moment, I had still been basking in the euphoria of the phial, but it all seemed to come tumbling down around me. I suddenly had doubts about all sorts of things. What was it doing to me? What had I become? I don't tend to suicidal thoughts as I've told you, but I have to admit that on that afternoon, there on the floor of Church House, I could very easily have swallowed the lot.

I awoke and it was dark outside. I was cold. I managed to get myself up from the carpet but collapsed on the wing chair and sat there for a long time in the gloom. I had to take stock of things. Was I letting all this take over my life? I tried to figure out, honestly, whether I was developing an addiction to the liquid, and I honestly concluded that that was not the case, though quite what criteria I used I've no idea, because from where I see things now, in those early days that's what everything pointed to. No, I concluded that it was a habit, and not an addiction. Nevertheless, I felt this had been something of a wake-up call. Just keep in control; that's the main thing.

I thought I needed to be prudent and firm and I waited about a week before I tried it again. Life still went on; I went to South Molton on the Thursday bus; I ate and drank and showered and washed my clothes but during those few days I felt I was a hollowed-out shell of my former self. It was cold turkey agony, I'm now convinced.

It was with some trepidation that I resumed my tried and tested regime on a Sunday afternoon in late January and I'm glad, and am very relieved to report that everything was back to normal. I was done with experimenting. I changed my routine, and instead of imbibing every day, I restricted it to Sunday afternoons. Everyone should have a routine on a Sunday afternoon. I look back very fondly on those times. It was a period of great enquiry and learning for me and most Sundays I would take away from the experience sufficient new impressions to fuel a week's deep thought.

But as well as indulging myself in fancies of other dimensions, parallel worlds and the rest, I was still itching to make the connection to the festival. What role did the potion play? I guess at that point, I hadn't much hope of getting very far with this. After all, Godfrey was long gone, and so was the guy with the photo, and I felt I'd already sucked Harris dry.

I was being very stupid, wasn't I?

I'm sure you've worked it out, as usual, and was wondering when I was coming to it. I'm sure I would have got there, too, but it doesn't matter because one afternoon in mid-February, it all came knocking on my door, literally.

It was one of those very rare occasions when I was actually expecting a caller. I'd been round the community shop earlier that morning; I was probably one of their best customers because most villagers got their food from the big supermarkets in Barnstaple, more fool them. They had no eggs and the shop girl said she'd pop round later with half a dozen when they'd been delivered, so I was expecting her.

It wasn't the shop girl with the eggs, of course. You know who it was. It was the quiet child's father waiting for me on the doorstep. The 'other guy', as I've been calling him.

At first, I didn't recognise him. It was out of context, after all, and I hadn't ever really got a good look at him. It had been dark and I'd been agitated and preoccupied with avoiding some painful retribution.

He just stood there looking at me in an intense, unnerving way with his fuck-off eyes, and then I realised who it was. I wondered what to do. How to react? Was he going to hit me? I asked him what he wanted and he replied sheepishly that he just wanted to talk to me. I don't normally invite anyone, especially strangers with unknown agendas, into my house. The last time I had a visitor was the lad who came to install my computer, and I couldn't see any way round that. I hesitated while I tried to think it through. I had no idea what he wanted to talk about, but of course it had by then struck me as it struck you some time ago that it might just be about the festival or the sacred grove and I was certainly curious. I felt I had no choice but to ask him in.

He took his wellingtons off at the door. He evidently hadn't dressed for the occasion and smelt vaguely of silage and sheep. He was wearing a navy boiler suit and a NYC baseball cap. I'd put him at about fifty. His leaden face told me he'd spent his life outside in the Devon rain; it was weather-worn and life-weary. I showed him into the kitchen and he looked hapless until I gestured for him to sit down on one of the dining chairs. I think he would have preferred to stand but I didn't give him the option. I leaned back on the Aga rail and looked down on him and was smug that I'd managed to orchestrate this opening gambit so seamlessly and shamelessly. I already felt I had power over him; he was that sort of bloke. Was he a bit simple?

My thoughts returned to the confrontation in the graveyard that night of the solstice and I had to conclude that I had no notion of the man's demeanour. I'd heard some of their heated argument before I was discovered, and wondered how protective he was going to be of his son. Did he now believe I was a paedophile leading the village lads astray? Because as I recall at the time, he obviously feared that I was no mortal, and he wasn't waiting around to find out.

He just sat there, cap in his lap. He was finding this difficult. Finally, he simply repeated that he needed to talk through some things that were bothering him. He started by admitting that he'd behaved foolishly on the night in question and that if he hadn't run away then things would have turned out differently, so we got that out of the way. He then continued that Ted was no longer speaking to him because of the incident and was being actively aggressive and antagonistic towards him and his family. My good fortune, rather than his, I fancy, as otherwise I might have borne the brunt of his anger; I had certainly warranted it.

He then proceeded to tell me his life story, just like that. It all came out like a burst dam. He was variously, in turns, angry, wistful and contemplative and I warmed to him and took the chair next to him at the table and made a cup of tea for us both.

It gave me further great insight into village life. I'm talking proper village life. The way it's been lived for generations and is now lost to us, except in these little pockets where a vestige clings on. The man sitting in front of me was a throwback to those times and his like will die, in England at least, before we are aware of the loss. A way of life will have vanished for good and no one will be left to nourish it, nor to participate or even observe. It will be gone for good.

He was an Uglow.

You've come across that word already, but I haven't told you who they are.

The Uglows are one of the oldest families around here. You see the name everywhere, on gravestones and war memorials, in farming chronicles and the parish records, in local papers and in framed photographs of long-dead bellringers. They're embedded in Crow's Nymet and word has it that they have six toes on each foot. They quarrel and they fight and they ostracise and they are what the word dysfunctional was invented for, but they are still here, and they are all around me as I write.

This Uglow was called Peter, he told me, and he was an only child. He grew up with his widowed grandfather in a worker's cottage just outside the village, after both his parents had been burned to death in a barn fire when he was eight. The wider family were not supportive, for some reason, so Peter and his grandfather became close. Long winter evenings in front of an open fire and blissful summer nights in the cottage garden were times of great congress and intimacy. It was the manifestation of the great oral tradition in its purest form.

That's also a practice that's long gone for most of us now, sadly. Peter said he rarely talked with his son any longer, although he'd tried to pass on to him all he knew of the old country ways. He wasn't interested. He'd sought to excite him with stories from nature or from local lore from a young age, but he felt he had wasted his time. Most specifically, he had spoken to his son many times of the Rousing and now he was a teenager he had finally started taking an interest. Sadly, it turned out it was drug induced hallucinations that had attracted him, not incarnations of green men.

Peter spoke at that kitchen table without pausing for breath for nearly an hour, but he didn't actually offer much more of the festival than I already knew, and that was disappointing. There was one thing, however, that really aroused my interest, and it was this that had fed the son's pharmaceutical ambitions and got Gavin grounded indefinitely.

It was this. Peter told me that there was indeed a magic potion, and that this was an intrinsic part of the festival, as I had surmised. The villagers in the know always referred to it as their Physic. It was indeed supposed to raise spectres at the time of the solstice and it was also the mysterious shaman who was responsible for making it. But this was the explosive bit. He told me the recipe for the Physic could be found in the church itself.

Well, actually, it was more cryptic than that. Nothing should be too easy. It was all down to the bench ends and the bosses in the barrel-vaulted ceiling. I told you a bit about them at the beginning. That seems like a long time ago; I didn't expect to be writing for this long.

I knew the bench ends were old. I'd put them just before the dissolution of the monasteries in about 1540, but apparently, they are older. It seems that this mysterious shaman had some hand in getting them made and installed in the church, and he did it as a way of enhancing his position at the expense of the official Church laity. He paid for them and specified their design and oversaw the carver's work. He must have been an imposing character. Anyway, the depictions on the bench ends were meant to represent some sort of riddle. I think he was playing with the peasants again.

With his sudden demise, the riddle, such as it was, went with him to the grave (or wherever he ended up), as did the Physic.

Oh, no it didn't.

There were factions who wanted to continue as best they could without the shaman, but there were also those who thought the time was right to abandon the whole thing. There was great unrest in the village and there was talk of ripping out the carvings and making a bonfire of them.

The more I hear of this shaman guy, the less I like him. He was bad news for the ordinary folk of Crow's Nymet.

Anyway, that didn't happen, so they're still there. But they were left with the riddle. There were many theories, but it seems no one had ever got anywhere with it.

Peter and his grandfather had spent hours and hours trying to interpret the bench ends but the best they could come up with was a motely list of possible ingredients for the Physic, and it was this that Peter had ill-advisably given his son.

This news whetted my appetite, but I may as well tell you now that I've never even figured out what the riddle was, let alone solved it. I don't want you to be anticipating some intriguing twist that isn't coming. On the other hand, I did get a bit fired up. I like a good mystery.

I asked Peter what was on his list and he rattled off a whole load of plant life in both the vernacular and the Latin which lost me. I asked him to write them down and I handed him a pencil and paper. He came up with about eight names in schoolboy boilerplate script that I resolved I would Google as soon as he left.

There didn't seem to be much more that he wanted to say. He was consumed. He looked drained. I wasn't sure what he'd wanted to get out of this meeting, but I guessed that it had been cathartic and that, like me, he had nobody else to tell it to. I'm afraid I didn't contribute as much as I could have done. I most certainly didn't tell him about the phial, although there were times when I was tempted, just to see the expression on his face. It would not have been a good idea.

He left without fuss, shaking my hand limply, but we both knew that an unlikely and curious bond had been established between the two of us. I had little reason to believe we would ever meet again, but even then a little grain of an idea was emerging in my brain. If I was going to try to repeat a re-enactment of the Rousing in the summer, then Peter would likely be a willing and enthusiastic participant, especially if I told him I had some of the proper Physic that he could try.

I've told you a bit about medieval vernacular carving in West Country churches, haven't I? I hope you've remembered everything. Did I mention that the subject matter won't be religious? It'll portray common lore in the guise of fantastic beasts, mythical figures and ordinary simple country craftsmen and their tools of the trade and local eccentrics in the semblance of grotesque caricature. They'll be carved in a very primitive style with naïve characterisation, apart from the rood screen which will be fine decorative latticework just to show you the quality these guys were really capable of. There are lots of books about them and plenty of online forums if you're interested.

I knew that St Rumon's was renowned for the green man roof bosses. There are about six of them and they're all different. They figure in quite a few antiquarian books and are well documented in some recent research papers and I've seen visitors who come to the church specially to see them. They're on a mission or pilgrimage to view and absorb these images. They're special. Some set up cameras on tripods with fancy lighting to accentuate shadows. I actually had a chance to examine them closely when the scaffolding was up inside the church, which I consider was a rare privilege. They are fascinating, every one of them.

I have to admit, though, that I never really paid all that much attention to the bench-ends. And neither did anyone else, apart from Peter and his grandfather, because I couldn't recall them being mentioned in any book. Sure, they're fine examples, but I guess carved bench-ends are two a penny round here.

When Peter had gone, the first thing I did was to Google the ingredients that he'd written down in his little list. Most of them were poisonous plants of the type you're advised not to grow in your garden by well-meaning celebrity gardeners. Even if you don't know much about plants, you could probably reel off half a dozen yourself.

Come on, try.

Yew, obviously, henbane, foxglove, deadly nightshade, fly agaric, laburnum, ragwort, and those are just the ones your mother told you not to pick. I wasn't convinced by Peter's list. It just seemed a random table of poisonous plants, any one of which on its own would give your insides something to think about. It was as if someone had said, look, mix me a nice cocktail of all the most dangerous flora that you might encounter on a nature ramble in the English countryside and then knock it back and see what happens. I can't believe that Peter suggested this to his son, either, and I certainly wasn't about to try it.

So, I was sceptical, but I went over the church that night with a torch and inspected the bench ends with renewed curiosity. There are about two dozen of them altogether, in varying degrees of survival. It was evident that some were missing and had been replaced by plain chamfered ends, and others were so weathered and decayed that it was difficult to make out much at all of the pictorial content. I wasn't all that impressed. Also, I couldn't really see all that well with the torch. I would have to come back in daylight. I did take photographs of them all with the torch at different angles but when I put them up on my computer screen later, it was obvious that it was nowhere near as clearly defined as the real thing. I was a bit disenchanted. I had become quite exhilarated at the thought of concocting the long-lost recipe for the Physic from a cryptic message, the legacy of a powerful, mysterious shaman who had lived half a millennium ago. Over-imaginative, I now realise. All I had was some primitive carvings and some silly stories and some reckless conjectures.

Nevertheless, I did persevere. I took to spending time in the church during daylight hours and I believe this excited the vicar into believing that I'd got religion. He tried to befriend me once or twice, but his timing was unfortunate as I wasn't in the mood for theological debate. Conversely, the lady who did the flowers and the other one who vacuumed the carpet and dusted the pews would not even share the same space with me, even with the strength of numbers on their side. The first time they disturbed me I was on my back, prone, across the aisle inspecting a low-lying artefact on one of the bench-ends. They had come in from the back door of the vestry and were chatting and laughing and one of them was dragging an uncooperative Henry, but when they saw me lying there they both shut up their faces, spent just a hesitant moment in a considered response and without uttering a word backed off the way they'd come, tripping over the Henry as they went. That wasn't very Christian of them, was it? I could have been having a stroke, or a miraculous religious experience.

So I had the place entirely to myself most days, which was how I liked it.

I wondered what I was going to do. I could see how Peter and his grandfather had compiled at least some of their list. Other entries, I thought, were a tad speculative. There was one that patently showed a digitalis (a foxglove to you), I don't think there was any denying that, and another that was unmistakeably ivy. There was a representation of a yew berry and a needled branch accompanied by a tree with many stems that was almost certainly meant to be Yew Magna, so that was exciting, and for a while convinced me I was on the right track. Finally, there was a posy of liberty caps, again unmistakeable and menacing, but that was about it. Everything else was either unclear or ambiguous or disingenuous, so not much to go on, and I wasn't particularly confident that I wanted to try any of these things. In fact, it got me thinking. Was this all part of the game that the shaman was playing with his unfortunate parishioners? What was the point of it, otherwise? Was it just to big him up? Because he could? I think those poor sods were up against it. I began to think that there was very probably some foul play involved in the shaman's untimely demise.

I did feel I was on fairly safe ground with the magic mushrooms. At least I knew they weren't going to kill me.

I'd never seen any growing around here, but I had a good idea now where to look for them because I'd heard Peter's lad telling the other two on that December night. I knew the place, a wet field further down the valley, but I had never ventured there. It wasn't on one of my normal routes, because it didn't lead anywhere interesting. I determined to make a point of staking it out, and took the opportunity a few days later when I was walking Rosie one afternoon. I found the field and spent some time mooching around until Rosie got bored and made it known she was looking for something a little more physical.

Not a sausage. Not even a hint of a fungi of any description.

I could have saved myself the time and effort, of course. When I got back, I Googled it and sure enough, you're not likely to find anything until August, and even then it's got to be the right growing conditions. As you can imagine, the WWW is full of dubious knowledge of the subject, mostly expounded by contributors who have maybe spent just a little too much of their free time imbibing the little blighters. How I love the internet.

It was all a bit depressing, actually. I never figured that being a card-carrying, unhinged shaman or full-time potion-gathering alchemist was such a long-term commitment. Just about nothing on my list of suspect plants was around in early spring, except the ivy. I would need to be gathering and preserving and preparing until next Christmas if I wanted to pursue this avenue, and with the strong likelihood of abject failure, it wasn't particularly appealing to me to put this much effort in.

I discerned I was on one of my downers. I felt deflated. It was only March and a good three months away from the summer solstice. I'd got so galvanised at the prospect of experimenting with mysterious, druidical recipes, and my Sunday afternoon distraction had now almost lapsed into such routine, that I was bored. I would say I was at a loose end for a while, most unlike me.

Little did I know that something much more immediate was about to grab me by the throat. It was a very surreal little interlude in my otherwise insular and introspective existence.

I wasn't going to tell you about it. I don't feel entirely comfortable putting it in writing, but as with most things, it doesn't matter now at all, so here goes.

thirty

I think, in retrospect, it was just the sort of diversion that I needed. I was getting a bit bogged down.

It was Pinky, of course, wot done it, though it was me who set it in motion.

Considering I was still paying Pinky his $1000 retainer every month, I did have the nagging feeling I wasn't getting particularly good value for money. True, there were several occasions in December when I thought I might need him to get me out of a fix, but in the event it wasn't necessary. It had been very reassuring to know that I could call upon him, all the same, and I guessed I should really be looking on our deal as a sort of insurance policy. Maybe I should have been looking for a no claims discount.

This was probably at the back of my mind when one Saturday I was reading the paper and something caught my eye. It was presumably his name that jumped out at me. There was an article of about four column inches tucked away between an editorial and the overseas news. I could easily have missed it, but the banner proclaimed, 'Felix Marsland to be honoured for services to technology'. I was intrigued. Felix and technology were not two words that I would have expected to find in the same sentence. Felix and creative accountant, perhaps, or Felix and cunning bastard more likely, but in my experience, Felix couldn't identify technology even if it came care of guys with acne, glasses and white lab coats. I read on and was even more intrigued. I'd not heard of the man since the fiasco of the IPO. That was over twenty years ago. I guess Caspar might have told me what he was up to, but I wasn't listening. I had bigger things on my mind, like the death of my son and the end of my marriage. Oh, and a nervous breakdown.

We had parted in a reasonably professional manner, as much as was possible in the circumstances. I don't think I hated him for doing what he did to me. At the time. Over the last twenty years, I've had plenty of time to think about it. Too much time, by far. And now I hated him properly. In fact, I hated him in every possible way, not just because he robbed me of the company I had started and nurtured and loved; not just because he cheated me out of my life, stole my aspirations and my future, but because he was an obnoxious cunt who was blissfully ignorant and uninterested in anything to do with technical achievement. He shouldn't be getting any sort of award for that. His only love was money, especially his own. He used to describe it as his 'stock in trade'. I no longer liked him at all, or the memory of him.

It turned out the headline was a bit misleading. There were expectations that he would be knighted in the next honours list, but it hadn't happened yet. The article had been prompted by his daughter's appointment as Chief Financial Officer in the company that Felix now ran. This was presented in the piece as being something of a novelty, though in this day and age, I hardly think so. They were trying to make more of a story out of it, but had still only made the four inches. Cronyism's a habit; it's not news. I'd sack the PR team if I were Felix; he's good at that, at least.

I remembered Felix's daughter. She was just a little older than Angel. Felix had brought her into the office once or twice and had sat her down at his computer. She was a daddy's girl, all right. I think her future had been mapped out at birth.

Anyway, the two of them were doing rather well, thank you.

The article didn't add much more of interest, but I looked them both up and learned a lot more. It sounded to me as if they were both obnoxious cunts.

For an hour or two, it spoiled my Saturday afternoon. It simply hadn't occurred to me before how much I hated him. And now I knew about his awful daughter, I couldn't get my head round why she was enjoying a full and successful life, whereas my poor Angel was dead. Why does something like that happen?

I only started feeling better when I realised, as you have now realised, that this had the makings of an interesting little project for Pinky. I spent some time fantasising about how he might interpret my little missive to him. On a post-it I simply wrote, 'I do not like this man or his daughter at all', and I stuck it to the newspaper clipping and popped it in the tin. Oh, and on a whim, I took twenty $500 bills from under the bed and attached them to the note with a paper clip. Rather impulsive of me. Presumptuous, too. And generous, or so I thought at the time. I was just feeling in that sort of mood. It gave me a warm feeling inside that this money came from the pot that Felix never managed to get his hands on, but I guess that it made what happened more of my fault than it might have been, and like I say, I don't mind telling you that, now.

It didn't take long for Pinky to take the package. I did wonder how often he looked, and I pondered how, after all this time, I still had absolutely no idea who he was, or whether I'd ever seen him or even knew him. He remained an enigma. A complete mystery.

I mused about how he would get news to me of his mission, and indeed about what he might come up with. Would I even know? It was all pretty obvious with Mrs Gogwell's cat. It was on my doorstep and I couldn't have missed it if I'd tried, but this was a bit different.

Felix existed in a different world. A parallel world.

In fact, nothing at all happened until the second week in April. To be honest, I'd gone off the boil by then. The novelty of it had worn off and I was bored fantasising. I was also a bit unhappy with the impetuousness of my $10,000 investment. So when I noticed the quarry tile on the wall, I was in no hurry to examine what was there. It was no longer something I felt I wanted to savour. I felt a little let down over the whole thing, actually.

I looked in the tin later, as I was walking around with a bottle of beer in my hand at the end of the day. There was just a folded piece of paper inside. I hadn't known what to expect and I have to admit that a frisson of anticipation aerated the hairs on the back of my neck as I put it in my pocket. I think I was savouring it, after all.

It simply said this. Your presence is requested at … and then it gave a date and a time and described a lay-by on the road to South Molton where there was a stile marking a public bridleway that I knew well. It was on one of my routes. It ended up by saying, 'transport will be provided'.

Hmm. This was two nights hence at half past eight, so round about dusk. I wondered what to make of it. To be honest, I didn't have a clue. I had no idea what Pinky had in mind.

Now I really did feel a sense of anticipation, and there was certainly plenty of frisson about.

I have to tell you, I was nervous. Wouldn't you be?

When the time came, I started out earlier than I needed to. I locked the doors to the house and left my study desk lamp on a timer, as I always did when I went out at night. I was virtually certain that nobody was taking note, or was even interested in my comings and goings, but there was no point making that night different from any other. As usual, there was nobody else around. They were all watching Eastenders. I could get to the bridleway by climbing the bank at the bottom of my field and then just following the hedge to the gate in the corner. From there, apart from crossing a quiet lane, it was all fields. This was why I used it a lot. It was dead convenient for ways West and North and there was good cover and no farms all the way to the next village about three miles distant.

I approached the lay-by from the field at about a quarter past eight. There was nobody there. I stayed hidden behind the bank, next to the stile. It wasn't really a stile, I suppose, it was one of those galvanised gates that you can open while still sitting on your horse. In theory, at least; it all looks a bit tricky to me.

The hedges haven't really got growing much in April. They've greened up a little, but in North Devon they're mainly made of beech, oak and ash, rather than hazel and hawthorn, so while most of the country looks summery already at this time of year, in Devon in April it can still look like spring has yet to put in an appearance. So, the hedge wasn't providing me with much cover and I had to duck down behind the bank on a couple of occasions as a pick-up and then a Land Rover trundled past.

At eight thirty on the dot, a car pulled up and switched its engine off. It was just the other side of the hedge and I couldn't see the driver. I decided to bite the bullet. I calmly stepped up to the gate, released the catch and walked through, leaving it to slam behind me with a clatter. I could see the driver, now. He wasn't fazed by my entrance and stared ahead with an expression of disinterest. I opened the car door. It was a Golf of some age and it looked tatty inside. I didn't think my muddy boots would be a problem. I had been wondering. I took off my coat and threw it on the back seat. There was no one else in the car, which I felt was probably a good thing at this stage. As I sat down and put my belt on, the driver started the engine without a further movement of his body. He was still looking straight ahead, expressionless. I decided to play it cool and I just sat there as well, saying nothing.

Now, I suppose I should have been asking myself was this guy in the driver's seat Pinky, but I sort of knew instinctively that it wasn't. Pinky had gone a year without revealing himself; I was sure he wasn't about to now. And I was equally sure that I wouldn't be seeing him later, either. He was a facilitator, not a doer. I doubted now he'd even dug the cat up himself.

The driver looked to be about thirty. He had uncombed mousy hair that needed cutting and a two-day stubble on his chin. He looked a bit rough, actually. I wondered where Pinky had found him. I had no idea what his brief was, obviously, and I guessed that at some stage he would need to talk to me, but for now we both just sat there trying to look composed and in control of things.

You have to understand that just sitting in the front passenger seat of a proper car was a complete novelty for me. The last time I had been in a car was when I exchanged my 'S' Type for the Land Rover, and that must have been well over ten years ago and was in itself a bit of a scary episode as my confidence was still shot. I only had to drive to Chulmleigh in the Jag, but I remember going round every corner at a snail's pace and I found it difficult to judge the width of the vehicle around the narrow country lanes. The guy I was doing the swap with didn't look very impressed with the car. He'd not seen it; I had just told him the age and the mileage and that it had had an easy life and was in good nick, but the trouble was that after several years in the barn it was covered in algae, dust and bird shit. I hadn't thought to wash it. Anyway, I think he got a good deal, and it must have looked a lot better after a hose down. The Land Rover was all I now needed. A workhorse. It's still at the bottom of the garden under a tarpaulin. I use it maybe once or twice a year if I need to shift anything heavy and it takes some hand-holding to get going, but I've never been much further in it than South Molton. You don't see many police around here, and there are plenty of Land Rovers on these roads that look far less roadworthy than mine, but it would be just my luck to get stopped. I keep a low profile if I can, and only drive it at night.

So, you can see just what a novelty it was to be sitting in the passenger seat after all this time, even if it was just an old Golf.

I worked it out. Since the day I drove down here that Christmas twenty years previous I hadn't been further than Barnstaple, just ten miles away, and that was on the bus, and only the once. That's quite a thing, really, for someone who used to clock up a regular thirty thousand miles on the road most years. When I was a jet-setter. Who could guess that, now?

I was tempted to ask my driver where we were going. It would have been nice to know, but somehow it didn't seem proper to break the silence that had been established between us.

He struck me as being a good driver and I had no worries that he might try and show off. I guess he had his instructions. We slipped easily through South Molton. There's only one traffic light in the whole place, and that's at a pedestrian crossing that nobody uses. In the Midlands, I used to hate wasting my life sat at red lights. One after the other. It was funny how it was all coming back.

South Molton looked unfamiliar in the dark, and it was empty. Just the other side of the urban sprawl of the metropolis, we picked up the link road that took us as far as the motorway junction. The M5 was quiet, too. It was nine-ish and most people had got to where they were going. It was eerie; the motorways I remembered were choked with traffic.

My driver kept religiously to seventy miles an hour. I guessed that was part of his instructions, too.

Bristol came and went. I was mesmerised by the lights of the city. I had forgotten. The road looked foreign with its variable speed limits and lane changes and camera warnings. I was glad I wasn't in the driver's seat. It never used to be like that, did it?

We settled down to a gentle plod, but then surprisingly we exited the motorway just east of Gloucester. I wasn't expecting that. We took the A417 to the Air Balloon roundabout, then headed South to Cirencester. This had been my stamping ground in an earlier life, and I knew the area reasonably well. When I'd just passed my test, we used to meet up at the Air Balloon and then drive to one of the cider pubs that you could still find in isolated villages round about. I bet they're all gone, now. Long gone, along with all the cider apple orchards.

We didn't get as far as Cirencester. We took a sharp left off the main road onto a single-track lane that wasn't signposted. At first, I thought he'd gone wrong and was turning round to double back, but he carried on along the track. It struck me as a bit odd, but what did I know?

A little way down the track, we pulled off and headed into an entranceway to a wood. It looked like a loading area for cut timber because there was a big pile of freshly sawn logs. I could smell the pine. Next to the pile was another car, a black Ford Ka, and we parked by the side of it. There was no one else inside this one either.

Up to this point, there had not been a word exchanged between us, but now he turned to me as if I had just climbed in beside him and not been there for the last two hours and he explained to me that we were going to change cars here and I was to swap my boots for some shoes I would find in the back, and I was to leave my coat in the Golf.

I asked him where we were going and he replied simply that it was going to be another two hours, so I should make myself comfortable.

It was round about this time that comfortable was not something I was becoming. I suddenly realised that this was a much bigger deal than I had hitherto appreciated. A change of cars? A convoluted route, four hour journey? Changes of clothes? It was all adding up to a very big deal indeed, and one in which traceability, or rather a lack of it, was an important consideration. I didn't feel there was any option to back out now. Pinky had patently gone to a lot of trouble on my account, but I was beginning to have serious misgivings that this was maybe a little out of my league.

In the light of subsequent events, that wasn't the half of it. Probably not even the tenth.

The Ka was cold and felt damp inside. How long had it been there and who had brought it and who knew about it? Was I ever going to see my boots again?

We picked up the A429 North of Cirencester. This was also very familiar territory; we were on the Fosse Way. If you look at a map, it runs straight as a die. It's a Roman road; it would do. Up close on the ground, it's now actually a series of many roads, some big, some small, and they're all joined together by new, traffic-friendly junctions that allow the sedate traffic that typically uses it to mix seamlessly with the racier stuff on the trunk roads. It's signposted Fosse Way from just north of Bristol to Leicester and it's the road I would use to get home from Loughborough as a student. My first car wouldn't go faster than fifty and lost power up inclines, so it made for a less worrysome route, avoiding motorways and fast roads as it does. I remember there was a hill where I had to change down to first gear to climb up it, no matter how much of a run-up I was able to get. There was no synchromesh on my first gear, and I never did master double-declutching, so I had to wait until the car came to a standstill to slip it into first before it started rolling backwards. The hill's still there. We had passed it a mile or so back. That's what got me thinking about it. The Ka went up in fifth, and it's not what you'd call a powerful car.

Not so exciting an episode in a modern vehicle, perhaps, but tonight I reckoned there would be plenty of excitement without the need to be rolling backwards down steep hills.

A few junctions had been 'improved', and parts were wider and had properly marked kerbs where before there had only been grass. There were a lot more double lines and road signs and speed restrictions than I remembered. It had lost a lot of its charm. It didn't look to be the calm motoring experience it had been in the seventies, but it still managed to pass between the conurbations of Rugby and Coventry without you even realising they were there.

The Fosse Way was always a quiet road. I once drove the whole length of it in fancy dress after a party and was so drunk when I got to my parent's house that I couldn't get the key in the door.

I wonder what on earth they thought of me?

You observe, my mind was wandering. I was all over the place. It was a very strange, unsettling journey. If I could have just stepped out of that car and walked away, I think I would have done. I was a bit uneasy.

I guess I'd figured out that we were on our way to meet Felix, either at his house, or somewhere else, and our route was intended to make our tracks as clean as possible. I'd read a lot about cameras; I'd taken an interest in the surveillance society and I'd seen news items and the odd crime drama where video footage plays an increasingly crucial role in apprehending villains. I'd been amazed at all the cameras on the M5 gantries. It never used to be like that. The odd mobile speed camera parked on a bridge and that was about it. There are no cameras in South Molton.

The largest place we'd been through on this journey was Stow on the Wold and that skirted the main drag. I didn't see any cameras there either; it was a clever route.

We left the Fosse Way at High Cross and were weaving our way past Hinckley through the back roads, and then we took the A447 for a few miles. I had no notion where Felix lived and started to speculate as we homed in. We were criss-crossing Charnwood Forest and I supposed that we might be heading for Rothley or one of the affluent southern outposts of Leicester, but I sort of lost my bearings a bit and was surprised when we came to a halt in a quiet, dark lane. I was disoriented. My driver was looking intently ahead, squinting into the murky darkness beyond the dipped beam. He flashed the headlights and almost immediately this was answered by another vehicle about a hundred yards away, facing us but off the road. We gingerly approached and passed through some fancy rusted ironwork gates, one off its hinges. There was room on the gravel to do a full circle and we came up behind the other car, which turned out to be a black Range Rover. Of course it was.

My driver turned to me. 'These guys are professionals. Just let them do their job. Your role is strictly as observer, so don't do anything and don't say anything. It'll be much better that way; we really don't want any slip-ups.'

Looking back with hindsight, I suppose I could have put a stop to it then and there. It was my show, after all, wasn't it?

Probably.

I was pretty sure something awful was about to happen and I was the only one that could have prevented it. I could have walked away, but of course I didn't.

You knew I didn't.

I was well out of my comfort zone, but I loved it. I didn't want it to stop.

We got out of the Ford and my driver opened a rear door of the Range Rover and gestured for me to get in. He got in the other side. The two men in the front were dressed all in black and were both wearing balaclavas, the sort with just peepholes for eyes and a screamy hole for the mouth. They were like Milk Tray men, but much, much more menacing. My driver and I were each handed one of these things and a pair of black latex gloves and told to put them on. It felt good. It instantly gives you power. Maybe I should get one for Crow's Nymet, I thought.

No. Not a good idea.

I felt as if I needed to keep what was happening tonight as far away as I conceivably could from my real life. Was this even going to be a possibility?

We all got out the car, the four of us. It looked like this had once been the drive of a Big House. I was told that we'd have to walk for half a mile. We turned off the drive and headed across fields. The Leicestershire pasture was much dryer and easier going than the heavy Devon culm land that I was used to. We came to the edge of a group of very smart houses. Most of them were hidden behind big fences and electric steel gates, but the one we headed for had an open drive.

If this was Felix's house, I saluted him. I hate electric gates and high fences and closed communities. Hate them. Always have.

There were a number of cars in the drive. I counted five, big German SUV's, and there was a pretty little Audi convertible. We all crept very quietly through the garden in a line. I was amazed there were no security lights, but I imagine some preparatory work had been done, and we did seem to be sticking to a pre-ordained route. We all stopped in front of some French doors. There was light from within, but there were some lacy curtains covering the whole of the window from floor to ceiling.

How very fifties, I remember thinking. How very fifties.

Because the light was coming from inside, and we were up close to the windows, the curtains had the opposite effect to their usual purpose. We could see in, but no one could see out. It made us invisible. We stood there in a line, peering in and it was the weirdest feeling being able to do that.

Nobody bothers to pull curtains in Crow's Nymet, unless it's to keep the cold out.

We could see that there were eight people sat round an oval table talking and laughing. Man, woman, man, woman it went, round the table. It was obviously a dinner party and by the look of the number of bottles on the table, it had been going on for some time. It was gone midnight, after all.

The witching hour.

I saw Felix straight away. He was holding court at one end. It sent shivers through my spine seeing him again. I suddenly felt a bit sick. Opposite Felix was a woman of about thirty who was obviously the daughter. She looked just like him, especially when she laughed. I had no idea who anyone else was but they all looked 'well to do' as my mother would have said. You can bet your life they were well to do; they wouldn't be there, otherwise.

The two milk tray men reached into the insides of their coats and pulled out handguns and held them against their chests. An escalation, then. I should have realised that it was inevitable they would be carrying arms. How else could it have worked? Threatening language?

On a nod of the head, the bigger of the two jumped at the glass doors, his right shoulder making contact with the frame where the windows met at the centre. They burst open with a huge bang, and one of the toughened panes splintered into a million pieces of crystal. It was lucky they opened inwards, I mused; you can never be sure with French windows.

There were screams and one guy started choking, but no one had time to stand up from the table or make any sort of move because the milk tray men were pointing their weapons menacingly in their faces with a two-handed hold in the manner of American TV cops. They were big guns. Most alarmingly, though, and this made me all tingly and frightened, too; they both screeched with this macabre, high-pitched trill. It took me totally off-guard; it made my flesh creep. How did they do that? Did they have some sort of concealed electronic device that altered the modulation of their voices or had they been inhaling helium or something? However they did it, I have to say that it was very, very effective. It scared the fucking wits out of me.

So we stood there, and they sat there. I think my driver was playing a dual role. He was acting as a sort of back-up. He had a gun too, though not such an impressive one, but he was also looking out for me. One of the male guests shouted the classic chestnut, 'Do you know who I am?' and went to get out of his chair, but we never did get to find out who he was because he was hit over the head with a pistol grip and there was lots more screaming and an endless stream of high-pitched expletives and threats and the white table cloth was splashed with blood and red wine.

If you have a high-pitched trembly voice like a banshee and you're wearing a balaclava with pokey eye holes and a screamy hole for your mouth, you don't particularly need to sound aggressive, you just need to sound scary. There was certainly shock and awe in spades, but there was also fear and dread and terror and it was all a bit other-worldly, very surreal.

It was, in fact, pandemonium, what with all the crying and shouting and groaning and screaming, but then the big milk tray man sort of took command. He pushed into a space between two of the seated figures and did something with his gun that looked as if he was preparing to fire it. I don't know anything about modern firearms, but you see people do this in films all the time. He pulled something back on top the barrel and it clicked. Anyway, whatever he had done, it did the trick, and everyone became still and quiet. I wouldn't say they were calm, more terrified. The man with the gun announced that he would shoot the next person to make any sort of noise. I have to say, he did come over rather convincingly.

Then he took what looked like a Sainsbury's For Life carrier bag from his jacket pocket and threw it on the table where it unfurled. 'You', he said, pointing to the guest opposite him, an overweight individual wearing a DJ and red bow tie with a stupid waistcoat who was sweating profusely, 'slowly empty all your pockets on to the table and then put the contents into the bag'. 'Slowly does it', he needlessly added for further emphasis in his falsetto voice.

Out came the car keys; some loose change; a comb and a hankie; reluctantly a credit card wallet; some loose notes and a phone. It all went in the bag. Next up was the woman sat to his side. She had to empty her handbag onto the table. It was funny how all the men leaned forwards to get a better look, me included. There was some weird stuff in there and some things I couldn't identify, and the woman was plainly embarrassed. The

English would rather be terrorised than embarrassed. We went round the table like this and it was a fascinating microcosm of the human condition. We all took an unhealthy interest in what came out of these secret, denied places, a man's pockets and a woman's handbag.

Then from his other pocket, the big man took a packet of nylon cable ties. They were white, about twelve inches long and there must have been about fifty in the bag. He gestured for the nearest woman to get up and then he told her to put a cable tie on the wrist of the man next to her and pull it tight. Incredibly, she didn't know how a cable tie worked and had to be shown and the man eventually had to put it on his own wrist. She was shaking a lot and found it difficult and it took a while for her to get round all the men, both hands. Then the next bit was trickier as she had to loop new ties underneath the ones already on the men's wrists and tie them to each of the women's wrists until she was the only one that wasn't attached. Then she sat down and the driver completed the circle by looping her wrists with her neighbours, so they were all sat there around the oval table attached to each other by their wrists. With reduced mobility, most of the men were growing red and sweaty with indignation. Steam was almost coming from their ears. It was fascinating to watch. For good measure, the driver put an additional tie around Felix's ankle and looped it round the stretcher of the table leg.

'Fine, now we can all relax', said the big man, and he gestured to his partner to take a look around. It became apparent that Felix's daughter, although up to that point being one of the most composed of the group, had now become the least relaxed. She was trying very hard to keep it all together, but not quite succeeding. She was very worried about something and I thought I probably knew what it was.

It took about ten minutes before the other guy came back. It was a long ten minutes, but I enjoyed it very much. There was no talking allowed. I appreciated the opportunity to scrutinise the faces of the guests, and especially I relished Felix's agony. I noticed a discrete nod from the guy who'd been looking through the house. It said something like, 'mission accomplished'. The big man slipped his gun back into his jacket, while the other two still pointed theirs intimidatingly. He approached the table and stood behind Felix's daughter. She was wearing a low-cut silk dress and had a very fetching sparkly necklace round her neck. The big man brought both his arms forward and I thought he was going to unclasp the jewellery from her nape. Instead, he put both hands down the front of her dress and left them there and then started gyrating them so that it was obvious that he was squeezing and massaging her breasts. I'll never forget the pained expression of vexation and resignation on her face. It was a picture.

It quite turned me on, actually, and I wondered if I was going to get a go and where it might all lead, but then he suddenly pulled out and grasped the cleavage of her dress and ripped the whole front of it apart, exposing her breasts. Instinctively, she went to protect her modesty but of course her hands were tied to both of her partner's and for a moment it looked just like they were both making a play for some of the action, and all four hands were desperately trying to cover her chest. It was very comical. I would have laughed out loud, and I almost did, but I'd been told not to utter a sound, just watch. It was very funny.

She was told to put her hands on the table, so we all took the opportunity to look at her breasts some more. They were very handsome breasts, actually.

The big man then got his gun out again, and the other disappeared back into the house. There was great unease. I sensed it. When he returned, he was carrying something over his shoulder. Whatever it was, it was quite heavy and was wrapped in a duvet. It was about the size of a … child.

Felix stood bolt upright and shouted something very obscene. He was a bit hindered with his physical expression by the cable ties and I'm sure this made him even more angry. The big man walked calmly up to him with the gun laid across his chest, and just stood there and then sniffed the air in a decidedly theatrical manner. 'You've shat yourself, you dirty old man', he announced to all, and we could surely all see and smell it now; Felix had indeed soiled himself.

I was delighted. It was more than Felix could bear, and he slumped back into his chair and started crying.

The big man went across to the stereo system on top of a low dresser. It was an expensive looking one with big, floor standing speakers. It had been burbling away to itself the whole time we'd been there, but I'd only just noticed it. He rejected the disc that was playing and selected Led Zeppelin, their first LP, my favourite. He started it on Dazed and Confused about three minutes in; this guy was on the ball, and he motioned for us to leave as he turned the volume up until my insides started melting. For good measure, he switched the lights off and stamped on the Wi Fi router.

We were out like a flash, back the way we'd come. The small man's burden didn't slow him down, and I had difficulty keeping up with them. The driver had the Sainsbury's bag with him.

I guess it would be true to say that at that stage I hadn't really taken in what had happened, and what was likely to come. I know it sounds silly to say it, but it was so surreal that it just wasn't real at all.

The two cars were waiting where we'd left them. The bundle was laid in the back of the Range Rover and we were off. There was no melodramatic Sweeney-like getaway; we both pulled away sedately and drove in convoy, about a hundred yards apart, for ten minutes or so without meeting a main road, then we stopped. It was a dark night, but I could see that we were next to what looked like a disused airfield. There were several derelict concrete block buildings and lots of barbed wire and broken wooden panelling. There were notices warning of guard dogs and security patrols. I don't think so.

The Range Rover tailgate opened, and the small man took the bundle over his shoulder again while the big man carried a canvas tool bag and the Sainsbury's For Life bag. We left my driver changing the number plates on the Ford and found the gap in the wire perimeter fence and shimmied through. The two men weren't saying much, but I was relieved they were talking normally now. I'd had my fill of the scary stuff, and it would have been really creepy out here in the open. We went over to the far building, about two hundred yards from the road across a concrete yard. The door was ajar, but the big man kicked it further open and produced a torch. Inside, it was a bit squalid. There was mud in one corner where the asbestos roof was leaking and some graffiti on a wall and some discarded Red Bull cans and other detritus next to it.

And then there was the cage.

It was actually two gabions that had been joined together, and one of the hinged faces had been left loose. It was about five foot by two foot six by two foot six. As the small man leant down to place the bundle in the cage, he pulled the duvet back and the big man shone his torch on the face of a little girl; she looked about ten years old. She looked at rest. What I mean is, she didn't look troubled. I was assuming she was alive. I was going to touch her skin, but I wasn't fast enough as in the cage she went. The big man got a pair of pliers out of his bag and a coil of stiff wire and wired the door of the cage shut. Then he took out two plastic bottles of water and pushed them through the mesh. Finally, we left the Sainsbury's bag in a bucket of muddy water on the other side of the room, and pulled the door tightly closed on the way out.

And that was it. Over. Done. But of course, it wasn't, was it? The first bit was over, but the second bit most certainly wasn't done; it was just beginning.

There wasn't much of a goodbye. I got the impression that the two milk tray guys considered themselves a bit above us. I guess all they were concerned about was if we mucked up, somehow, and made things more difficult or precarious for them. As far as I was concerned, the whole night had gone without a hitch. All very professional, and I was impressed.

Pinky had certainly come up with the goods.

My driver was waiting in the Ka with the engine running and we both drove off in different directions. I just sat there in the passenger seat, head back, eyes closed. There were so many questions I wanted to ask the driver, but I knew he would not be for talking on the way home. For him, the less said, the better. I was just left with my thoughts.

And what thoughts! I'm not stupid. I realised the enormity of what had just happened. This was going to be big news. You don't get many kidnappings in this country. If you don't count family feuds or domestic quarrels, then there's probably ... none. It just doesn't happen. And when the victim is a young, innocent child, the daughter of wealthy parents with influential friends, well you have the perfect storm, don't you? The police would throw all their resources at this, and then some; the public were going to be whipped into a frenzy and the press would go ape-shit. It was all high-octane stuff, and I was loving it. It was what I was put on this Earth for.

Really? Was this really how I felt at that moment at the start of the return journey to darkest Devon, sat there in that passenger seat being driven home to my lovely hermitage, my sanctuary? A big smile spread across my face which I think gave the answer.

My mind drifted back to the dining room of the big house. What would have happened the moment we had slipped out through the French windows? Well, I think, confusion initially. With the music blaring and the darkness and the cable ties, it would have been difficult for anyone to take charge. You need a leader at such times. I bet it was just chaos for several minutes while they tried to free themselves from the table. Even if they clambered over the top of it from one end, they were still attached to it by Felix's ankle. The ties were done up tight, and they would have been painful. The first thing to do would be to turn the music off and the lights on and then try and calm everyone down and start thinking coherently. That's what I would have done if I was in charge. Then I would have got something to cut the ties. There would have been kitchen knives and scissors about, so we would all have had to crab over in our little circle to find one and then I would have figured some way to let the wider world in on our predicament. There had been eight phones in the Sainsbury's bag, but I'll bet there were more in the house. The kid probably had one by her bed. There might have been one on the landline, too. I'm not sure if that had been disabled or not. Then, there would be the neighbours. They were all in for a bit of a rude awakening, behind their high walls and their locked electric gates.

So, I mulled over to myself; probably more than ten minutes for the first emergency call to go out, three or four minutes to get past the operator who would be trying to weed out the hoax calls and time wasters and drunks, and then finally, when someone believed the caller or figured it wasn't worth their job to ask any more questions, all hell would be let loose. It would be a major incident. The biggest career opportunity ever for a lot of guys.

But by then, of course, we would be miles away and minding our own business.

And then I got to thinking, eventually, if we would really all be likely to get away with it.

As far as I was concerned, the whole operation had gone faultlessly. Any number of things could have happened, but they didn't. Nobody got in the way, and nothing unexpected turned up. I'll bet the two milk tray men didn't know who I was or who my driver was, and I most surely knew nothing about them. Even if my life depended on it, I couldn't give any sort of description, no clues whatsoever. I knew what my driver looked like, but that was about it, nothing more. Sure, he was a bit of a weak link in that he knew who I was and where I lived, but I imagine Pinky's arrangement with him would help ensure his silence.

I have to say I was beginning to feel invincible and it was a marvellous feeling.

We were back in the Golf in no time at all. It's like that when you're thinking hard, I find. Another quick number plate change and we were on the road again.

I did wonder about the cars; I thought perhaps Pinky might have stretched to a different one for the return journey. I wondered why the driver hadn't torched the Ka, and who would be coming for it. It would be a couple of low-lifes, and all the vehicles would have been nicked, even the Range Rover. Especially the Range Rover.

But I have to tell you, there was some unease niggling away in my head. It was obvious my $10,000 wouldn't have gone very far. I wouldn't have put my neck on the line for that sort of money. Milk tray men with squeaky voices don't come cheap, I'll wager. I'm guessing you'd have to add another zero on the end, at the very least. Why did Pinky choose to do that for me? He didn't have to.

I didn't like the idea of being in his debt, and I wondered if he would want repaying in some way.

Anyway, I had my own boots back on and I settled down. I noted that we were going back a different way but then I lost interest and fell asleep, and it was only when we pulled up in the lay-by next to the bridleway that I woke up.

What an unreal experience that was, as well. It was almost as if nothing at all had happened. It all just seemed so distant, so detached, so unconnected somehow. A truly parallel world.

It must have been about five-thirty because I could just see the horizon lightening. It was overcast and damp and one or two birds had started singing and I could hear the distant cockerel. I had enjoyed my adventure, but I was glad to be back in Devon.

I thought I'd take the shoes with me, just in case. You never know. I'd put them in the wood-burner as soon as I could. All was quiet on the way back and not even Rosie stirred when I let myself back into Church House. My wing chair looked inviting. I poured myself a good tumbler of Laphroaig and sat back and went through the whole party again in my mind until I fell asleep with the empty glass on my lap.

I don't have a TV, I've told you. I watch things on my iPad now and again, but not much. There's not a lot I can get excited about, and I'm afraid I don't do ads, so I have to restrict myself to iPlayer. I also have my Sony Digicube on my bedside table and there's an old mains FM radio in the kitchen that's permanently tuned to Radio Four. If I ever wanted to listen to anything else on it, I'd have to take the back off and move the tuner by hand, so I don't bother.

The bell of the grandfather clock woke me at midday. It sounded urgent, for some reason. Sometimes it sounds like that, other times it says, it's alright, no need to get up. Today it requested my attention. The empty tumbler was still resting on my stomach and I rescued it and transferred it to my desk. Ah yes, last night. It was a hell of a night. Did it really happen?

I had trouble collecting and collating my thoughts.

I wandered into the kitchen and the radio beckoned for me to turn it on. There was a news update about a kidnapping. So it was all true of course. I knew it was. I listened intently to see what I could learn. I learned lots, and as I had predicted, all hell had been let loose.

I learned that the man who wanted us to know who he was, was actually the Deputy Chief Constable. Wow. That would be adding just a little pressure to the police operation. I didn't know what I thought about that. Just how confident was I that I was immune from all this?

It seems amazing to think back to this and tell you that this really was the first time that I had even thought of the implications of getting caught. I most certainly wouldn't be able to cope with that, no way. I just wouldn't. What had I actually got myself into here? At that moment, it suddenly seemed as if I had risked everything I held dear on this very foolhardy and very unnecessary adventure. Was it worth it? What a question, and a bit late to ask it.

I had to conclude in the cold light of that very pleasant spring Devon day, of course, that it wasn't. What had I been thinking of? It quickly became obvious to me that I desperately needed some checks and balances in my life. I hadn't had any for twenty years.

I guess the thing that amazed me most of all was that they hadn't found the girl. What were they playing at? The police forces from the whole of Leicestershire, Nottingham and Derby, and the rest, were out there crawling all over the place. What were they doing? It can have only been five or six miles away from the damned house.

At first, I thought it must be some sort of bluff, to try and trap the kidnappers somehow. How could the police be so stupid? But then they played some recording of shouting and screaming, and I recognised some of the voices and they all sounded pretty authentic.

It had been just about twelve hours since we had left the girl in the derelict building. Surely in that time they would have searched all the local hiding places. Perhaps they judged that professional kidnappers who had gone to so much trouble would be very unlikely to hide their victim nearby, and the more I thought about it, the more this had to be true. Still, all the same, you'd have thought they'd have had all bases covered.

I gauged that when (if?) she woke up, she'd have started on the water straight away. Kids today, especially rich, trendy kids, seem to be always holding on to water bottles as if they were an extension of an appendage and are always drinking out of them whether they're thirsty or not. Those two bottles wouldn't have lasted very long. She'd be getting hungry, too. Also, I imagined it was chloroform or something that had knocked her out, so she probably wouldn't have seen it coming if she was asleep. When she woke up in the gabion cage it would all have been a bit frightening. Just a bit.

I made a sandwich for lunch and took my iPad and went and sat back in my study. I was right that it had stirred the press up. It was more or less constant updates on the news channels. I was becoming fascinated with this. It made me tingle inside that I knew more than anyone who was being interviewed by the media. It was such a shame I couldn't share it with someone. I found myself shouting at the device. No, you stupid idiot, I was saying, it couldn't have possibly been like that because … ; don't you realise that if … ; no, of course it wasn't Islamic terrorists. Look around you; look for the clues.

The police weren't giving anything away. They hadn't even made a statement, and there was speculation verging on the ridiculous in the press. From the look of the video clips there was a whole encampment of TV vans outside the house, churning up the neat grass verges with their vehicles. They couldn't get to within a hundred yards of the gates because of the police don't cross lines and were very busy trying to find neighbours to quiz. It looked like they had all chosen to stay safely behind their locked gates, besieged.

I was beginning to enjoy it. I felt so involved, but so detached. Unlike the other millions of viewers glued to the news flashes, I knew everything. I was absorbed.

It was headline news on the BBC at six o clock and the police had had to release a statement. I wondered if it might

407

be the Deputy Chief Constable himself who would be doing the talking, but it wasn't. It would probably have broken some protocol or other. I wondered, casually, if he would welcome the sudden intense scrutiny of his private life. I wondered what he had to hide. And Felix, for that matter, and all the rest. I wished we'd kept their phones.

Basically, the statement said that the girl was still missing and they were fearful for her life. It didn't exactly say that they had no leads, but that's what you would infer. The spokesman looked nervous.

It had become a circus and the animals were performing as they'd been taught, but the clowns were looking on and the audience was becoming restless.

I had a good night's sleep after all the excitement, but when I woke, I was incredulous that they still hadn't found her. I was beginning to feel sorry for her. After all, she was just an innocent child; none of any of this was her fault. By now she would be hungry and thirsty and she would be lying in her own urine and excrement. She would have been petrified through the long, dark night and wondering why she had been abandoned. That's if she was still alive.

It wasn't really very fair, and I considered if there was anything I could do. I thought through all the options, but I couldn't come up with anything that wouldn't be hugely risky for me. I thought maybe I should try and contact Pinky and let him know that I thought we'd gone too far, but that would have been seen as a weakness, and would still be hazardous. I would just have to hope that plod would get his act together.

You're thinking, didn't you learn from the hanging in the wood?

That was different.

Angel was the same age as the girl when he died, I suddenly thought.

Midday news and still nothing. Another statement, even squirmier than the first, and a disconsolate, desperate press conference. Despair from everyone involved. Incredulity and incomprehension that there had been no credible ransom demand, nor admission of responsibility. It was a complete mystery.

Apart from my nagging concern for the girl and the realisation that if she died then they really would leave no stone unturned, I was entranced.

Then, at about five pm came the news that everyone had been hoping and praying for, but that no one had really expected. The girl had been found alive.

There must have been spontaneous rejoicing on the streets and in the pubs and living rooms across the country, probably the world. I guess I was happy for the girl, but for me it did represent the end of an interesting little interregnum in an otherwise humdrum sort of existence. The panic was over, and everyone lived happily ever after.

Apart from the nightmares that would follow for some of the players and would never, ever go away.

I did continue to listen to the news updates and I watched the six-o-clock news on catch-up for the next few nights until it got knocked off the top spot by something else. They still had no leads, no motive, no nothing, although they didn't describe their incompetence quite like that. I wasn't so naïve as to think that would be the end. It would always be there on someone's desk, if not in their in-tray, for ever. The Deputy Chief Constable certainly would never forget it.

I got a bit of a fright one morning in May, it must have been towards the end of the month because I remember that the honeysuckle draped across the trellis around the front door was just starting to come out. I like honeysuckle. It smells so evocative at dusk in summer; there's really nothing quite like it. Stood on my doorstep were two people I had never seen before, a man and a woman. They were dressed smartly; they weren't from around here. The man had a blue suit on and the woman wore a sober grey skirt and an almost matching jacket. They looked to be both in their mid-thirties and came across as purposeful. At first, I thought they must be from the council, and then I thought maybe the Inland Revenue or even, stupidly, the DVLA, but no, the man took from his inside pocket a little wallet with an ID that announced they were from the Leicestershire Constabulary, CID, and could they come in please. The woman showed her ID, too. She was a Detective Constable and he was a Detective Superintendent, but I instantly forgot their names. I do that as a nasty habit and have never been able to correct it.

Well, there was no alternative but to ask them in. I didn't want to leave them on the doorstep in full view and it would have come over as churlish and suspicious to have not invited them in. After all, they had probably driven down from the East Midlands that morning. I hoped they had come in an unmarked car and had parked it in the parish hall car park, out of the way.

I've said before, I do pride myself on my ability to remain cool when faced with unplanned uncertainties. My mind works fast under pressure. I decided instantly that no matter what was coming, my demeanour should be one of simple politeness and country bumpkin ignorance. I would play the Devon card.

I took them through to the kitchen and offered them a drink. They declined. They looked as if they intended to keep things formal.

Now, I've told you, I don't watch much TV, but when I do, I often go for crime dramas. English ones, not American imports. They don't interest me. One of the things I've often wondered is do real detectives actually call on suspects without warning? The fictional ones are always doing it. I can obviously see the advantage of surprise and unpreparedness, but what about the practicalities? How likely are you to find people in? And if they are in, what are you going to do if they pretend they're not in and they hide and won't come to the door? Especially if you've just driven two hundred miles or have stayed overnight in some grotty Travelodge at the Constabulary's, and ultimately the taxpayer's, expense, and you don't have a warrant? It doesn't really add up to me. What happens in real life? I guess they need to keep coming back, but then that doesn't make good TV. It cramps style and stymies dramatic flow, I would think, though I'm not a director.

So I was wondering what my two detectives would have done if I hadn't answered the door, as indeed I might not have done instinctively, had I known who they were. That would have been a big mistake; I'm sure they would have knocked at a few neighbouring cottages until they got a response, and then where would we all be? I didn't like to think about it.

They wouldn't sit down when I proffered the dining chairs. Professionals, damn. Anyway, I leaned back on the Aga.

Firstly, they wanted to reassure me that this was just a routine enquiry. Had I been aware of the kidnapping of Felix

Marsland's granddaughter in April of this year? Of course I had. Everyone in the country had. I told them that I didn't have a TV and didn't really keep up with the news but yes, I had followed the incident with some interest because Felix had been a friend and colleague of mine in the nineties. Ah yes, they said, this was the reason for their visit. As a matter of routine, they were checking all associates, past and present, to rule them out of the investigation, or something like that. They added that they were concentrating on acquaintances that might have some reason for doing harm to Felix or members of his family. They understood that Felix had fired me from a company of which I was a major shareholder and did I perhaps harbour vengeful thoughts towards him? I told them that was twenty years ago and I'd made a new life for myself in Devon.

I believe it truly was routine and that they had no knowledge of the subsequent breakdown of my marriage that I might have attributed to Felix's actions. They continued to probe around the sacking, but I think I reassured them that as far as I was concerned it was just a sound business decision on Felix's part, that I had accepted at the time and was simply the result of an unfortunate series of events that had conspired against me.

I wondered what words Felix had used to describe the episode to them. How did he actually feel at the time and what did he think of me now? I was surprised he even remembered me. Perhaps he was scraping the barrel by the time he got to me. I suspect it was quite a big barrel.

Then they asked me a bit about my life in Crow's Nymet. What I did now, and how I occupied my time. I told them life was good. I was a keen walker and I enjoyed gardening, and the rest of the time I read books and tried to keep my mind active. It was all true. And then, inevitably, they asked me what

I was doing on the night in question and I replied that I was reading in my study until midnight and then I went to bed. And no, of course no one could corroborate that; I live on my own, read the book on my own and went to bed on my own, and in the morning I got up and had breakfast on my own. I didn't put it to them quite that emphatically, but they got the message. They had walked through the village and seen what a sleepy place it is.

I had already told them that I hadn't driven a car for twenty years. I don't think that anything I said to them sounded remotely suspicious in any way. How could they have possibly associated my insular life down here with a brazen kidnapping two hundred miles away?

After some initial trepidation on first seeing them, I was now beginning to enjoy the experience of my interrogation. Luckily, I realised that I was getting a little overconfident and had the good sense to keep my mouth shut when I was sorely tempted to throw in a cryptic clue or two. That would have been very silly and unnecessarily foolhardy. All the same, it would have been fascinating and good fun to have pitted my wits against the combined might of the nation's constabulary, especially as I was so sure of my cover. It would have been interesting to discover how stupid they really are.

So if you're one of them reading this, of course you'll now know just how stupid you are, without me having to tell you.

thirty one

The way I've been telling you this story, you probably think that my life has been one long string of stimulating incidents and adventures, but you'd be wrong to think that. I'm not telling you about the boring bits when nothing happened for weeks on end. It wasn't a problem for me most of the time; it's like that for everybody, I think.

The kidnapping was a high point, and I often think of the excitement of it when I've had a drink or two. It was exhilarating for some time, but I've put it on the back burner now. I don't expect it to come back.

Just as long as the driver keeps his mouth shut.

I was, I have to admit, becoming concerned about what I was going to do when the Physic ran out. I had inevitably been using it as something of a crutch, and I've told you about my worries about getting addicted. It was going to leave one hell of a gap in my life when it was gone, and I had no notion what I was going to fill that void with. My life would be very empty for a while. Another thing that was bothering me was the viability of continuing to live in this village. I had racked up a lot of hate, what with one thing and another. I guessed at some stage there was surely going to be some form of reckoning. There were a lot of people out there who would be happy to give me a good kicking. I felt it was bound to happen, and I wasn't looking forward to it at all.

I was trapped in this place.

So I ended up focussing on the forthcoming summer solstice to take my mind off it. I thought it could be a final blow-out. And who knows, I mused, something interesting might happen.

This time I was going to take a dose of the Physic with me and I was going to swallow it on the stroke of midnight, lying there on the soft moss at the foot of Yew Magna. I wouldn't dress up this time. I looked on that as a bit of an indulgence, now, and seriously creepy. I'd got over that. All the same, I would go with an expectation that if anything ever was going to be stirred from its long sleep at the Clump, then this would be the occasion for it.

I did actually contemplate drinking all of the remaining liquid in one go and be done with it, one way or another. It might kill me, but that wouldn't necessarily be a bad thing. I felt I was quite ready for that. I was confident I knew what was waiting for me if that's the way it turned out, but I sensed it would be cheating and I didn't care for that.

For the week or so after the detectives' visit, this is what I was indulging my time with, and I must admit, I was beginning to get aroused by the idea. It was my focus. I like to have a focus. I've always been a project-oriented sort of person. Not goal-oriented. It's not necessarily the end that counts for me; it's the means to the end. My focus was the Rousing; my means the Physic, and the end, such as it might be, was yet to be determined.

So when I noticed Peter in the graveyard one Tuesday afternoon in early June, my focus turned back to all he had told me.

I hadn't seen him to talk to since that conspiratorial little chat in my kitchen earlier in the year, when we juggled poisonous ingredients with magical symbols and riddles that ultimately came to nothing. My brain was working hard. Was there mileage in having Peter come along with me? I know this had gone through my mind at the time he was telling me everything. I think he could prove to be a steadying hand if things started to go unusual.

He was digging a grave. A man of many talents, then. I could see now that he was among the Uglow graves. There were lots of them. They'd been around for a long time. Their patch was in the South East corner of the graveyard. Their graves were the first ones you saw when you came through the lychgate. The more recent burials were all well-tended and one or two had vases of cut flowers on them. Garden and hedgerow flowers, not florist's gaudy hybrids or faded plastic tat. In fact, it was the prettiest part of the graveyard all year round, what with the spring primroses and bluebells and campion and dog roses in the hedge and then, later, a mass of amber montbretia in the bank and purple honesty or sweet rocket and then there would be yellow jasmine and snowdrops in the winter. They'd had centuries to get comfortable. They liked it there, where things didn't change much. The flowers were very much at ease with the Uglows.

I thought I'd go and have a word with him. I would imagine he was half expecting it because every now and again I saw him cast a surreptitious glance in the direction of my kitchen window. He knew I was inside watching him.

I don't know much about gravedigging. I probably know about as much as you do. I guess in principle it's just a case of digging out a hole that's about seven foot by three foot, by six foot deep, keeping the sides nice and square and neat looking and piling the spoil nearby on a tarpaulin and then tidying it all up a bit for the ceremony. It's probably not that simple. I know I wouldn't fancy doing it. I would think the deeper you go, the harder it becomes and the more effort it is to chuck the dirt out. I'll bet it's getting difficult to find a traditional practitioner nowadays; one with a spade rather than a mini-digger.

It must be interesting going through the various layers of earth. There'll be lots of curious things to find. Bones and stuff and the odd keepsake that went in with the corpse. It's fascinating to do a back-of-the-fag-packet calculation on body count in an English churchyard. Let's say the place has been a graveyard for one thousand years, and the parish has had a population of about a hundred people for all that time, and they have an average lifespan of fifty years each and they've all been buried in the consecrated ground, then there would have been about two thousand burials over that period. I think that's probably a conservative figure. No wonder the ground level rises after a while. I know it all sounds a bit unlikely, but you can't deny the maths.

It's only relatively recently that graves have been marked, so the ones that you now see in churchyards are rarely more than a couple of hundred years old. All the rest are in there somewhere, on top of each other, side by side and rotting down, all pointing in the same direction, east to west.

Peter had got down to about two feet so his head came up to my chest. It was a bit awkward, so he got out. He had a denim shirt on that was open a few buttons at the front and it was wet through with sweat. He looked every inch a man of the soil. He was panting and his throaty breathing betrayed a lifetime of smoking. He really didn't look up to the job.

'I shouldn't be doing this', he confirmed.

'It's Ted's job, but he won't do it. His ankle's never really got better. He's still off work'.

Peter told me that in their family it was a tradition that the son dug the grave of the father. He had even helped bury his own father after the fire, though he was just a child and couldn't wield a proper shovel. He had got down on his hands and knees and clawed at the earth until his nails bled and his grandfather had dragged him away. He was standing next to his parents' grave as he spoke. It seemed like it was from a different world. It was physically here with us as we looked at it, but it belonged somewhere else, lost in the faded memories of a little boy bleeding dirt.

So, Ted's father had died, and he was being buried the next day. It would be a big funeral. There were lots of Uglows, and lots of cronies and hangers-on. Ted and Peter still weren't speaking to each other, evidently, and I gathered that there was some hope that the funeral might be the catalyst to them reconciling their differences. Fat chance, I thought. I'd seen the way they looked at each other. That chasm had been around for ever and it wasn't going to go away any time soon. Even though Peter had agreed to dig his uncle's grave because Ted couldn't, I could sense that it wasn't from some wish for family unity or a gesture of appeasement. It was because it had to be done. It was Peter's choice, but in the end, he really had no choice at all. He had to do it. I could see that.

'He could have helped me, but as you can see, he's not here. He could have done something'.

418

Was Ted maybe not there digging his father's grave because he was scared of seeing me again? I can't believe that, though it was something of a puzzle that almost six months had passed since the altercation with the pissing and the foot down the mole hole and Ted still hadn't come calling for some score-settling. It was unnerving. I didn't understand it and it unsettled me. What was going on in Ted's mind, and would some heavy drinking at the wake tomorrow with his mates trigger a pressing need to end the waiting?

And what was I going to do about it?

I was sure I would think of something; I was just in that sort of mood.

I asked Peter outright if he'd had any more thoughts about the ingredients of the magic potion. This had been our main topic of conversation the last time we met, and I was curious to know if Peter had gone away that day with a renewed interest or whether the catharsis of the telling had put to rest any ambitions he may have harboured. He was a little taken aback by my abruptness. I could see it in his eyes. It was as though he thought of the episode as a clandestine rendezvous between us that was now complete, done and dusted and moved on from, if not entirely forgotten. I was disappointed. I thought it might have fired his imagination. I guess, on reflection, that if that had been the case, then he'd have come back to see me before now, to see how I might be getting on solving riddles and brewing potions, but then he could just be anxious at what might be unleashed. Who knows?

Do I overanalyse people and their actions, do you suppose? Do I give their cognitive skills more credit than they deserve? Do people think as much as I do?

Peter was hesitant in replying. I couldn't really work the guy out. He said he'd spent some restless nights going over what we'd talked about. He said he'd spent his whole life with all this as a backdrop. It had always been there, part of him, but mostly tucked away out of sight and mind. He'd never been able to shake off this feeling that his life was anchored to Crow's Nymet, and his every thought and action was somehow influenced by the legacy of the place, by its history and its pre-history. Those weren't his exact words, but that was what he was trying to say. He was telling me what I had surmised all along. Peter and Ted and their family were rooted by the superstitions and the stories and the folklore of the area and were inseparably hefted to the wooded valleys, the church, the Clump, Yew Magna and the Rousing, and to Crow's Nymet itself. They were all part of the same thing.

I was fascinated. It was at that moment that many things became clear to me. Things that had been churning around, bothering me, ever since I arrived in this place. This must have been how it was everywhere at one time, and now there was only a tiny vestige left, just under the surface but still there in the hearts and minds of the local people and propped up by the continuity and cohesion of the land and the traditions and the memories. I was witnessing a little bit of what it was really like to live in those far off times. Something we've all lost to the modern world. It's just hanging on as a parallel existence, but only just, as there's hardly anything left of it. I was lucky, at that moment, to get a tantalising insight into another life, a sort of ephemeral amalgam of the natural and supernatural worlds that is surely receding from our very souls before our eyes.

I'm rambling, again, but I'm telling you that that was a Eureka moment for me. They do come along when you least expect them, don't they? And they do tend to last just a moment. But in that very brief lapse of time, everything becomes clear.

That's what it was like.

I knew, now, that I had to tell Peter about the phial.

When I told you about it, I needed to explain quite a few things beforehand, like where Church House and the smoke blackened thatch came into the scheme of things. My guess was that I wouldn't need to do this with Peter. Even if he didn't know, specifically, about these things, I felt he would be able to 'sense' the concepts; that they would all fit together seamlessly and intuitively because they were already there somewhere, in his brain, his genes, his cells.

I believe that his response showed I was right. I wasn't disappointed. All I said was that I had found the sooty stone jar full of brown, viscous fluid hidden in the blackened roof timbers of the house.

He was stood there in front of me, leaning on his shovel. I watched his face. He was having some very deep thoughts. A bead of sweat trickled down his temple into the stubble of his cheekbone. I'm not saying he was sweating from anxiety or fear. He was calm. Completely calm, actually. It was as if for a moment he had transcended into another existence. It was a Eureka moment for him, too.

When he came down, he asked me if I had drunk any of the liquid. Now, of course, I was expecting this question, and had been mulling around in my mind how to respond. I had become more convinced than ever that I wanted him with me on the night of the solstice. I felt he would be a link, a conduit to whatever was going to be there.

I told him, no, I hadn't tried it. I was waiting until the solstice and then I would try it.

I added that I'd like him to join me at the Clump at midnight, and together we could discover the long-forgotten secrets of the Physic at the time and place for which it had been intended half a millennium ago.

It was difficult to discern what was happening inside Peter's skull. He wasn't giving much away. He looked wistful, but his brows were furrowed and his limbs were held tight and braced with his hands fisted and his eyes were empty and bottomless.

We stood for a while like that. Thrushes were singing and the sun was washing the colour from the campion and the scent of the cut grass was heady and sickly in my nose.

'I've got to finish this digging', was all he said, and he jumped back down into the grave and struck the shovel hard with his boot into the heavy, muddy shale. He turned his back to me and unloaded the spoil by my feet.

I knew we weren't done.

I walked back to the house and let myself into the kitchen and made a cup of coffee and stood there looking at him labouring at his commitment.

You can tell when a man isn't concentrating on his work. He was in turn erratic and aggressive, and then fatigued and listless. He looked stoic, then angry, then circumspect and then drained. Of course he did. He had lots to think about. A lifetime of thoughts.

He wasn't making a very good job. The heap of earth was all over the place. I watched him for an hour until all I could see was the point of his shovel every now and again. How deep was he going to go? Finally, the spade was thrown out and Peter scrambled up the side of the hole and sat there upright on the untidy pile. He put his elbows on his knees and his hands on his forehead and sat there in the early evening sun, lost in his thoughts.

I had enjoyed my afternoon. It was a good feeling to be in control.

The next thing I knew, the kitchen door flew open and Peter was standing there, all mud and sweat and consternation.

'I'm going to have to ask my grandfather', he said slowly.

'He'll know what to do'.

Now, I have to say that I did find this rather amusing, although of course I didn't show it. In my mind, I saw Peter sat round an Ouija board asking the question, or whispering at the side of a grave for inspiration from a long dead ancestor. How would he reply? In a ghostly voice from the long grass? Had Peter already been talking with his grandfather out there in the churchyard?

He hadn't, actually, and there was a very good reason why he hadn't. The old boy wasn't dead yet!

You could have knocked me down with a feather. I think my jaw must have dropped both melodramatically and metaphorically.

I did a quick calculation. It didn't really seem very likely. It would put him in his mid to late nineties.

I supposed on reflection, it could actually be possible.

Peter said he was in a nursing home. Funnily enough, I knew where it was. It was in a big house a couple of miles the other side of South Molton. It was on the top of a hill and the rendering was painted a dazzling white. You can see it from a long way away.

My mind was racing. I had to talk with this guy. What a link to the past. I'd had no idea he was still alive. It hadn't entered my mind when Peter spoke of him.

And then I realised that I'd have the perfect opportunity to speak to him the next day at the funeral. I said to Peter that maybe he should bring his grandfather along to meet me and we could all talk about the summer solstice together. I felt sure I would be able to inveigle them with some subtle deception and flattery.

Peter told me the old man wasn't coming. He hadn't even been told about his son's death. He didn't know anything about it.

Apparently, Gramper Uglow, that's what everyone called him, was, and always had been, a strange sort of bloke. Sure, he was now the lone surviving patriarch of a prodigious local dynasty, but it was a dissolute and dysfunctional family, rife with infighting and had been for as long as anyone could remember, including Gramper Uglow himself who had grown up in the thick of ructions and strife. He had lived as a widower and a virtual outcast for many years, alone in the outlying cottage where he was born and where he'd brought up his grandson, and had been happy to live a self-reliant life just within the curtilage of his untidy family estate. However, it seems there had lately been a series of unfortunate psychotic episodes that had resulted in some unpleasantness, and the family had finally succumbed to putting him in a home, out of the way until he died.

Now I came to think about it, I knew the cottage that Peter was talking about, but I'd never associated it with him. It was unoccupied and overgrown and was falling down. The tin was flapping off the roof, letting the rain in and washing away the walls. I remembered the old man when he lived there. I used to have a cubby hole in the bank at the bottom of the garden from where I could watch the cottage. I remember one night I watched for hours as he sat there alone in the garden, shaping something with his knife. I remember the blade reflecting light from his oil lamp in staccato bursts.

So that was Gramper Uglow, all along, and I never knew.

Peter was trying to make excuses for the family. The old man was too frail; it would kill him. He would be too upset by his son's sad demise (probably because there'd be no one to bury him when the time came, now both sons were gone). But it seemed to me that the obvious reason he'd not been invited was that everyone feared that he would end up making a scene.

If only they could have known.

Anyway, after Peter had gone, I got to thinking seriously about all I had learned, and I knew that I had to go and talk to the old man. It would have to be at the nursing home.

Now I guess I could have walked there. It was only six or seven miles away after all, and I was used to walking that far and back. The thing was, though, that I was a bit afraid that when he got to hear about the funeral and his exclusion from it, I thought it might tip him over the edge. A good idea would be to visit him before the funeral, and that meant turning up at the home the next morning. I wanted to be back in time for the interment because I wanted to see who would be there, so I hatched a daring plan. I would drive there in the Land Rover.

Luckily, I keep the battery on a trickle charger in the barn. All I had to do was to carry it down to the bottom of the garden and connect it up. I hadn't started the engine since before Christmas when I needed some bags of aggregate to fill a hole in the yard. It took a bit of persuading and I had to unbind the clutch with the starter motor. It felt odd in the driver's seat and I was nervous, so I drank a cup or two of whisky before I left, and I felt much better.

There wasn't any need to venture onto the main road, so I stuck to the back lanes. I know them well, but all the same it was compelling seeing them passing by at speed in the daylight. I parked up in the corner of the car park. It was surfaced with gravel that had algae and moss growing through it. There was an air of neglect and decay about the place, and it was manifest that it had seen better days.

Despite the fact that it had been built on the hill and was in a rather exposed spot, there was a lot of greenery in the grounds, mostly rhododendrons and holly and laurel. All good evergreen cover. I didn't like the place. I wouldn't like to end my days somewhere like that. I shuddered as I got down from the cab. I guessed it was going to smell of urine and stale medicine and old people.

As it happened, I didn't actually get to find out, as I never got past the wretched woman on the front desk. I don't know what I was expecting, but I wasn't expecting a front desk. It was only a small place; they couldn't get many visitors. Was she sat there all the time waiting to intercept strangers like me? From her smug expression, I fear so.

I realised that I didn't know Gramper Uglow's first name, so I referred to him as 'old man Uglow' in as familiar a manner as I could muster in the confusion.

I think she saw through me straight away. I guess it was her job.

'Who are you?', she asked.

I told her that I was an old friend of his and was up here for the funeral. I guessed, correctly, that she knew about the funeral and she knew he didn't.

'I won't tell him anything about it', I added quickly, but it was too late and it was clear I was wasting my time.

'I have strict instructions from the family that Mr Uglow should have no visitors today'

'But I've come a long way specially to see him. He'll be upset when he finds out you've turned me away'

It was apparent that she believed he never would find out anything of the sort.

'I don't know when you last saw Mr Uglow, but he has become mentally unstable and has recently developed psychopathic traits that make unscheduled visits inappropriate'

That all sounded bollocks; she was reading from a script.

'Leave now, please, or I'll have to call security'. She looked at her phone on the desk.

I wondered what 'security' was in a place like this, but I decided I'd rather not find out. I gave her my finest mad old man grimace and turned and walked back out the door. Stupid, I thought, as I walked down the steps. She sees those faces every hour of her working life. I should have tried a different approach altogether. If I'd thought about it beforehand, I was sure I could have come up with something better. Stupid. You're not as clever as you like to think. So what are you going to do now?

I walked round the corner where the bitch couldn't see me. There was a fire escape leading from a first-floor balcony. I could try that.

I have to tell you, I was doubtful that I could handle that sort of thing. The door was bound to be shut on the outside and I'd have to force it and make a lot of noise and security would come and escort me forcibly from the premises. And even if the door were open and I could just walk in, how was I going to find the right room? I'll warrant they don't have names on the doors. I wasn't very confident, you can tell, but I was going to give it a go, anyway. I wasn't going home empty handed.

I started climbing the wrought iron staircase. It was rusty and it wobbled horribly and something was making a zinging noise as the treads vibrated against the stucco of the wall. It shouldn't be like this. It's not like this in films. I stopped, and the zinging stopped. I looked around. Now that I was a few feet above the ground, I could see over the tops of the laurels that there was a conservatory bolted on to the rear elevation, and in said conservatory there was an old man sitting on his own in a rattan armchair. It looked to be an original part of the building because it was in bad repair and needed some prompt preventative maintenance to the rotten wooden frame before it fell down. I could see that it had proper encaustic floor tiles and ancient heating pipes and massive green terracotta pots with dying ferns in them and borders with voluminous unruly planting. There was bougainvillea and plumbago and a top-heavy jasmine pulling off the wall supports. It was just what you think of when you imagine a faded Victorian conservatory in an Agatha Christie. Not a polycarbonate panel or tasteful wood stain in sight. A proper glasshouse, just how I like them.

And there was Gramper Uglow sitting there waiting for me, eating a toasted teacake for his elevenses. I recognised him. I was sure it was him.

That's more like it.

I pushed my way through the laurel and made what must have been a spectacular entrance through the open double doors right in front of him. He looked at me, but didn't flinch, or indeed make any movement. I did just need to check that he was still alive. He was, indeed, an ancient crone, but he was still breathing and staring at me intently.

We were alone, the two of us.

I asked him if I could sit in the empty chair next to him

and he nodded and motioned with the palm of his hand for me to pull it up.

He was a really old person. Let me try and describe him to you. He was short and lean, like a stringy root vegetable left out in the sun and a lacerating east wind. He was wearing a dishevelled blue suit with a white shirt and striped tie; shiny black shoes and no socks. No socks? He had one of those lumpy old chins where no matter how long you spend with your wet shave, you can't quite clear out all the white stubble. His warty nose was flecked with surface veins, as were his ear lobes and the backs of his hands, and his skin looked like rice paper. He had a good head of hair which was combed in a neat parting to the side and his eyes were very, very bright. They were sparkly, despite all they'd seen.

Where to start? I told him I lived in Crow's Nymet, in Church House and I said I remembered when he'd lived in his old cottage because I used to see him at his vegetable garden from the footpath. I said I counted Peter among my friends, a slight exaggeration, I accept, but I thought it might be a point in my favour.

He said he knew who I was. Of course he did.

He didn't say it in an aggressive or negative way. In fact, I was quite encouraged.

His voice was gravelly and hoarse as you'd expect in a man of his age. He spoke in a very broad local accent which I'm not going to try to reproduce for you, so you'll have to imagine it. Just try not to associate it with BBC West Country speak, because it's nothing like that. It floats in the air and is a real pleasure to listen to. Once you get the hang of the mis-cased pronouns, it's quite easy to understand, as well.

I didn't need to tell him that Peter and I had spoken about the formula for the Physic earlier in the year. He knew all about that, too. He knew how Ted broke his ankle, and why Gavin was grounded. I wondered who he had heard it from, and if it bore much resemblance to the way I remembered it.

He asked me what I wanted. Why was I there?

I got straight to the point. I told him I hadn't realised that he was still alive until yesterday and I wanted to talk to him about the Rousing. While I still could, I could have added, but didn't.

He became guarded. He must have been expecting it, but I was guessing that if he was going to play ball, it was going to be a very big thing for him, telling me things that he perhaps felt in his heart should remain unsaid, or at least unsaid to strangers or outsiders.

He maybe felt he hadn't got much left in his life apart from this. How precious was it to him, and would sharing it reduce its potency?

Anyway, I was watching his expression intently, and it suddenly changed, as if an uncomfortable weight had been lifted from his face. I could see the lines on his brow soften and his eyes widen and dilate.

It was at this point I knew he was going to tell me everything. And what he had to say was not what I was expecting at all.

So where shall I start? Because you should know all this stuff, too.

Well, actually what he did first was ask me what I knew about the festival, so I told him everything Godfrey had told me, that the old guy had told him. I said I had a copy of the photograph and that it had the name Uglow written on the back. Then I said I'd met Harris at the library and he'd revealed still more. I could see the old man's eyes glistening as if they were smiling at me, laughing perhaps. He was taking it all in.

Then I told him that I'd found the Clump, and Yew Magna,

and I'd discovered the spring and the Celtic cross, and I saw his eyelids tighten. This was obviously of more interest to him; I was starting to push his buttons.

I'd been deliberating on whether to mention the phial, and I decided that I wouldn't. Not just yet, anyway. I would hold something in reserve.

I couldn't think of anything more to add. It was his turn.

This is what he told me.

Most of what I'd been spun, he said, was rubbish. He said that there were two festivals, quite distinct and separate, and that I'd managed to get the facts all mixed up together, like many before me, until what I was left with made no sense at all. He would explain, he said.

The only important festival was the original. The other one was an aberration and a distraction from the real thing.

The original festival, the Rousing, had its origins well back into pre-history, just as I'd thought. There was a sense among those who had practiced it that it had long preceded any involvement that they or their antecedents had passed on. Just a sense that it had always been there; and I was right, the spring was the key to it all.

Now I was conscious even as he spoke that most of this was still just conjecture. It's all very well talking about 'senses' but there was no proof; nothing tangible as evidence; nothing written down or preserved.

I got the impression that it was only when the shaman finally came along in the early sixteenth century that the oral tradition could be counted as any sort of reliable foundation to support the accepted wisdom.

Anyway, where was I? The mists of time. The Rousing was always a fertility rite, held twice a year on the eves of the

431

solstices. It was centred on the spring, which then became the Clump, and Yew Magna was the physical manifestation that anchored the Rousing to the place. It was a rite performed by a select few, chosen probably by their lineage, not more than a handful of participants and all local to Crow's Nymet or its environs. No outsiders allowed. It seems to have been a simple rite. During the year it was one man's responsibility to assemble the ingredients from local sources to be brewed into a magic potion (yes, I know it sounds corny, I can't remember the words that Gramper Uglow used, but it didn't sound corny when he used them). The brew was distilled into a concentrated fluid. At midnight, each man would drink from the spring and drink from the potion.

The main idea, evidently, was that this allowed the participants to commune with the spirits of the woods and the surrounding countryside, and that being as one with the natural world, being an integral part of the whole ecological set-up would ensure prosperity both of the family and of the field; children would be born healthy and thrive, and crops and livestock would flourish and the land would be fertile and productive. That was it; it was just as simple as that. No dressing up, no chanting, nothing creepy, all pretty innocent stuff and strictly very localised and not harming anyone.

And then the shaman came along.

I'm still very aware that all this is based solely on the oral tradition. It's why I tried to make something of it earlier on. It's very important, and why it's such a huge loss that it's virtually disappeared from our lives today.

Just think about what I'm saying for a moment. This shaman character turned up five hundred years ago. Nobody wrote anything down about him. He doesn't appear in the

432

church records and his name isn't on the list of vicars of this parish which is hung in a nice frame on the wall of the nave, which goes back in a continuous line to 1243.

And yet, after those five centuries I can tell you many things about him because this information has been passed down from generation to generation, maybe twenty generations or more. That's incredible, isn't it?

It might be all bollocks, of course, but I don't think so. It could have been embellished in the telling, Chinese whispers and all that, but again, what would be the point? It was only for local consumption, that was clear. There was no one else to impress or frighten.

This was Gramper Uglow's take on the shaman.

He just turned up one day as a young boy. He was a foundling. Nobody knew where he had come from, and he wouldn't say. He claimed to be the seventh child of a seventh child and that this gave him special powers. He was taken in by the childless lady of the Big House and given a sound education by tutors brought from London, but he remained other-worldly and distant and made no attempt to assimilate either with his adopted family or with the wider community. It seems he was an oddball from the word go.

Evidently, he had no interest in the Church, or indeed any vocation that his erstwhile parents might have wished him to pursue, not politics or the military, agriculture or even trade. He was only interested in the natural world and spent all his time immersed in a life of scouring woodland and hedgerows, moorland and rivers for material to enhance his understanding of his chosen passion.

Then one day he announced that from that moment he would sleep in the church house and would be in charge of the

433

ales and all the secular activities associated with the church. It seems this all came as a bit of a shock to the villagers and was presented to them as something of a fait accompli, and I guess they didn't want to upset the squire or his wife, so they went along with it.

As always happens, once in place, he set about reinforcing his position, sticking his fingers into more and more pies. I was beginning to get the measure of this man, I think. My guess is that he had the Rousing in his sights right from the word go. I reckon he had settled on the formula for the magic potion and knew what it was capable of doing and he wanted to use it to exert more control over his little empire. That's my theory. I think he added a few of his own ingredients to the medicine to spice it up a bit, too At some point he does all the stuff with the bench ends and probably the green man bosses as well, just to give himself more of a shamanistic aura. More kudos. And just to fuck the peasants up a little more.

I could tell Gramper Uglow was warming to his story. He was enjoying telling me all this. He was coming to a good bit.

The shaman announced to the villagers that the forthcoming winter solstice was going to be of great significance because there was going to be a full moon, and this happened only rarely and was special. To prepare for this event, the cross in the churchyard was to be carried down to the Clump and erected so that the rising sun cast its shadow on the face of the spring.

I think this was all claptrap. I think it was just the shaman exercising his power over the villagers. It was just another way to subjugate them. He wasn't interested in a Christian cross. He just wanted them to cast it from their consecrated ground and trust it to his protection. It wasn't a well-received order. I remember when Godfrey first told me about the shaman. He'd gone too far; he was in danger of misjudging the mood of the peasants.

Anyway, the rest you already know, and Gramper Uglow couldn't add anything to this part of the story.

The cross was erected as commanded. The Rousing went ahead as normal on the night of the full moon, and the shaman and two of the villagers never came home. No one would ever say what happened, and no one would go back to the Clump to look for the bodies.

I've already told you, more or less, what happened then. The shaman was out of the way so things could get back to normal. Everyone was in shock, but nobody was prepared to say enough was enough, and that it should mark the end of the Rousing for good. There was too much at stake, what with all the superstitions and omens and all. So it sort of went underground. Everyone knew it went on, but didn't really care to get involved if they didn't have to. I guess it was looked on as a necessary evil by all concerned.

It probably came down to one or two families to keep it going, and I bet it acted a bit like a glue for them. The cohesion was something they had to live with. They were stuck with it, or to it. All the same, five hundred years is a hell of a long time. You'd have thought that disruptions like family feuds, plagues or emigration to the towns and cities might have resulted in a loss of continuity, but it seems not. The power of the fertility rite and the fear of the failure of the harvest was sufficient to keep it going.

Until about 1870, it seems. This is when things took a quite different turn.

It's hard to imagine, but evidently there were some bright young things in the village. Let's see, 1870; there wasn't much going on. No wars; no disruptive natural events or political strife anywhere nearby. Some of the brighter lads, the vicar's sons, perhaps, or the squire's or sons of the more upmarket farmers would be a bit bored. Not much for them to do. They would have known a little bit about the Rousing, I expect, although I would think that most of it was kept from them. I'm sure there would have been a natural divide between the landed owners and the tenant farmers and their workers.

Well, you might have guessed it. They decided that they would invent their own festival, but this one would be a bit twee. It would incorporate all the traditional folklore and customs and it would be a merry jape. A jolly wheeze, twice a year, and probably a good excuse for a piss-up afterwards, or more likely a nice supper party with the girlfriends and wives where daring stories would be told of the evening's capers.

This was the festival that the photograph showed. Gramper Uglow stopped for a dramatic pause and to finish off the last of the toasted teacake.

'You can imagine all this didn't go down very well with the old families', he chirped between crumbs.

It turns out that one of the leading lights of these old families at the time was none other than Gramper Uglow's grandfather. Now, there's a thing. Again, I found myself doing some quick mental arithmetic. Gramper Uglow said his grandfather was a young man when the Rousing was commandeered by the trendy elite of the area. He could see me concentrating on my sums, and he added with just a sly glint in his eyes,

'It's true. We were a big family. Lots of brothers and sisters and aunts and uncles and cousins. I too am the seventh child of a seventh child. That's why my grandfather took such an interest in me.'

I don't know about you, but I was beginning to think all this mystical witchcraftery stuff was starting to get a bit out of hand. I was going to ask him if he had magical powers, too, but I managed to bite my lip in time. I knew it would have come over as patronising, but now I wished I had asked him. I'm sure he could spin a yarn, but I would have liked to know all the same.

There was some consternation in the village and a lot of ill feeling. I think these young toffs must have stirred up a hornet's nest. I bet it came as an unwelcome surprise to them that they had unearthed this venom.

Gramper Uglow had been given the chronicle of those turbulent times by his grandfather, and the gist of it was this.

Basically, there really wasn't room for two festivals. It would have been a bit crowded at the Clump with all these players from both camps trying to do their own thing. The peasants backed off, as they always do, with their tails between their legs, but they weren't happy. They were particularly unhappy later on in the year when crops failed and there was an unexplained stillbirth in the village. It must have been a traumatic period in the history of Crow's Nymet and it went on for some years.

I expect the young Turks thought it was a great hoot, something like a mummer's play or a carnival or procession followed by merry making and revels. The exact antithesis of what the Rousing had meant for maybe a millennium or more.

The problem was, it took place in a dark, spooky wood at midnight, and wasn't much of an inducement for well-to-do ladies in their finery and Sunday best, so when they picked this up, they took it out of the wood and placed it on the square

437

outside the pub where they danced around a bit and persevered for a couple of decades. It was never a winning formula. The real locals either weren't interested or were too disheartened and afraid to be part of it, and the village was too remote to get punters to drive from Barnstaple in their phaetons, or even up the steep hill from the railway station.

The famed photograph showed the very last of the Victorian festivals when there was an attempt to return to the roots and to hold it at the Clump, albeit on a Sunday afternoon. A photographer was hired for the occasion and set up his equipment while the characters acted out a charade for the camera.

Meanwhile, sad to say, the heat had gone out of the old village stalwarts. The hiatus had unsettled them. After the first two or three years when just about any misfortune was attributed to the failure to complete the Rousing, it was eventually generally acknowledged that maybe it wasn't all it had been cracked up to be, and they could get along quite nicely without it.

It was all very sad for those who had held great store in it. Gramper Uglow said there were various attempts to get the whole thing going again in the traditional way, but it never really gained enough momentum or enthusiasm to sustain it. It became just a story that men would tell their children, as indeed had the stories been passed down to Gramper Uglow and to Peter. That was all that was left of it.

It was a bit of a low note to end on. We both sat there deflated and in need of some uplift.

I felt it was maybe time to tell Gramper Uglow about my phial.

thirty two

I knew this was going to be a big thing for the old guy. If he believed me.

Can you imagine? All those centuries when they were trying to keep the thing going. All those times that they sat there in the Clump on the bough of Yew Magna, feeling just a little inadequate and out of it, as if there was something vital that was missing. And it was there, just a few hundred yards away, hidden from them and waiting to be found. All that time, and they didn't know.

I had been wondering how to tell him. I didn't want to send him into some sort of fit or seizure. It might kill him. In the end, I asked him if he'd ever considered how things might have turned out differently if he had been able to come up with the proper recipe.

He was wistful. He said he and his grandfather had tried everything they could think of. His grandfather had hoped that he, Gramper Uglow junior, was the one to revive the tradition of the Rousing, being the seventh of the seventh and all that, but it wasn't to be. He went to his grave a sad and unfulfilled old man.

'What would you say', I said, 'if I told you that I had some of the Physic?'

'I would say that you were a liar', he replied instantly. 'I don't care how clever you are, you couldn't do it'.

So I told him.

'I don't mean I've discovered a way to make it. I'm saying that I've found a bottle of the very Physic that the shaman himself created, and it works'.

He didn't believe me, of course, and it was obvious he was becoming indignant and rattled and if I wasn't careful that would be it, I would lose him, so I had to quickly describe the circumstances of its discovery. That shut him up. He was lost in his deepest thoughts, weighing up this and that; trying to figure out if I was making fun of him, or whether I was just a tedious waste of his time. But I could tell that there was this nagging doubt in his mind. He wanted to believe me.

He sat there slumped in his chair for some time, and I kept quiet and let him think. In the silence, I could hear some activity in the room behind us and I feared we were going to be disturbed. We must have been talking together for a good half hour, probably more. It would be a bummer to be interrupted now. It wouldn't go down well with anybody, especially if the old guy turned against me.

He was oblivious to anything outside of his head. I believe I noticed his eyes becoming tearful.

He looked up suddenly and said, 'I don't believe you. I don't know why you've come here to tell me these lies. Why would you want to upset an old man like me?'

Then he stood up, quicker than I would have thought possible for a man of his age, and I thought he was going to call out, so I got up too, ready to make a hasty retreat. He didn't call out. He took one step towards me and then he grabbed the collar of my jacket with a skeletal hand and pulled me forward so that I had to turn my face to avoid butting him. He held me there like that. I could hear his panting and feel the heaving of his chest on mine and smell his old man smell. And then he whispered in my ear.

'I need you to show me. I need to see your phial, and I need to drink some of the Physic. I need to be sure. We have to do it now.'

I've told you, I'm not much good at dialogue. It was much more dramatic than this. He was literally hissing and sort of screeching in my ear. It was quite unnerving. He was a very threatening, frightening old man, and he made me feel as uncomfortable as I have ever felt. I figured he hadn't often been aroused in his life, but on those occasions when he had, he would have been a formidable force, someone you wouldn't have wanted to get on the wrong side of.

Why I'm telling you this is so you'll realise that I felt I had no choice but to take him home with me. I wouldn't have done it otherwise.

We slipped out of the conservatory and stalked our way round the greenery to the car park, where my Land Rover was the solitary occupant waiting in the corner for me. It was a real effort getting Gramper Uglow up into the passenger seat. He could only just manage to get one foot up on to the running board and he had no strength at all in either leg. I literally had to grab him round the waist and launch him on to the edge of the seat and then push him over far enough to shut the door. I looked around me. There was no indication that anyone who cared had seen us. This was certainly a weird place, this home. Surely someone must have noticed the Land Rover parked there? Where did they think I was, on a nature ramble?

441

As we drove down the drive, Gramper Uglow's reaction did seem to reinforce this impression.

'I'm never going back there', he mumbled. 'I'd rather die'.

I shuddered, and the Land Rover shuddered down the lanes as Gramper Uglow held tightly on to the grab rail and started humming a quiet tune to himself, his eyes focussed on some faraway object known only to his mind.

Now, of course, I realised that I was in a bit of a pickle, all things considered.

I had just abducted a psychopathic old man from his nursing home against his family's wishes and soon we were just going to rock up at his son's funeral, that he knew nothing about. I do seem to get myself into some unfortunate situations. I pulled into a passing place and turned the engine off. He looked at me in some surprise.

'There's something more I need to tell you', I said.

And so I told him. I was afraid that two existential shocks, one after the other, might be too much for him. Instead, he started laughing. Was it the irony of it? A nervous reaction? I wondered if he was still properly with us.

He told me that he hadn't spoken to his son for years. Their relationship had never been comfortable and there had been some major falling out decades ago that had never healed. It was not his loss, he said. He told me he'd waited a long time for this and thought it would never come. All the hurt. The bullying. The cows of wives and the strangers of children. Who was going to be there? I thought I knew the answer. Everyone except him. Except, now he was going to be there too. This was going to be fun.

I could see as we passed the parish hall car park that it was full, and cars were parked all along the road as well. St Rumon's would be packed. It was big for a village church, but it would be full to bursting with all these people.

I guessed, correctly, that the service would be in full swing. There was nobody about as we pulled up at the lychgate, not even the undertakers. They'd all be inside, too. I could see that the empty grave had been dressed with green matting and there were bunches of cellophane-wrapped flowers stacked untidily to one side.

I lifted Gramper Uglow down from the passenger seat. He was a bit unsteady on his feet and held on to the door handle until he got his bearing, but I could see that he was still weeping and he was still smiling with that knowing look in his eyes.

Basically, I left him to it. I wasn't about to gate crash this funeral and I certainly didn't want to be there when they all came out. I was probably the last person they would wish to see.

I left Gramper Uglow pottering off towards the church. He looked like he could have done with a stick to support his frail frame, but he seemed in no hurry and was waddling along down the path at his own pace. I drove the Land Rover back to its bare patch at the bottom of the garden and went and put the kettle on.

I was expecting to enjoy this.

By the time I settled down at the kitchen door, coffee in hand, there was no sign of him. I wondered what sort of entrance he had made, walking uninvited so startlingly into the middle of the service. Was he giving them some fire and brimstone or was he prostrating himself on the coffin with a histrionic gesture, perhaps? Whatever strategy he had adopted, I knew from the mood he was in that it was going to be a good one. One to remember.

I wished I could have been there to see it.

Whatever was happening inside the church, it wasn't leaching out into the churchyard. I couldn't see or hear anything that suggested there may be trouble inside. In fact, I had finished my coffee by the time anyone appeared at the door, and then it all looked like a normal, respectful funeral procession. There was no sign of Gramper Uglow anywhere. Had he just been ignored as an embarrassment at his estranged son's funeral? I began to feel a bit vexed on his behalf. These Uglow people were indeed an unusual lot.

Everyone was disgorging out of the porch behind the pall bearers and the coffin and the vicar. There were loads of them. They were sombre and black; even the kids were long faced. I guessed they'd probably be making up for it later at the wake, but for now they were morose and serious, all of them.

So, you have to try to imagine all these dark, deep people following the coffin out towards the prepared grave. They all looked the same. Same gaunt features. Same eyes. Same six toes, probably. No one was crying, or even red-eyed, but they were all grim. And then, the leading female mourner, it must have been his widow I suppose, let out this truly blood-curdling scream. I didn't realise it was physically possible for a woman to scream as loudly as that. It was quite an achievement; it made my blood curdle, I can tell you, and I was listening from the comfort of my kitchen.

It did rather change things quite dramatically, as you'd expect.

I was pleased with myself that I realised instantly what was going on. Gramper Uglow had only gone and got himself inside the open grave. How did he do it? The old bugger certainly had some balls, I'll give him that. What an entrance.

I imagine he must have lay down by the side of the hole and then sort of swung his legs over and down and hung on to the matting as he slid precariously into the grave. Yes, that's possible, I guess. If he'd managed to do it without breaking anything or knocking himself out, I'll bet what he did next was to lie down and place his hands across his chest as if he had been laid out. In fact, I know this is what he did because I've heard people talking about it since. I'm sure it's a scene that will never fade from some memories.

Anyway, the scream seemed to act as an unspoken stimulus for most of the other females at the graveside, and there was a tumultuous outpouring of caterwauling, a communal sharp intake of breath among the men and wide-eyed, open-mouthed horror from the children. Basically, there was pandemonium. And then, at that very moment, who should turn up but the bitch-nurse with two burly men nurses, all in the same green and white uniforms. It was great, but what happened next was even greater. All three stepped up to the grave and looked in together at their lost charge. There was some shouting, and then the wife of the deceased, the owner of the scream, launched herself at the bitch-nurse and punched her so hard on the jaw that she fell back comatose. She was out cold before she even hit the freshly mown grass. It looked like one of the male nurses was going to be the recipient of the next left hook, but he managed to grab the woman's fist as it hurtled towards him and deflected it away from his face. Unfortunately, he then decided to try to restrain the woman, and this was a bit of a mistake on his part because it attracted the protective instincts of several of the deceased man's friends and relatives, including the six pall bearers who unceremoniously ditched the coffin on the pile of spoil.

There followed the kind of melee normally associated with

western saloon bars. It's not the sort of thing you usually see at funerals, at least not before anyone's had a drink. It was a wonderful spectacle to watch. For some folk there, it clearly turned into an ideal opportunity to settle old scores and overturn familial injustices.

It was difficult to see how it would all end; even the kids joined in.

There was something entrenched and lingering in their bloody faces and flailing limbs. Each kick and throttling arm-lock was testimony to a deep feral outpouring. They were wild animals, all of them and it was a sobering prospect to witness from my ring-side seat.

The first of the walking wounded to limp from the scene of the fracas were the nurses, the two of them supporting the third in a comical threesome. I thought that Gramper Uglow would probably get his wish. I don't think he was ever going back to their home again. The crowd began to thin out, although some were still brawling. They would be slinking away to lick their wounds or were heading for the Druid's for some liquid sustenance before the wake.

Someone got a stepladder and they put it down the hole and one of the younger lads climbed down. I couldn't see what was going on because the graveside was surrounded with those weary of the fight.

Then, and this looked really funny from my kitchen, everyone sort of jumped back in unison and there was screaming again and lots of women with their hands over their mouths and wide eyes. It was very Edvard Munch. I've gathered since that the young lad was bending down trying to find a heartbeat when Gramper Uglow, timing perfect, opened his eyes wide and let out an unearthly cackle. The old sod.

I think when everyone had recovered their composure they now started tiring of the whole debacle. They were losing patience. They just wanted to bury the coffin and get on with the drinking. The next thing was that the youth had Gramper Uglow in a fireman's lift and was climbing out of the grave with him over his shoulder. He dumped him ungraciously and rather roughly on the grass. I don't think he had been amused by the eye thing.

Up till that moment, the vicar had been keeping well out of it. Now he ordered the pall bearers to take up their burden again, as he tried to get back on track. I think he was looking forward to the drinking, too.

So finally, the body was laid to rest. Just at the best bit, the ashes to ashes stuff, a couple of paramedics arrived rather like the Keystone Cops (though it was interesting that no one had thought to call the police; they like to keep it in the family down here). They acted as if they were in charge of it all, and they started shifting people around mid-ceremony so they could get their fancy stretcher in place, which didn't go down very well.

Gramper Uglow was motionless as they lifted him on the gurney. Either he was really dead, now, or he was still playing to the crowds.

I was cheered to see that a trio of young girls went off with him in the ambulance. Great-granddaughters, probably. At least he wasn't unloved by the whole family, unless the girls had predicted that a few hours in A and E in Barnstaple would be more fun than watching their boyfriends get legless.

As soon as everyone who was left had had opportunity to throw some good Devon loam on the coffin, they all buggered off pronto. Nobody stayed to fill the hole in. That's a bit odd, isn't it? There could have been some more fun still to be had for those with an inclination.

On an impulse, I thought perhaps I might do it myself. Some would say it was the least I could do. Fortunately, I did think better of it. I rightly guessed that it was Peter who would come back to do it.

He left it late; it was nearly dark and he was pissed. If you hadn't been there in the afternoon, you'd have thought it looked a bit creepy. It's not the sort of thing you want to come across if you're taking a short cut through the graveyard at night. As it happens, I'm the only one who does that in Crow's Nymet, apart from the bellringers on practice night, and they always put the outside light on first.

I needed to speak to Peter, but the time obviously wasn't right. God knows what was happening up at the parish hall. They'd all be munted as dizzy rats. Would they be coming to drag me out of my home and string me up somewhere? They would be working themselves up into a lather, that's for sure.

He must have been out there for a good hour trying to fill that hole. He was staggering around and every so often he'd stop shovelling and stand and shout something at the moon. He looked pitiful. When I went out to him, he still had some way to go.

The man still had his dark suit and his patent leather shoes on and the black tie hung loosened round his neck. He was wearing one of those old-fashioned shirts with a button-on stud collar and one side of it had sprung off and was flapping crazily, just like you see in old films where they're trying to make the protagonist look pitiful. His hands were covered in mud and sweat dripped from his nose and chin like someone had left a tap open. He was wild. What a day. He was in no mood to talk to me.

He told me to fuck off several times. I stood there and watched him. At one point, I thought he was going to come at me with his shovel, so I stepped back into the shadows and from his line of thought, such as it was. I could see in his face that he was struggling with demons that had been there all his life. They were lurking in dark corners and waiting for the right time. They would never let him be. I could see it; he was a pitiable soul. I hoped that the part that I had played had eased it, but I fear that this was almost certainly not the case; quite the opposite, I'm sure you're thinking.

I was still there watching him like this, fascinated, when who should turn up, but the vicar. I'm sure he'd been in the Druid's like everyone else, but at least he looked like he was still sober. I don't know him very well, but he's always seemed to me to be a little odd for a man of the cloth, coming over as more worldly-wise than your average cleric. He didn't live in the village, Crow's Nymet being a far-flung outpost of his family of churches, but he seemed to take a special interest, and was often visible in the community here. He was a big man with an authoritative, purposeful voice that served him well in sermons.

He told Peter to fuck off home and that he would finish the job for him. Like I say, it came over authoritatively. Sadly, not authoritatively enough, because although Peter thrust the shovel roughly into the vicar's hands, I fear he'd decided that he was not going home at all but back to the Druid's for a nightcap or three.

The vicar turned to me with his worldly-wise expression on his face. He wasn't in the mood for talking, either. He said that things were getting out of hand in the pub. He'd never seen the like in the Druid's and feared that the landlord would throw them all out and that they would then come looking for me for some late-night amusement.

But here's the funny thing.

You'd have thought that this would have made me feel fearful. It should have, shouldn't it? In fact, I remember thinking that at the time; I should be feeling very fearful about this, because some bad things could happen to me.

I don't know if it was because of the way things seemed to have played out over the last couple of days, played into my hands, really, in the sense that I naively thought I still had some sort of power over these people. I was inviolable. They couldn't touch me. Everything pointed to it. Is that how the shaman had thought? Just before his downfall?

Whatever. Anyway, what could I do? I guess I could have run into the woods. I could easily have escaped them in the night, but that wouldn't make it go away, and they might decide to ransack my house, or even burn it down.

Fuck 'em. I wasn't afraid of them.

I could confront them in the public bar. Just walk in and see what happened. It would, at least, put them on the back foot for an instant or two. I thought it was an interesting idea. Just to add a little frisson, I thought I might just go back home and put my djellaba on. I had this odd feeling that it might be just what was needed for the occasion. My heart was thumping in my chest. What exhilaration. What a way to live life.

I was very fond of my djellaba. I hadn't actually worn it since the Christmas Eve, but I'd put it on a hanger and hung it from a nail in a beam on the landing, so that I saw it every time I went upstairs to bed. In fact, if you didn't know it was there, it could have given you a fright because it looked just like some ghostly hooded apparition floating along the corridor. It gave me a comfort to take it in.

I put the thing on and went and sat on my bed in my little green sleeping chamber. My mind was weirdly empty. I was, unusually, totally sober; I hadn't had a drop to drink all day. It was a funny time. I knew that something special was about to happen.

I waited on that bed until I thought the time was right. I knew when to go.

The vicar had finished his shovelling. I could see from my kitchen door that he'd removed the matting and was starting to arrange the flowers tastefully on the heaped mound, but he became distracted and stood looking up the lane from the lychgate. I could hear them, too; the mob was coming for me. I was too late for the pub.

He took several long strides and met the unruly crowd at the entrance to the lychgate. He still had the shovel in his hands. It was a masterful stroke because it's so narrow there that no one could pass him, and he held his arms up like Moses parting the Red Sea and I could see they all stopped abruptly in front of him, then kind of stumbled forwards like unsteady penguins because the ones at the back couldn't come to a standstill in time. You see it in cartoons. There were about twenty of them, men and women, all Uglows, surely. Ugly Uglows; ugly in face and ugly in attitude. Very ugly. They didn't have pitch forks and long dangerous sticks, or lengths of rope with a slip-knot on the end like most peasant mobs, but they were certainly ugly.

I was curiously calm. I held back. I couldn't hear what the vicar was saying to them, and there was some jeering and shouting and cat-calls and some pointing of fingers in the air.

I thought they needed to see me.

I was under the lychgate roof, just behind the vicar, with my green hood up shrouding my face, and they saw me. The vicar turned around and I don't think he was very pleased. I think he felt that it probably made his job a little more difficult. He was between me and them and they would have to get past him. The whole crowd went quiet, and there was murmuring in the ranks. I looked at them over the vicar's shoulder. They were a sorry bunch. They were all drunk, but it had been a long day, and there had already been plenty of fighting. Some of them looked droopy-eyed and others needed help just to stand. I didn't think they were up for much more. They could hear their beds calling them home to their outlying farms. Peter was at the back. He looked like the living dead. The thing was, they didn't have a natural leader among them, there was no one to rally the troops, no orator to stir the soul and see the job through.

I think it surprised the vicar, too. It must have made him feel powerful, just like it made me feel. It's what it must be like to realise you can take control of people as simple as that, if you want to.

The vicar took advantage of the hiatus to gather up the front runners in the long reach of his long arms and shuffle them back up the lane. He looked a bit like Jesus in those renaissance paintings. There was posturing and some petty threats and one or two of the young lads pointed at me, stabbing the air and mouthing obscenities. Fuck 'em, I thought. I'm not scared of you, and you know it.

So, what an anti-climax, you're thinking. The Uglows simply staggered back to their cars and drove off into the night, humbled by formidable words from the shepherd of Christ.

That's what they did, but I can tell you it wasn't an anti-climax at all.

No

I watched them all lurch up the lane, herded by the Jesus-made-incarnate vicar, and then they wearily dispersed and went their separate ways and I just stood there taking in the wonder of it all.

And then I turned around to go back to my safe, cosy kitchen sanctuary and there was Ted, standing on the fresh mound of his father's grave, treading flowers into the dirt with his posh shoes. You knew he was going to be there, didn't you? You noticed how he hadn't been around lately and I hadn't spoken of him. You knew he'd be there somewhere.

He was snarling. He was spitting. His eyes bore into me and the veins on his forehead almost popped. He looked even bigger stood there on the mound than he normally was.

I'm no fighter. I've never tried, actually, but I think you've got to want to do it to be any good. Even faced with Ted like this, I didn't want to fight with him. My heart wouldn't have been in it. I don't think I would have wanted to hit him back if he'd lunged at me with his fists or his kicks.

But nothing about the night had changed. If anything, after the turning of the mob, I was feeling more invulnerable than ever.

I stood my ground. I guess I was about three or four strides from him. Then I started shouting at him. I shouted all sorts of things; where was it all coming from? I could see he was taken off-guard, but that he was waiting with his menacing anger for me to finish. I invoked Peter and his grandfather and then Ted's own father (whom I never met, by the way). I told him how he should be ashamed of himself for not digging his father's grave

453

and that he would never have forgiven him, and more, all crap. I waved my hands in the air and pointed at him and the flowers and the tributes in the manner I'd recently seen of the rough Uglows. It must have been all a bit sad, really; I wasn't quite hitting the mark and I knew it.

And then the most unlikely, gobsmackingly fucking terrifying thing happened.

This emaciated arm burst out through the grave and grasped Ted by the ankle. His bad ankle. I'm not kidding you. There was a look of abject horror on Ted's face. I've never seen anything like it. His whole face shook, like there was something inside, in his mouth and cheeks and eyes, that was trying to get out. It was horrible. Mind you, I imagine my face probably looked very similar. I can tell you, it is the most frightening thing that I have ever seen in my life, by far. When you think about it, I don't suppose you could get anything more frightening than that. Primordial is the right word, I think. You don't get anything more primordial than a freshly dead corpse coming to life and grasping you in its cold fingers from the earth in which it had just been buried. Especially as it now seemed to be trying to pull Ted down into the grave to join it.

It must have been even more awful for Ted than it looked. It went on for ever. He tried to get it off, but it just wouldn't release its grip. Ted was on his hands and knees now, trying to scramble away rather than be dragged down, like the squealing piggy guy in Deliverance just before he gets raped by the hillbilly. He was screaming and gibbering and crying. He was moaning like a frightened baby. It must have been all echoing around the village and I bet it caused a few sleepless nights behind closed curtains.

I've spoken to you before of bowel-loosening, I think. I have never been more frightened, but in a funny sort of

454

disengaged, other-worldly way; difficult to explain. My bowels had been truly loosened; I was in danger of losing control of them, but I still felt curiously detached from it all, as if I was looking in from the outside again onto something that was not quite of me. I was not a real part of this, but I felt I had mastery of it, somehow. That was weird.

I really did feel like I could do anything at that moment. I stepped forward and I looked right into the depths of Ted's terrified eyes. Through the eyes and into what lay beyond, and then the hand released its grip and the arm returned to the earth from where it had risen, and Ted crawled past me on all fours and pulled himself up the gatepost of the lychgate and limped and staggered away, still whimpering and moaning a death rattle, leaving me alone in the churchyard.

So.

I expect you're thinking, hmm, that little episode marks something of a departure from the otherwise entirely plausible narrative of my story. You're probably a little uneasy about it. I think you have some decisions to make.

How can we explain, between us, what happened out there in the churchyard?

There are a number of choices, I think.

Firstly, what Ted and I witnessed was a supernatural phenomenon. Thus far in this story, there have only been hints that there may be supernatural forces at work and I've been able to explain everything else rationally to you. Then again, you've probably not read to the end, yet, so you don't know if I'll spring something on you in the final pages. This might just be the start.

I could be going mad. I could have imagined it, or hallucinated, or otherwise extracted it from the murky depths of my addled psyche.

I might just be lying to you, just for the hell of it, because I can. I think you should regard this as very likely.

However, I can explain everything, so you also have this last option open to you.

When I had recovered enough to actually put one foot in front of the other and make my way unsteadily back to the kitchen door of Church House (giving the grave a wide berth), I headed for my supply of Laphroaig and took a big slug, straight from the bottle. It didn't do much, so I took another.

I didn't believe in ghosts. Don't believe, sorry, I may be misleading you. For a moment or two in that dark kitchen, though, it did make me question whether I wanted to be out on my own at night any more. I didn't want a mysterious scrawny arm coming and grabbing me and trying to carry me off somewhere. And if I was really going mad, that wasn't good news, either.

Much better to find a comfier answer, and then there it was, unfolding in front of me as I stood there in the dark with the bottle of whisky in my hand.

It was the vicar. He was back with his shovel.

He crept furtively up to the fresh grave and he dragged the matting back and gently scraped the loose soil from the mound on to it, and then he dug a little deeper until a man emerged from the earth. He staggered to his feet and I could see him shaking himself down. He was wearing a loose shroud over his head which he removed with his bare, scrawny arm. I couldn't see who it was; it was too dark. Both men then returned the earth to the grave and mounded it up again and replaced all the floral tributes and tidied up the matting, as if nothing out of the ordinary had ever occurred. The two men stood there for just a moment and then the vicar stepped away, slipped his cape back on and flounced through the lychgate in the direction of his car, whilst the other figure took the shovel and matting and headed for the back door of the vestry.

And that was it.

Decision time.

I know it's all a bit corny, maybe too embarrassingly corny for me to have even bothered to make it all up, but you are probably thinking that it's just about possible.

If I'm telling you the truth, then it almost certainly means that the vicar is some sort of mole or stooge for Pinky, and he's been keeping a closer eye on me than I knew. What are the implications of that? I think, big ones.

I understand my explanation has weaknesses, and you've probably now taken them into account. The whole charade was a bit of a long-shot, wasn't it? and it was very convenient that Ted of all people just happened to be standing there where he was at the right time, but that's just the way it goes, sometimes, I guess. It could have worked differently, but I figure the vicar always had in mind for it to be a crowd-disperser, even if in the end it wasn't. All the same, a bit speculative on his part; it could easily have all gone wrong.

So what do you think?

thirty three

One of the most dispiriting things about living in your own little world is that it's very difficult to pick up news.

In the days following the events I've just described, I kept myself even more to myself. I thought it would be wise. But I was eager to find out what had befallen Gramper Uglow and I had nobody to ask. I got to thinking that it had all been rather a shame for him. Sure, he had enjoyed himself at the funeral while it lasted, that much was plain to see, and it had certainly been livelier than a typical day in the nursing home. The shame was that he now knew of my phial, but there would never be that opportunity for him to indulge himself with it. Christ, what a way that would be for Gramper Uglow to go. Gramper Uglow was who I should have been getting to join me at the solstice, not Peter. If Gramper Uglow couldn't get the spirits of the natural world aroused, what with his special powers and his stoic, ninety-six-year-old determination, then who could?

I guessed I'd really screwed up that possibility. What a shame and a waste. Peter would only ever be a second-best option, now, and there was a strong possibility that even he might not be up for it.

I suddenly felt overcome by self-pity. After a lively, optimistic few days, I sensed an overwhelming feeling of bathos and lost opportunity. Basically, I had screwed the whole thing up. I had first, Peter, then his grandfather, in the palm of my hand, and I'd let them go. I'd not played it clever at all. I hate it when I screw up.

Poor Gramper Uglow. Even if he survived his hospital visit, what was he going to do now? The family would find him an even grimmer nursing home somewhere far away, where he would live out what remained of his life in solitude and isolation, and where eventually he would die, just like his grandfather, an incomplete and unfulfilled shell. I didn't think anyone would be coming visiting him, not even Peter.

Peter. I needed to see him. If he was still up for it, we had to make plans. The days were ticking by. I wasn't going anywhere near his house or his wife or any Uglow, but fortunately, as it turned out, I didn't need to.

It was only a few nights ago actually, but it seems like an age. A different age where things were not the same as they are now.

It was a wonderful evening. Of course it was; it was the middle of June in the Devon countryside. The sun had been beating down all day and was now just touching the blue green hills in the North West towards the coast. The air was alive with insects of all kinds, and birds were out busily feeding their hungry young and there was the sweet scent of summer in the wind. Blissful.

I was out walking with Rosie on a nearby bridleway and taking all this in and trying to put thoughts of self-loathing and failure to the back of my mind.

I hadn't intended to be out long and I'd worked out the circuit I would take home to get back a little before dark. There were other walkers about on this balmy night doing the same as me, but I'd managed to miss them by keeping to the more overgrown tracks. Rosie was in her element; she loves this time of year as much as I do. She's in and out of hedges, up deer leaps and chasing pheasants and shadows. She'd just leapt over a low bank in front of me into the scrub beyond when I sensed that she'd suddenly stopped in her tracks. She growled. Rosie very rarely growls at anything; she'd much rather go and make friends. I was alarmed and stood motionless while I decided what to do. She growled again, and I heard movement in the undergrowth; it couldn't have been anything other than a human making that much noise.

Well, it won't come as a surprise to you that it was Peter, because I've just implied that I'd seen him again, but what was he doing there? He was petting Rosie and she was wagging her tail. He looked a bit haggard. His hair was unruly and greasy, and his breath smelled. He said it was a good job I'd come to him, because otherwise he would have had to try and find me at home, and he wasn't keen to be seen to be doing that.

He told me to follow him, and he set off through the young holly, brushing it aside as he pushed his way through. I knew the wood, of course; I'd been there many times, day and night, and then I made the connection. Silly me; I'd been a bit slow. It was the copse at the bottom of Gramper Uglow's old garden. We'd been coming at it from a different path than the one I normally took when I was going that way. It was an acre or two of coppiced hazel and scrub with some large old oak standards and a tall stand of small-leafed lime. I should have recognised it; you can see the limes from anywhere in the village.

The boundary to the garden was an old earth bank and we scrambled over it easily. The garden was a shadow of its former self. I remembered when it was orderly rows of potatoes and carrots and broad beans and peas, and there had always been a row of runner bean sticks just where we stood. Now, it was full of nettles and thistles and docks the size of rhubarb. The fertile soil from a lifetime of Gramper Uglow's hard toil had eagerly fed the weeds in this hidden lost world.

Peter kept up a brisk pace, and I had trouble following close behind. He hadn't cared about scratches from the holly on his bare arms and he didn't seem troubled by the thistles or stings from the nettles, some of which were taller than him and in their prime. We'd been walking through the old vegetable beds on a crumbling brick and cobble path that had been disturbed by the new vigorous swelling of the unwelcome roots, and when this came to an end and Peter stood and brushed away the remaining nettles with his arm, I smelled the fire before I saw it.

It was clear that someone had taken a scythe to what had been a flagged courtyard and cut the offending growth and brushed it into a pile of dried grass and herbs in the corner, and there was the fire burning inside a makeshift hoop of rocks and bricks, and behind it was Gramper Uglow sat in a deckchair looking at me, his eyes as intense and deep as ever.

It was quite a shock. Ridiculous I know, but I hadn't seen it coming. It was the last place I expected him to be. A near-centenarian cripple, lately of the North Devon District Hospital in Barnstaple, sitting next to a camp fire in the middle of a wasteland clearing.

Of course it was him.

The courtyard was inside the 'L' of the two arms of Gramper Uglow's old cottage. One arm was the cottage itself, the other was an open-fronted workshop. I recognised it now. There were many nights during my wilderness years when I would sit beyond the bank at the bottom of the garden and watch the old man in his kitchen, and I remembered he often brought a deckchair out and sat well into the early hours in his little yard. He used to smoke a pipe. I would be able to smell the sweet tobacco from my hiding place if it was a still night. I wouldn't have been surprised if he had it in his pocket now.

There was another empty deckchair next to Gramper Uglow where Peter had been sitting, and he beckoned for me to take it, and he went inside the kitchen and brought out a dining chair which he brushed off with the back of his hand and eased himself on to. Rosie made herself comfortable on the far side of the fire.

Have you got an image in your mind of the picture the three of us made there?

It was bucolic. It couldn't have been more bucolic. There was nothing about that scene that would have made it more bucolic, except the aroma of Gramper Uglow's unrubbed shag on the cool night air.

This was where Peter grew up. It was where Gramper Uglow was born, and his gramper, probably, and his too. It was made from the earth several centuries ago and was now returning to the earth, and soon there would be nothing left except some broken glass and rusting tin. That's how it should be, I think, in the English countryside.

The cob walls were crumbling away where rain had found its way through the holes in the tin. It looked to me like the sheets had been clamped down through the original thatch underneath it, because I could see straw reeds poking out under the eaves where the sparrows had pulled them out. I wonder who had harvested that wheat. It would have been an Uglow, that's for sure.

Most of the windows were still in place, though some had slipped and broken. There wasn't much paint left on them. The doors looked secure enough and I could see there was still furniture inside. I knew there was, actually. I'd taken a snoop around as soon as it became apparent that no one was living there anymore. I'd never associated it with Gramper Uglow, though, obviously; I didn't know who he was then. I thought he was just some old man, I suppose, who had gone away.

There were the beds in the bedroom. God, they weren't living here, were they? There was clearly no electric and the oil tank had been pushed over and was empty and smelt of tar.

I settled into my deckchair and Peter handed me a can of cheap cider. It had started to get properly dark and birds had found their roosts or their nests. There was a tawny owl hooting somewhere close. The air was heady with the scents of midsummer all around me. I could smell the oregano and thyme crushed under my feet, and the minty fennel and dill against the wall next to me which I squeezed through my hands. Further afield there was the wild honeysuckle, at its zenith in the June night, and there must have been roses and other garden escapees.

It was a mild night, but not stifling. We didn't need the fire, but it was just perfect there, the glowing embers and wispy smoke curling into the air and the smell of hot, sappy hawthorn. I opened my cider and took a long swig, and we all stared into the intoxicating flickering flames.

I was halfway through the can, when Peter broke the silence.

'The old man was only in overnight', he said. 'Just a few bruises, and then I think they wanted the bed back'.

I couldn't work out whether Peter thought this was a good thing, or if he was berating the NHS.

'He had nowhere to go; they would have left him on the seat outside the pub if I hadn't got wind of it. They dropped him off at my place and he was already sat in my armchair next to the TV when Jill got back from Tesco's. She wasn't best pleased. They've never got on. Anyway, what could we do?'

'Well it only lasted two nights, and then she threw the both of us out, just like that. She'd had enough, she said. She pushed Gramper out the door and slammed it behind him'.

It took longer for him to tell me all this than just a couple of sentences, and now and again Gramper Uglow would put his oar in to add some colour of his own to the story. It was a sorry tale. It had been Gramper Uglow's idea to come to 'the old place', as they called it. I guess they didn't have any other crash pad in Crow's Nymet. They'd been there a few nights already and reckoned it was working out well.

I don't know who they thought they were kidding. It was obvious this couldn't go on much longer. I didn't like to think of the hygiene arrangements. Still, I guessed that until someone happened to mention it to social services or some other busybody, it was probably going to be like this for a while. It might have been a bit different if it was January.

Anyway. There was still the elephant in the room to be addressed. I knew it was coming.

Since his discharge from hospital, Gramper Uglow had spoken to Peter of little else, it seems. He wanted to be there. He was going to be there, no matter what. Nothing was going to get in his way. It had taken over his life.

I wasn't surprised. The only thing I was surprised about was that it had taken them so long to tell me. But I could see it in Gramper Uglow's eyes, now. That's all there was there, the Rousing.

Well, it was fine by me. It's what I was hoping they would want to do.

We made a plan, but it was a very simple plan. Peter and Gramper Uglow would make their own way to the Clump and would meet me there at a quarter to midnight. I would bring three portions of the Physic with me on wafers, and we would take them at the crack of midnight and see what happened.

How could we be sure no one else would be there? We couldn't, obviously, and if there was, then we'd have to improvise. It would only be us that would have the Physic.

It was plain that Gramper Uglow was very satisfied with our plan. He sat back in his deckchair and closed his eyes. Only the sides of his mouth twitched, now and again. We got ourselves another cider.

I thought it was odd why Gramper Uglow wasn't more curious about my experiences with the Physic. The other thing that was nagging me was why hadn't Peter told me more about the Rousing than he had done, right at the beginning? He must know as much as his grandfather. There would surely be no secrets between them about this mutual lifelong infatuation.

I confronted him with this, and he simply said that I'd chosen not to say anything to him about finding my phial, and in the same way, he'd decided to hold back some stuff from me. And he added, a little ominously I thought, that Gramper Uglow actually took a bit of a dim view of me taking the Physic at any time or place that wasn't the right time or place. Especially when it was so precious and irreplaceable and it wasn't really mine.

'I think he feels that anything you've already experienced will be as nothing to the real thing.'

And then Gramper Uglow opened his eyes and turned and looked at me.

'Are you prepared?', he said.

'Are you ready for this?'

Then he closed his eyes again.

'I am', he added. 'I've been ready all my life'.

And he looked serene and at peace there with his eyes shut, and yes, he looked like he was ready.

'There's something that neither of us have told you', Peter said. 'It's about the Green Man'.

I know about green men. I've told you about them. They're there, in the church roof.

'Gramper and me, we've never seen the Green Man, but Gramper remembers talk of him among his grandfather's friends; talk that came from beyond anyone's memory, because none of them had ever seen the Green Man, either, but there was talk of him, all the same. Because, you see, the whole point of the Rousing was always that you became a part of nature. And it became a part of you.

'It's how things used to be once, for us all. We were all part of nature once, and not just on the eve of the solstice. We were simply a part of it. All the time.

'We're too bloody civilised, now. We've lost that connection. Look, you're not really allowed to be part of it anymore, even if you were aware of it and wanted to be.'

I'm trying to remember how Peter described this to me. The way he said it, it just seemed to settle into place naturally in my mind and made everything suddenly much clearer.

466

Nature, red in tooth and claw. Eat or be eaten. What he was saying was that that's how nature works. It's how it's always worked. That's why we're here, and it's why everything else is here. And we've lost our connection with it.

We're all here because we're lucky enough to have evolved on a planet that has been stable for four billion years, and finally, evolution by natural selection has produced us, an intelligent life form. What are the chances? (and don't use that as an excuse to invoke God. I've told you, he doesn't exist). You and me, and the others, we just happen to be living our lives at a very interesting cusp in the history of the world. There's a lot happening. We're that lucky. We've become intelligent; we are conscious and sentient; we like to think we're civilised. We're all these things, and they're all good, but it does mean that we've lost this connection.

Your reaction is probably going to be, "So what? Does it matter?"

Well, it matters to every other living thing that we share this planet with, because we're fucking the place up in just about every conceivable way, and we've been doing it ever since we acquired our consciousness and the rest, but now there are seven billion of us and we need feeding and clothing and we need our iPhones, and we seem to have decided that we have some sort of right to do pretty much anything we want to do with the planet.

Where is it likely to end? Well, I think that we're due a correction and it will be part of a natural process, probably a viral infection or something. It seems to me that nature has an inclination to correct mistakes. It'd better do it soon.

You didn't expect that rant, did you? I didn't see it coming, either, but now it's down on paper, it's staying.

But the thing is, it has only partially answered your question.

That lost connection matters a lot to you as an individual, because it affects what is left when you die. That's why you have to keep reading, so you'll know.

thirty four

We're getting close to the end. I'm going to tell you what happened yesterday morning. Is it still yesterday? I've lost track. Anyway, it was on the morning of the eve of the solstice. The 20th of June. It was on Monday; I remember that because that's the day they take the recycling and there were some brown bags piled up against the lychgate.

It started with a mysterious figure walking into the churchyard. Don't groan and yawn; this wasn't some ghostly apparition. I'm not going all supernatural on you again so soon. This was a real person.

I was stood at the Aga drinking a cup of instant coffee, looking idly out of the window. I was in a bit of a daze, I think. I felt unusually smug and pleasingly contented with life. Everything seemed to be aligning in the way I had hoped. It was all coming together. I felt good. I could sense that whatever happened at the Clump at midnight, it was going to be a gamechanger, one way or the other. And I felt like it would be a final outing for me, and probably for Gramper Uglow, too. I couldn't see my life beyond it.

I watched this person come through the gate. It was a girl of about thirty. She had walking boots on and wore a canvas day sack on her back over a cagoule. She had in her hands a folded piece of paper and was stood looking at it on the path, then she looked up and straight in my direction. I knew she wouldn't be able to see me through the kitchen door window. She was too far away, and the kitchen was too dark. I've done experiments, so I know. Nevertheless, she stared for quite a while and it was a bit unnerving. I didn't recognise her. I reckon I know all the villagers by sight and she wasn't one of them. Villagers don't usually dress as if they're going on a day's walk, even if they are. She would be looking for family gravestones, or green men, or rare flowers, not trouble.

I watched her as she pocketed the paper and carried on down the path. She went into the church and was gone from view. I was vaguely interested in a detached sort of way. Intrigued, rather than interested. I would be intrigued to know what her story was and what had brought her to St Rumon's. I realised that just her presence had nudged me from my dreams. Life goes on, I guess. You never know what's coming next.

I took my coffee outside and stood among the lichened graves and the long dewy grass and the red campion that had invaded the shady areas. The flowers on the Uglow grave had faded and shrivelled and looked forlorn. I had more or less decided that I would intercept her on her return journey to the lychgate and engage her in conversation, but I waited until my coffee went cold and she still hadn't come out. I threw the dregs on a gravestone and put the mug in my coat pocket.

Then a bell started ringing. That was against the rules. In order to ring one of the bells, you have to release a wooden hub to which the ropes are attached and bring it down on a pulley so that it's within reach. It's normally hung out of the way, so kids can't get to it. It wasn't being rung properly, just a side to side toll that sounded melancholy on that misty summer morning. If the tower captain heard it, and he almost certainly would because he only lived on the other side of the wall, it would tweak his ulcer and he would be out in a proprietorial flash to investigate. I decided a tactical retreat was in order and I slipped back inside the kitchen door.

I was right. He still had his slippers on but was marching down the path at a spirited pace. Probably nothing as exciting as this had happened to him since that fateful wedding peal. He didn't like anyone touching his bells without permission and there would likely be a bit of a rumpus. I heard he had become a little oversensitive since the incident and had taken umbrage and responsibility in equal measure, although they didn't sit comfortably together.

When I next saw them both they were standing outside the porch and they were talking animatedly. The tower captain then pointed over to Church House and the girl made a beeline for my kitchen door.

Now I really was intrigued. She was the one now looking purposeful. I watched her as she approached. There was something familiar about her. I suddenly saw it in the shape of her face as she trampled some long nettles into the grass. Before I knew it, she was rapping at the glass on the door in an insistent, pushy sort of way. I hesitated just long enough for her to try the handle. The door wasn't locked, obviously; I'd only just walked through it myself. It swung open and she stood there looking at me. And what do you think she said? Have you guessed? Are you keeping up? She said, 'Hello Dad'. Of course she did.

I guess I always knew this was going to happen one day. In fact, I'd been expecting it for about ten years, but I still wasn't prepared for it. And this day of all days, when I had other things on my mind.

We stood there looking at each other across the kitchen. She'd turned into a fine young woman. She looked very presentable. Not particularly attractive, as such, but smartly turned out and homely in a girl-next-door sort of way. A bit Felicity Kendall-ish. She didn't look as bohemian as her mother had done at that age.

What did she expect me to do? Kiss her and hug her and embrace her into my bosom? Or was she still a little pissed off that I hadn't said goodbye when I walked out of her life without warning? A bit tough on an eight-year-old, I freely admit. I hoped she would be circumspect; I didn't want any emotion. I don't do emotions very well. Awkward, I can do, and it was. It was awkward for about ten seconds, which felt like ten hours, and then she said she had come to wish me a happy birthday. I said it wasn't until tomorrow and she replied that she might stay, if invited.

It probably wasn't what I should have done when confronted with a long-lost daughter who I hadn't seen for twenty years, but I am ashamed to say that my thoughts went straight to what I was intending doing that night at midnight, and I instantly knew that we would do the whole solstice thing together later. She would be there along with Peter and Gramper Uglow. I was making plans in my head when I should have been welcoming her into my life.

My mind was racing. There was so much I wanted to say.

We managed to overcome our awkwardness and our shyness and our unknowingness, but it was hard going at first. It took a while, two cups of strong coffee and then I opened a bottle of pinot grigio that I had in the fridge and put it on the table with two glasses.

At first, I wondered if she knew anything at all about how I had spent the last twenty years. Presumably, she knew that I was still married to her mother, but I could have gone off and started another family. I could have done anything, really. She knew me as a businessman and an entrepreneur, even through eight-year-old eyes; I might have started another company, invented a must-have gadget and made millions, or become a teacher, or a scientist or a politician. Instead, I had had a nervous breakdown from which I was still trying to recover, two decades on.

It quickly became clear that she knew nothing at all, except that I was still living in the holiday home. Who told her that? My name had evidently become taboo in Georgia's household and among her extended family and within her circle of friends. I had disappeared, and I no longer existed. Miriam never questioned this, evidently, although she must have had difficulty reconciling her memories of me with her new life. It must have been desolate at times and I wondered if I had truly fucked up her life for her, or whether she had been able to shrug it off as if I had never walked the Earth. Well, she was here now, so there must be a vestige of my influence in her still, or maybe I was just being kind to myself.

I can tell you this. We sat and talked for about four hours around that kitchen table, non-stop and without repeating ourselves or becoming morbid or sarcastic or vindictive or sorrowful. It was wonderful, actually. I'm glad it happened. We reminisced about holidays and school events and birthday parties, memories that had just lain dormant in my brain all these years but were still there waiting to be tickled. What good times we had had then; I had quite forgotten.

She told me about her life. She had gone to college but hadn't settled afterwards. She'd done burger flipping and waiting at table, but it never worked out. She hated it. Then she'd tried her hand at ceramics and fell upon a basement studio where she turned out nice pots which nobody wanted to buy and so she had finally quit and was going to travel the world for a few years to find herself – my words, not hers. I told you, there was no sarcasm between us (but between you and me there can be).

This trip was a sort of trial run. She had already been on the road for a week or so, walking some of the South West Coastal Path in Cornwall, and had decided, on a whim, to take the train from Exeter to Crow's Nymet to try and find me. It's a long haul up from the station to the village on foot, she'd probably forgotten.

I asked her if she was married or had a boyfriend and she said no, she'd never had a long-term partner. Was this something else that was my fault, I wondered. So many questions, so few resolutions. It's the same with my life.

It had been intense. We'd hardly come up for air. I hadn't had the opportunity to think through any practical stuff. I wasn't used to guests, and I would have to hunt out some clean single sheets and a duvet for the spare bed. Where on Earth would I find them? Then there was food to think of. I wasn't used to entertaining either. I hoped Miriam would accept all this. She hadn't batted an eyelid when she saw the state of the house, because I watched her face when I showed her through to the toilet. Of course, she could remember where it was, but I wanted to see how she reacted to my home and how I lived. She didn't flinch, I'm pleased to say.

For one wild moment, I considered taking her to the Druid's. The kitchen opens at six nowadays and I understand the food has won awards recently. Punters come from far and wide to sample it; I watch them turn up in their posh 4x4's which they park untidily and inconsiderately outside the pub because they can't be bothered to walk twenty yards. I've never plucked up enough courage to eat there, not even as an experiment, but I thought briefly that having Miriam by my side might give me the confidence. On the other hand, it would be fraught with uncertainty. Who would be there? I didn't think such a visit would be likely to end happily, so I quietly forgot about it and hoped Miriam wouldn't suggest it. In any case, I didn't want people to know who this mystery girl was. That was my secret. Mine, and possibly the tower captain's.

We had to make do with Spam and cheese on toast. Miriam was most amused because she told me that that had been the only meal she ever remembered me cooking. I used to splash Lea & Perrins all over mine and Miriam and Angel had done the same to be big just like me and had always eaten it all up even though the Worcestershire sauce made the toast soggy and reek of anchovies. We had tinned peaches for afters which was evidently also a favourite stand-by of mine when Georgia was out, and I had to feed the kids. All the little things you forget when you're on your own and have nobody to connect with. And how little some things change.

We had a bottle of red with the Spam. It was a cheeky little Tempranillo from Spain and pleasantly complemented the saturated fat of the chopped ham. It was a bit on the cold side because it had been in the barn, so I brought another couple of bottles in and put them on the Aga to warm.

I had seriously enjoyed our chat. We'd even talked about Brexit, for God's sake. In fact, it was the most stimulating thing that I had done for as long as I could remember. However, we needed to move on to other things.

We took our wine and went and sat in the living room. I very rarely use this room, though it's easily the best in the house, and it embodies what these ancient Devon farmhouses are all about.

It's very original, and of all the rooms, it has changed the least. There are crooked slate flagstones and cobbles on the floor, and along one side is the black oak plank and muntin screen with a massive arched doorway leading to the passage where the farm beasts would be led. On the other side of the room, fastened to the bulging cob wall is more old wooden panelling and there is an elm bench that runs against it and into the window alcove and turns in on itself across the chimney breast, so that it seats about a dozen eaters around a gargantuan, arthritic oak table that is far too big and heavy and fragile to ever move. You'd have to take the window out to shift it. This is where the farmer and his family and all the farmhands would have eaten three times a day for centuries. Think of the stories they would have told each other.

And then there's the huge fireplace. It takes up half the outside wall and is so big you can burn a tree trunk on it. I know; I have.

I keep the fire laid in the hearth and I put a match to it. Even though it's early summer, there can still be a chill in the air in the evening. In any case, an open fire is comforting, and the thick cob and stone walls of Church House mean that the inside temperature doesn't change much, no matter what it's doing outside. It can feel a bit like a cave sometimes.

We pulled up our armchairs as the flames licked through the newspaper kindling and the dry birch twigs, snapping and crackling as they caught. I was burning some old alder roots from a stump that I'd pulled out of wet ground at the bottom of the garden with the Land Rover and a chain and hook. It had taken some doing and they were heavy to haul up to the house. I had laid the largest root resting on the back of the carbonised sheet of plate steel that served as a fire back and it started hissing as it warmed up. It was still damp. The other roots were all piled up on both sides in the hope they might dry out eventually. Bit of a fire hazard, I guess, but I loved the strangled and dancing shadows they cast on the sidewalls.

We put our glasses on a painted elm milking stool that was positioned there for that very purpose and I balanced the second bottle of red on the slate hearth against one of the firedogs.

I felt very at ease, something that I hadn't experienced for some time. I had loved talking with Miriam; it was so easy to do. I would never have guessed.

She knew I had something in mind for later on; I had sort of hinted at it several times over the last few hours, and although she hadn't acknowledged or enquired or probed, I knew she had taken this on board. The time had come when I needed to tell her what I wanted to do, but I realised that I would have to tread carefully. I didn't want to frighten her off; that would have been a tragic disappointment. I was almost beside myself with anticipation and couldn't believe everything had seemingly come together just at the right moment.

I have to say, the atmosphere was perfect for tales of shamans and ancient mystic rites. As the light faded at the end of the day, I lit some fat church candles that were sat on the table in saucers. I'd found a tin of stub-ends in the vestry and helped myself. If it was windy outside, the candles would flicker from the draughts that sucked through gaps under the ledge doors and sometimes even blew them out altogether, but tonight the flames were still and upright. It would be calm outside. It was going to be a wonderful night, midsummer and not a breath of air and with the heady perfume of a million wild flowers and blossoms. Why would you want to be anywhere else on such a night?

Miriam was expecting something from me and I wanted to make it good, but it was difficult to know where to start. There was so much.

So I told her all about the festival, except I may have made it all sound a bit more like a village May fair than how I believed it had actually been. You know, country dancing with morris men and children around the maypole, laughing and singing and merrymaking and feasting and drinking. I perhaps overdid it a bit. She must have realised. I told it as if all this had been going on as a village activity since time immemorial but had recently died out because of apathy and the lure of more sophisticated attractions.

I could see she was only mildly interested, and I realised that I had made a mistake. What was the point in not telling her the truth? Sooner or later, I'd have to get there.

I was mulling this over when she said, quite matter of factly, that that wasn't exactly how the man in the church had painted it. He'd told her that evil men had used the festival for their own ends and had unleashed the power of the devil on the village for ever more. I wondered why he had volunteered this information, and marvelled again that knowledge of the Rousing was much more widely disseminated than Godfrey had originally led me to believe. I guess Godfrey didn't know. He didn't know everything, after all. The tower captain said it was something that needed to be laid to rest and left undisturbed. He added that those who sought to resurrect it would pay a price.

I figured if Miriam had asked the tower captain where I could be found, then he probably wanted to get in first with his disapproval of what had happened at the winter solstice, the story of which would have definitely reached his ears in some form. That was why he wanted to get his little piece in.

So I came clean and got the whole story out. The Rousing (the real one), the phial, the Physic, the near-death experiences. And then I told her what had happened in December and that led on to the troubles with the villagers and before I knew where I was, I was telling Miriam the sorry details of my breakdown. I was pouring my heart out to her.

She'd had no idea. It had never entered her head that this was why I'd left. She had assumed, all this time, that the marriage was failing and with Angel dying, I just hadn't loved her enough to stick around when all else had ended. She thought I'd just walked out of her life because I didn't love her enough. She said that if I'd loved her, I would have kept in touch and I would have sent her birthday cards and arranged to see her now and again. She couldn't, and still didn't understand. I just couldn't have done that.

There was a silence that lasted for ever. We both sat there looking at the flames, deep in our thoughts. I wondered if I had just been a selfish bastard, pure and simple. I appreciate that that's how it came over to just about everyone at the time. No one really understood what I had been going through. I guess nobody wanted to be on my side, and maybe that's why I had always felt even more isolated and on my own.

I reflected briefly whether I could have handled things any differently, but it was stupid to even go that way. I've told you, I'm not one for regrets. But even so, life could have been different for so many people that have had the misfortune to encounter me on their journey.

Miriam said she could remember me finding the phial, at least she could recall me bringing it home and telling stories of wonder about it. I couldn't remember ever doing that. She asked where it was now, and I went and got it from my study, and gave it to her. She sat there brooding, deep in her own world. She twisted the cork stopper off and smelled the contents, and for one ghastly moment I thought she was going to put the jar to her lips and swig it back.

'There's not much left', I told her needlessly. It was pretty obvious that the phial was almost empty. I added that I didn't know what I would do when it was gone, and it was true; I didn't, if I was still here.

She said she wanted to know more about my experiences with the Physic. I'd already told her about my Sunday afternoons and my ideas about atheism and the retreat of nature and the rest that I've bounced off you. She hadn't contributed much so I didn't know whether she was taking it all in or questioning it or secretly laughing at me.

Do you want me to tell you what else I told her? It's about what happens when you die. Look, I've written it in a different colour, so you don't have to read it now if you don't want to. You might like to come back later.

> *We all have a soul and it survives us on death. It's sort of attached to us, but exists in another dimension, so we are not aware of it until we die. So far, so standard …*

maybe. I know that it sounds like a million other theories. Let me explain further, just so you have some idea at this stage. I've written it all down much better on some separate sheets. It's what I've learned, but it's probably best that you leave reading it until the end. This will do for now, and this is complicated enough.

The other dimension, the soul dimension, is the key. Because it's a different dimension to the three physical ones that we're used to, it's very difficult to comprehend, and can't be explained in physical terms, but I'll do my best.

First, imagine a pinhole camera, a very simple thing. The upside-down image of a view is displayed on the back wall of the camera, because light travels in a straight line from the object to the image, and from all other points in the view in the same way. All the light that you can see in the image has passed through the pinhole. When I was a child and I read about this, I didn't think it would work and I gave the one I made a much larger hole so that it would work better. It didn't, of course, it was brighter, but it was blurred. It has to be a pinhole.

I'm going to call this a singularity, which is a bit cheeky and provocative, really, because singularities are themselves very complicated things and have several meanings. Just Google it and you'll find out. A mathematical singularity is usually something where things occur that are ill-defined, so I think it's appropriate.

So back to the camera. The image and the object both exist together, and their relationship can be said to be linear, both in the optical sense because, as I say, light travels in straight lines, and in the mathematical sense in that changes in one result in definable and reversable changes in the other.

Now, consider this. What about if the two spaces either side of the singularity were still linearly related, but in a much more complex way. In other words, the transformation between the spaces is still mathematically definable and reversable but it doesn't necessarily result in something that has a physically recognisable attribute. Tricky, eh? But it gets much worse.

Have you ever heard of a Fourier Transform? If you Google that and you're not a mathematician, you'll feel like packing up now, but stay with me; we don't need all that Greek stuff. I used to be able to understand all these Greek symbols and equations and formulae and proofs. I used them a lot when I was doing my PhD, because Fourier Transforms were a big part of the image processing research that I was doing. I've forgotten all the maths, now, but I still retain an intuition for two dimensional Fourier Transforms. If you work with something long enough, that tends to happen, doesn't it? I'm sure you can think of lots of examples. A driver's ability to read the minds of other road users is a good one.

I want to try to relate the Fourier Transform to the pinhole camera in an intuitive way, so if you're that mathematician, look away now, or you'll be offended.

A Fourier Transform 'transforms' a function from one space into another one, both of which have physical realities, for example, time and frequency if you're only considering one dimension.

I don't want to get any deeper into it. All you need to know is that all points on one side of the singularity can be mapped onto the other side in a definable way, but not necessarily in the same way that optical rays do in a pinhole camera, where one point on one side is mapped to another point on the other. In a Fourier Transform, a point on one side is mapped in such a way that a small part of it occurs at every point on the other side. That's the important concept to grasp.

Now let's try to relate this to the soul dimension. On the one side there is an entity that we are calling the soul that I'm saying we all have, and it's 'linked' to our bodies in some way. On the other side of the singularity, this entity has been transformed in such a way that a tiny part of it exists in every single part of the other side. Unfortunately, it's not quite as simple as that, because both sides of the singularity are in fact the same soul dimension and the soul can exist in both sides at the same time. And the singularity is, in fact, life itself.

When life no longer exists, that is, when you die, the singularity ceases to exist and your soul then only exists on the 'other' side.

I know, I know, that was a rubbish explanation, and even if you understood what I was trying to say, you're not really on board yet, are you?

There's lots more, of course, about how the soul evolved in the first place, but I'd better leave that for later. For now, all you need to know is that when you die, your soul is released or unlinked from your body and it exists in another dimension in such a way that it is everywhere in that dimension simultaneously.

I think it was a mistake to tell you like this, but I wanted you to have some idea of what happens when you *take the Physic. There's much more, and you should read the separate sheets when you feel brave.*

So back to last night. Actually, it was the night before, now. I've just realised.

Talking with Miriam was in a sense, dreamlike, but it had been a purgative ordeal for me. I can't tell you the sort of emotional turmoil I had been going through for the last few hours. There was so much to absorb, but I took from it an unfamiliar cleansing.

We'd managed to get through all three bottles of red, but my mind was still crystal clear. In fact, it was more than just crystal clear, I felt my consciousness had almost been elevated to a higher plain. I wondered at the daughter that I had abandoned for twenty precious years, and all the lost opportunities. No. No regrets. Stop it.

The fire had burned down to embers and it was glowing mischievously in the dark of the hearth. The warm roots gave off a pungent but not unpleasant odour and the candles were spluttering their death throes in the saucers.

The time had come. I had refined the way that I took the Physic, as it was a little unscientific to just dip my finger on the spout. I used holy communion wafers from the vestry. I thought it seemed wholly appropriate, somehow. If I held one under the lip of the jar and tipped it up carefully, I could ensure that just one drop soaked into the little circular wafer. It made no difference if the liquid had dried out when I swallowed it; it was having the same effect on me. I'll bet that's how the shaman did it.

I put the four prepared wafers in a little hinged wooden snuff box of my grandmother's. That seemed appropriate, too, though I don't know why; I don't think she would have approved. I popped it safely in my shirt pocket. Miriam had been watching me with great interest while I was involved with this, rather like a junkie looking on while her fix was prepared, though in this case it was me who was the junkie. I guess it was all a bit like rolling a joint or heating smack in a spoon when I thought about it. It had become a gratuitous, ritualistic ceremony for me, I suddenly realised. Why had I never made the connection?

I'd told Miriam all about Peter and Gramper Uglow, but I hadn't warned her they'd be there waiting for us at the Clump. I wanted to, and tried to get it out several times, but the opportunity was never quite right. I felt very guilty about it; it was almost as if I was continuing with the betrayal. I thought she would question the four wafers, but she didn't. It would have been the obvious chance to tell her. Oh dear. Why am I such a failure at things like this?

She put a fleece on and slung the daysack over her shoulder. She hadn't made time to unpack it and I guess it had become part of her kit while she was on the road, and she felt undressed without it.

I'd considered putting my djellaba on, after all, but I was afraid it would freak her out. I know it looked a tad Hammer Horror-ish. I decided on the coat with long sleeves instead, which was marginally less scary. It was mild out, and I would be hot in it, but it felt somehow appropriate. She might even remember it from my workshop at Babel House, though it was looking a bit the worse for wear. Threadbare, and with the torn shoulder.

There was a hole worn in the lining on the right-hand side and now and again, when I felt like it, I had taken to pushing my wakizashi into the split, so it hung there innocently inside the lining, with the hilt up against my right breast. I felt like it tonight, but I didn't show Miriam.

I was right, it was a lovely night. Quiet and still with a little dew sparkling on the grass and summer scents in the air. There wasn't a sound in Crow's Nymet, nor a light to be seen. It was half past eleven on a Monday night and all were tucked up safely in their snug beds.

I took Miriam by the hand and walked her through the churchyard to the stile. I'd been coming this way a lot. It was my path, and it was easy going now the ground had dried out. The moon was up and cast precise shadows on the ground. It was almost like daylight. Yew Magna had become a regular haunt of mine, and I would sit on the bough sometimes for hours during the night just contemplating things. It always felt comfortable there, as if I was cocooned within a protective shell, somehow. Is that how sacred groves work, or was it a placebo all along?

I'd been tempted several times to take along some of the Physic with me, but had resolutely managed to resist the urge. I had been saving that call for tonight. I hoped Gramper Uglow was right; if anything was going to happen, it would happen here, tonight. Everything was aligned and was coming together. It just felt right.

I was nervous. I couldn't help myself looking anxiously around as we walked slowly and silently through the wood towards the Clump. I was alert for signs of things that shouldn't be there. I was good at that, but tonight I was exceptional. Things like people, or things like unexplained stuff that comes and taps you on your back when you can't look round.

I knew Peter and Gramper Uglow would be using a different path, so I wasn't expecting to come across them. I was curious how Gramper Uglow was coping with the tree roots and the stones and the soft leaf mould on the track and the difficult terrain. I didn't think any of that would trouble him tonight. He'd be floating like a Dalek going upstairs.

I could see as we approached the Clump that they were there ahead of us. They were both sat on the bough. How long had they been there? When was the last time that Gramper Uglow had sat on that bough? I saw them before Miriam did, and I clasped and squeezed her hand as I felt it tense when she noticed the figures.

'Don't worry', I whispered in her ear, and I told her who they were and that I was expecting them to be there. She was uneasy, and I can understand why. They both looked a bit thuggish, even in the moonlight. It was obvious they weren't pleased to see her, either; there was muttering and grumbling. I'm not bothering to tell you what they said because it doesn't matter; they just had to accept that Miriam was there, whether they liked it or not.

'I can smell the alcohol on you', Gramper Uglow said. 'This isn't a fucking party'.

I suppose he had a point. We weren't drunk, but I guess we weren't as sharp as we could have been. That was just the way it had panned out; I hadn't planned it that way.

It wasn't a good start, but they did calm down once they realised that was the way it was going to be.

I do believe the two of them had been taking this very seriously indeed. I think they'd probably been there for some time and had been mentally preparing themselves in some way or other. They looked quite trance-like before they saw us. What were they expecting, really expecting? Did they think it would be an ordeal or a picnic? A good or a bad trip? I guess the point was, they were trying their best to make it work, whereas maybe I had taken my eye off the ball. Note to self; Back off.

Gramper Uglow had what looked like a pewter hip-flask in his hand. He had filled it from the spring and said we should drink some before we took the Physic. He was taking it very seriously.

I took my coat off and laid it on the ground, spread open, and I gestured for Miriam to sit on it. I'd explained in great detail to Peter and Gramper Uglow what happened to me as soon as the Physic touched my tongue, but they insisted on keeping sitting on the bough. I think they'd got it into their heads that that was how it should be done. Well that was up to them; I'd warned them.

I have to tell you I'd always been a bit sceptical about the midnight thing, ever since Godfrey first told me. I always thought it was likely to be a red herring. Why should midnight have been of any significance? It had never felt to me like it belonged in a medieval rite. I had a sneaky feeling that it might have crept in with the first pocket watches because you wouldn't have been able to tell what the time was before that. How would you know when it was midnight? I reckon it was added to act as a focus, to consolidate the ritual and concentrate the minds of the participants. But a sunrise or sunset would do that better, wouldn't it, if it wasn't cloudy? Whatever. I didn't want to spoil it now with my doubts. We were ready at midnight.

Gramper Uglow handed his flask around and we all took a swig. It was cold, fresh, and unremarkable. Then I got the snuffbox out and handed a wafer to them all, and I lay down next to Miriam on the coat. The coat with long sleeves.

I was drained, spent. It was a solemn moment, for us all. In the light of what happened, I'm glad it was like that. Miriam and I said not a word between us as we lay there, but there was an intensity and intimacy that didn't need speech; an unspoken, mutual togetherness that transcended normal communication. It felt like that, anyway. It was undeniably sensuous and uplifting and it defies my literary powers to describe it accurately to you.

I think, perhaps, that for those few moments, for me, that had become the new high point of my life. Yes, seriously. I felt I had it all during those seconds lying on the grass with my lost daughter, now found, with the bright moon filtering through the yew needles, surrounded by millennia of history in my beloved Devon countryside, and about to experience something that had been forgotten for five hundred years. I felt privileged and special. Everything in my life had been leading up to this moment. It was the culmination of a sequence of events in my existence that had now become … clear. There was nowhere else I wanted to be and no person I wanted to share this with other than Miriam.

At midnight we placed the wafers on our tongues, and they melted in the way they do at the altar. I closed my eyes and passed into the soul dimension. And it was astonishing. I guess it was like putting on a pair of new glasses and suddenly realising that there was much more to see than you had previously been aware of. It was there all the time, but you couldn't make out the detail, so you weren't aware of it. A parallel world.

When I took the Physic on a Sunday afternoon on my study floor, I drifted into a sort of nothingness, but with the realisation that there were presences and influences all around me, but that I couldn't quite focus on. I've tried to describe it to you, I know, but it's very difficult, because it was all just these intangible feelings. Here at the Clump, it was totally different. There was so much going on all around me, still intangible and unstructured, ephemeral, but I KNEW that what I was experiencing was coming from the natural world around me. In particular, there was an overriding presence that I was aware was coming from Yew Magna itself. I could feel it and it embraced me in its power. It was everywhere and seemed to almost saturate similar weaker effects from all the other trees and undergrowth that surrounded the Clump.

I was aware of other things, too, that I could tell were fauna, not flora. I could feel the closeness of several deer, and a badger, and an owl, and further in the background more deer, and roosting birds, and insects and frogs and toads. But outweighing all this activity was an overwhelming feeling of togetherness and oneness with my Miriam. It's not that I could see her or speak to her, nor she to me. It was as if we were the same entity. We didn't need to communicate. We were one.

I think the thing that you have to try and grasp is that this soul dimension is not predicated on thought, or consciousness, or intelligence. There's no cognitive reasoning or intellectual structure of any kind. It all just sort of is. And it's is-ing all around you and inside you, or it would be if you existed. But you don't exist, as such. Your soul exists, but you don't.

And then suddenly, and unexpectedly, and completely, the soul that was Miriam's and my soul were as one with the soul of Angel. Angel, my boy, was part of me, my soul. There was this oneness and it was everywhere and it was all pervasive, but it was complete. We three were an integral part of the whole, we were one with nature, with creation. It consumed us and was us.

And then it was gone. I lay on the grass and opened my eyes wide and knew that I was returned. I remember thinking in that moment that I could not face losing Angel again. Just that. I don't remember any other thoughts or feelings, but I know my mind was struggling to cope. It was in turmoil with emotions of euphoria, ecstasy even, but somehow also fear and loathing, backed up and queueing. I turned and looked at Miriam's face in the moonlight. It was featureless. I shook her to wake her. I needed to discover if she had experienced the same as me, if she had found her brother there, but in that instant, I knew that Miriam was no longer living in this world. It's funny. I didn't need to check her pulse or her breathing. I just knew she was dead.

Why wasn't I dead, too? I wanted to be. If I'd had the little jar on me, I would have taken the lot, all that was left, and rejoined the son and daughter that I had lost, and then found, and then lost again.

But that was not to be. Why had I not thought to bring it with me? I lay beside Miriam's lifeless body. I could sense that it was getting clammy already. Her face was now curiously even less expressive than it had been when I first woke up. Somehow empty, as if her essence had just drained away. Which, of course, it had.

Despite what you might think, after all I've told you about funerals and the way I reacted after Angel's death, I've never been an emotional sort of bloke. It was always one of Georgia's grouses. I couldn't help it. I blame my dad; he was even worse. It's not something we did.

I lay back with my head on the dewy, mossy grass and my mind was now acute. I could think clearly, as I am able in a crisis. Maybe one is a consequence of the other; lack of emotion and clarity in chaos, I mean. All the same, I lay there for a long time, absolutely motionless apart from my wide eyes which were locked on to the moon as it flickered behind the branches of the yew. I can do that for hours and hours when I'm thinking. It doesn't have to be the moon. It could be condensation forming on a wall. Or paint drying.

I turned and looked at her face and I thought about Miriam. Who knew she was here apart from Peter and Gramper Uglow? Probably not anyone. She would have been noticed in the village, of course, and the tower captain had spoken to her. He would remember her. Did she tell him anything of herself, or of me? Doubtful. I wasn't sure if she was in contact with anyone back home. I hadn't seen her use a phone while she was with me. It would be easy to check, I suppose, but I knew I wouldn't look through her things. I didn't want to do that. Even if she had told anyone she was here, presumably she had only intended staying for my birthday and then moving on with her walk, so unless there was someone with whom she was regularly talking progress, it might be several days before any alarm bells started ringing. She struck me as being the sort of free spirit that wouldn't be bound by convention or commitment, so her absence might go unnoticed for much longer. Maybe.

I was lying there next to my dead daughter, indulging myself in these selfish, practical and introspective thoughts, when a noise behind my back alerted me to some odd movement. I just had time to turn my head upwards from Miriam's limp body when I witnessed Gramper Uglow throw himself on the corpse with my wakizashi held in his bony hands like a hara-kiri lunge as he thrust the blade clean through her neck and skewered Miriam to the ground through my coat in one fluid movement.

Fuck me; I hadn't seen that coming.

He lay on her body panting and crying and he was still holding on to the hilt of the sword and was trying to push it further into the ground by waggling it backwards and forwards to enlarge the red ragged slit in Miriam's throat.

It wasn't very nice.

To be honest, I had forgotten all about Peter and Gramper Uglow. They hadn't featured in any part of my near-death experience. That was odd.

I looked up and saw that Peter was stood there watching his grandfather grinding the sword. His face was impassive. White and milky in the moonlight and empty. As if there was nothing working it from behind.

Gramper Uglow was breathing furiously and retching. I thought he was going to choke. He was dribbling on Miriam's blouse. Then he let go the sword, just lay there like he was dead himself for a moment, and then pushed himself off the body as if in post-coital torpor and lay gasping for air next to her.

Was I still priding myself on my clarity of thought and my calm response to unexpected excitement?

Yes, of course I was; I was thinking very clearly indeed. I did suddenly have some concern for my own safety; I thought perhaps I might be next. Not that dying held any fear for me just then, but I would want to have some say in it.

There were lots of things to think about, actually. I realised I was unnecessarily vulnerable laid on the floor as I was, and I got up and pushed Peter back onto the bough with the palm of my hand on his chest and I sat next to him and we both watched Gramper Uglow struggle for breath. Blood from Miriam's throat glistened in the moonlight.

'You shouldn't have been here. Especially her,' Peter said, pointing at Miriam.

'You were spoiling it. You weren't welcome. You can never be part of it; you shouldn't have come', he repeated.

That was all he said. As if that explained why Gramper Uglow had seen fit to run a sword through my daughter's throat. He didn't attempt to excuse it further, as if there weren't further cause.

A few days ago, I would have been longing to know about Peter and Gramper Uglow's experience under the influence of the Physic, but do you know what? All of a sudden, I wasn't interested any more. I didn't give a damn what they had experienced. In fact, I think I agreed with Peter. It was their festival, not mine or Miriam's. I didn't care any longer what they did with it, or how their fucking crops performed.

But I was interested in my experiences. I wanted to get my Angel back. I wanted to be with him again. And with Miriam.

I'm telling you all this so you might understand why we did what we did next.

It might have been an impetuous decision, but it did seem like the right thing to do at the time.

I told Peter to go and get a spade from my shed.

Look, I could argue the logic with you, if I could be bothered. Peter was in deep shit, no matter what happened. Gramper Uglow couldn't give a shit, and was on his last legs anyway. I think his life was done. My life was over. I no longer wanted to live this existence any more. It held no attraction for me. And I certainly wasn't going to be helping any policemen with their enquiries. I resolved that as soon as I got to Church House I would pour the remains of the phial onto another wafer or something, and keep it on my person at all times, ready. It would hopefully be sufficient to ensure a swift and permanent departure from this life.

If we buried the body in the woods, it might take some time before it was discovered. Even though Peter had some recent experience of grave digging, I didn't think he could get down to six feet with all the roots and stones. It would be a shallow grave. The body wouldn't stay hidden for long; there are too many badgers and foxes around for that, and then it would start smelling and it would guide dog walkers to it, like a siren's call.

I did wonder if we should try and carry or drag it back to Church House, or even to the old place. I could keep it wrapped up in plastic for a long time or we could bury it in the earth floor of the barn or the workshop, but what would be the point? Someone was going to come looking for her at some stage and they would start by knocking on my door first. And they wouldn't go away until they found her.

So when Peter came back with the spade, we carried the body deeper into the wood, using the coat as a stretcher, away from the tracks and paths. The body was heavy, and I'm not as fit or as strong as I used to be, and I had trouble keeping my end up, so we only managed about a hundred yards downhill where we came to a natural corpse-sized hollow in the hillside. I was right about the roots, and the bedrock was only just below the layer of leaf mould. We didn't do a very good job. We wrapped her in the coat and pulled the body into the hole and covered it with the mould and the leaves. It was a waste of time, I think. I rammed the rucksack into a foxhole until it wedged tightly and then I stuffed a rock into it and covered that with leaves, too. I couldn't bear to leave my wakizashi, so I took it home with me with the spade.

Gramper Uglow was still lying there where he'd rolled, but his troubled breathing had subsided. I said nothing more to them. I left them there and made my way home. I wasn't even sure if they'd taken their Physic yet.

thirty five

And that almost brings us back to where we came in, doesn't it? It's turned out to be much, much longer than I expected when I started writing. Sorry about that. I wasn't going to include anything about the company or my early life or Ralph Ralph but it all just sort of came out, and I suppose it does make my story more complete. I've found it cleansing and purgative, and I've mostly enjoyed it.

If you're reading this in the original manuscript, you'll notice how I ran out of lined paper and had to start using the plain sheets from my printer. I'm sorry the writing's a bit wonky. The ink changes colour a couple of times as well, where I had to swap pens.

It's now Wednesday night, it seems. I've been writing continuously for almost forty-eight hours and I'm exhausted. Dog tired; never been more jiggered.

I've seen and heard nothing of the outside world since I returned from the Clump. I've hardly looked out of the windows. At least that means the body has yet to be discovered. It's going to be a bit frenzied around here when that happens.

As soon as I got back, I tore out a sheet of pink blotting paper from a Basildon Bond pad that was my mother's. I cut out a square about two inches across and laid it in a saucer, just in case there was more Physic left than I thought. There wasn't. I counted six drips only and then the jar was empty, though there was a sticky residue left around the rim and on the stopper. The stain on the blotting paper spread to about the size of an old penny. I folded it twice and put it in a little plastic wallet that had held a medal announcing University Table Football Champ, 1975, and I put it in the top pocket of my shirt. It looked innocuous enough but felt good next to my heart.

Then I started writing and waiting. Who's going to come knocking first?

Although my awareness of the presence of Angel's soul had been brief, almost instantaneous, during that intense interlude a myriad of things happened. Like an arc-flash of comprehension, but not, because as I've said, the soul dimension isn't about cognition or intelligence. But it was this sense that a sort of ephemeral, intangible knowledge was being imparted to me, which at the time didn't mean much, but when I got back to Church House and had time to think about it, I realised that there were revelations that I had been privileged to be party to that explained to me all manner of things about the soul dimension that I hadn't fully appreciated. This was proof for me, but unfortunately, it won't be for you. You'll just have to take my word for it.

I've written it all down, but I've kept it as a separate postscript so you don't have to read it until you feel you're ready, although if you're a policeman I guess you'll be obliged to now for completeness. I don't care if you believe any of it or not. I don't see why you should, actually. Like I say, there's no proof. I was lying to you before. In actual fact, I guess, by its very essence it is unprovable, and that perhaps is the whole enigma of the soul dimension, at least for us humans.

So, are there any loose ends to clear up while I'm sat here thinking, with time on my hands once again? Anything unexplained that you're unhappy about? Any inconsistencies making you uneasy? I can't bring anything to mind that might be troubling you. I think I've been pretty good at explaining stuff as we've gone along, and I believe there are some conundrums like the Green Man that are perhaps best left unexplained and cryptic.

Fucking Hell. There is something. Fuck it. All this time and I never realised.

I bet you're a clever dick and you worked it out long ago, and it's been staring me in the face for twenty years and I never saw it. Fuck. What an idiot.

OK, it's later; I've calmed down and I've thought it through and I'm going to write it down.

For completeness.

Did you guess? It's how Angel died. I never realised, and it's bloody obvious. The phial was in my study; Angel and Miriam weren't allowed in my study, but I must have left the key in the door when I left for El Paso, and they would have gone in and found it. I'd told them all sorts of stories about it, Miriam said. They must have been curious.

Miriam must have known. She's known all this time and didn't let on. She knew about the Physic before I did. Why didn't she say anything on Monday night? We talked through all sorts. She had plenty of opportunity. I thought we were telling all our secrets. Did she tell me and I wasn't listening?

Fuck. I've just thought of something else. You probably got that, too. It's only when you're disturbed that you die. It must cut off the soul, somehow, and not allow it back.

Miriam (or Georgia after all) killed Angel and I've just killed Miriam. What a fucking mess.

epilogue

The day started cold and bright and in Crow's Nymet parish hall there were uncharacteristic signs of early activity from about six-thirty. Villagers were busy milling around purposefully, when normally at this time on a Thursday morning there would be no more than a lone enthusiastic jogger or perhaps a dog walker up with the lark.

Referendum day. A historic moment in time.

In the churchyard, a figure dressed in casual tweeds made his way to the kitchen door of Church House. He put his elbow to the glass pane and shattered it loudly. It disturbed the tranquil air of the graveyard and momentarily caught the attention of a robin and a blackbird that were busy with the business of raising their young, but it went unnoticed by the human inhabitants of the nearby cottages. The man put his arm through the broken glass, released the latch and pushed the door firmly open and went inside in one smooth accomplished action. As he stood taking in the kitchen, another man stumbled in and confronted him. This other man looked startled and a little wild. He had an unruly, uncombed beard and was wearing a dressing gown over a crumpled shirt and dishevelled trousers. He was old, early sixties, but had alert eyes and an upright countenance, despite his choice of clothes.

Neither man made a move, both seemingly reluctant to take the lead, then the older man carefully and meaningfully took from his shirt pocket a little package folded inside a transparent plastic wallet, and was somewhat impetuously attempting to open the flap to release the paper when the man in the tweeds said,

'I'm Pinky'

This simple statement had the effect of slowing down time altogether for a few moments while the two men stared probingly at each other in silence. The stand-off was broken when the older man said, 'Take a seat', and he pulled out a dining chair for the other to sit on. He returned the package to his shirt pocket and leaned back against the Aga rail.

The seated man in turn took something from his own pocket and placed on the table three passports which he arranged in a fan, face-up.

'Pinky thinks you might like the use of one of these', he said.

A raising of the older man's eyebrows betrayed the fact that this turn of events had been unexpected. He took each passport separately and flicked through them. The photographs in each were completely different but all undeniably showed the older man.

'Impressive', was all the man said.

'It would be best if you chose just one of the three, then you can build your new identity around it. Choose one that will suit you for the rest of your life. Pinky's idea is this. Once you've decided who you'll be, we arrange transport for you. Pinky thinks perhaps New Mexico would be a good choice.

502

We'll be told when it's all been sorted and in the meantime you can clean yourself up, get some suitable clothes on and do some packing. Best to travel light'.

Some time later the older man appeared from the bathroom with a smartly groomed and trimmed goatee, wearing a clean shirt and pressed khaki chinos. He carried a small suitcase downstairs and placed it on the study desk, and then he opened it and looked around reflectively at the full bookshelves. In the end, he took only a small stoneware jar with a cork stopper from a shelf and popped it into the wet-bag alongside his toothbrush and flannel, then he put the case to stand by the front door.

He then went into the living room and pulled back a Turkish rug in front of the hearth and with a screwdriver he prised up a flagstone and laid it to one side. In the exposed cavity was a grey gunmetal box with a hinged lid. He gently eased it out and opened the lid. Inside was a large number of high denomination notes, many thousands of US dollars and English pounds. The man gazed at them for a while, as if musing over a course of action and then he selected a number of each currency and distributed them about his person and gave the rest to the man in tweeds.

Then he carried the tin box to his study and took a large sheaf of papers held together with two elastic bands and placed them in the tin. He returned to the hearth and deposited the box in its home and replaced the flagstone. It was a tight fit and needed tamping down with a measured stamp of the foot. When the gaps were filled with grit and ash from a dustpan, there was no longer any sign of recent interference, and the man rolled the carpet back into place.

Then the two men waited together in the kitchen without speaking until it started to get dark outside and the tweeded man took a call on his phone. He got up and went to the corner of the room where a dog was sleeping, and he deftly put his hands around its throat and squeezed until it stopped struggling. The old man looked on with sadness in his eyes and a tear on his cheek.

They left the house separately by the front door, the tweeded man going first with the case, and then the older man a few minutes later. As the older man passed the pub, he peered in at the throng, but his expression said nothing. There would no doubt be talk of Brexit all through the night.

In the car park the two men sat in the Volvo that had been there all day unnoticed in the hubbub of the voting and then they drove out into the dark night.

Excerpt from the North Devon Weekly Gazette, dated 26th April 2119.

MYSTERY BOX DISAPPEARS.

We reported last week that a box containing about four hundred pages of hand-written paper had been found in a fire damaged cottage in the village of Crow's Nymet, and that it had been handed to police to assist their continuing enquiry into the source of the blaze.

Barnstaple Constabulary issued the following statement yesterday afternoon.

'At 10:00 am on Friday 22nd April 2119, a sealed bag containing papers was stolen from Barnstaple police station. It is believed that intruders entered the premises from North Street while the storeroom was unattended. Nothing else was taken.'

The statement was met with incredulity by chairman of the parish council, Mr David Rose, who told our reporter that the manuscript represented a unique opportunity for Crow's Nymet to shake off its unenviable reputation as a magnet for occultists and pagan worshippers, following the unearthing under suspicious circumstances of an alleged sacrificial murder scene in nearby woodlands a hundred years ago.

'It seems they hadn't even put the pages through a Scriptreader before they vanished from the station, so there's no transcript or any record at all of this important document,' he added. Mr Rose further stated that the loss of the evidence amounted to gross incompetence and he demanded the resignation of the Chief Constable.

'There's something that doesn't quite add up here,' he concluded ominously, adding to the air of mystery and intrigue surrounding the discovery and subsequent disappearance of the written account.

Police and forensic teams are continuing their search for clues and the site has now been sealed off.

Transcript of article uploaded to America Today, dated 30th May 2119

News has reached us of an interesting item for sale on the eBayRetro online auction house that is attracting some furious bidding from unexpected sources. The lot is an archaic handwritten document of just under four hundred pages. Very little is known of the manuscript, and details have now been withheld and concealed by the seller, but there are plenty of rumours on social media concerning its content and origins.

It has been reported that the document was offered in a pre-auction private sale to the MyLife Order, but that the approach was rebuffed after claims that a vital appendix was missing. However, it is being widely speculated that the cult has now joined the bidding war and is pitted against trillionaire Randy Gonzalez and the pharmaceutical giant AWA Inc. Mr Gonzalez has had a run-in before with the Lifers when his daughter took her own life in the mass suicide during the great famine of 2096-9, when the cult surprised the world by breaking cover from its covert Arizona stronghold with an army of missionary zealots. It is estimated that over one million US 'disciples' followed their messiahs to an early death in the obscene hysteria that resulted.

In an intriguing twist, the sale has been frustrated by a moratorium forced on the auction house by the English Police Federation who claim that the document was illegally removed from their possession and that it contains important evidence concerning serious unsolved legacy crimes. All this has further fuelled conspiracy theorists who have long been convinced that the trance-like rituals characteristic of the MyLife regime have their origins in the medieval folk medicine of the West Country of England, and that the document may shed light on the enduring mystery behind the baffling emergence of the founder of the cult, known and self-proclaimed as the Foundling.

We'll bring you more news as the story develops.

author's note

I returned to my West Country roots with my wife Liz four years ago and we live in a barn conversion on a working sheep farm. We wake up to the wide expanse of Exmoor with its colourful patchwork of ancient fields and moorland, wooded river valleys and historic farm buildings. We are lucky to have made many good friends with incomers and true Devonians; villagers and farmers alike.

It is from this backdrop of bucolic landscape and local character and tradition that I constructed 'Coat with Long Sleeves', my debut novel.

It is self-published and has not had the rough edges broken off it. It is not perfect, but it remains the book I wrote, faults and all. I hope you enjoyed it.

I want to thank Liz for her stoic endurance and endless coffee over the three winters it took to write; all my proof and beta readers, especially Ali, Josie, Lynn and Judy for their considered observations and enthusiasm and the countryside and people of North Devon for my inspiration.

Coat with Long Sleeves is not an ordinary book. It explores many threads which may have given you cause to sit back,

512

think and wonder. I hope you have been entertained but also frightened, upset, heartened, provoked, inspired, patronised, offended and extended. But mostly, I want you to have come away with a renewed appreciation of the extraordinarily fragile heritage we currently enjoy but risk losing forever.

If you would like to discuss anything, particularly what might have been in the missing appendix, then I hope you'll visit my website www.geoffduckauthor.com. And if you've enjoyed the book, but also if you haven't, a review on Amazon would be great, too.

Geoff Duck